MAYA

MAYA

Blessed are those whose
arms are held open.

Happy 53rd Ian.

Simon

x

Simon Wolfe

authorHOUSE®

AuthorHouse™ UK
1663 Liberty Drive
Bloomington, IN 47403 USA
www.authorhouse.co.uk
Phone: 0800.197.4150

Published by AuthorHouse 02/16/2016

ISBN: 978-1-5049-4073-3 (sc)
ISBN: 978-1-5049-4074-0 (e)

Print information available on the last page.

Any people depicted in stock imagery provided by Thinkstock are
models, and such images are being used for illustrative purposes only.
Certain stock imagery © Thinkstock.

This book is printed on acid-free paper.

Back cover art: 'father and son on the day
of his barmitvah' by Amelia Jane

Contents

Preface ix

PART 1

Hello 3
Beginnings 11
We Have All The Time In The World 19
Where do the children play 26
Kids in America 37
Different for girls 43
Strobe light 47
Geno 53
Scarborough fair/In Shreds 64
Golden Brown 68
Riders on the Storm 75
Hey baby 85
How I wrote Elastic man 92
Food for thought 94
Holiday in Cambodia 102
Down in Brazil 108
Hanging on a string 119
My Old Man 136

PART 2

The Soldier Stood Alone 149
The Changeling 163
Hard Headed Woman 175
Movin' On Up 183

The Chain...192

Imagination Limitation................................205

Cantaloupe (Flip Fantasia)...........................208

Don't Let It Pass You By 218

A Forest...227

In the Waiting Line....................................233

Torch 237

In a Rut 241

88 Lines About 44 Women...............................253

Cocaine 269

Six Underground 280

Summer's Almost Gone...................................288

Rival Tribal Rebel Revel..............................294

Supersonic 300

The Sea..308

PART 3

Days Go By (Acoustic) 313

The Needle and the Damage Done.........................315

Slide Away..319

Oh Bondage, Up Yours 332

Penthouse and Pavement 335

I Don't Want To (Go to Chelsea).......................340

Sing Our Own Song......................................343

Coming Down...350

Can't Stand Me Now.....................................356

Father and Son...359

Bernadette 368

Moondance 374

Dobro Ladies 381

Columbia..389

About a Girl 399

Walk This World (Acoustic) 407

You Do Something to Me 410

Polka Dots 417

Love Her Madly 426

Sunlight in the Rain 433

Three Lions on a Shirt 437

Smells Like Teen Spirit 445

Something in the Way She Moves 451

Don't Be Afraid of the Dark 457

Dragonfly Summer 461

Just Now 466

Lament 1, "Bird's Lament" 474

Thirteen Days 479

Fate of a Fool 489

Preface

I had taken it for granted that I'd be our family's literary pioneer until, out of the blue, Dad told me he was writing a book. This revelation disappointed me at first but before long I reasoned that with my project long dormant, waiting for the insight I trusted age would bring, if he'd beaten me to it that was probably fair enough. More than that, it would be something that the two of us could share, and reading his manuscript really inspired me. His tale was one of facts laid down, a story of his life and times entirely the way that he wanted to tell it, and it brought clearly to me the kind of book that I wanted to write: one very unlike his which I hoped would shimmer more around life's uncertainty and carry in its pages that intriguing sense of eternal mystery which my favourite authors alluded to.

During the draft period – about four very full-on months which were followed by a couple of years of part time editing - it seemed as if the book was writing itself. Now that 'Maya' is complete I wonder if I should have planned the structure more consciously, thought more about what I would include and what I actually wanted to say. On balance, I suspect that the message I've had bubbling inside of me for most of my life would only have come by this process of my telling it and anyway, the twists and turns that did develop, the various interwoven sequences and the final coda which completes a number of the earlier passages, makes a finished work that I find reassuringly pleasing.

With the salting of licence 'Maya' is the telling of my tale and a heartfelt expression of my scant understanding. Laced with the sounds that embellish my life, it is a nod to the people I care about and a salute to all who have stuck in my mind for a variety of reasons. I hope I've managed to show a little of what I see when I gaze out on the world, knowing that my perception is mainly a reflection of what comes from within. A number of people have told me that to write a book is an achievement and it's definitely for others to decide if mine is a worthy one. Whatever the final judgement 'Maya' is presented to you now as the fruition of a dream long dreamed. That kind of fulfilment is something even I can be proud of.

Part 1

... and yet, in black night's chill,
does shine no light on still night's path.
Not sound, nor even rustling wind does stir,
nor breezes shake discretion's mask
of hush.

Unhassled and unhurried I,
can swagger, pensive,
down my way to mystery step.
Soft footed, quiet, leaf wandering,
this way unknown to my mind's map.

A hooting!
Does it call my name, or call instead illusion false?
For those there are to break my stride with promises,
or change the course
I've chosen, for me safe to be,
lest drown in this thick forest deep.
Oh how I long to reach the sea –
for now salt tears I dare not weep.

Hello

Night hung thick in the air like a gloss fresh painted as I crossed over the Roman road at Highbury and Islington and stepped onto the fields. The vintage metal street lamps which lined the Edwardian pavement shone their deep yellow light, a glaring clash with the night's rich darkness, as helicopters held steady high above, the cutting report of their steel rotors playing a 'mega-city two' soundtrack. The venerable townhouses waited as they always did on these countless occasions; these times stretching back to the days of my father and his father's before him, ready to bear witness with that straight-bricked dignity which seemed so richly befitting of such an institution's attendant; of such an animus whose name resounds far beyond this place, all over the world and through history itself. It was all set to be an amazing evening, and the jangle of my anticipation was already stirred as I continued on my way.

Not far from this very field, just a blink away really, was where it all began. Not only my entrance into this world in the old hospital which once stood near Mare street, but equally significant and enduring my early introduction to a lifelong passion; a colour and a flag and a pole to dance around, as chosen for me in my grandparent's little flat in Amhurst. Those earliest memories are not one's own, but are borrowed instead from monochrome photographs; white bordered miniatures taken with a suspension of disbelief that the fat-faced subject really was another you, yet I swear that I vaguely recall the time when the men of my family convened and the choice was made official. What followed soon after was my maiden visit; my initiation at the home of the hopes of all my fathers. Even on the day itself it was a blur, but my presence there and the promise that I too would one day belong, and so belonging serve the memory of those before me, wasn't only for me: it was an homage too for those no longer around; a joining of our line. This is part of our destiny, and one day I would see history repeated, repaid and replayed in the acts of my own new offerings, carrying the little ones on high myself just as more distant forefathers once did on dusty African plains, a tradition that endures the millennia.

Overwhelming excitement are the flashes of memory from the old iron stadium, my mind's images very much in colour; very much in red. The noise of the crowd, as if a growling from inside the earth itself, was all overpowering as I cowered by the sanctuary of my father, who then seemed huge. Both of us were guests of the Arsenal captain who was a regular in the West End boutique where Dad worked as manager, and whose number five I wore on the back of my shirt. To my left, completing the protective sandwich around me, sat a female supporter: kindly and indulgent in my memory, she seemed to like being part of my first visit. I listened half afraid and half in wonder at the single voice shared by innumerable throats, rising and swelling impossibly loud; smooth and rich and tonal, and fading back gently in a soothing wave of sound. I remember a Charlie George penalty which was followed by my own contribution of a verse of 'Good old Arsenal' smuggled low beneath my breath, lest I should be heard. The game seemed to last for hours.

I can hardly recall the thrills afterwards as I joined the players in their very own tea room, exhausted as I was from the hyper stimulation, but those photos tell their unmistakable story: a new recruit, all smiles and few teeth, with hair as wild as it only can be on a father's outing. Pictured beside me are various of my now sober-suited heroes, camera-patient stares on their faces as I stood there resplendent in their colours; the white bordered neck line which set off my deep red cotton shirt where the little white cannon was sown and proudly worn, marking a deep planted allegiance which from that day on imbued my heart.

Fast forward eight years. Little boy is now little man, and he's running in tears down the high street as an assured victory is snatched from his grasp by the cruel football fates. Dad by that time had his own menswear shop and I had started spending Saturdays there with him; doing a bit of folding, a bit of dusting, and obeying orders to 'make yourself scarce when a punter comes in'. I would be sent to fetch soup and rolls, and fudge cake at lunchtime. Afterwards, I would often spend the afternoon lingering by the record shop on the high street, entranced by the infinity of album covers and always hoping to find the next 'big thing' in the wooden racks.

Today was special however. As he always did on cup final day, Dad carried into his shop a little black and white television for the purpose of watching Arsenal vs. Man United. He would perch the portable set, with the aerial on top that only served to frustrate, on his black wooden desk amidst the percolator and card files. For both of us the work thing was an exercise in reaching out to each other. Too few were the easy words our fledgling father-son relationship could share but football was a cause we could both understand; a cause where we could join together as equals without any confusion or difficulty.

The two-nil lead had made me blasé, and I was swanning around the shop awaiting inevitable victory impatient for the whistle to blow. I was looking forward to watching the teams climb Wembley's famous steps for the presentation and then seeing our boys in red and white waving the big silver trophy in the air. Hardly bothering to watch the game as the clock ticked down, suddenly it is two-all and my desolate heart is breaking, my tears in full flow for a promise denied. Dad is half laughing, half disappointed himself, and my predicament is too much to bear so raging against the world as only a thirteen year old can, I'm out of the door, rushing down the street in hurt and tears. But then Dad's in the doorway waving me back with his two eyes still fixed to the little television, the header replayed and a victory score restored. What a day to remember and a lesson and a warning that I should have taken better heed of: that love is full of grief and joy and barely a whisper between them.

Sitting on a pile rug in the middle of the lounge, I recall the family meeting together, one side of our clan red, the other white, to choose my colours. The occasion was untypically good-natured, devoid of contention as this result was never in doubt, for both sides it seems accepted that a father's casting vote was all but cast-iron. Now, long after those early urn movers are gone, more than a century after the first of our name made their local choice, my own sons are wearing the same jersey.

Though these memories are dimly lit, the image of my grandparent's flat holds stubbornly firm: its tiny rooms, impossibly small for the lifetimes that were spent there; days lived and relived to their end and always, in my mind, in black and white. The huge television set that dominated the room really was black and white, as were the old photos which stared, Slavic and critical, from their positions above. Though even the wallpaper stays monochrome in my mind, I do remember the glassy orange glow of the faux flame on the bar heater as it wavered, set to shimmer, fixed there below the glass mantel and ornamental mirror on the wall. This faced out to the low two-seater sofa, and my papa's cracked leather armchair, deep red and forbidden, the chair and the glowing heater providing a little colour amongst otherwise sepia views.

I remember Nana breaking into wistful song with a faraway, dreamy light shining in her eyes.

'You'd be so, nice to come home to, home to, home to', she sang, taken back to a time long gone by an advert for a 'real fire', the song a sound of her youth before she was married and the family came here, inching north east from the slums around Shoreditch. To my young eyes this bricks and concrete environment was another world: so different from the modern one where I was ensconced with my parents. I recall huge metal bin stores where you didn't dare go, and the viaduct at the back which carried the heard but not seen railway line, shutting off absolutely from this London ghetto any access to the Hackney downs. A single curved railing in front of the concrete hallway outside the flat offered me the only suggestion of playtime equipment. It was something to swing from perhaps, but only in my fertile young mind. To all intents and purposes my grandparents' home really was another world, a place that was cast and set in another time, before the war came to change everything; to make places old and people too, they who shortly would live on rations and baited breath, as they waited those long dark war years while men like Papa, men of his class, served time and country in the heat of a hell I know little about.

My grandfather's act of returning from the war was his final word on the subject, leaving that last ring of hell behind him and shrouding it in silence rather than unburdening. Those horrors I suspect cut him short, short as the time we would have to get to know one another. I'm told he never really much conversed, expressing himself in clipped, enigmatic epithets which have been handed down and are regurgitated even today whenever a fitting opportunity allows, thus keeping alive his memory. I was fascinated with his pipes and his pipe rack; the wooden curiosity which was the source of many a recurring contention as he wasn't allowed to smoke in front of us children, but I recall my grandfather mainly through his sudden parting, and a wet linoleum floor in our kitchen that came to be half covered in our tears; my mother's, my sister's and my own, perhaps my first that were actually worthy of shedding. I remember guessing at my father's grief upstairs which was too painful and too private for us to be part of, life's grim reality intruding for the first time into my heart as my mind filled with wonderings of how high this water beneath me might rise.

Visits to my grandparents' flat were often, especially before Papa died, and were always a welcome return, this going back to a place ever unchanging and warm with my family's love. Christmas is a time I remember most clearly, so it's mostly from those times that there are memories to unwrap: the early morning journey which would find me in deepest despair, with my still mysterious presents teased and stolen away; locked in the car boot. I'd be filled with the gnawing, biting fear that somehow a villainous lock may come undone and my presents somehow spirited away; all hope thus lost. Pleas and then tears were more or less futile in my early world where rules were made of stone. Crossing the river with the tunnel roof lights above darting past my eyes, I'd lay across the back seat and gaze through the top of the window, toughing out my sentence as we drove through the bleak concrete roads and pavements of Shacklewell, close to where my grandparents lived, where trees were sparse and most always bare. At last, turning off Amhurst road, we would reach the barren court where the flats stood; where my father had been but a son; where again he still could be.

As soon as the car drew up, the curtains in the ground floor flat would twitch: my nana always found waiting there just where we'd left her. What hugs I'd get at the doorway as I stood halfway up giants in their tight warm embrace, the time apart always too long for them with their pinching and squeezing. Ignorant, and hardly understanding who meant what, I stole hungry glances at those boxes which were carried past me to the lounge, still wrapped in magic. Nana seemed to become a little girl again when it came to unwrapping time, and if she could steal herself from the kitchen long enough her uncontained excitement would see her joining in unbidden in your business of unwrapping if you should only pause or linger too long.

Some kitchen! Just a stove, a larder and a table crammed between, but what industry; what energy was expended there; a veritable factory that fuelled a family. Here, never ending meals were made. Chickens boiled and skimmed or roasted. Egg yolks grated to garnish the livers chopped, and beetroots souped, all my dad's favourites. Pots, pans, plates and silver cutlery were washed, dried and lovingly stored. Nana's old radio was as much a feature as she was; blue with the make in gold letters and a big white dial. Its place was by the plant on the frosted back window sill, and although long past utility it was too much of a fixture to be replaced; too many were the memories on the dial to change to a newer channel. I did buy her a new one for a Christmas that came some years later but it came that year just a few days too late.

Boxes and games and scattered excitement would be all about the floor in the evening, once we'd dispatched the dinner in the room at the side which had been my dad's bedroom and was now furnished with a table. Constantly refreshed with tea, the adults would already be waiting for the inevitable follow-on sandwiches; a tradition which each year would always come too soon as they sat bloated and dull around me, captivated by the box in the corner. Even as a small child, I remember the clock as it chimed every hour, and I recall the minstrels on the TV, as bizarre then as now. The younger men would engage each other haughtily, sometimes pleasantly but often goading; more lectures than discussions or else admonition and some seething ire. It was often over inanities such as who was the world's best guitarist, just as Hank playing 'Ghost rider' beamed from the television amongst his shadows. Dad's cousin invoked Hendrix to which my uncle, simple and sneering, offered his smarmy rebuke: the arguments always as black and white as the television itself, and not mind enough there for even the most modest meet. Papa back then was a mere spectator: he'd had his fill of fighting, and would sit quiet and pipe-occupied, not actually smoking but just tapping and cleaning. My mother, not yet used to this kind of display and who hadn't yet shed her too soft skin, also played onlooker as the men acted out their warring game in too small a space, replaying a loop without tire which led inextricably to a family breakdown, a reconciliation from which death would deny.

Perhaps a continuous moving on is inevitable, but at least when the old folk were transplanted from their old country and later when they moved up from the squalor of Whitechapel, they moved together as a package. Their place of worship was found on the main Amhurst road where the markets sold the kosher food and the familiar fare that the community lived by. My grandparents met their friends in the street and had family in the shops and on the pavements. They identified with their environment and that identity gave them peace. My parents would seek for themselves something different, however, and not seeing beyond the earliest and most immediate consequences, their decision to move would contrive a mould of more awkward fit for my formative years. As early as then; as early as those days of black and white, the theme of belonging was set and had become a desire that filled me and hunted me in my sleep. Even to this day as I bask in familiar, warming seas, delighting in the moment with the love of those I've learned to trust, I still feel sometimes afraid; still catch myself fearful for that untimely wrench which at any moment might come to cast me out, into the cold.

Beginnings

Who were they then, my parents, that they should forsake both their history and their peers, and snap with tradition? What was it that made them so bold, or so spiritually cavalier? For a start, it wasn't in the dance halls of the East End, or the coffee bars of Stamford Hill and Hackney that they met, living in the same part of town and so bumping together as they went about their existence, but rather it was 'up West' where their paths serendipitously converged.

My father was a menswear man, by then, after a brief apprenticeship as a diamond-mounter in Hatton Garden and a spot of door-to-door encyclopaedia selling. He got a start on hosiery at 'Glass' on Upper Street after he'd done his good time of National Service in the signals corps at New Market. Even back then he wasn't one to shirk. Such was his drive and presence, and no little ability, he was pretty soon breathing the rarefied airs of Piccadilly, specifically Brewer Street, in charge of the suit department in a new Fenton store and earning a salary that, albeit a pittance to my decimal ears, a year earlier he might have thought would have bought him a yacht.

The shop was just down from Carnaby Street and fed heartily on the late sixties' fashion maelstrom; the ground-breaking excitement which was so loudly spewing forth from its epicentre just a little further along the road. Various privileged dandies, actors and footballers were drawn into the store, perhaps by the waft of fresh brewing coffee, or even by the clothing, itself so much a part of the period jigsaw. More likely, it was the company therein that was both the stimulant and lure, the opportunity to mix with the locals whose diverse and unconventional characters added to this special time of change. One 'face' whose image would later be etched on my young mind was the man with a tap stuck to his forehead, just one of an entourage comprised of various degrees of 'bum', some of whom were already quite lost to hope while others, as time would show, would be just about to make it. Inevitably too, there were the junkies. All-in-all this daily show was enlivened by the various sounds from the trusty eight track; the 'Beach boys' and their long-haired summer sound, or 'Moon dog', with his strange orchestral cacophony, or perhaps 'Sergeant Pepper's' whose irreverence to these times played so well amongst this fast-living audience. This throng of characters shared a stage and set as their particular parts allowed and together patronised the establishment, either looking for, or providing, authenticity.

So here's my father, born and raised a product of the East End Council, and glad to aspire away from it. Mother knew a different start. She had spent her dreamy childhood as the exalted princess of doting parents in leafy Surbiton. Coming to Farleigh Road in Stoke Newington in the early fifties was a wrench that would not be without consequence: she was always looking back from her latter day enclave to her idyllic suburban childhood. Even though she had her family close around her, the auntie and cousins whom she loved, still she longed to return to a life that was so distinct from this dreary one in the East End ghetto; that ghetto of the mind where things were all done differently, and where the people were all the same. This frustration of her intellect would make retreat quite inevitable. As a youth she did not share my father's determined ambition, but clever enough she prospered in the local grammar school, winning points for her essays and her presentation, leaving there as well equipped as one could be for the life of the pampered sixties housewife that was meant for her. Societal change was in the air, however, and such preparations as these, indeed such assumptions as they were based on, were to prove less than satisfactory.

As I said, my parents met in the West End one night, mum going to find her older brother so they could travel back home together on the red number thirty eight. She was working as a radio controller in a mini cab company, her attractive feminine personality making up, in the drivers' eyes, for her lack of efficiency on the phones, and was based not far from the Brewer street shop where her brother was a department manager alongside my father. It wasn't the first time she had gone in to the shop to meet him, nor the first time that my father had noticed her, but as a family gem she was kept under wraps, and Uncle was what you might call 'protective'. By Dad's account his future brother-in-law was a closed book back then, even inventing for himself an array of domestic fantasies so he could project something more than what he felt was his mundane reality, and he wasn't prone to openness for even the most innocuous enquiries: those concerning my mother were especially unwelcome. Realising this, dad knew he'd have to bide his time; make his own introduction when the chance should arise, and that's how it happened.

One summer's evening mum sashayed into the shop a little earlier than usual looking for her brother. He wasn't around. It was one of those quiet mid-week days that seemed to drag. Having served the long standing hours with cleaning and straightening of the garments until they looked crooked; doing and redoing the in-store displays until they looked blurred, it seemed only right to her brother to take a 'vader' up the road and have a look see what the local competition was up to. With a fresh pack of 'Woodbines' and time to kill before closing, Carnaby records' siren call inevitably prevailed and a few minutes of absence from the store stretched to an hour. Dad was near the back of the store in the middle of serving when she came in looking for her brother. It was only because dad's charge was changing; trying on and admiring himself in some latest items of swimwear, that he was able to race to the door and apprehend my mother, getting there just as she turned on her heels to start a solo journey home.

"Are you looking for David?" he enquired at her elbow, all nonchalant and casual, though he'd almost broken his neck to get there. "He won't be long you know. Just up the road for a packet of fags," he assured her. "Would you like a wonderful cup of coffee while you wait?" There was something intriguing in his tone that convinced her to stay.

Returning, her big brother was none too happy to see what havoc his absence had wrought. My father, that uppity little twerp from the flats, and someone my uncle had long since determined was not the 'right kind of person' for my mother to associate with, was sitting there cross-legged on a wooden shoe cupboard bold as brass, playing my mother his careful selection of the latest and coolest tracks. Chicago's 'Beginnings' was on, a favourite one at going home time, and she was all smiles and admiration for his entertaining and charming best. Unfortunately, the swimwear prospect had long since left in search of that 'je ne sais quoi' which only attended service can properly reveal. As could be expected, the siblings' leave taking was a swift one. The bus ride back to Dalston was mixed: my uncle was brooding sullenly, while my mother rattled off questions too quick to answer, hardly noticing that they were left there to hang anyway. The damage was done.

After the wedding, they lived in a small flat above the barber in a run of shops at Hackney Downs Station. This comprised a single room with a big white bath tub which they filled using large pans of boiling water brought carefully from the little stove. Unlike his own parents and parents-in-law both, and despite their advice, Dad had resolved not to be a life-long tenant, and as soon as his place on the mortgage waiting list had come up at the National Bank in Berkerley Street, he bought a three-bedroom 'semi' in a leafy Stanmore side road, complete with an actual bathroom, a stone chip driveway, and a little garden which I remember always smelling of mint. I was born soon after they moved in. There wasn't the money back then for curtains, nor carpets, but hope is high at the beginning of an adventure, and so it was here. For my father at least, life's course was plotted and planned and most satisfactory.

For mum, though she didn't know it at the time, this was not to be the life that she desired. At home with a child and soon enough two, she mixed with the other women at the mother and toddler groups and coffee mornings. As her own truth gradually developed, she went through the motions, seeing that mostly the other women were of a type, and it wasn't hers. They seemed to her so at home, as if the time they spent there was fulfilment itself, rather than a means of passing the long day until hubby returned. Relative penury might also have been a factor; the lack of a washing machine and the greater freedom that one brought meant she felt more keenly the lack of 'appliance joy' that the others were so proud of.

More sinister, she was disturbed by how the women spoke of their relationships. Perhaps it was talk, perhaps not - naive as she was she couldn't really tell - but the women sometimes spoke of their partners in terms which my mother felt unkind, and all the more so as increasing familiarity within the mothers' circle made them less guarded. The focus of their happiness seemed solely to be on the latest household purchase or trinkets received. She took personally the disparagement that was meted towards a husband who could not provide; the criticism this entailed seeming harsh and unfair. Partly due to circumstance, but also to her nature, she couldn't even pretend to take part. She grew to resent the snipes that were taken at her own beloved husband, as well as the looks of pity, or scorn, when she maintained that the two of them were in this together and that life must be about more than what's put in your hand at the end of the week.

Just as this little world was closing in all around her; just as it seemed that no light and relief from the tedium could be found and the strain of her unhappiness was beginning to seep through to her own relationship, hope was reignited in the shape of a new friendship. One afternoon, as I trailed after mum in the local Spa, dragging my feet sulkily as my baby sister rode in the shopping trolley seat that I felt should be mine, I spied a plastic tool kit containing a hollow red hammer, green screwdriver and yellow mallet. My heart was set. Uniquely, perhaps because she just couldn't take any more of my whining, or maybe she understood the harrowing effect of displacement which the late arrival of my sister had caused, she bought it for me. As we left the store the tool kit was put in my hands, a perfect diversion while mum wrestled with the various straps of the big 'Blue Cross' pram in which I would otherwise have been crying to share a ride.

I remember my happiness at this unscheduled providence, the hammer especially, as red had already been chosen for my favourite colour. I remember the thick bulbous handle and its big fat head. Taking it from the box and holding it, light but firm in my hand, I felt a strange sense of power. I knelt and started to tap on the paving stones, concentrating hard and making sure they were all flat and even. After a moment I noticed an older boy standing near me, watching with his hands thrust deep in his pockets. I glanced up at him and we exchanged shy smiles, and going back to my work, he too was pretty soon kneeling. Though I would absolutely have refused to relinquish my hammer, mum handed over the mallet so he could share in my labours.

As we continued to do the work of the council, our mothers made new acquaintances of each other while my baby sister, to my delight, lay forgotten above us screaming in the pram.

Acquaintance turned to invitation, and dad was looking forward to meeting this Stella of whom he'd already heard so much. At the dinner table another couple made six. With their babies looked after and out of the way, the young group sat into the night adding Kummel to Cordon bleu and positing on all the wrongs of their generation, pleasantly surprised to find they had so much in common.

"But ah," said the hostess, as they poured scorn from high upon the perceived small mindedness and vacuous self-satisfaction of their peers, "it's all very well sniffing and snorting that you'd do it all differently, telling yourself that you're not like them, and something apart, but are you? Are you really?" she challenged. "Do you actually want something different, or is it just the talking about it that works for you?"

"Well of course," said my father, "talk is cheap. But what are you getting at?"

"Next Sunday we are heading down to Kent. There is a new development near the racing track at Brands Hatch that we simply must see; modern housing for modern people, and a completely different environment. If you really want the life you say you do, then you must come and see it with us."

"Yes," said Bill, who was Judy's husband and father of their two boys, "why not? We're going, and if it's anything like it sounds, it could be a real opportunity. Here everything's the same; just the East End transplanted to two up, two down, and everybody knowing where you've come from and what you've got. If you really want to live your own life; plough your own furrow as it were, this might be just the thing. We can be pioneers," he laughed, and the date was set.

The things we do for love. Dad was ambitious, and a battler-where he came from he'd had to be. But the better life he had envisaged while pulling himself up was something akin to what he'd always known, only more so: a house; a car; friends to rely on; the respect of the community and, by no means least, plenty of food on the table. These were the near stars he gazed towards. Defying a tradition that was unconsciously so much a part of his life, so much a part of his integral make-up, had never been part of his agenda. Suddenly, a realm of possibilities presented themselves to him, and many were uncomfortable. Where would they find kosher meat? What about the synagogue and the children's religious education? Could they even breathe the air down south of the river? Above all, he knew that mum had never really found her niche in this suburbia. When our lives seem to call for courage, we are often too quick to confuse doubt with fear. At times like these, it is easier to be brave than it is to be wise.

We Have All The Time In The World

Like the Rubicon, which once crossed was a commitment and a statement of intent, the three families put behind them a community and a shared gene pool. Fording the Thames in convoy via the singular tunnel of Blackwall, they left their erstwhile dream of North London, the 'semis' and their neighbours and friends who, thinking they must have lost their minds, thought no more of it. Just three months after that chance meeting at the bottom of Honeypot lane the conversion was made. Six little children woke in their new beds the following morning in a new world where swathes of woodland yet prevailed, a 'modern village for the seventies' made up of a series of neighbourhoods where planners had kept green spaces everywhere; orchards that were free for the picking; pathways which meandered away from the menace of cars. A local pub on the outskirts of the development became the non-denominational meeting point, and the adults would commune there on Sundays for some 'rest and relaxation' after the parties of the Saturday nights. With people coming from all over the south-east and further, from all walks of life, a vibrant and colourful existence quickly took root.

Going to a nearby nursery, the church school and then, as the local amenities further extended their reach, the village primary, life flowed as planned. We kids were left pretty much to our own devices, once old enough to be so left. Mum realised her dream by opening a boutique in the village, in partnership with Stella's overbearing shadow. Dad bore his daily commute, picking up a train to London at the mainline station a few miles down the road. Able to find our own way about the area in relative safety, us kids could come and go as we pleased, a freedom we were hardly equipped to appreciate. We'd knock for each other and cover the ever expanding village with endless games of 'hide and seek', meeting up at one of our houses, or in the shops hours later, to find out where the game had taken us and what we'd ended up doing there. We rode about on our bikes and if we needed some help, or lunch, or a little maternal attention, we could go to mum's boutique shop where the room at the back was equipped with a portable television set; a fan too for when the weather was stifling. With our mums spending so much time there, the room was a useful port, and though we didn't make use of it especially often, it was good to know that we could.

Living in a liberal and unquestioningly welcoming middle-class society meant that we never seemed to think upon anyone else's heritage, and least of all our own. Were it not for the rabbi's fortnightly visits (gradually tapering off as the journey from London became too onerous for a man of his advanced years, not to mention the prohibitive cost of a nineteen-seventies tank of petrol) or the weekly reminder of the Friday night Seder, sitting around the table with a half can of Coke before 'It's a knockout' or 'The Virginian', my sister and I would have had no clue that we were anywhere other than where we were always meant to be, growing up as we were in this non-sectarian Utopia. Inevitably though, it is what lies beneath that comes last to the light.

Turning eleven I left my gentle village school and moved on to a nearby comprehensive. This brought a shock that I wasn't prepared for. Due to my surname, and perhaps also my looks, some of my classmates seemed to view me with suspicion and as an object of prejudice. It dawned on me that most of them shared a common origin: one that unfortunately I did not. It became natural for me to feel jealous of the 'smiths' and the 'fords' - anyone in fact without a 'z' in their name. For the first time, though not the last, I resented the letters of my own family name which clearly spelled out 'intruder'.

This realisation was a blow. Now speaking my name a little quieter; holding my head lower as I tried to avoid undue attention, the disruption of moving from the school I'd known and loved was greatly exacerbated. Questions started coming to me, and I began to wonder who I was. My grandparents, especially my mum's mum, 'Bubi', who was foreign, and the extended family who remained steeped within the Jewish community, seemed somewhat different to me now. With them lay a truth that set itself firmly against the new normal I longed to be part of; here were implications that I wanted to ignore.

This sense of isolation was not mere paranoia. Hanging around on my own one lunchtime, eating some fruit that I'd brought with me, one of the boys in my year invited me to join in a game. I was shy, but delighted to be asked and included. I took my place more than willingly against a wall where the game was explained to me. I was told I had to avoid the tennis ball which would be thrown at my head, bending to the left or right to do so. I cheerfully obeyed as they led me exactly into position. Ducking sharply to my right on the third or fourth throw, I smashed my head against a metal pipe that I hadn't noticed. I stared at the blood soaked hand which instinctively I'd moved to my head to test the damage. Despite the hefty clue of the other boys' laughter, it didn't occur to me until much later that this had been the point of the game. Feeling even more keenly the unwanted outsider, from that time on I tried to keep myself safe during the breaks in that big scary playground by staying unnoticed and out of the way, longing for the end of each day when the coach would arrive to take me back home.

Is pleasure greater for knowing its opposite? What happy times they were when we'd stay for a few days with our grandparents. My sister Gloria would stay with Nana in the little flat in Everlyn court, while I would be just around the corner with Mum's parents. The two matriarchs never really saw eye-to-eye; Bubi somehow frowning upon her counterpart as something of a 'good time girl'. I've no idea how she conceived this idea but resentment had been brewing between them since the very beginning. At Mum and Dad's engagement party, possibly the first time the two sets of parents had actually met, my excited nana, good naturedly as ever, asked my bubi what she thought of 'her David'. What she got by way of reply - that Bubi 'was hoping for something a little better for her Janet' - wouldn't have been the best 'ice-breaker'. It wasn't the only time that a clash of cultures caused a rift between them. Dad's mum was born in England and was quite anglicised, whereas my bubi was born in Poland. Only arriving in England as a young adult, she brought with her a strong accent and a penchant for very straight talking.

Some old silver candle sticks that had been cleaned up and polished were given to my parents as a wedding gift. A sucker for punishment, Nana couldn't help but ask what her counterpart thought of this gift that had been made by one of her close relatives.

"Had I made such a gift to my daughter," the other responded proudly, "she'd have spat in my eye." Consequently, though the distance between their residences was slightly less than a ten minute walk, they never became friends and my sister and I spent the duration of our visit estranged from each other.

As evidenced by her daughter, my bubi was anything but deficient as a nurturer. Perhaps too devoted a mother, she was certainly a splendid grandmother. Both she and my grandad would spoil me rotten and treat me like a little prince. Even as I got older, I'd be happy to stay for weeks at a time. I have memories full of days spent lying on the sofa in the lounge, my de facto bedroom, watching endless runs of black and white movies on the television. 'Abbott and Costello' was a particular favourite, while my every wish was delivered to me supine, just as I liked it. In the earlier days, I remember how I'd wake up before it was light and join them in their bedroom. We would all keep warm in the winter by snuggling under the home-made electric blanket, listening to my grandad's tireless renditions of 'Paddy McGinty's Goat', or concert hall favourites like 'Burlington Bertie', and my Christmas time favourite about 'Minding an 'ole in the road'.

My grandparents lived in a slightly run down three storey town house, complete with a basement. They could never afford to heat it all, so large parts of the house remained a mystery to me. I never went down the dark, dusty stairs which creaked away behind the cellar door - Grandad warned me off with convincing tales of dogs there that guarded, their eyes 'as big as saucers'. Never mind that I thought he'd said 'horses', which I pondered for quite some time before finally challenging him on it - I think he was amazed at my gullibility. Naturally timorous, I never ventured alone past the first floor landing, nor to the work room where they used to do their dress making and tailoring while both were still working. This room had large sash windows that looked out over the garden. When it became a store room, it was filled with boxes and books and all manner of excitements: an old electric razor that Grandad kept; a mechanical mincer that to me was a living 'meccano' set; the 'Peanuts' cartoon books that I started to enjoy.

One time when I was playing out in the garden, scratching around in the dirt flower beds and abusing a particular leaf that I found there, Grandad informed me that I should be careful with it as it was edible. I was baffled: an edible leaf! I didn't think it possible. I was even more fascinated when I watched them boil it and saw it wilt in the pan. Because of that eye-opening introduction, spinach has a special place in my heart, and I never taste it without thinking of my grandparents.

Their kitchen also was a hive of activity. My favourite dishes were matzo-brae; scrambled eggs mixed with sugar and matzo, and the salads they made plain; ones not swimming in the oil and vinegar that my parents insisted on at home. I loved that they always concurred with my sneering for the 'rubbish' that Mum and Dad made me eat, plying me instead with the plain things I wanted. I loved that Grandad's chocolate drawer at the bottom of the fridge was always ready stocked: always my first point of call as I pushed past them at the front door on arrival. I knew it was slightly bad form but I was fairly sure that Grandad appreciated the joke.

A lot came down to chicken soup in my family: such was the effort required to create it that it was more of an investment than a mere dish, but the dividends were paid liberally whenever we were with them. Whereas Nana's soup was always consistent with the same wonderful taste and quality, with Bubi you never quite knew what the latest batch would bring. Though I always enjoyed her soup, steaming up at me at the grand polished table behind the sofa in the lounge, the moment before the first spoonful was always full of suspense and trepidation, such was the range of different flavours that she achieved through her unconventional seasoning and her absent-mindedly forgetting to add this, or otherwise neglecting to include that in its preparation.

Already quite old when I was born, my grandparents were well into their seventies by the time I was staying with them, but this was paid nothing by my youngest of minds. Blissfully insensitive, I never lifted a finger but allowed them to fetch and to carry, rewarding them merely with grateful smiles.

My cotton wool world received a shock one day when my uncle turned up to find my grandparents running about me, tending my every desire as I reclined on the sofa. His deep, angry voice at odds in that environment, he boomed a warning that 'I should think more of his elderly parents', his finger wagging home his point. When he was gone I made quite a show of my hurt and upset, huddled in Bubi's comforting bosom. Nevertheless, I knew he was right, and I continued to revere him.

My uncle had the luxury of an extended childhood, marrying my aunt and having his only son when already in his forties, and perhaps it was this that allowed him to continue so long playing the wild man that his half-Polish blood had made him. Spinning around town, he lived life to the extreme, whether playing his beloved tennis to kill or telling his bosses the way it should be. Not being my father, he was easier to admire. The relationship between my uncle and my father was always antagonistic, regrettably reaching a loving understanding only after many years had passed. For my part I always looked up to him. I wanted nothing more than to be crazy just like I thought he was, inevitably finding much in my make-up that reflected what I saw in his. A great affection always thrived between us, and is no less strong for the passing of years.

Beyond question, amongst my family I felt truly loved. My relationships with my grandparents and my uncle David was all I could wish for. Although far from my friends and the vast green village with its familiarity and freedom, and despite only an inner-city garden and the no-go roads lined by the strangely foreboding, knobbly and barren trees, I never felt happier than when I was staying there. My grandparents were looking after me; with them I would always belong.

Where do the children play

In the centre of village, just down from the recently extended run of shops where our mums had taken premises, a new more central pub called 'The Beaver' was built. This pub overlooked a huge square field which served as the grassy heart of the area, something like those medieval squares that the towns of Eastern Europe were built around. It was called 'The Minnis', and it ran away from the shopping area as a hill to the south, bordered at the bottom and to the west by different neighbourhoods. At the eastern edge began a scrubland which, growing thicker and denser, became woods. Beyond this was some farmland which marked the boundary of the development, land which had been here for eternity and which quietly seethed in the face of our ugly modern invasion. Stella and David had bought a house which overlooked the Minnis from the west, with the rooms of their children, Lionel and Barbara, looking out onto the field where we would meet and play, joined by any other strays that would appear on any particular evening. Many were the summer nights that we spent in the shadow of their kitchen window, throwing to and fro a frisbee as daytime would fade into darkness.

One June Saturday, a month before my thirteenth birthday, the village committee initiated an inaugural celebration. It was planned as an annually recurring event with the highlight being 'Village Day Saturday'. The week preceding was a build-up of activities for adults and children alike: a massive treasure hunt; sporting competitions, plays and film screenings to name but a few, all culminating in a huge fete that would fill the central field. Gloria and I spent the afternoon of the main day itself with Lionel and Barbara, wandering about from stall to stall in the sticky heat of the hot summer's day. We spent our money on the lucky dip and having a chuck at the 'smash the crockery' stall. Once penniless, we stood watching the tug-of-war and breathing the candy floss air; smelling the hog roast that was an aroma we never knew at home. Sometime during all the excitement we bumped into Rachael, a girl we'd known since primary school, walking around with her older brother. When he headed home she stayed with us, and as the afternoon wore on we continued to run into friends. Our little group carried on growing accordingly, until there were about twelve of us.

As things started to wind down at the day's end; the stalls and the fete all being cleared away on the field above us, we found ourselves gathered around a bench at the field's bottom corner. The boys were on the grass, boasting and trying to outvie one another; to see who'd done the best on the coconut shy (despite none of us actually having dislodged a coconut). The girls were all squeezed up on to the bench itself, none of them wanting to sit on the grass. Seeing the group segregated like this, it struck me that there was something different now. Running into any one of them previously on our rides around the village, I'd never given it so much as a second thought - whether it was Linda, John or Christine, it was just running into another friend; it didn't make any difference. Now I felt that something really had shifted. We weren't really being ourselves and it was as if we boys were trying to put on a show for the girls as they sat before us on the bench. I myself felt an inexplicable desire to be noticed and a few of the other boys clearly felt the same. I couldn't put my finger on what was causing this twist in our interest, but none the less all the chest-beating and braggadocio suggested we were pretty consumed by it.

Rachael had been carrying a cassette player that we now started listening to, us boys getting in closer and draping ourselves around the bench. After a while we got restless again, and a couple of us started lashing the frisbee; ripping it through the air at each other like a lethal weapon, close enough to the bench of course so that the girls would keep watching. Soon all the boys were joining in, and as Rachael got up to play, a thought suddenly occurred to me. Gathering up a couple of cardigans which lay thrown about on the ground and removing my own tee-shirt, I used them as corners to mark out a huge grass square on the field.

"Listen up," I cried, excited by my plan and full of self-importance. "I've got a brilliant idea. Let's play frisbee hee."

"What's Frisbee hee?" said Lionel, "Never heard of it."

"See this square?" I replied. "Everyone, come inside. Come on, Christine, you'll like this." Although it was about seven pm, *it was still w*arm and it felt great having my tee-shirt off, not just marking out part of the area but also serving to mark out myself. So different from being at school, I loved being the centre here. The others mooched over to the area and waited to hear the instructions.

"Two of us start as 'it'; me and Lionel, and everyone else has to move around inside the area keeping away from the frisbee. If you get hit by it then you're 'it' too, until in the end everyone is working together to hit the last remaining free person."

"Just run up to someone and hit them with the frisbee?" said Barbara. "That's stupid, I'm not playing that!'"

"No; it's not like that. When you have the frisbee you can't run; like netball. You can only throw, pass, or catch. Got it? And don't worry," I said grinning, "I promise I'll only throw it gently." From then on a game was born, and so too was a gang. On most summer days after that we'd meet by the bench after school, and more often than not we'd play frisbee hee. From her kitchen window Stella could watch our game, and sometimes while doing the washing up she saw that I didn't always throw that frisbee as gently as I'd promised. I guess aggression was a way of dealing with certain issues, and I was also starting to find my clumsy feet as a man.

The school holidays came and we continued to spend our time together, messing about in the Manor house gardens, or playing all day tennis marathons at the local courts which were always left unlocked and otherwise vacant. But now it was late August and that dreadful day of reckoning, the beginning of term, was drawing near. Thankfully for me, the prospect was not the dismal one it could have been as I was starting at the Grammar school in Gravesend, a change that for once I could whole-heartedly embrace. I was truly euphoric to be leaving behind the unremittingly ghastly experience of my previous two years of education. Even so, I was no lover of school work, and would happily rewind the few weeks to live August again if only I could. Although the days had become repetitious, and maybe the same old, same old of the summer months was growing heavy on us, like too much of a good thing, we realised that what we had here was special. Amongst us all there was a growing despondency that our holiday was coming to an end.

Since we'd all started knocking around together, our little gang had developed a dynamic that had palpably changed each one of us. We all felt somewhere that by developing our own micro-society and making our own decisions we'd got closer to becoming adults. Instead of whiling the days away listlessly watching cartoons alone on the television, or picking through 'TV Comic' for the umpteenth time, as we'd done for the countless summers before, this year we'd had such a time of it. We played less and postured more than previously perhaps, but each day we'd be round at a different house; some days going out early and waking others up, or else being woken up ourselves, but always part of a bigger crew, traipsing off in a convoy of mates to see who else could be gathered for the day's entertainment.

I don't remember rain. Perhaps indicative of the mood in this time of my life, the memories I have are of the sun always shining. Whenever the fancy took us there was always a quorum for an adventure somewhere in the village, even if a few of us were missing. Hanging out at the playground we were sometimes too self-conscious for this place of childish innocence, asserting all moodily and self-aware that our presence was an ironic protest; too grown-up to admit that we still actually enjoyed swinging and sliding. At other times, however, moving as we were randomly around that indistinct border between childhood and adult, we'd find ourselves again just happy to play there. If the mood took us, we'd brave claustrophobia and crawl into the under earth tunnel on our hands and knees; meeting at the middle of that dark dingy world with a fellow crawler who'd come in from the other side, only the twin openings of the semi-circle as evidence of the pipe which snaked deep buried beneath the grass mound. At those simpler times the climbing frame would be used just for climbing; the 'chin-up' contests that were waged at other more grown-up times eschewed. On the swings we'd maybe just sit there and swing, without making it a test of strength; of who could swing highest, forgetting for a while our former renunciations of these pure pleasures past.

Our gang had a loose, tacit hierarchy. Rachael was the unspoken queen. She was the oldest of the girls and three weeks older than me. She was always bubbling with ideas and adventures and when she wasn't about, the imagination of the gang was palpably lacking. The other girls looked up to her and though we boys liked to think we were running the show, we always needed her seal of approval when someone else concocted a plan. If Rachael was up for it then it followed that all the girls would be. Naturally something of a 'tom-boy', as she liked to call herself, she'd always be found in the vanguard wherever we went.

The pecking order among the boys wasn't as simple. The four of us couldn't help butting heads. Unlike the girls, who seemed naturally to settle into an easy order, it was a thing taken for granted that all of us hoped to be the king. Lionel was my oldest friend, one of the children I'd moved down with from London all those years back. Just by dint of being the eldest, a full school year ahead of the rest of us, he should have been granted a certain position. As it was, he actually fell behind as we got older when it became increasing obvious that he was the least sporty of all of us: these tests of strength and feats of sporting prowess became more and more important in establishing a pecking order. Socially too he was awkward, perhaps overwhelmed by the effective loss of his father, who he saw less of now as his parents had separated. Maybe he was just born that way, but I guess living with his sister and his extraordinarily overbearing mother must have been hard for him. Perhaps he was more prone than I to the negative effects of our experimental transplant: his black curly hair and more ethnic appearance making him stand out for what he was that little bit more. Perhaps our relationship never quite moved on from its inception; the two of us still banging our toys on the pavement and trying to make the most noise. Whatever the reason, things naturally became more complex as we grew older and we grew further apart. Gradually his presence was suffered more from loyalty, and then from a mixture of pity and guilt. In a very few years our association would die out completely.

Monty was a different case: very much a peer, and in my class at school. I suppose he was the 'clever one', set to follow in the footsteps of his older brother who was away at university studying science. On those rare occasions when his brother came home, Monty would bring him to see us. It was like the visit of a god. We'd all flock about hanging on his every grown up word, hoping that in his knowing dialogue he might reveal some of life's mysteries.

Monty and I each had a racing bike but he took the sport much more seriously and was the first to make the shift from the standard five-gear model to the super ten. I'd often see him darting along the village paths on some mission or other, always too hurried to stop but flashing a wave as he passed. His favourite obsession was whether one had a 'cycle' or a 'bike', and how one 'cycled' or 'rode'. Once, on the huge car park on the outskirts of the shopping centre we'd held time trials. Giving my all to catch his record I'd mistakenly pulled my rear brake going into a turn. Before I knew it I was sailing through the air, bike and body parallel to the ground. On landing, I slid along the gravel with my thigh an unfortunate buffer that protected my red metal frame from the worst of its scars. It was a spectacular crash, celebrated by the intake of breath from the watching pack. Scraped raw from hip to knee, I was helped to the shop for my mother's comfort. Significant in my personal history, I did not cry as I was helped on my way there: something of a miracle. It used to rile me enormously that Monty insisted on grading me deep below his number one in the rankings, but looking back I guess it's fair to say that among us, in this arena, he did wear the yellow jersey. He was always ready and able to push his machine that little bit further, no matter what risk to life and limb.

For all his speed and skill in cycling and despite his 'beg to differ' attitude, I didn't really take Monty seriously as a challenger. He was smaller than me, and being small myself I gave that no quarter, and as our young bodies developed at their different rates I would use the advantage of strength over him whenever I could. I only became aware of how important a factor this was when my sister told me that the female bench panel were unanimous when discussing my chest and my shoulders - of course I was delighted.

However, the definitive battle between Monty and I came with the frisbee on a long, warm evening about a year after that first 'village day' meet. Since these holidays had begun, the two of us had been growing increasingly chippy, with a climax building on this particular night. We had already had an incident: Barbara taking a carelessly hard shot and going off crying, thus bringing out an irate Stella with washing-up gloves still on her hands, confronting us and ordering that we clean up our act. Instead, we got more and more competitive; more and more aggressive with each other. As a game was ending, Monty was the last man standing. I was getting more and more angry as he darted around the square, diving this way and that to evade all throwers.

At last I found myself jumping to catch a pass from John and landing right by Monty, determined to make my point. Spinning around as he fled, and whipping the yellow hard-back across the grass from low down towards him with all my might, I watched as the disc made its way. Shaking furiously as it span through the air, it was rising to the level of his neck, and as Monty turned to look back and saw it coming too fast to avoid, he jumped to take the blow on his chest. At the moment of impact, as if willed, it gapped up and caught him mid-air in the throat. He fell crumpled to the ground with his mouth wide open and his tongue sticking out, choking as he held his neck. After a little while of panic he was able to breathe normally again, and was led shakily away to the bench supported by a concerned group.

Deep down I was irritated by the fuss. I was irrationally galled by the attention Monty was receiving. Not so deep down I was wearing a huge smile, convinced I'd won the 'final conflict' and almost beating my chest in celebration. The excitement and the adrenalin had trapped me deep in my ego; the beat of my heart like a background of tribal victory drums. When I think on it now I wish I'd been mature enough to understand the difference between play and pain. Who knows, perhaps Monty and I could have been enduring friends. It might be that I'm too harsh in hindsight, but looking back I think I was better equipped to create enmity than friendship.

John was a different case. Though younger than me, he was the sportsman; a footballer and county standard tennis player, encouraged and driven by attentive parents. He was often away at camps or playing in tournaments, but when he was home we'd meet at the tennis courts where he would demonstrate the latest shots he'd learned, some of us playing while others sat in the corner with spangles or opal fruits to share. John's mum didn't work, and being an only child we were always welcomed at his house with easily the best selection of chocolate biscuits; clubs, bar sixes and wagon wheels, and plenty of them. I often found myself round at his for dinner where, compared to the eight pm bell at my place, it was served comfortingly early. I also loved the way the dinner was dished out, his mum putting the food out in a 'build-your-own' style where bowls of potatoes, carrots and peas were set out on the table, along with a huge jug of steaming gravy, unlike the pre-plated methodology at my house.

Different to me in looks, John was blond with fair skin. He also seemed to have a different way of dressing, with his Fred Perry and Sergio Tachini tennis gear starting to feature as fashion choices. His age notwithstanding, I kind of looked up to John and thought of him as the coolest of our crew. This was a friendship based on a mutual respect, without the need always to be challenging each other. As it turned out, our friendship petered out a few years later over a girl. I'd taken John's side, naturally believing him when he told me that talk going round was just malicious gossip. When it transpired that he was the liar, my shock and feeling of betrayal left me reeling, and the wound to our mutual respect was left to fester. It proved fatal: the gap it created at the centre of our friendship was one we never managed to find a way back across.

Kicking our heels at the bench in that late August sunshine and not knowing what to do with ourselves to make the day worthwhile, inevitably by default we were drawn to the playground which was situated towards the main road. When Barbara suggested we play 'Desert island' the rest of us were too lacking in inspiration to resist, not to mention quite grateful that someone else had suggested it, and we fell to it easily. In the few months since the beginning of summer the physical changes had seemed to accelerate, and by appearance the boys and the girls had grown even further apart. Trying to ignore these changes, some more obvious than others, it was a relief to hide away in our imaginations. We could explore the park like some kind of mystical kingdom, rather than try to work out what our own physical changes might mean. The swings were transformed into a hut on a desert island; the surrounding park was an ocean with the thick, big leafed border bushes a mysterious, uncharted landscape. Finding food was our mission and our salvation, as the inventory was worth barely two day's supply.

We formed ourselves into small search parties, Rachael picking the groups and directing each into the furthest corners. Each group was warned to be cautious and call for help if they encountered trouble. Rachael and I set then off together; she directing me into the jungle and entering just slightly behind me, both now crawling on our hands and knees and moving very slowly as we kept down and out of sight. We marked our faces with dirt to disguise us, and full of the day's fantasy we were again those happy children; now negotiating the dense undergrowth; now crossing an infested river with stealth to burn. Truly lost in the moment I had no idea there wouldn't be a time like this again; a time of such beautiful innocence. We were scavenging for food in a hostile landscape, the two explorers alone and on heightened alert, afraid that each leaf, each river, might hide from us those silent dangers that we must strain every sinew to avoid.

Slowly edging towards a clearing I bade Rachael with a silent hand to wait while I sneaked closer and closer, keeping low and camouflaged against the green. At the edge now I looked out upon a vast plain with gazelle, antelope, elephants and other animals I didn't recognise, waving Rachael in closer now to see for herself. Through my binocular hands I scoured over the plain to the mountains beyond. Where was she? I looked around and didn't see her, then turning my head to the right she was there above me, seeming to trip and landing on me with her knee in my side, knocking the wind from my lungs.

Winded and half-covered with her hair, I stared at Rachael's face which was just inches from mine, momentarily stunned. Then our lips were touching and we were kissing; open mouths all teeth and saliva, interrupted immediately it seemed as Barbara and Monty came close by, almost treading on the ground where we lay. The spell of our play was broken; our imaginary world fractured by this sudden physical reality. We held each other's gaze for just an instant, looking but not really knowing what we saw, before jumping from the bush together in ambush of our friends, laughing and suddenly bored with the morning's ruse and looking for something else to do, the moment forgotten like it never occurred.

Kids in America

Summers go and summers come, and summers go again. Two years had passed since we first formed our innocent little holiday group, and again it was June, this time after what felt like an interminable year of study. In reality, I'd spent the school year shirking my homework assignments until the very last moment, then rushing on the morning coach journey to complete the barest amount of work acceptable with my exercise books sliding around my lap, making my way too quickly again to school and my recurring doom. Consequently I'd spent much of the year on report for lack of diligence. The months since the last summer holiday were mostly an unseemly blur of dodging and disgrace, but there is a scene I do remember from the beginning of the year.

Staring into the window of the toyshop as I waited in the cold morning for the coach to arrive, I noticed that the song 'January' was playing from a distant speaker. It was very much of its time: listless and drab in that late seventies fashion, with its weak stab at bravery and a simple, almost pathetic tune. What stung me was the realisation that I'd been in exactly the same place a year before, doing the same thing and listening to the very same song. This was the first instance that a concept of passing time properly grew flesh. Where previously I had blithely perceived time as something endless, and with that perception saw my life the same way, there suddenly appeared a chink. There was now a jarringly palpable point of reference and it's grown more and more obvious the older I get, as time itself, for me as an individual, runs faster and faster.

People talk of time as the fourth dimension, and I had been captivated by the concept as soon as Lionel introduced me to 'The Tomorrow People'. It was, again typically for its time, a low-budget but high-concept children's programme. I was hooked by it, rapt by the special powers of the characters, all of them outsiders, and especially by their ability to travel through time: the premise of a thousand games we then played for years around the village. Trying to rationalise, it seems to make sense that each year makes us older but becomes a smaller and smaller percentage of our overall life lived. The perception of our speed of travel through time therefore increases accordingly. Whenever this theory comes back to my mind I think of that kid again, cold and stamping his feet in the frosty mist of a January morning, hearing a ghost of a tune which was the dawning of a true revelation.

Winter was gone and spring had come, and the long holidays were once more upon us. In June, the village prepared for a third annual celebration. Posters and leaflets had been put up everywhere by the social committee; on lamp posts and trees and hallway mats, all declaring an even greater offering of events than the previous years. The excitement was building. Teams were being put together for the various sporting tournaments: bumping into John unexpectedly one day on our way back from school he told me proudly that he'd been picked as the star striker for one of the football teams. Another mega-treasure hunt was prepared, this one to encompass the nearby hamlet of Ash with its flint stone church and little nursery where I'd first raised an infant hand for the register. Mum had got us tickets for a kids' screening of 'Bugsy Malone', scheduled for the Saturday morning of 'Village Day' itself, before the real centrepiece and coming together of the entire week of celebration: another huge fête to be held on 'our' field.

When the morning at last came around, Gloria and I took our tickets and went excitedly up to the village hall for ten o'clock, passing through the shopping centre on our way where the shopkeepers were frenziedly buzzing about with their last minute preparations. There were many stalls set up outside the shop for the big day, a long line of them on the walkway giving the place the feel of a market. The stall holders themselves were made-up and in various costumes, which was funny to see. Dressed in a huge busty corset and crinoline skirt, Bob the local fireman smiled back at us as we laughed and waved: clearly even the adults were infected by the carnival atmosphere, all of us sharing in the sense of community and the day's special excitement.

The delicatessen had a crepe iron and a freezer full of home-made ice cream outside. The toy shop's trestle table had on display some of its cheaper items: balsa wood planes; pencil top rubbers and cartoon transfers. The owner of both the toy shop and the adjacent book shop, a woman I remember as decidedly un-child friendly, had also set up a lucky dip, though for us it was prohibitively expensive: I'm sure her plan was that only she would get lucky. Further down, the greengrocer had set up a huge barrel for apple bobbing, also putting out toffee apples, popcorn and fresh lemonade. As we continued along the path we passed face-painting and hot dogs. Outside the pub was a huge 'guess-how-many' jar filled with some kind of bean, the prize being a week's free patronage. Waiting for what seemed an eternity in the line which wound its way from the village hall door, we met up as planned with Lionel and Barbara. We were also joined by many of the others that we'd spent so much time with over the last two summers. Sitting together nattering quietly at the back, catching up throughout the film, we arranged to meet later at our bench to spend the afternoon en masse.

Though we'd been absent for what seemed like a lifetime, the bench was our own again in no time at all. We sat there swapping tales of the fun we'd had last year, and the year before that; that first year becoming known officially as 'last summer', always recalled as if nothing again would ever live up to it. We were looking forward to the adventures that lay ahead and just sitting there together seemed to fill us with promise; as if good times for us were just waiting to be claimed. Involved as we were in our reminiscences; so happy to see each other and with so much to tell, the afternoon's fair was in full swing before we decided to take a break and enjoy the action.

A few of the boys made for our favourite stall, the coconut shy. After spending most of our money trying in vain to dislodge those hard, hairy fruits, the stall owner took pity on us and told us to return in an hour. It was early evening when we did, and time to pack up, and he gave us three bottles of Pomagne which we took proudly back to the bench, all sworn to the story that we'd won them. None of us were drinkers and thinking them alcoholic, we weren't sure what purpose we could actually put them to. Rachael, who I'd hardly seen since last year and who really did look a lot more than a year older, and pretty with it, was once again the inspiration provider.

"We'll have a party round my house," she said, "next Saturday at five o'clock." How grown up we were, our gang was to have its very first party! So five o'clock then, round at hers in the room designated as a 'den', with only her mum and dad to persuade first.

We watched from our familiar vantage point as the fête was packed up; the stalls disassembled and the animals, donkeys and goats and other small creatures carefully led back by their handlers to where the transports were waiting. It was like déjà-vu, and the only activity that remained was the less than enticing prospect of a 'womble-thon'; tomorrow morning's official close where some of the younger villagers had been recruited to scour the field, removing the assortment of litter that currently was the only decorative reminder of the festive scene. It could have been melancholy seeing the 'Minnis' disrobed of its tents and now hollow of the crowds of people who'd thronged but an hour earlier, even more so with the light going down and a fun-packed week drawing quietly to its close. Bubbling with our plans for the weeks ahead, we were far too full of excitement and anticipation to mourn the passing of this albeit long-anticipated day. Finally, summer was here!

The green-light had been given, and we met at Rachael's for our first party. These Saturday night gatherings quickly became regular, our very own little night-club in the room which was a perfect hideaway for the lot of us. The family 'den' was an annex at the side of the house, the sofa there now augmented by several bean bags. Rachael's parents solicitously kept themselves distant in their own lounge on the other side of the house.

The den also had a television and a stereo, and though we can't have had Michael Jackson's 'Off the Wall' on a permanent loop, it is mostly all I remember, along with 'Funky Town' by Lips Inc. At the end of the night, when the curfew of ten o'clock was upon us, '10cc's 'I'm not in love', or 'It's Raining' by The Darts would accompany our chaste close ups as the lights were dimmed. Sentimental pop music mixed in the air with the sweet, unfamiliar smell of skin and the swoon of cheap eau de toilette. At the first few of these get-togethers some of the more daring boys got drunk on Pomagne, staggering about a little bit as we experienced our first taste of inebriation, until we discovered that it was just a sparkling soft drink. With the dangerous idea already planted in our heads however, we moved on to the hard stuff; a couple of 'Babychams' maybe, or even a 'Shandy Bass' smuggled in if the proprietor of the off license turned a blind eye.

The long summer holiday was again filled with each other's company, a family of cousins roaming the village with always somewhere to go. It felt as if those eternal months would never end. Inevitably, September's cloud was too soon looming on the calendar, and with it a sense that we had been terribly let down. In the final week, after spending another day mooching around the village, we found ourselves drawn back to the bench where we all sat around bemoaning our depression; too down even to raise ourselves for a game of 'frisbee hee' as night again drew in to separate us. Even Rachael seemed uncharacteristically glum and not quite herself. What was needed, someone suggested, was a final 'hoorah', an end-of-summer extravaganza, and it was quickly agreed that the following day we should go for a picnic, meeting back at the bench at noon and then heading off to the 'Wizard tree' for a final grand adventure. We made for our homes that night with our heaviest moods lifted; something to look forward to, and the end of the holidays temporarily forgotten.

Different for girls

Dozing in bed the next morning I heard the doorbell ring, an early contingent arriving for the day's excitement, and Gloria must have let in whoever was there. I lay looking through the glass of my window at the trees outside; a little outcrop of nature amongst the grass banks that bordered our neighbourhood's perimeter path. Birds came and pecked a little, then hopped and darted to another branch, or off to another tree which lay outside the little window of my view. I just stared unmoving at nature's vignette, capped as it was by a bright blue sky and complete with a couple of slow moving, puffy clouds. I was lost in a beautiful, thoughtless meditation.

Hearing feet pounding up on the stair carpet I closed my eyes getting ready to play 'asleep', watching now the veiny lines on the insides of my eyelids as they swam against the light; trying to hold still the shapes that appeared in my vision as they slid this way, now that way, slipping across my line of sight as backwards and forwards I moved my eyeballs. I heard my bedroom door open and I knew that it was Lionel. He stopped a few feet away and I could feel the scrutiny of his eyes as I kept dead still. More footsteps and Barbara had joined him, whispering in her nasally tone before their weight settled near my feet at the end of the bed. They started opening the cupboard and searching, I suspected, for my diary. Things were being moved; doors slid this way and that and then closed clumsily; certainly not softly enough if they hadn't intended on waking me. I smirked to myself: the book was safely hidden, and with the search frustrated I could hear that they'd now moved on to inspecting the records; the stack that was alphabetised on the floor below the record player.

That stack of records was to me the main feature of my bedroom; a true statement of the 'me' that I wanted to project. A carefully assembled, highly prized set of vinyl emotions; badges and treasures in sound and picture that I used to display: each one of them in some way a self-validation. All those Saturday afternoons I used to spend endlessly rifling through the empty sleeves at the bottom of the high street; the record shop where the people looked different, knew different things and did things differently; where I could quietly exist while the otherwise slow passing Saturday afternoons would painlessly fly. Sitting here at our favourite park bench a lifetime later, many of those happily rediscovered sounds are waiting here with me, distilled for the modern age and digitally translated on the iPhone in my pocket. I remember how excited I was; how auspicious it seemed as I unwrapped for the very first time this most modern invention, even before the advent of today's ubiquitous iTunes, realising that from now on all of my music; some of my best friends, could always be there around me in my car, or in the gym, and in my ears whenever I wanted.

Music from old was ever my faithful running partner, and without even leaving my room I'd end up in places that were far, far away. I recall always listening to that first record player with its clear vinyl lid and the crooked black arm that sat above the turntable, down at the far end of the shelf that was meant to serve as a desk. It wasn't far enough. Wilfully I would lose myself; embrace the distraction of sound and be infinitely transported from my duties; from my responsibilities and the rigour of my homework, yet without such diversion I could barely sit at my books at all. These records were a world I'd constructed and I loved them. Despite the retrospective judgements I make on some of the content today, I very much identified myself with that soundtrack of my early youth, going to a lot of time and effort in discerning and tracking down the things that I thought I should like; sending off to catalogues to fill the gaps in my collection as I felt appropriate, and then proudly recording each single or album I collected as an entry in the exercise book that I kept on proud display. It was one page to each letter, though for reasons known only to alphabeticians the 'S' section was twice as big as any other.

Apart from the pride of ownership and from their intrinsic vinyl beauty; those thick shiny discs which were black but for the few that were coloured, or even translucent, my relationship with music was in its way pernicious. Being a sensitive soul, full of questions that were coming from everywhere and nowhere, and trying to work out my place in the world, I laboured back then under a very dangerous misapprehension. Being incredibly moved by the tones and the melodies and the words themselves that seemed to speak directly to me, I was convinced that the world's secrets- all of its ultimate knowledge- was held therein to be discovered if only I could perceive it; if I could only stretch a micro-grasp beyond my natural intuition and make it my own. In every line and in every cadence I expected, no, almost tasted something universal. Just like my Latin translations, where my impatience and aversion to study had me grasp at any convenient glimmer of a possible meaning, invariably choosing the wrong one and setting off with it down the wrong path, so too in the music did I lift the meaning to suit my mood, instead of realising that the passion, the urge, was something that was especially mine.

Buoyed by my faith in what I was hearing I pushed further into the emotional world. Revelling there in my weaknesses, I allowed the music to confirm for me a path that was already leading me wrong. My failure was to realise that what I loved in the music; the richness of the feelings it engendered, was not so much the music itself but rather the depth of my own confused sensitivity that it revealed. Missing the point of my perception, I blatantly mistook the world around me.

There is no one truth that works for us all. Rather, we each of us have our own truth that marries where we are, where we've come from, and where we're led to go. Long lives are spent just trying to catch a merest peek of something that makes sense to us, so that in the end we might pass in peace, calm in the knowledge that whatever reason we were here for, ultimately we will have been harmonious with whatever it is that sent us. Whether or not this is a palliative, back then I had no personal philosophy; no inkling of a path which seemed to point towards anything of meaning; no meanest hint. Fool that I was, I really believed that the things within me that were moved by music could lead me towards a true light, or at least an understanding of what it was to be a man.

Joe Jackson's 'Different for girls' was a case in point: a haunting, echoing pop song which seemed to be talking directly to me; to where I was; to the very fundament of my point of existence. I hungered for the message and wisdom it alluded to; a message that would unlock for me the vagaries of my not so nascent interest in the male/female relationship. Rather than understand that it was just entertainment, I thought that my inability to make sense of its message was a sign of my ignorance. I just needed to be a little smarter, a little savvier; perhaps over-think it a little harder, and ultimately I'd get it. Of course it never did happen that way. Trusting the romantic leads that led me to nowhere, I ended up going places I should never have gone. The irony is that later a musical message would indeed come to my rescue, and finding me then ready would resurrect in me a life affirming emotion; reignite a flame that was long past ready to burn. However, I still had a long way to go and plenty of tears to cry before I'd come to be the man who could re-join the path I'd been made for.

Strobe light

The muffled sound of voices that came from my sister's room next door told me that Christine was in there with Gloria: she must have come along with the other two. After a minute they both joined the melee in my room. Gloria came over to the bed and poked me to get up, so I made a big show of stretching, feigning a look of waking surprise as I purportedly returned to consciousness. I shuffled myself and my pillow to the upright and sat up against the painted brick wall. Christine came and sat by me on the bed, holding in her hand the 'A4' sheet where I made notes of the songs I'd heard and liked on the night time John Peel show. From the time that I got my first clock radio I'd used his ten p.m. slot as a consolation for having to be in bed. I'm still listening to many of the bands I heard him play today, 'The Fall', 'B-Movie' and 'The Chameleons' to name just a few. I'll never forget the dark excitement I felt when I first heard the 'Adam and the Ants' song 'Puerto Rican' on there. Whenever I replay this sound of my youth, this echo of my teenage ignorance, the beat and his vocal challenge is alive again in the pit of my stomach. Happily reacquainted with my ears in the digital age, these old friends still inspire those same feelings of wonder, rage and indescribable passion, and I remember gratefully that I first became aware of them back then when I lay unsleeping, listening to the legendary DJ.

The piece of paper Christine was holding was a rough, scruffy one, written all over in whatever pen was to hand at the time. Blue, black and red ink shared the disorderly page, its scribbled entries hard to decipher sometimes even by me.

Strong...enough....to...make love to you?" she read smirking, and her words gave me a bit of a start, lying naked as I was under the duvet with the weight of her body pressing close to my hip. "Is this some kind of a love letter? What is this?" she said leaning in, and pressing further. Christine's proximity made me pause, flushing, to take command of myself. I'd known Barbara for as long as I could remember, and though not unattractive she was younger than me, and the deep familiarity meant that I thought of her like a little sister. Christine, however, was something else. She was a couple of days older than me, and slightly taller. For one thing, or two, in the last year she'd gone and grown breasts. Suddenly she seemed pretty much like a woman, and that really changed things. What also attracted her to me was a recently developed propensity to faint: an incident of her swooning on a trip to the London Dungeon sticks in my memory especially. To my chivalric nature she seemed like some kind of classic damsel to be swept up and shielded, if only I knew how.

Sometimes she stayed over with Gloria on a Saturday night and the three of us would be left alone in the house while my parents went to a party, or more often now to Gravesend where they paid regular homage at a favourite Indian restaurant. We'd sit on the bed in my sister's room watching a film, and if Christine was tired she'd rest her head on my lap. I loved it when she was tired: the experience at once unnerving, frustrating and exhilarating.

"It's the 'B-52s'," I said. "See?" pointing at a scrawl of the numbers, "I heard it last night."

"What's this then?" she pointed disbelievingly, "It says 'make love' doesn't it?" There was a knowing emphasis in her words, and her increasing playfulness made me squirm even more, feeling especially uncomfortable that my embarrassment was being played out in front of such a wide audience. "Come on, tell us, what's this really about!"

"They kept singing it," I protested. "It's called 'Strove light', or 'Strobe light' or something. Look here, it doesn't say 'Strong enough'."

"Really? That says 'Strobe light?'" Her disbelieving look was set in a frown.

"Let's see," chipped in Lionel, taking the paper and casting his investigative eye over it while Christine, enjoying my predicament, leant ever closer with a big grin on her face. Gloria, most often a nuisance but now a godsend, saved me. "Everyone out," she cried. "Let him get dressed 'cause we have to get going. Come one," she said turning to me, "you can't stay in bed all day." For once I was happy to take my sister's direction.

The five of us left the house and headed down the hill. I had a couple of 'sandwich spread' sandwiches, and some chicken roll that I'd found in the fridge, along with a cold flask of chocolate nesquick and a frozen bottle of 'R Whites' that we'd left overnight in the freezer. I'd also risked Dad's wrath by sneaking out a six pack of coca-cola which I'd found in the room we called our study, really just the place that he kept the various 'goodies' brought back from the trips to the 'cash and carry'. At the bottom of the hill were the townhouses where Linda lived and though she hadn't been about for a few weeks we rang the doorbell just in case, waiting outside for signs of life as we stood twisting our bags. After a decent pause we rang again, but still there was no answer, so we set off towards John's, walking through the Manor house car park and passing the tennis courts where we spent so much of our time, then crossing the one main road that bisected the village. John's mum answered the door, cheerily as ever, and told us he'd gone ahead. As we turned to go she shoved a bounty of club chocolates into our bags, despite our well-mannered but easily yielding protestations. It was like Halloween come early.

As we got to the end of the path and reached the corner where our bench was situated, John was the first person I laid my eyes on. He was standing in front of Monty with a tight grip on his handlebars, while the daredevil himself was standing tall on his pedals, leaning out from the bike and making a show of himself for Rachael and Lisa who were laughing as they watched his antics with a cooler bag on the seat between them. James was there also, a classmate who'd moved up to the village just a few days after 'Village day' last year, his family leaving behind a more rural hamlet just a couple of miles down the road. He'd run into us at the bench the following weekend and had been one of our number ever since. The girls had been impressed, which was a bit unfortunate, and I had to admit that with him around the natural hierarchy of our group was changed. Knowing him from school as a thoroughly good guy; kind, friendly and considerate, this change of status wasn't too bitter to take. Physically, James was far and away the biggest one of us; a senior in our class due to his September birthday. With his semi-permanent five o'clock shadow affording him the early blessing of swarthiness, he already looked quite the man.

Standing slightly away from the others and facing our approach, James was the first to see us. Grinning, he called out. "About time too!" followed Rachael in mock sarcasm, which Monty took as a cue to make a show of looking at the new digital watch which graced his wrist, partly sucking up to Rachael but also to show off what must have been a birthday present. He'd just turned fifteen, and we'd all clubbed together to buy him a book that he wanted; a 'Dungeon Master's Guide' to expand his fledgling 'Dungeons and Dragons' collection. The gang had been none too impressed by the 'Ian Dury' inspired acronym I'd insisted on writing inside the front cover.

"Are we ready to go?" she said, "I'm starving."

"What are you doing with that Bike?" I asked Monty. It irritated me that he and his metal machine were almost inseparable. "You can't take that with you in to the woods."

"We're taking it back to James's. See you at the tree," and so saying he started off, surprising John who was still holding the handlebars. Released, he rounded the bush and whizzed back the other way along the path that ran behind the bench, with James running on after him.

The sun was bright as we went, picking our way carefully through the scrub with high lifted steps and looking out for the briars, the odd crisp packet and even a bottle or two there embedded in the tight gorse web. Batting away the annoying clouds of midges that were suddenly buzzing about us in the warm hazy air, the woods soon began to thicken and it grew darker as the fully-leaved trees kept out the sunlight above us. We continued to make our way towards the far clearing where our big tree stood, its picnic canopy high up in the branches. With Monty and James not around I felt I had to take the opportunity to grandstand, so I declared that I would lead us by a route that I'd discovered while exploring on my own the previous summer. It was slightly longer, but it ran along the north side of the chalk pit, which was always cool to visit, and from there along the boundary fence of our old middle school. Forging on purposefully without giving any time for Lionel or John to object, the group fell in behind me, but after about thirty minutes, I started to wonder where the path that I should take had gone. I was sure that I knew the way, but now back amongst the trees the light wasn't great. I didn't fully recognise the features around me as we walked on with our bags getting heavier- a year can look like a long time in nature.

We'd started out smiling and full of excitement; sharing ideas about what we could do after our picnic and talking about the games we'd played over the last couple of months. We compared these to the ones we'd played during that legendary 'Last Summer', a period that James had long grown sick of hearing about. As we continued deeper, the darkness grew thicker; the shafts of light which pricked through from the sky above becoming more stark and more sparse. Somehow the mood among us seemed to change; an uneasiness seeping from within as the world around continued to grow ever more sinister. Rotten old leaves squished in a damp slushy mulch beneath our feet. Branches here and there were lying broken and rotten on the ground. Others hung pendulous, cracked and twisted against a trunk, stump-ends all gnarled and chewed and decomposing.

The thick air had turned musty and unwholesome and my uneasiness was laced with guilt as my confidence faded with the path's growing unfamiliarity. Worse than getting lost; worse than letting the others down was the galling thought of Monty's sneer, his jeers unanswerable should we have to turn back now, if we could, and come at it again from the shorter, regular way. Just then looking about me, to my relief I saw that the orchard we used to pass, albeit on its further side, was just across a bridle path. Thank God! All we had to do was get over to the other side, and then we'd be close. Adjusting my path as if the whole time I'd known what I was doing I turned in that direction, choosing to ignore Lionel's suspicious looks that followed me as I did so.

Geno

At last back on the path I could relax, but as I did so I realised that it wasn't only the surroundings and my orienteering that had been making for a feeling of uneasiness. Once again we'd all had a brilliant summer together but something was very odd today; something I couldn't put my finger on. Perhaps it was the end-of-holiday mood but somehow, the dynamic was unusually off. John was John. I knew him well, spending as much time as I did round at his place (his mum's hospitality saw to that) and Lionel and Barbara, and Gloria of course; Christine too was as I would have expected. Rachael though, who was always plotting something and always so full of fun, seemed uncharacteristically quiet.

Now that I thought on it, though I'd been around her pretty much every day of the holidays, we hadn't been alone or shared a private word. It seemed such a lifetime ago that I could hardly believe we'd kissed, if that's what it was, way back in the bushes in the park. We had hardly even looked at each other since that fleeting moment when for a few seconds our gaze had caught deep in each other's eyes. Before leaping away in hurried denial we'd been so close to a real connection. In fact, I realised now that what had occurred that day almost exactly two years ago, inexplicably, had scarcely crossed my mind until now. Having the memory coming back so vividly half startled me, involuntarily looking behind to the path where she was coming up from behind. I could feel my face reddening as I recalled the close up of her freckles and the strawberry mark on her cheek; the smell of her bubble-gum and the mischievous flash of light in her eyes. I felt weird.

"What are you doing?" said Lionel pointedly, appearing next to me and bringing me awake. "Do you know the way or not?"

I didn't even realise I'd stopped walking. Looking about, I saw Gloria and Barbara were waiting as well, with Christine and Rachael coming up behind with Linda; the three of them talking conspiratorially together, and then looking up surprised and suddenly silent. This started John laughing but he was cut short as we heard a booming voice which made my blood run cold.

"Well, what have we got here?" mocked Baxter, coming out from the orchard. When I had laid eyes on the orchard moments earlier I'd thought it meant deliverance, but now that idea was mocking me. Instead of a nagging unease I stood at my worst nightmare, trapped in the midst of this dank and now justifiably foreboding forest. "Oh look; if it isn't the famous fucking five! What have you got in those bags? Something nice for me?" Lionel and I stood the nearest, motionless and sullen, and I could feel the others moving closer together behind us. Baxter's horrible dog waited by his side, unleashed and drooling, and the ghost of a memory which had long lain hidden, of it biting me, now rose up from my stomach and made me feel sick. When it's not going your way, it's not going your way. This was living proof.

Quite a few years older than me, Baxter had been 'the bogeyman' for as long as I'd been able to explore the village without supervision, living close to our house in a nearby neighbourhood. Whenever I could I'd take a longer route round rather than pass through his territory. On the occasions that I did go by the run of terraces where he lived, mostly with my parents, even passing the other side of the grass strip opposite caused a shiver through my body, relief growing as the distance between us was stretched again. I hadn't been able to remember exactly what had caused my phobia, but seeing his animal before me I recalled running the few minutes home to where mum and dad were sunbathing in the garden; wailing with my hand bitten blue; pierced and throbbing on a sweltering Sunday afternoon, so many summers ago: innocence shattered and a lifelong fear of dogs set down by my first meeting with Baxter. They went round to speak to his parents, but coming back with no joy and finding no shared set of values, they warned me to steer clear of him. I'd managed quite well until now.

I don't know what his story was. I think he spent long periods away from the village, and I could go for months or years without seeing or hearing anything of him, but when he was about he always meant trouble and I did my best to hide from it. I'd heard stories about his violent tendencies, and was so wary of him that once, when a friend told me that one of Baxter's neighbours had a set of cartoon stickers to sell; stickers I really wanted, it took me a week to pluck up the courage to go round there. I felt so guilty about my cowardice that I couldn't confess it to anyone, but shaking and anxious all the way; watching all around me and afraid of the alleyways and bushes that I passed, I arrived only to find that I was too late. I was gutted to have missed something I'd really set my heart on. Now here I was; stuck fast like a fly in his web; paralysed by fear if not by venom.

"Give it here," he said, motioning to the bag that I held, now resting on the floor at my feet. He took a step towards me and his animal, this Cerberus, stared menacingly and slobbered.

"No," I said. "Come on Baxter, leave us alone." My intended defiance sounded more like a plea, but I'd found the will to stand up to him and I felt myself growing tall with a surge of pride in my chest. He sneered and came a step closer but I stood fast before him, standing up for all of us. It was so important now to be brave in front of the others.

"Arghhh!" I'd involuntarily released the bag as he grabbed my shoulder, twisting me round in an arm lock. The sudden pain contorted my face; my arm helpless in his grasp feeling like he could snap it with a flick.

"You think you're big enough to front me do you? I'll break your arm! Get on your knees." The others looked on, Lionel and John in front of the girls, and I felt their pity making me smaller as I desperately tried to stop my legs from giving way.

"Let him go," said Gloria. "Pick on someone your own size." Baxter laughed, tightening his grip and pushing more of his weight down on my arm. I winced again as the pain shot deeper.

"I will break your arm," he asserted. "Are you an idiot?"

"No," I said through my gritted teeth, tears welling into my eyes.

"I said get on your knees!" He pushed down harder, and I had time for one last, semi-defiant 'No', as my resolve withered away, and with the pain growing too great I gasped and let my legs take me down to the ground, kneeling on the floor as my friends looked on. Baxter laughed; a big victorious laugh, and pushing me face down into the dirt, he picked up the bag and marched off still laughing, his dog following behind.

I stayed lying there as the pain in my shoulder subsided, hiding my tears in the dust and enduring the pain of my humiliation as the others gathered around. There was no damage done but I felt that once again I was humbled; my pretence of strength and manliness shattered in front of the very people that I wanted to believe in me. This day was going from bad to worse, but at least Baxter was gone. I got myself up and wiped the dirt and bits of bark from my face and tee-shirt, just as an apple whizzed past my head from behind me and almost hit Christine.

"Quickly, get behind a tree!" shouted John as he scrambled for cover. About twenty metres away a group of lads from the gypsy camp, somewhere beyond the borders of the village and yet another place I'd always avoided, had decided it was their turn to torment us. Apples were now coming thick through the air, from right in front and from the flanks as well as they moved around us. We watched out to avoid the incoming projectiles, keeping low on our haunches behind a tree. All the girls except Rachael backed off to find deeper cover. "Come on then," implored John, picking up a couple of the apples around him, "let's give some back". Taking his lead, first Lionel and then Rachael started to hurl the green missiles back to where they'd come from. Still deflated and useless, not ready to move on despite this new threat, I took to picking apples up from the floor and passing them on. This went on for a few minutes; volleys exchanged and then lulls, while I just felt bruised and picked on, wishing they'd go away and leave us in peace.

The apples were coming slower now; the volleys more sparse and only from the front, and it seemed that those throwers who had been flanking us had done so only in passing us by. There was just one group of diehards left, about fifteen metres in front of us behind a couple of trees. As the lull went on we started to wonder if they were still there at all, keeping ourselves hidden just in case. Waiting with the forest quiet around us, the situation now seemed far less precarious. My spirits were coming back and I was kicking myself. A chance to join the others in making a fist of it and stupidly, lamely, I'd let it pass by. I poked my head around the tree trying to make out if I could see whether they were still there: I could see no-one.

"Damn!" I thought. "Bloody typical," as I bent down and picked up an apple. Although it had a big bruise it mostly felt hard, like a cricket ball, and its weight felt good in my hand; as if holding it there I was now somehow loaded. "Why did today have to turn out like this?" I thought bitterly. I looked up at the quiet tree ahead of us, now just that; no longer a threat and the trouble passed. Suddenly swinging my arm with all of my might I released the apple; all of my anger and frustration and rage packed neatly with it, tied with a bow and delivered with the furious arc of my swing. It flew through the air away from me, its path about head height, marvellously straight and flat as I followed its trajectory, on and on unerring. Suddenly, at the last moment a face; without warning a head popped out from behind the tree looking and the apple struck right smack on the forehead. A moment; the head frozen there with open eyes still staring, and then falling away; falling back out of sight.

Rachael turned excitedly to face me, seeing what I'd seen, but I couldn't quite believe what my eyes had shown me. I smothered a feeling of panic that I might have made things worse. Keeping a look out from where we were hidden, and whispering over to John and Lionel, we were all trying to work out what was happening behind the tree ahead of us and what the rustling and the muffled voices meant. After a minute we saw three of the boys moving away from us to the side and out of the orchard with a fourth carried limp on their shoulders. One of his legs was hanging down, swinging gently as they went.

"We've won," I thought as I saw them retreating, though admittedly I felt a little unnerved and guilty at the sight of the unconscious casualty. We called the girls forward with big whooping forest shouts. As they came up Rachael was full of the tale of the apple, and how I'd knocked out one of the boys with a throw. The others were happy too, because we'd won. Our little gang was not used to the flush of a victory. Each one had their own little detail; their own favourite part of this piece of a morning that was already folklore, told and retold as we made our way to the clearing full fresh with excitement and ready for the rendezvous with the others.

As we approached the wizard tree, holding sway as it was in the middle of its own clearing, it was a sight to behold. Ancient, twisted and grey, with a cove in its hollow trunk large enough for three or four of us to squeeze into, the lower branches were spread wide like arms, and wooden knots like eyes in the middle made an overall impression which gave the tree its name. A circle of creepers hung down on the far side which formed a high-curtained chamber, one Rachael last year had claimed as her own; one where boys had been strictly forbidden. There on the bouncy branch, growing out about five metres to the left sat Monty and James, both balancing cross legged. Monty was looking our way smug with his green rucksack behind him on his back.

"We didn't think you were going to make it," he said. "We have got the right day?"

"I never doubted you," said James, and as he hopped down to the ground Monty almost bounced off the branch as it recoiled, suddenly lightened. Grappling to keep his seat on the branch he hurriedly got his legs astride, shooting a look of annoyance at the back of his erstwhile branch buddy. James was unconscious of the ire he'd provoked and was already doing a round with the customary offer from his packet of polos.

It was an easy tree to climb, the many branches making it possible even for Gloria, the smallest of us. We soon sat high on the platform that we'd discovered when climbing it last year. It was located so high up in the branches that passers-by might go right under the tree without knowing anyone was up there, though in truth not many people used to come this way. The sandwiches were put into the middle and were happily shared, fortunate as I'd lost mine and Gloria's, but the Baxter trauma was behind us now. It gave me real pleasure to see the jealousy in Monty's face when the great apple blow was again recounted, and we wondered if the victim was okay.

Once we'd eaten and got tired of sitting up there, and most of the chocolate bars that John's mum had given us had been suitably dispatched, we climbed down by one and variously amused ourselves. Some of us were swinging on the creepers at the bottom; running down the slope with one held tightly in both hands and jumping out into the air, then swinging back and running to try and stay upright: invariably ending up scraping along on our behinds. Others were sitting and bouncing on the special branch, or else scratching around the ground with twigs, looking to find the assorted marks that we'd been cutting into the tree and its neighbours since the previous year. Some of us were looking for branches; bits of wood that would make worthy articles for a sword fight, and then someone, it was John I think, suggested a game of 'forty-forty'. We were up for it, and nominated 'it' he leant his hand-covered face against the tree trunk, already counting as we began to scatter.

Looking around I caught sight of Rachael who was waving, signalling for me to follow her. As I made to do so she set off ahead, running away to the east, opposite from where we'd arrived. In a few strides I'd caught up and we were racing each other, darting through the woods together with now her in front, and now me, weaving in and out of the trees; jumping over branches and pieces of wood that were scattered over the ground as we went. Shooting sideways glances at each other as we pushed on with our contest we ran further and further, only slowing down as we came up to the perimeter fence. Reaching it first, I hopped over the stile and stopped, Rachael just behind me, the two of us now at the edge of the wheat field completely out of breath. Full of our race, we stood facing each other with big open-mouthed grins, our hands on our knees bent over as long deep breaths gradually caught up with our fast-beating hearts. Slightly recovered, I lifted a hand and placed it gently on her shoulder, and close together, looking into each other's eyes, once again we were connecting like we had all that time ago in the park. Something sad; a look of strange inevitability was in her eyes. Caught there staring at each other for a moment I felt that weird feeling come again to overtake me and my heart started to quicken. Standing up straight, she smiled and held her hand out to me, and taking it I noticed how soft it felt; how hot and sweaty too. For a few more moments we stayed set like that, maintaining our dumb gaze, and then slowly and deliberately she started off into the field. Still holding her hand I followed.

The sun had leaned back past the woods we came through earlier, and it was late afternoon rays that now reached us; the tips of golden prisms shining through the tree tops and the long grass to play patterns in our eyes on our half-shuttered eyelids. Laying side by side on our backs and gazing up into the sky, the warm air felt easy as it caressed our naked skin, listening in silence to summer's natural hum: the click of the crickets rubbing their legs; a far off tractor, with every now and then the sound of an engine from a passing car, distant and fading on the road below. That strange feeling of ignorance which overwhelmed me before; the 'what now?' that had gripped me, just dissolved when she placed my hand on her tee-shirt, and moving still closer put her face next to mine. I remember the feel of her skin: so smooth and taut, our eyes still open, our lips just meeting, and then slowly, meltingly falling together, our faces pressed and then eyes closing, held by each other as our hearts beat with love.

I turned my face towards her and watched as she stared at a lone cloud above; the freckles dotted above her pretty nose, more now than earlier in the summer; the little strawberry mark on her cheek; her brown eyes, and something of cheekiness in her smile as she chewed on a blade of corn, the head casting its long shadow down past our toes. Lost swimming in time and peace with our soft hands together, suddenly I was jolted back to life as she turned her face for the corn head to slap me on the chin.

"It's rude to stare!" she laughed, jumping up and quickly grabbing her clothes to put on. Suddenly I felt cold and naked, but I didn't think I'd ever feel ready to leave that place. I reached out for her hand. "Come here, please, let's not go," I pleaded, trying to pull her back down.

"I have to go," she said, and then paused, looking down sadly at me I thought. "Come on," she said more brightly. "We must. It's getting cold. Get dressed now. Come." I didn't argue. I just sat up, and finding an errant sock I put it on, pulling on my shorts, tying my laces and untangling my tee-shirt as I stood up beside her. I bent forward to kiss her mouth but found only her cheek, and she pecked me back, giggling in my ear. We turned and walked slowly away hand in hand, leaving the secret spot of flattened grass in the field behind us. Climbing over the stile we crossed into the woods, and making our way back my heart felt both heavy and light; retracing our steps to the tree which was now deserted, and then on to her place. By the time we got there it must have been quite late as there was a tinge of darkness already in the air. I stopped at the top of her path and watched as she went to her door and picked out her key from the faux rock there with the white number four on it. Going inside she turned back and smiled at me, and gave a little wave, and then closing the door she was gone. I never saw her again.

Scarborough fair/In Shreds

Sitting here at the bench that I always choose to wait on when I arrive before Tommy, I can't help but marvel at the beams of light that will shine out one day from somewhere behind the tall houses to the north, from the vicinity that will boast a new stadium, searching around the dark night sky like something remembered from a batman cartoon. The stream of people moving along the road has grown thicker by now, and with my gaze I follow a selection of the passers-by. Some are running, competing for pace with the leisurely bikes and their flashing red lights and orange jacketed riders; while others stroll, or pull a suitcase behind them, fresh from some outpost far away. The whirring pitch of those little wheels and the metal heels that click on the tarmac mingle to mark the air with short little scratches, adding a light metallic line to the soundtrack of the night.

Ungloved hands are thrust deep in my pockets to find a warren against the cold, waiting here amidst this maelstrom of times; where future and past converge, yet where outward appearances seem uncommonly neat to my eyes. Not just the lines of people straight making their way, but a deeper orderliness that speaks of planning; of structure. The great trees themselves, each one a long-time resident, seem so perfectly spread, and older even than the lights which so well illuminate this much-trod thoroughfare; those orange glowing casements that begin just beyond the grey stone statue on the very first corner; a corner I've passed some hundreds of times, bedecked in its wreaths of laurels and small iron cannons, just like those that we take to our hearts.

Even now if I think back about Rachael leaving like that, about a dream cut short, it makes me feel old with a tired, heavy sadness. I remember going off into work with my dad the next day, happily distracted, and then that evening not knowing what I should do; should I call or go round, in the end choosing to do nothing. Sunday seemed to pass in a blur, spent mostly in sleep and thoughts of her made absent by that impending dread of school the next day. Though sometimes I ask myself why I didn't reach out, I know the answer. What happened between us had mystified me, and not knowing what our next move was; who each of us should be, I didn't want to act like a novice.

I thought perhaps that Rachael would be waiting for me at the shopping centre on that first day back at school. I spent all day in class dreaming about her; imagining her there when the coach came. When it did, she was not; nor was she there on the second day, and not seeing or hearing from her all week, on the Saturday morning I went up to the little flat above the shops where Christine lived with her family. I knocked all casual with my words rehearsed; ready to ask if she fancied going round to Rachael's with me. I didn't know why Christine looked so angry when she came to the door but I started my speech anyway. Tongue-tied and barely begun she cut me short, almost spitting at me like it was my fault that Rachael had gone; that she hadn't wanted anyone to know about her dad's transfer; how they'd just left for somewhere up north wanting no goodbyes. I stood on her doorstep cold and stunned right through, and seeing how shaken I was she seemed to soften but it just made me feel worse: my world was spinning. Not wanting her to see me cry I hid my face, too late. I turned and ran.

Looking at the world about me now; feeling the cast of that pain which time has rubbed smooth, I can't help but think how permanent this place seems; so ancient and unchanging. The fields; the trees and the houses, just as they'd been a hundred or two hundred or I don't know how many more years ago. Only the parked cars are out of place, where carriages and horses before would have been; where ladies under parasols might stroll on an evening jaunt, and gentleman, tail-dressed like characters from a Dickensian novel, would doff their top hats to each passing opportunity. How different are the lives lived here today I wonder. You've got to be lucky to live hereabouts, then and now; very lucky. As long as the fields remain; the very soul at the centre of this place an unbroken line to time immemorial, perhaps change can be held back forever. How did these lucky few in their marquee homes come to hold such privilege? City wheeler dealers perhaps, or silver-tongued 'Rumpole' lawyers. I'm just glad to be here, however temporarily; to have found my way back to this place where I'll always belong, sitting on our bench on the field where my ancestors have been before me; watching where the trail of their paths once led them as I wait here for Tommy, remembering.

Life went downhill after Rachael left. Wounded; heart-broken as I proudly insisted, I contrived to make my pain a handicap, moping around and compounding my misery like some faux-Romeo who we just happened to be studying in school at the time. Romantic plays and poets were a dangerous place for the impressionable young Milo. Taking pains to wring out the last drop of my emotions; to prove my own standing amongst those miserable greats, I'd sit tear-soaked with music guaranteed to bear me even lower, my room darkened with 'Simon and Garfunkel' as I feigned hopeless misery. I would pass on my parents' concerned offer to join the family for a meal out and instead spend Saturday night after Saturday night alone, preferring the sympathetic company of my own special woe. At first they were all understanding, and Gloria must have hinted something of what had occurred, whatever little she could surmise, but as weeks turned to months my affectation wore heavy, and the house had to move on. Christine, from whom at first I'd tried to hide my real feelings, now saw me at the lowest ebb of my contrived theatre, and if not already as close as a brother, it pretty much ensured she'd never again see me for anything else. Before I knew it I'd dug myself a hole: the friends that I'd pushed away had now withdrawn. The gains I'd come by so slowly growing up; the respect that I'd earned, was indulgently squandered.

Just remembering those dark shameful days I feel like I'm sinking back into them, as I sit here on the bench. So long passed, they should be leavened by now with relief when they return to me, but to think on it is somehow to be there. There's nothing more self-indulgent or easier than to trace the fingers of my memory around the scars they left; to press down deep to find their bruises, and bring them back to wallow in again. Lifting my head and perversely enjoying the weight of my heavy heart, I turn my gaze outwards and sit here just watching. It's still early and I know that Tommy will be here, by my side in the midst of these fields that will later carry tens of thousands; now still relatively sparse as Barbour-wearing locals, celebrities some, walk their dogs: obedient on leads and mannered as their genteel owners. Others are taking their evening jaunt by the long, thin cut paths that criss-cross the fields, lay lines disguised, as part of their regular routine. Real lives, rich in peace and quiet, are lived around this field you see, even under the ever looming shadow of a football carnival which, with its excuse to excess, rolls into town every ten days or so. When it comes, for those that remain it comes as an occasion to scurry; to get clear before the comfortable norm is swept away. Match night with its attendant hordes is to our locals just a gargantuan blip; close your eyes and it will pass, until the next barbarian wave, as life in between returns to civility.

Golden Brown

My self-torment was bottomless. I shake my head to think of the extent to which I contrived such misery, set on this low path by my own stupid ideas. Was it just that I needed something to hold on to; something that I could relate to and thus somehow make sense of myself? If that's the case, I must have felt that any dumb conviction was better than no conviction at all. My daily routine didn't help much. I didn't look forward to school, and was left very much to my own devices in the morning; waking to an otherwise sleeping house as my sister would be taken to school later, my parents themselves not early risers. I'd leave the house without a word shared, unless I appeared forlornly at their bedroom door to offer a sorry-for-myself word of goodbye, and my walk across the village to catch the school bus was habitually tearful: even becoming a source of remark and humour to those of my parents' friends who used to see me. I'd cheer up a little once I met with my school mates, sometimes playing a game of tennis-ball football as we waited. Even if that translated as being stood against a wall, at least this time I'd be parrying their shots as goalkeeper.

Winter wore on with each day beginning in the same unhappy pattern, but one morning a few weeks into the Spring term I noticed a girl I hadn't seen before, waiting in the spot where the girls' school bus was due. I fancied that I kept catching her looking shyly at me, and there was something about her crooked smile, exacerbated by the braces she wore, that attracted me. I saw her again the next day and the next, and soon I'd be looking out for her; hoping she'd be looking out for me. I had grown sick of myself and the world I'd created, and this shy newcomer could be just the break I needed; a rebirth and a perfectly timed redemption. I had a new plan now, and hope was reborn.

I started to hang around the shops after we'd been dropped back from school so I could bump into her. On the third night of trying I did, seeing her walking along with Linda who lived a few doors up from Lionel and Barbara.

"Hi Linda, how are you?" I said over-eagerly. The words jarred somewhat as I'd walked past her with my head down and without so much as a nod of recognition on many times since the picnic last summer. Though I addressed her, I was actually smiling at the girl she was walking with.

"Oh, Milo, wow!" she said sarcastically. "You remember me now do you?"

"I..Um..You know, it's..Um..." I was stung by the deep scorn in her voice and didn't know how to proceed or what I could say by way of excuse. Her gaze was even worse; disdain sharpened by pity, and looking away from her eyes and down at my feet my worn out shoes struck me; as scuffed as I felt inside.

"Are you going to walk us home?" said her friend, sticking out her hand to introduce herself. "I'm Maddie by the way, I've seen you at the bus stop haven't I?"

"Yes, I've seen you." I said recovering myself. "Can I?" I said, looking at Linda, who shrugged as they started to move away down the path, Maddie passing me her school bag. I didn't so much walk with them as follow, but the gratitude I felt was like that of a drowning man handed a hold at the last. The encounter had me almost skipping back home, full of the joys like Romeo starting from the sycamore grove; right after his 'Whipped and tormented' speech was tellingly interrupted by the change in the wind. Assuring myself that this could be it, I determined to ask her out at the bus stop the very next morning.

Next morning I stood scared stiff at the bus-stop as I awaited a chance to make my move. I kept sneaking looks to find her and my bravado- while the other lads ignored my protests and nagged me to take up position for their shooting practice. Over anxious, the narrative in my head said that the bus would arrive early and ruin my life. Then I saw Maddie, and starting over too quick, set myself up for a chorus of whistles and shouts.

"Oy, where's he going?"

"Where you going Mo?"

"Mo's got a girlfriend!"

Half way across I checked myself to a pace that was more casual, and tried to block out the furore. Locked on course and red of face, my legs felt awkward and gammy but my autopilot carried me across the car park to the spot where she stood facing away from me, engrossed with her friends. As soon as I got there it felt all wrong. I got no response from my croaky 'hello', watching the amused grins grow wider on the faces of the girls she was talking to, marooned as I stood there for what seemed like ages. I started to toy with my blazer button as my green parka was open, stuck without any way to retreat as the boys continued their cat-calls; whooping with enjoyment at my anguished predicament. I began scrutinising the brick pillars, counted the coping stones, and at last she span around, like something theatrical, all friendly and superior.

"How are you? How lovely to see you," she said, talking it seemed as much for the girls around her as for myself.

"I wanted to ask you...."

"Yes?"

"Ummm...Can you come over here a bit?" She didn't seem to understand; just kept on beaming at me with her big smile, enjoying herself tremendously.

"Do you want to speak to me about something?"

"Yes. Can you come.." I gestured.

"I'm busy now Milo. Why don't you come to my house tonight?" she said. "Then we can have a nice little chat."

I nodded assent as the girls around her went past the sniggering, and gave themselves up to hysterics. "Six pm, see you later lovey," I heard as I walked away, feeling at least like I'd proved myself in the fire. Surely this meant that I'd get the prize that I wanted; a proper girlfriend, and a way back to a bit of respect for myself. I fixed a big smile on my face, but I couldn't help feeling pretty stupid as I returned to the others who were enjoying themselves no less than the girls at my expense. 'Desperate time loves desperate measures,' I thought, 'and tomorrow morning I'll be the one laughing.'

I rang the doorbell, pulling myself straight and self-consciously lifting my chin and smiling, or grimacing anyway, my lips tight and wide. The house was the same model as my own; a four-bedroom 'semi' of modern design, with the same boxy utility that most of the village shared. I waited, not wanting to ring the bell again too soon; not wanting to seem rude or impatient but eventually, after hovering my finger over the bell and counting to twenty, slowly, I rang again. Looking up, I saw the curtains twitch in the bedroom above the kitchen; my bedroom at home, and I sensed movement in house. Eventually, through the glass panel beside the front door, I saw the hallway door open and then there she was, standing before me.

Dark brown wavy hair, cut short but now grown longer, her deep brown eyes widened by blue make-up at their outside edges, her mouth reddened by lipstick and her eyebrows shaped precisely, Maddie smiled down at me, the hallway higher than the pavement outside. She looked considerably older with her hair down, also by the fact that she was made up and no longer in her school uniform.

"I didn't keep you waiting did I? I was finishing off some art homework and so engrossed I just couldn't pull myself away. I hope you don't mind." It wasn't really a question. She had on a white knitted jumper, sleeves hanging low off her wrist and bulky enough to give away nothing of the girl underneath. Her skirt, pleated with folds and long to the ground, was the colour of mustard.

"No, no...it's fine," I said, shaking my head to dispel any appearance of objection, and then blurting straight out with it. "I just wanted to ask you if you'd be my girlfriend."

"Come in, yes, come in," she said laughing, not at all put out. "Have some coffee." I wasn't really a coffee drinker, but it didn't seem a good time to spoil the flow. I'd done it; I'd asked her. It felt as if the battle was already won.

Stepping up into the porch, I followed her heroically to the kitchen where she filled a cafetier with heaped spoonfuls and added the boiling water. "I think I'm drinking much too much of this," she said, when she poured the steaming dark liquid into two cups, "but it tastes so good." I took a sip and agreed. "How well do you know Linda?" I asked, using the only piece of common ground I could think of, and wondering how I could guide the conversation back to the point of my call.

"She's lovely isn't she? Told me all about you," she smiled, raising her eyebrows, signifying I wasn't sure what, but it couldn't be great. "She's been in my class since the third year."

"Oh, so you've been at the school all this time," I said surprised. "How come I've only just seen you this year then?"

"We've just moved here. I was living in Denton, but my mum and dad split up, you know, and my dad and the evil step-monster shacked up, and they wanted to make a new start somewhere different." I found out that she had a younger sister, a brother and couple of step-brothers, though where they all were now I couldn't tell. We sat for a while at that long wooden farmhouse table; very different from the modern 1970s furniture that I was used to at home. Time passed quickly as she talked and I listened, still wondering how to close the deal. Finally, with the time on my watch close to eight pm, and needing to be back for my tea, I asked her again.

"Yes, I would love to be your girlfriend," she replied, looking over the table and into my eyes, and smiling as she took the hand that I reached out to her, "but things are a little bit complicated at the moment." I sat there, my limp hand in hers. "It's nothing, really, but I've sort of got a boyfriend in Denton. I mean, he's not my boyfriend, of course, but he sort of thinks he is, and I need to let him down, gently, you know what I mean. I wouldn't want to start going out with you and for there to be any confusion."

"Yes, yes, that's good, yes. So...what..."

"I'm going back there next weekend, and I'll tell him that it's all over. Then we can be going out. Okay?"

"Okay," I said, pushing away a nagging feeling of doubt, and assuring myself that we'd be an official item very soon.

Heading home, through a short cut involving a crouching scuttle through a set of bushes that ran on one side of the tennis courts, I resolved that Maddie would be my Lesbia and I would be her knight.

"You're going out with Maddie from Denton I hear?" A big lad with an Irish accent, probably the first I'd ever heard, suddenly appeared in front of me as I hung around outside the school building the next day in first break, his attitude one of amused menace. He was a couple of years older than me, and I'd never spoken to him before; hardly even noticed him, and suddenly I'm on the spot. "Er, well, not exactly," I replied. "Not yet."

"You're hanging around with her though aren't you? What's going on?" The challenge in his tone was making me nervous.

"We're just friends at the moment," I said, adding defiantly; "but I will be going out with her."

"Will you now?" he sneered.

"Why?"

"There's someone at home who'll be very interested to hear that." He certainly wasn't trying to be friendly, and though I wanted to seem untroubled my face must have told a story. The adrenalin was running through me and making me feel queasy.

"You just watch yourself," he laughed again, "You'll find out why."

Riders on the Storm

With the fates stubbornly refusing to turn enough for our star to rise, pretty soon a pattern was set between Maddie and I. My supplicant attendance at her kitchen table went on and I would listen eagerly while she filled me in on the latest minutiae of her excuses, along with other confidences that were befitting of our special bond. Many weeks went past like this with Maddie still finding herself unable to clear the way for us, but with me declaring my worshipful undying love. Through these evenings listening to her promises a friendship was born: one like that between a princess and her eunuch. In time, when I was far enough lost to my original purpose, I would be afforded the odd chaste kiss as reward for my wonderful patience, not to mention my unquestioning faith. I hated that her brother, the oldest of the three, used to greet me with outright hostility but looking back it was the least that I deserved; such a pathetic creature I must have seemed as all the while, chief confidante and cheer leader, I kept myself close thinking how lucky I was to be where this dead end had brought me, quite unable to tear myself away.

It was one Saturday morning on the phone that Maddie told me, and the plan at long last was going to come right. Maddie informed me that today was the day: it was definitely happening, and by tonight that poor deluded fool whose ignorance we often mocked would be out of her life for good. I begged Maddie to let me see her later and though reluctant, she at last relented. My day was spent in a nervous state of heightened excitement, but when the evening finally came it wasn't the celebration I expected: Maddie wouldn't even let me come in. She said that she just felt too sad; that it was so awful to see his hurt when she told him, and it broke her to have been the cause of so much distress. Even though she'd been as kind and as gentle as she could, he would hardly understand her.

"He's not like you,'" she said when explaining that it had ended in tears and recriminations.

"We'll have to put 'our thing' on hold of course," she went on, "for just a little while longer, to let things settle down." I protested, but she said she simply couldn't think of it at this time, consoling me that it wouldn't be good for us to begin our relationship proper in such tawdry circumstances; with her feeling so disenchanted with relationships; with life and things in general. When I told her that I could make her feel better, and tried to put my arm around her, she pulled away from me angrily before admitting that she was almost fainting with tiredness, and it was time for me to go.

The next day some of the boys from my class were going to the local swimming pool. This seemed just the opportunity to get Maddie out of herself; help make her feel better. It would also give me the chance to parade my physique. I was aware that the rugby I was playing at school was helping to shape me favourably, and the spring weather wasn't warm enough for me to impress this point around the village. To my delight, when I phoned Maddie and told her about the plan and who was going to be there she said she'd come along. Arriving at the bus stop with Gloria and Christine we all met up, costumes wrapped in our Swiss roll-like towels, with our drink and snack money folded deep at the centre. James was there too, and that was quite nice as I hadn't seen him out of school uniform since the summer. Maddie mentioned nothing of yesterday's torments, and around the others she already seemed in much better spirits. We all shared a good laugh on the journey peering down at the cars and the people from our place above the driver, streets coming rolling towards us and the bus scraping against the occasional over-grown branch as it made its juddering turns.

It took about forty minutes, and we got off at the stop which was just a short walk from the building; a huge red corrugated iron structure which dominated its surroundings. It must have been designed by post-post modernists; to my untrained eye easily the ugliest building that I still have ever seen in my life. Once changed and around the water it was the usual charging about; both feet on the ground so we wouldn't be called up for running, and all the boys spiking in to the water almost on top of each other, without actually 'bombing'. As usual, the boys' general horsing around was played out in clear sight of the girls, feigning disinterest as they huddled whispering together on the steps at the side. Alan and Buzz were there, as were a couple of the others in my class who lived more locally, along with some mates of theirs that I didn't know.

We started taking turns on the low diving board, and when I was up, climbing the steps and taking my position, I looked over to make sure of my audience. Priming the board and propelling myself through the air as far as I could, I aimed to demonstrate with sheer power and the grace of a perfect dive what a fine man I'd grown into. In my excitement, I neglected to check the water I was landing in, and demonstrating beyond contradiction what an idiot I was, I smashed my face on the skull of an unsuspecting swimmer. It was painful and messy, and though the guy I'd hit was shaken up, I'd come off worst by putting my teeth through my bottom lip.

Once the staff at the centre had tried our home phone number and found no-one there, Gloria and I were accompanied by the 'first-aider' to the local hospital where I got stitches in my mouth. The experience seemed other-worldly. I felt displaced, as if the world I was used to had somehow transformed and become darker; more dangerous. Of course I felt completely foolish, even a little guilty, for the damage I'd self-inflicted. Abandoned by the others, I was very grateful to have my little sister there looking after me; she was even insisting loyally to anyone that would listen that the accident was just bad luck. Afterwards, when we'd been put on to a bus that would get us back to the village, I remember how wobbly I still felt, sitting beside her self-consciously with my lip all swollen and sore. Staring forlornly out of the window as we passed the glowering leisure centre that housed the pool, Gloria holding my arm, I wondered if I'd even been missed.

Maddie didn't appear at the bus stop the next morning, but I was busy anyway, showing off my stitched up mouth which proved quite an attraction; the big lump on my lower lip where the teeth had cut in, and the four black jagged stitches. When I got to school and sheepishly entered the classroom, the boys there also crowded around me, again wanting to inspect the damage. I showed off a loose end of the thread that hung from my mouth, like a limp spider's leg, that was driving me nuts. Asking about the remainder of their afternoon, Alan said they'd gone on to the fish and chip shop with a couple of the girls in tow. This struck me as odd but before I had a chance to ask anything further, suddenly everyone had to be elsewhere.

James sidled up to me during Friday afternoon's registration and very diplomatically mentioned that after the swimming at the weekend he and Buzz had taken Maddie and Christine home. Buzz was one of the oldest in our year, and having just passed his test, was the only one of us that could drive. Jim told me that Buzz dropped him off after they'd seen Christine back, and that he had then gone with Maddie to hers. He said they seemed to be hitting it off, and he wanted to let me know. I hadn't shared all that was going on with Maddie and I, but I guess from what Jim had seen at the bus stop he'd worked out that we were a couple. I could see that as a mate he thought he should probably warn me. I thanked him for looking out for me, but assured him it was all fine. As far as Maddie was concerned I told him, I was an insider, and I knew her state of mind. Anyway, I'd be seeing her that evening, and I was pretty confident of how things were going to be between us now. There wouldn't be a problem.

I burst out of her house, slamming the front door and almost breaking the glass as the jeers from that family's other tormenter steeled my heart with anger, delaying the imminent teary capitulation that my anguish would not be denied. Predictably, once I was across the road and out of sight, and no longer defending myself from the slights of outrageous insult, I gave way to a flood of tears, bending over the petunias on the pebble pathway.

"I don't want to lose you," she'd said. "What we have is so special, you know that. Milo, you are my best friend!"

"But I want you as my girlfriend," I protested weakly, starting to feel choked as the tears rose, the full awfulness of the situation starting to confront me.

"Nobody loves you the way I do. You promised, and it was all lies."

"No, I will be Milo, you know I will be. We are so close but this isn't the right time for us, I know you can see that." She put her hand over the table on mine but I pulled it away. "There's just too much going on in my life at the moment. Later, when things settle down, then our relationship will actually be something that lasts, not like this. Buzz," she said mockingly. "He's nothing compared to you; just a silly fling. It's just a rebound; I know that's not what you want."

I felt her hand again, looking blurry on mine as I stared down, averting my face from her. Blinking away the tears, each drop that fell sat there proud on the dark brown table like a tiny Perspex dome; the light that shone in from the patio doors reflected and highlighting the wooden grain that it sat on. Her soft words continued to reach me: the voice I'd worshipped for so long, convincing myself that we were the real thing; stronger than strong. Her hand on mine was comforting but tantalising; almost burning, and though I wanted to push back, I couldn't. I didn't dare. "...and he's not like you Milo," she continued. "You mean everything to me. I need your help; to share my thoughts with. How do you think I'll live without you?" Now she was squeezing my hand to make better her point. "I don't want to ruin that. Come on, not now, not until we're both ready."

"Oh look, the Jew's crying!" announced Thomas triumphantly, bursting in through the kitchen door.

"Get out Thomas, leave him alone!"

"Oh ha ha, who's a poor little didums," he continued, and I stiffened, lifting my chest with a huge intake of breath through my nose, as best I could in its semi-blocked state, and frantically wiping my eyes with my arm as the hurt turned to anger. I shot her the most theatrically defiant look I could, leaping away to round the table and flee past him at the kitchen door.

The final insult, just to make sure I knew that fate conspired too in my misery, was to find the front door locked and impassable. After pausing for a few moments in outright disbelief as I weighed up my options, I had to return indignantly to ask for the key.

"I'll get it," said Maddie, glowering at Thomas, who was having the time of his life. "Why did you even lock it?" she said to him angrily.

"Don't worry," he said innocently. "I've got it," and walking out of the room, he unlocked the door and beamed at me, pushing it open and showing me the wide outdoors with a sweep of his arm. Out I went, pulling the door shut behind me.

On the way back I resolved it was over. This time Maddie had gone too far, and if she didn't realise what she'd lost then soon she would. I didn't need her. I could go back to my friends and forget about her, and she's not even that nice anyway. I went to my bed and slept, sound in my decision and safe in my anger. When I awoke the next morning I felt so very alone, and there was a hollow pit in my stomach. My life had had one purpose, one comfort and now it was bereft. And what if she was right? Maybe this isn't the right time, and anyway, if I don't have her, what else is there for me? We are so special together: she knows that, she can't bear to lose me.

Later, I found a card she'd dropped through the letter box. The picture on the front was a red phone and red flex, an old-style home phone of course, made up repeatedly of the words 'Call me' as a collage. On the back was that extravagant hand which was so recognisable, where she'd written; 'Please call me, even if it's just to tell me how much you hate me.' 'Ha' I thought, 'that's right, I should hate you! She needs me as much as I need her, and if I do stay close then surely it will only be a matter of time'. I let her sweat, and tightening the screws I didn't call her until that night, imagining her waiting for me all through the day, and when I did I was proud, and haughty. She said she was sorry, and that she was sure I understood, which I graciously conceded, and she promised to make me a special tea the next day. So glad to be won over by her care for me that promised so much, I fell back into line. On the Monday morning she summoned me over to her side of the car park, as we waited for the coach, and in well trained obedience I went. Returning to the boys' side, I batted away their vulgar insinuation; they didn't understand what we had between us; how could they? Now our relationship was set: I the confidante, her jester; she the goddess, untouchable. My dreams became ever more distant as she grew ever more exalted and far from my reach. I'd made my bed and I slept in it, alone.

'Seek, and you shall find' they say. I was so deep in my malaise, so discouraged by my various failures and so ignorant of my deficiencies, I didn't even realise that I should be looking for a remedy for the ignominy that I'd made of my life. Nevertheless, the universe will have its way, and whether I was seeking or not, one evening it found me. At first, it was only as a dull sense, but a chink of hope managed to reach me; an idea that there was something other than what my meagre life calculations had allowed for. Alone one night, sitting up late and watching anything that was on the television, a documentary about the rock group 'The Doors' called 'No one here gets out alive' was about to come on. I vaguely recognised their name as Dad had a couple of their records, but mainly through sheer boredom I began watching it. As the story unfolded I found myself captivated, and more than a little bewildered. This band were pushing the boundaries at a time of youthful discovery, going to the edge of what was then acceptable behaviour, and seeing how far they could go over it. They were also questioning the very boundaries of the mind itself, the idea that our perception can go only so far, and no further beyond. The lead singer, Jim Morrison, seemed to be their inspiration. His very persona was a challenge, and his looks bewitching, but what really set the seed deep within me was a ring of authenticity; a feeling that their mission was no mere stunt but one clearly born of a drive and a yearning - one that made fundamental sense to me. I went to sleep that night with an unformed thought in my mind, and as soon as I awoke I sent off for the book of the documentary. Gradually my interest increased, and it would grow to be a driving force in the new construction of my life.

I dug out Dad's 'best of' compilation, but that Christmas, knowing the thing that was so exciting me, Maddie bought me a copy of the band's final album; 'L.A. Woman'. Listening to the rich sound; the heavy rock beat overlaid with an unusual array of different instruments, quite alien from the catalogue of pop music that otherwise I'd fed upon, I was entranced. Jim's deep voice was gruff and laden with mystery, speaking of things ancient and eternal in 'WASP', a musical exhortation, or the carnivalesque celebration of love lost that I thought so wonderful in 'Love her madly'. It was the tender pathos of 'Hyacinth house' that struck me, and 'Riders on the storm' was a song as familiar as rain on glass - I guess I'd always been hearing it but strangely not noticed. Now, I appreciated its clearly expressed understanding of displacement; that sense of haunting disconnect that I knew so well. 'The Changeling' came with an explicit suggestion that we could be somebody different, and that really inspired me. As the song built to its irresistible crescendo, Jim's screaming defiance hit exactly the note, and offering hope he became my hero, right at the time one was so badly needed. Looking back, this was the beginning of a process; a massive clue that another way was possible, if I could only find the path.

The following February, all sugary-sweet Maddie handed me a homemade valentine's card, something I treasured while I valued myself so little. All the same, it was a nice card. White, with three red hearts painted on the front, and words that read; 'to a dear friend, with love x'. It was the postscript that pretty much told everything salient about how our relationship had developed: 'p.s. I looked and looked for a card that was right' (this 'right' she underlined) 'to give to you, but I found them either impersonal or just wrong' (again, the 'wrong' underlined) 'to give to you - I mean, you're not my 'boyfriend' exactly, are you? But I want you to know that I appreciate and need you (though I don't show it very well) and so I made you this one, I think it's more personal.'

Sitting at her farmhouse table sipping coffee, with the card stood between us, I listened to Maddie go on about her latest beau; by her starry-eyed account a local scene hero. She told me how amazing he was and how amazing he must have thought her, surely, when she'd gone back to his from the cinema a few nights earlier. Complaining that he hadn't called, and that she didn't know where she stood, I admired him just for putting Maddie on the back foot. Truly, I felt too much in awe to be jealous.

"I wonder," she said. "Tommy's a hair dresser. You could go along to him and do some digging for me. You don't mind do you? Anyway, you need a decent haircut. Yes," she went on, "you can be my spy. I'll make you an appointment when I'm in this Saturday." So much her fool, I'd have jumped under a bus for her if she'd asked me. I shake my head just to think of it now. As it transpired, this meeting would be timed perfectly for the change in my life and incredibly, a friendship would grow to eclipse all others.

Hey baby

My parents upped and moved us all away from the village, finding a new home on the south-eastern outskirts of the great conurbation. They had to drag me kicking and screaming, and I never got settled in this relocation. The suburban pubs and green roadside spaces which, in the sunshine, would be thronged and overflowing with crowds of people who all seemed to know each other, ever remained to my eyes a foreign country. I just didn't have the skill set, the tools or the confidence, to find the way in there. As I seethed and watched what felt like my eternal home stripped and transported, I wilfully embraced a new abject surrender, total and unconditional, convinced I'd had a towel thrown in from behind me at the very moment I was starting to come out on top.

Our village had grown way beyond its original conception and the change in ethos that accompanied this meant that the idyll my parents had bought into had long since turned rotten. Looking back, I can see that the move was the right one. Despite this, though I'd left behind precious little save my familiar misery, it didn't stop my empty protestations: that their cruel, selfish move had dashed what I could now insist would have been inevitable success with Maddie. Accordingly I despaired that my whole world was lost, when all that I'd lost was my way.

Man lives to belong, and what price can we put on those friendships that are forged in our youth? Carried and nurtured through the wiser years that follow, in the end they make up the tail of life's comet: blazing and warm in the light that's behind us. Failing to appreciate my friendships until I'd lost them I'd squandered my chances, and fool that I was there was only hardship now, lonely and hopeless in a place that didn't even have a fix on my misery.

I'd sunk so low that being the depressed tool of a bullying supermarket manager was now the extent of my ignorant ambition, and I didn't even know that the world turned without me. While Jim was off at University enjoying his après-class, and Maddie, silent, was who knows where, I was training as a dead-beat and wallowing miserably through solo evenings. Taking slug after burning, mind numbing slug of the whisky I kept in a cupboard in my bedroom, screwing my face and the lid back on as I stared blankly at the ceiling, I would wait for the drug of my temporary relief to take its slow hold.

Quite unexpectedly, what served to sustain me through this mire were my visits to Tommy, the hair-dresser Maddie has asked me to spy on. Though seldom, and marked by an imponderable distance in our characters, these meetings somehow left a thread of hope in the back of my mind; they kept me going. Like a ship bound for the comfort of a friendly port, the thought of seeing him would lift my true spirits, keeping me afloat through this near-friendless time.

I'd sit in the barber chair feeling awkwardly unworthy again and again, marvelling furtively at the comings and goings behind me in the mirror; at the demigods who shared Tommy's space. I was desperate not to reveal the sad truth of myself as I looked out for learning, wondering if perhaps some greatness might rub off from those fingers and in through my hair. I wondered too if one such as I really could read those 'right' magazines; those mystical, bible-like publications that were so much a part of this select, invitation-only world: magazines, with a finger on the pulse, such as I hardly dared ruffle. All the while amazed at my own impudence just for being there, Tommy's mellow nature would gradually put me at my ease; his casual friendliness starting to reach me. Perhaps I even started to feel a tiny bit worthy as the visits became something that I genuinely looked forward to; as they started to become something for me.

On the fifth visit, washed and wet I sat waiting for what seemed like ages. The pace there was always languid, and Tommy would appear when he appeared, unhurried and unapologetic. The nerves that originally had paralysed me here were passing now; the nerves that had made me question whether I sat quite right. I started to wonder irritably how long I'd have to attend; how long before the great man himself would find time for me. All the while I listened to the music that turned a provincial salon into a worldly treat. Tom appeared in a little while relaxed and smiling.

"Hello Milo, how ya doin?" he said in his friendly way.

"Fine thank you," I smartly replied, quickly back to attention and forgetting the irritation of the long wait.

"Go on then, surprise me," he said, and suddenly I'd never been so unprepared, so challenged. It was as if a microsecond were an hour. What should I say? Oh my Lord, what should I say? I felt a moment was upon me, and I wasn't equal; a chance for I did not know what was expiring in my silence.

"Fuck you!" I blurted out in my panic, and his eyebrows rose.

"That did surprise me!" he laughed, and I joined in with him, trying to act like this was just another Saturday afternoon; as if I was used to jesting with giants and wasn't jumping inside with excitement.

Perhaps because it was so unlikely; a friendship between the two of us the last thing I could have imagined, that one actually developed. Clearly he was everything that I was not: attractive; assured; exciting. I couldn't have felt more unworthy back then, sent there by she who I'd allowed to drive me so low. My erstwhile hopes were now long since passed, and like them I was frustrated and lost. Somehow Tommy must have seen something in me; something worth knowing. Those awed, whispered tales I heard of him that floated back and amazed me as my ears pricked up in the salon, second or even third hand, but the talk of the town. Mad nights in the locals; volleys of popcorn in the Odeon down the road or a late night whim, dashing a break with the crew to the glitter of London; to the clubs and the glamour; rubbing shoulders and turning the heads of the stars; holding court in King's road's gilded restaurants while playing it crazy like Larry; like it was all of his own, and then the devil-may-care life testing races back down the 'A2' which delivered him home.

The more I heard, the more unimaginably amazing Tommy became, and the less I could even dream of the life that he painted. There was something about him, to my mind a spirit that stood for the same sense of defiance and adventure that Jim Morrison lived for. I couldn't help it as the images of my two heroes started to merge. How could I dare to breathe the same air as him, I asked myself; the same air as this arbiter of the zeitgeist; this prince amongst mortals.

Just being around him was a tonic and it lifted me: it was the very thing that I needed. I remember returning home fresh with a buzz cut one Saturday night and surprising my parents; eschewing my habitual retreat to the solitude of my room and consenting instead to watch a Woody Allen film with them. It was called 'Play it again Sam', a 1970s paean to the classic Humphrey Bogart film 'Casablanca'. It was unlike anything I'd seen before and resonated enormously. The main character, played by Woody Allen himself, was a 'nebbish'; awkward and clumsy and obvious, but the humour and the philosophy seemed so pertinent, so 'Jewish' and came so naturally to me, it was as if I belonged in the movie. However virtual, just to feel this sense of belonging stirring inside me, an innate recognition that seemed pregnant with a clue to who I really was, transformed my lonely sense of not belonging into one merely of misplacement. It brought an implicit suggestion that there was something I too could be part of.

Speaking to my mum like I never had before over the next few weeks, I seemed able to verbalise those deeper feelings which, now proven, were bubbling up inside me. She told me that what I felt was not unique; that investigation may lead to discovery, and to that end she gave me a book to read, 'Steppenwolf' by Herman Hesse. I read the novel almost reverently, not quite getting a full understanding but clearly sensing in it an echo; an allusion to something I felt I must have forgotten; something I knew that I'd never been truly aware of. The very mind and ideas of the author enthralling me, hungrily I devoured his pages, and when I finished it I sought other books by Hesse. Each one was different yet seemed of the same soul; each one with the same inescapable insinuation that somewhere out there a door did await me; a path that would lead me from my misery and into the light.

This new philosophy sunk deep into the blank that had been my spirit. Filled now with the sense of a truth that was greater; a thing worthy of faith, I started to sense that good times would come. This revelation, coinciding as it did with Tommy's influence in my life, was what made him such a powerful force for change. It gave me the freedom to reject all the old certainties that I had clung to, and like nothing else in my life, his opened my mind to all manner of possibilities. Tommy's very nature showed me that things could be so different from the mundane miseries that had tightened like a noose around me and which were so impossibly weighing against my hopes and my imagination. This new discovery was liberation, awakening in me at last the acceptance that I too was worth something; worthy at least of the self-respect that I'd long since surrendered. Just by having a friend like Tommy who liked me for who I was, made me see myself anew.

I remember the very first time that we spent a real evening together as mates in his bedsit above the pet shop. It was long since Tommy had first started cutting my hair, but even so I still felt like a novice, sitting there on the floor as he and his painfully beautiful girlfriend pulled each other around laughing on the bed. She was so pretty I felt like a fool, but she was good natured and indulgent, like most of the people that seemed to orbit around him. In no time I relaxed and started to enjoy the laughs for real. We were chatting about the album 'Troubadour' that was playing, the first time I'd heard 'J.J. Cale's mellifluous sounds; those which would become the sound track of my life. I was lost in the gentle tones that filled the room and sank into the walls around me as Tommy spoke on the phone. Suddenly, he's gripping the handset and shouting like a maniac.

"Come on then! Come and get us; what you waiting for?" he said, and then a pause while I stared at him. He listened intently to the voice at the other end of the line, and sitting in horror with my stomach now iron-gripped and ice cold it felt like our future would be determined by what was being said. I turned to Carina for reassurance, trying to return her smile with a leaden-mouthed one of my own as she chided Tommy like he'd put a cup down without a coaster. I didn't want her to know how scared I was. I didn't want them to find me out.

"Oh yeah? Well, when you fucking do, let me know!" and then that laugh; deep and conspiratorial and booming. "Won't be seeing ya!" At that, still laughing he bangs the phone down and falls straight off the bed. I'm stunned, but deep down I know that if I ask what the hell is going on I'll only give away how unsuitable I am to be here; more afraid even that I should be found unworthy than of the impending shitstorm that I may soon be part of. Tommy is too busy laughing to realise an explanation might be in order, and I'm thinking 'if this is the world he lives in, this is where I want to be.'

Inevitably, Tommy bore the brunt of my new found enthusiasm for life. I was often over-excited but this seemed only to please him, and somehow he endured me. The friendship was augmented by evening battles at his squash court and it grew stronger still. Sometimes, parked comfortably on the corner by a house as he finished with someone else's hair I'd end up dozing, listening to the radio as I waited there past time to fetch him, but he never let me down. His friendship continued to inspire and educate me, giving me something of value that was worth holding tightly; preparing me so that when next a chance of life might come along, I'd be ready to take it.

How I wrote Elastic man

Time's getting closer, and the north-bound foot traffic; the ranks of supporters who are making their way in the direction of the stadium, are starting to swell. Despite the greater numbers that now fill the main route at the edge of the field, passing as they do across my line of vision in their infinite variety, still it couldn't be easier to pick out my lone wolf among them, lumbering over from the station at his own pace and now turning, swaggering here towards me. Unmistakable, and even from a distance larger than life, I feel a lift the very moment my eyes make out Tommy's familiar, grizzly form. It isn't that I seek to be beaming like an idiot the moment he gets here: I just can't seem to help it. Perhaps it's all the memories, or maybe nowadays it's always too long since we last were together. Whatever it is, when I do see him, the swell of my heart is all over my face in my broadest, happiest smile.

"Hello my mate," I say, feeling in my body that sense of calm satisfaction which his appearance always brings. "Hello my brother," he returns, set to a chuckle. Standing at his chest in the warm hug where I feel I belong, I'm smothered by his big overcoat and the blended smell of leather and patchouli, an aroma that for all these years is his hallmark, the association in my mind with a dark strength; a mysterious excitement.

I look forward so much to these nights; the entertainment and the ceremony, and am ever mindful that while millions tune in on the television to watch from afar, I'm here at the centre where it all takes place: a pitch side seat and all of it happening around me. To be so invested in the spectacle itself is outstanding, but what takes these occasions, and their time old associations beyond mere superlatives, is the fact they are shared with the man who as an adult I've grown up with; who as my best friend has been with me through some of the best times, and some of the worst. The very spirit of our friendship is constantly mingled and mixed with that which takes place on these nights, until the two different strains become quite indistinct. What icing; oh what a cake!

We move along in our tiny perfect unit, quietly enjoying the green features of the field that we pass beside; the flower beds, the grass and pavements. Regarding some of those faces that approach and pass we hand to and fro the hip flask, sharing nips of Jack Daniels to help us move things along; shift gears to the highway of the mind that tonight's action requires. Regardless of the alcohol, I always feel like I'm in a warm cloud when I'm floating next to Tommy: memories that stretch back seeming to hang nodding around us in the air, affirming their good cheer like old friends who can't be forgotten; built in the very lines in our faces; laden in our smiles and the sparkle of our eyes.

This night long in coming has finally arrived and we head off together across the fields to the Barn. As we make our way the initial stage is for 'catch-up': what's going on with the family at home, just to make sure that nothing is missed. If there's anything special to tell we must cover those bases good and early, before the night's tone changes and we put on the clothes we must wear as 'lads'; what we need to cloak around us for the challenges of the crowd that lie ahead. Now is the time for these things which soon will be incongruous; a time of respect for the realities that are our anchors; those things that speak of who we really are and to where, when this night is over, we'll take ourselves back. From here there's a new sense about to take over.

Food for thought

For quite some time I'd been hearing the siren call of the bench that had once been the centre of my heart, and for the first time since I'd left, I was back in the village where I'd grown up. Walking down from the top of the hill; down from the shops and the village hall that stood prominent behind me, it was remarkable how the magic was gone. The field that I recall as the embodiment of my childhood happiness was now just so much grass beneath my feet; green and tired, empty of the spirits that one time had lived here; those smiling, laughing winds that had warmed us those many summers back having long since blown away. I didn't know exactly what I had been expecting, or whether it would be helpful for me to return. Either way, the temptation had grown too strong and I had to answer it. Being here now; descending this field of my fondest memories and the ghosts of those memories that must still be playing out somewhere in a parallel time, it seemed a long cold time ago.

Driving earlier up and down those country lanes which surrounded and shut this place off from the rest of the world, the roads were all broken and pitted in disrepair, just as I remembered them. Wide cracks were filled deep with brown muddy water, and the passage, barely sufficient for the passing of a car, was further impinged by sprays of scratching briars. These made the lanes narrower still, as if no way through should ever be sought, and each ill-fated attempt would itself be a mortal insult against this intractable landscape, a herculean adventure through dormant evils that lay long inactive yet bristled still with the dark threat of destruction; the fear that at any moment the brushwood should spontaneously reawaken to claim back its right.

Emerging from the tree-choked darkness, I stopped momentary at the 'T' junction and marvelled at the sight of the village approach. It curved around against the fields to my left where, much to my surprise, the archaic garage was as it always had been, even in my day an empire throw back with its handy pump service and Christmas calendars. To my right the church spire rose, my earliest memories of nursery there, before our little village had grown to dwarf its dowager sister.

My first point of call, inescapably, had been the house where I used to live: the little box so odd compared to the more regular builds I now knew. Strangely feeling no desire to enter, I sat outside without even undoing my seat belt. The study window which faced me was huge and modern and all of the wall, drawing light to the small room within where my nana once stood, stunned as the 'joy- riders' span the corner in her view and lost control, crashing into the gorse out front. It served us well indeed that day as a natural barrier from the road outside: no mere sponge for the noise of occasional cars that made their way through the village. The three-panelled front door stood in silence, as if it had forgotten me, but I well remembered that wooden mid-panel. It was still the same glossy brown between the frosted glass panes above and below. I banished myself once, and for an extended period of days, when in outraged teenage temper I smashed that lower pane by carelessly hurling a slipper towards it, aiming for Dad's goading presence taunting me by the doorway. An argument had begun when my resentment boiled over: his nightly request to fetch his slippers, to my mind like a dog, finally too much to bear. Roaring, and matched as he roared me from the house, our argument spilled to the path outside in a decently separated impasse, but when he commanded that if I was going I leave the offending piece that I still held in my hand, I really let fly. The slipper moved through the air and its flight turned to horror in slow motion as its course locked on a mid-pane impact; the glass splintering and falling away with first a dull thud, then a tinkling and sprinkling of glass rain. We'd both held pause, the surprise of the moment for a split second transcending our petty squabble, before I spun on my heels and set off I knew not where. Condemned by fortune, Nick Lowe's song 'I love the sound of breaking glass' was playing in my head as an untimely, ironic misnomer.

Behind the front door was the porch, protruding from the rest of the house and onto the roof of which we used to climb from the upper bathroom window; granting our games the excitement of an elaborate but relatively safe escape. Beyond that, the windows of my old bedroom still looked upon the gorse woods opposite, and it struck me how plain they were: all utility and clean, with neither architrave nor embellishment; just long wide panes and the metal casing where I'd stare out from my bed as Sunday morning's radio played family song after family song. Those innocent favourites: 'Three Wheels on my Wagon'; Cape Granada'; 'Beep beep'; 'The Laughing Gnome'. How I used to wait and hope that one of these would be next up, and if it wasn't I'd stay prone regardless, lazily waiting for the next pick to be announced by our avuncular presenter. If only we'd known. I remember the Christmas that came with the addition of sound; the advent of my first clock radio, and hearing then for the first time Rod Stewart's Christmas hit 'Do ya think I'm sexy': to the darkness of my mind so charged with the mysteries of adolescence; the hidden secrets, and strains of those mood confusions are preserved in memories as clear and immutable as if set in formaldehyde. Half sleeping and half awake, I would gaze at the world beyond that window.

I turned around in the little car park just beyond our old garden, and I remembered standing there with my angry fists clenched at the vehicles: at the idea of their privileged owners whose club I couldn't imagine ever joining. Leaving that thought, I headed back out of the neighbourhood and took the road around to the main car park by the shops. But for a couple of cars and the bushes that grew tall between the rows of marked bays, the huge lot was empty. Here was our old bike circuit and the gravel I'd come so closely to know. Parking up, I stepped out to the greeting of the loose stones grinding beneath my feet; to the smell of their dust rising around me. I looked about and took in the old familiar places. There along the top was the raised pedestrian avenue that, lined with trees, would carry me across from home to the shopping centre, and to the parking lot annex on my right where I waited for the bus to arrive: coming each morning without mercy to take me to school.

I'd started to walk, opting to bypass the shopping centre itself, where we used to play with our ten pence balsa airplanes, for the few moments at least before they took to the air propelled by the tightly wound rubber band and then splintered on landing; where mum's shop had been our haven and refuge, filled with the muddy sounds of Motown and giggling, semi-clad ladies; where we'd go upstairs to our friends' mum in the antique store, who would serve us from the kitchen at the back warm minestrone amongst the curios. Instead, I passed by the entrance of the 'stage two' service road which ran behind a second wave of buildings. My path took me behind the village hall, still replete with those bricks we'd sponsored and written our names on, and then out on to the top of the Minnis, by the pub. I just stood there: the scene as I'd remembered it, so familiar yet somehow a mere shadow as I stood there gazing down from the top, all the way to our little bench that was still at the bottom.

My senses tingled unusually as I made my way over the field. Each step that led me juddering down the hill seeming to bring me lower emotionally, and lower again, shaving another layer of strength until close to the bottom I realised with a thud that the seat in our fabled corner was no longer our own. The little encampment looked the same. It was still framed from behind by the bushes that grew there, but where before our throne had been of three long wooden slats on a rough metal frame, now it was replaced by something modern, all rounded and smooth. I felt like something had been ripped from me, and it felt like treason to seat myself on this new bench. At the top I'd been feeling so calm and so possessed of my blankly neutral state, but now I felt weak and defenceless. Although everything around me suddenly felt disjointed and wrong, still I couldn't deny those old aspects that were whirling about me; apparitions of reminders of times gone by, attended by the memories I'd long since neglected.

I looked to my left at the house where Lionel and Barbara had lived; where our old school teacher had moved in with Stella to add to their confusion after their father had been kicked out. I remembered those evenings when a warm fire was burning and warm advice offered on the rare occasions when 'Auntie' could look beyond her own needs. She and my father were always sparring, the loyalty and affections of my poor confused mother uncomfortably split between her husband and the woman who posed as her best friend and was her business partner: neither of these two powerful characters were born to give way. Though Stella's house was often a good place to come, my growing frustrations too glad of her alternative viewpoint, when all's said and done she was no devotee of the truth, and time makes clear that there's nothing as destructive as a selfish liar.

To my right, the scrub that bordered the field looked just as it had before, marking the start of our many great adventures on the way to the 'Wizard Tree.' I thought it would have been nice to go there, but actually now in place I could see I was wrong; like an adult trying to recapture past pleasures in the simplicity of a playground roundabout, or a slide that was now too short or too narrow, the briefest glimpse quickly overtaken by a righteous sense of the foolish. As I sat there quietly it seemed that nothing much around here was happening; nothing moving or any semblance of the life that my memories now recalled and dangled before me as if from a dream. One older couple walking from the vicinity of Rachael's neighbourhood - it would always be remembered as hers - did come along and passing behind the hedge they made their slow way up the hill to the shops. I watched as they eventually disappeared over the brow, thinking what I would have given to hear Monty whooshing past on a break neck bike mission!

As I sat and tried to reconcile the feelings I'd had about coming here; about what this had once been to me and no longer was, something from the poem of 'A Shropshire lad' crept into my heart; 'an air that kills' slowly seeping through my very being. I felt a profound kind of sadness mixed with the futile longing of nostalgia, but also a sense of completion; suffering's end that brings with it comfort, even if the comfort of death, never to be retraced. I'd had to come here but now I had seen for myself that its wonders were no longer, and I got it. It was enough, and gripped by the perfect feeling of closure I was ready to go; to never return. Full of resolution, I got up too sharply and had to pause for a moment as I steadied myself, the blood running light in my head. Just then I realised that a deep voice behind me was calling my name.

I couldn't believe it, but there was James coming towards me, very much as I remembered him. He seemed a little taller now and not quite as lean as the boy he had been. The 'Desperate Dan' patch of shadow on his face was more pronounced than before, but his hair was still the darkest brown. His blue eyes were as bright as ever; still bearing that same quiet confidence. He stood with an amused look on his face, clearly enjoying the fact that he'd caught me unawares. The little changes that had occurred in each of our appearances melted away before our eyes as we regarded one another. I almost expected him to proffer the packet of polos as he always used to back then: his signature trick that the girls had bought into, a symbol of the well-mannered politeness that he typified. He finally broke the silence. "Well, how are you old chap? It's been a long time." Still I could only stare and shake my head, dumbfounded. This place seemed less of a lie than it had just moments earlier. Putting my hand out and still saying nothing we shook. I sat as he bade me, finally finding my voice.

"What are you doing here? I thought there was no one still around."

"I'm just back for a few days visiting mum and dad: needed a break from the parties and the drinking," he laughed. "The course is starting to interfere with my social life, so I thought I better get away for a couple of days. What about you? Didn't you leave ages ago? I remember John telling me that you'd moved up to London or somewhere with the family. You look very well," he added, in typical James style. "What's the story? What are you doing with yourself now?"

I told him I was working in the supermarket and to my surprise added that it was just as a stop-gap while I puzzled out what I really wanted to be doing with my life. I said that I hadn't gone to University as I was too hungry to get out into the real world, and then he asked about friends. I said that I wasn't going out that much, explaining that I was pretty knocked out when I got back from work.

"I've been wanting to come down here for a while," I told him. "Somehow I felt that I'd left something behind, but being here now I realised that what was here was all us, and I guess we've moved on." We talked about the old times and how it was strange that the gang had just drifted apart; about Lionel and Barbara, and the girls; Linda and Christine; about Rachael. With a sympathetic smile he asked if I'd seen anything of Maddie, and I grimaced slightly as I told him that I had not, trying to indicate that I knew what a fool I'd been.

"Look," he said as we parted. "The campus is party central and there's plenty of room for you to stay with me. Get yourself down there." Handing over a slip of paper that he'd scribbled his phone number on he told me to call him. "I promise you won't regret it. It really is very good to see you." We shook hands energetically, and despite myself I couldn't help mirroring his evident sincerity, strolling up the hill together as we were both going the same way: he to the shops and I to my car.

"How long ago it all seems," he said in parting. "I used to think life would never get better than those summers, but well, we know differently now don't we?" I so wanted to be able to meet his satisfied smile with an honest one of my own.

Holiday in Cambodia

For a couple of weeks I danced nervously around that little piece of paper like it was a baited hook and I was scared to be taken, yet I prayed I'd be ringing those numbers from the second that Jim had put them into my hand. Thinking on the enormity of it however; the vastness of the world out there that I had to enter, I was overwhelmed and it weighed upon me. Each and every night when I took those rolled up blue numbers from my treasure box; holding them in my hand with a fresh determination to call, I'd just sit there by the phone staring blankly at the unfurled bit of paper; the marks upon it as incomprehensible to me as magical runes. I'd renew my resolution to try the next day, once again feeling myself filled with relief as I put them away. I was terrified that my ignorance would be easily uncovered; found out by those others who knew all the rules, and that I'd be despised, or laughed at, or worse.

The more I thought about it and the longer I delayed, the greater became my fears. Every night I'd sink exhausted back into a deep sleep where my subconscious had prepared for me a recurring nightmare. It wasn't clear at first exactly where I was in the dream but there was a happy mood, reminiscent of my pre-school at the church just up from the village. I was a young child again, painting contentedly. The air was gently laced with the smell of children's paint. Before me an easel stood heavy with sheets of thick white paper which hung from the two large clips at the top. My palette was full of rich, bright colours; thick pastes with reds and yellows, blues and greens, and I used them all as I drew on my sheet long thick lines from the top to the bottom and then thinner ones across. Each stroke I painted was neat and separate, carefully considered. Continuing to build my web of happy colours, I felt quietly pleased when one of my young class mates, a pretty little girl with long golden hair in a clean white dress, walked around the easel to see what I was doing. As she did so I realised at once: it couldn't be! I'd forgotten to dress, and completely naked I burst in horror from the classroom with her growling sneer upon me. As I ran endlessly down the pathway outside, the eyes lining up on the other side of the windows were staring and gloating in evil delight.

Eventually, after weeks of prevarication, finally I did it. I rang the number and spoke to James, arranging to go down there the following Saturday.

"Get the coach down," he said, "and give me a call. We'll go from there." Full of excitement, and no little feeling of achievement, I put the phone down and planned the rest of my life. I arranged with my boss at the supermarket to work the Friday night shift so I could get Saturday off, and coming home at nine am had a nice hot bath: also a large Kahlua coffee to calm my nerves. My bag was already packed with my toiletries and a book inside, and my walkman was flush with a new 'Peel' tape that I'd been recording. I even took some condoms with me which I hid in the zippered compartment, and after a late bit of breakfast I started on my way.

Once at Victoria I found the place to buy my ticket, still hardly believing I had the guts to do such a thing. Locating the pick-up point nice and early I boarded the coach, choosing a window seat quite close to the back. We departed on schedule in the early afternoon, and with the day a hot one, I found myself alternately staring through the glass and watching the streets pass by or else shrouding my face in an orange curtain screen that could be pulled across; peering out through the filter of its tangerine fibres when the glare got too much to take.

The metropolis ranged outside the windows on a repeating concrete loop, shops and cafes on the same grey streets again and again, with groups of youths all going nowhere together, kicking their heels and waiting on benches as they lived their lives for a few seconds under my hidden gaze. I didn't think too much about where I was going but just felt a little buzz that I was finally on my way. Checking now and again that the roll of paper James had given me was still in my pocket, I reflected that the setting off, the resolution made and executed seemed to make me feel braver. I dared to hope I'd be ready for whatever I would find there.

Later on, we finally broke from the town's thick embrace and the windows gave way to a pastoral reel; fields that whizzed by the motorways with their stationary cows, eternally surprised or gazing nonchalant: I couldn't tell which. As the greens and yellows melded and started to blur, and anaesthetised by the coach's gentle roll, I skimmed in and out of consciousness, looking upon yet more road for a few bleary seconds each time a bump or sharp turn roused me, disappointed, before slipping back again into fitful oblivion.

A gentle tugging gradually drew forth my conscious mind; something pulling on my tee-shirt. Lifting my squashed face from the window I turned to see a man there, the driver, telling me that we'd arrived. I must have been in a deep sleep, a hangover from the 'all-nighter', as the coach was already empty. Though the blankness of my rest sat heavily upon me I pulled myself through it, getting up and taking my bag from the rack. With it slung over my shoulder I stepped gingerly down from the coach and on to the asphalt. The queue for the phone inside the waiting room was already three deep as I entered the doorway, so I went on to the washroom and splashed a little water, the bright little beads of wakefulness bouncing off my skin and helping to lift the torpor. Looking at myself in the mirror I saw none of the anxious excitement I was full of. Now awake, my impatience returned and I speedily dried my fringe with a couple of paper towels, happy to find the phone now available as I went back outside. I put in my coins and dialled the numbers. It rang for about fifteen times before a voice I didn't recognise answered.

"Hello."

"Hello," I countered. "This is James's mate, Milo. Is he there please?"

"Hold on." I heard footsteps retreating, and then a couple of muffled voices, allowing myself the reassurance of a little smile. Then the phone was taken up again.

"He's not here, sorry." I was perplexed.

"Do you know when he'll be back?" I asked, a feeling of sudden panic taking the reins in my stomach.

"Hold on." Again I waited, though this time a little more anxiously. The plan that I'd made with Jim had seemed perfectly simple, though now I was beginning to wonder if it was a little too much so.

"He doesn't live here anymore; not sure where he's gone."

"Did he leave a number?" I asked, my previously casual intonation rising slightly to a squeal.

"Sorry mate, I don't actually know him."

"But how...?"

"I just moved in. Jill knows him but she's gone away for the weekend."

"It's just that I'm his friend," I pleaded, "and he said to come down and call, and I'd be able to stay there." I was rambling now with the panic I was feeling, my haven here suddenly evaporated and the bitter teeth of treachery seeming to have me by the arse.

"Sorry mate; no room here."

"But..." I started, and the phone went dead. I stared for a moment at the useless receiver and then like an automaton placed it back down in the holster, still staring at it. I was rooted to the spot and couldn't move, yet the whole world was swirling around me. I couldn't even think straight, cold harsh reality running freezing through my veins. Nothing was as it should be, and I just remained there, placed rigid. What the hell had happened? I looked at the numbers again but they just stayed blue, useless and mean on the little slip of paper. Taken with an impulse, outside the waiting room I ran up the path past the taxi rank and onto the main road, stopping there and looking at the cars about me. I didn't have a scooby, but running seemed to help, so I sprinted back to the waiting room and darted across to the window on the far side of the room.

"Excuse me; is there a coach back to London?"

"Yes," the man behind the counter told me happily, "seven thirty tomorrow morning."

"What? Tonight; how can I get back tonight? My friend gave me the wrong number and now I'm stuck." I was desperate, and starting to cry, the man on the other side of the glass partition regarded me with a mixture of pity and irritation.

"Hold on," he said after a moment of scrutiny, and disappeared into a small office that led out behind the screen. I waited, not knowing what he could do for me; wiping my eyes and thinking exasperatedly about what James had done, and how unbelievably angry I was. In a moment he returned.

"If you get yourself down to the mainline station at the other end of town quickly, the last train back to London leaves in just over forty five minutes. As I say, you had better be quick!"

Lights blurred orange and red filled my tear-stained vision as I ran panting hard down the central reservation towards the station. My bag swinging wildly across my back I ran like it was a race for survival, fuelled by bitterness that I should again find myself so ill-used; again fate's play thing. Tearing down the carriageway with cars close beside me as I darted around the traffic I made it just in time to pay a punitive fifty pound fare for the ticket home: about three times the price of a coach return. Sitting secure but exhausted on the London bound train I resolved that I would find out what on earth had caused Jim to play such a mean, expensive trick on me: whatever the reason, I would have nothing to do with him ever again.

Down in Brazil

"Pour me another," I slurred, half-hoping the next one might bring the antidote to this creeping feeling of nausea, despite that each incremental gulp of the own label whiskey was grating in my stomach as well as my throat. Smiling stupidly at me Jim began to pour, leaving his head hanging in the middle of a nod of assent and tapping the bottle repeatedly against the top of the shot glass like some kind of drunken Morse; splashes of the light brown liquid spilling over the table. The matches we were using as stake chips were mostly all on his side now, my losing tactics recently having become even more wild and reckless as I tried to recapture some earlier success. In truth, I was more focussed on when I'd be able to get my head down, willing the game to be over because the way I was feeling, sleep seemed like a perfect destination.

I'd worked myself up to livid, pure and simple, when I rang back the number that Jim had left for me at the supermarket. I have to say I was really looking forward to giving him a piece of my mind. I had even thought about putting some of my clearer thoughts in a letter, and delivering this by hand to where I remembered his parents lived, but I was damned if I'd make another wasted journey, even if that meant I'd be left seething with a burning load against him to the end of my days.

"I'm so sorry," he said after I'd been raging indignantly about my trip and how lucky I'd been to survive it. "I moved in to a mate's digs a week ago, and I'd told Jill you might be coming. It would have been fine but she was away, and I only found out on Thursday." I listened to his explanation and went on complaining about having the phone put down on me; how I was left friendless and stuck in the middle of nowhere. It was only because I'd already calmed down a bit that I didn't go mental when I realised he was laughing.

"That guy you spoke to," he continued, "he moved in when I left and actually he does sound like a bit of a knob. Honestly, I'm really, really sorry."

He carried on with his apologies as my pathetic report tailed off, and I felt at least that he was sincere. It was such an outrageous slight that I either had to forgive him or kill him, and I didn't want his blood on my hands.

"I came all that way, right after an all-nighter!" was my final summing up. "I didn't know what the hell to do."

"I'm sorry, really. Let me make it up to you. I'm flat sitting for a mate next weekend, not too far from your folks' place actually. Come over. Let's get together and make an evening of it. Come on; let me show you how sorry I am."

The least he could have done was let me win at some of these card games he taught me, but the night we'd had was so completely different from what I was used to it really didn't matter. The connection between the two of us was so immediate and happy that very quickly our little 'misunderstanding' of a fortnight ago was forgiven and forgotten. The flat was indeed only a few miles from where we had moved, and getting there was as simple as taking the bus. Jim paid for the Chinese take-away and buying us also a bottle of whiskey he made me feel truly wanted. Drinking it neat had reminded me of those solitary knock-outs in my bedroom, and it had gone down fairly rotten, especially now that I'd acquired a taste for Jack Daniel's and coke in honour of his namesake and my hero singer. Sweet or sour, I loved the thought that he had bothered to buy the whisky, and taking shots and putting hairs on my chest was better than rocking the boat: judging from his foliage I was a few cases behind. There was that wonderful feeling of relief as soon as I got flat and low, crashed out on his sofa. As he staggered off to the bedroom, Jim turned back.

"Top night mate, absolutely brilliant to see you again. See you in the morning." So saying, the door swung behind him and I heard the springs of the mattress heave with a squeal as his dead weight landed.

The following morning, over a couple of sausages, fried egg, bacon and beans in the cafe next door, we took turns reading bits of the day's 'Sun' newspaper, the food and the coffee gradually soaking up the previous night's excesses. Coming more alive; getting fresh coffees and mopping our plates with another round of the nice white toast, we talked a bit more about our lives and where we were in them. James did most of the talking as I didn't have much of my own to say, though I'm sure he picked up that I found the job I'd landed in the supermarket unfulfilling and bordering unworthy. I did mention my lately developed interest in a German author, but that didn't really go anywhere.

Jim told me that he had just got a girlfriend; someone he'd known for a while at University but had only just 'hit it off' with.

"It's nothing serious," he explained, "but she's coming round tonight with a friend in tow. Do you want to hang about and see what develops?" I think he must have noticed me blanch, before adding; "You'd be doing me a favour, mate."

I didn't tell him that last night was the first time I'd stayed out since we moved up here; that even now, by not phoning home in a pathetic exercise of childish petulance, I knew that my mum and dad would probably be worrying about me, nor that the very idea of finding myself with two strange girls was almost enough to send me scampering back into the arms of my parents, but it was amazing to be in his company and to be feeling like just any another adult. 'What the hey,' I thought, I was ready to make a weekend of it.

The time Jim had spent away at university had been fruitful. I could hardly imagine his world: the way he'd shared his life with all sorts of different people from so many different backgrounds; the different things he'd done, even skydiving for instance, a thing I'd once set my heart on but as realistic to me now as a moonwalk. I couldn't believe all the bands he'd seen and, from what I inferred, all the girls that he'd slept with. It really seemed to me like he was 'living the dream', and it made me wonder at my own lack of experience. In all his tales it was clear, however, that the process of learning itself had been somewhat secondary; very much taking a back seat as there weren't hours enough in the day to fit in everything that was on offer. Something inevitably had had to give.

"So," he went on as we were paying up, "I don't think I'll make it past this year. They warned me in case I didn't get the results. I could go back and retake, but I think I've done enough study. I'm planning to intern at my dad's place in August and if that goes well I'll go in full time. What about you? Fancy trying out with me? They're looking to recruit at the moment and you're not exactly enamoured with where you are now. You should think about it." I nodded, thinking that I actually might. "Before I start," Jim continued, "I was thinking about getting down to the coast for a couple of days. Why don't we go camping or something?" I was starting to get the feeling that I was now someone else. Clearly life had realised I'd been left behind and was pulling its boots on to give me the kick that I needed.

"Let's do it!" I told him, smiling in disbelief. "After all, some say you only live once."

Jim disappeared down the corridor and was gone for ages when the doorbell rang, leaving me to sit nervously as I watched the match reports on the television. Twiddling my thumbs, I took the fact that Arsenal had won as a good omen. The girls entered the room first, and standing to greet them I offered my hand quite formally. I could see from their reaction that this wasn't quite as expected, but we shook all the same and Jim made the introductions.

"This is Milo," he announced, "a very good friend of mine. Milo, this is Claire, and this is Sue. Milo is just about my oldest mate," he added, "and a veteran of our secondary school punching contests. He's still got the bruises to prove it." No one knew how to follow that and we stood looking at each other. "People," he went on, breaking the impasse and pointing at the sofa, "If you'd care to take a seat."

"Still got the bruises?" Claire asked, taking a bottle of Vodka out of the rucksack she'd just swung from her shoulders.

"Um, no, not anymore," I smiled. "I had them covered with tattoos. My mum went mad. Not really." I had added the denial much too quickly to achieve something of the comic confusion I'd tried for, but I was too nervous to hold the lie. I felt my face flush red.

"Anyone fancy a drink before we go out?" suggested our host as he flashed me a reassuring grin. The selection of alcohol that we'd purchased from the off licence earlier was out on the coffee table: a couple of bottles of white wine and a half bottle of Jack Daniel's. The girls had a glass of warm wine while I cracked open the Jack Daniels, self-consciously adding a little to a big glass of coke. Sitting around chatting, the mood started to relax.

Like me, I found that Sue was not at University, and I felt relieved not to be entirely in the company of intellectuals. She was a friend of Claire's from home who worked in a day care centre with young children. I didn't really have much to say about my own job but she seemed interested and asked me lots of questions about it anyway: 'Did I ever have to open the store up in the morning?' - I did. 'Did I get to unload the deliveries and ride around on an electric truck?' - Yes, and no: our pallet trucks were all manual. 'What was my most exciting experience?' Here I recounted an event that I still clearly recalled from a few months earlier when I had apprehended a shoplifter. I was working on the loading bay at the time, and looking up on hearing a noise I remember seeing a local kid, roughly my age, clutching a bottle and dashing across the yard to the car park. I knew instinctively what was occurring and suddenly I was tearing off in pursuit, bounding the little wall and heading across the car park with only the thought of catching up with him in my mind. He seemed to give up very quickly, bent over and out of breath as he turned towards me. It was only then as I started to get closer that the possibility of danger slowly dawned on me. For those few brief moments the world was the two of us; quite alone and separated from everything else by the shock and excitement. He gave a barely perceptible nod as I placed a hand on his shoulder, accepting his fate, and watched by random car park patrons who looked as stunned as we were, I marched him back to the supermarket. I described to Sue the massive sense of relief I felt when I realised that he wasn't going to resist, along with the wry, embarrassed smiles we exchanged with each other as I handed him over: as if through this mini-adventure we'd somehow shared something special. I was a hero returned, discharged of my captive and cooling off as I sat back on the steps of the loading bay, slowly coming down from the adrenalin shot; savouring the after-taste of this unusual afternoon.

We all had a few drinks and then returned to the cafe around the corner where only a few hours earlier Jim and I had guzzled and slurped our breakfast. Now with nocturnal lighting and a few other alterations it seemed much changed. Big grey curtains were pulled out across the front window and candles were lit in the centre of the tables. A whole new set of rules was in play in the more cultured ambiance and the gentler company also created something of a different consciousness. Full of the evening's propriety and not wanting to make the place look untidy we sat up instead of slouching, laying across our laps the useless little faux paper serviettes that were set as before in the glasses before us: a detail remaining from the 'greasy spoon' alter ego that would also have benefitted from upgrade. The food was simple but good, and was very well priced, and we even kept the bill a little lighter by passing the bottle of vodka about under the table, hid surreptitiously from management's eyes in the bag that we kept at our feet.

The girls were mixing their drink into the orange juice they'd ordered, while Jim and I ordered cokes for ours. It was the first time I'd tasted the combination and I liked it, a twist on my usual, and it went down great with the burgers and fries. Surreptitiously or not, pouring our own measures meant the night was a very relaxed one and we kept the theme going back at the flat, Jim joining me on the Jack Daniel's while the girls stayed with what they had left of the vodka.

There was a record player and some albums in the cabinet in the bedroom, and we were all treated to DJ James's 'moody' selection: I still particularly remember Echo and the Bunnymen's 'Heaven up here'. Having such fun and getting on so well meant the thoughts about 'later' were kept out of mind. I found that the surfeit of alcohol was neutralising the part of me that tends to over think; keeping me relaxed and helping me to act more or less like a normal person. I think I was even being pretty funny: everyone cracking up at a gag I made when Sue said something about how much she enjoyed working with the children, and asking if I wanted any. I don't remember exactly what I said to her but it was some smart-arse comment to the effect that I wasn't quite ready yet, grabbing my jacket and making to leave for added dramatic impact.

I hadn't looked too closely at her when I first saw them come through the lounge door: my eyes had been drawn perhaps to the prettier, more outgoing Clare, but Sue was getting better looking all the time. What stood out especially were her trousers; black, and baggy at the hip before tapering to narrow at the ankle, with variously coloured metallic threads that caught the eye as they ran sparkling like glitter down their length. More and more these seemed to catch the light as she sat at the other end of the couch with her legs out towards me. As we settled down from the joke-inspired ruckus that the alcohol had made so easy there was a pause, Jim shooting a look of enquiry at Clare and he seemed to get the nod he was looking for.

"Well, it's late," he said, standing up and stating the obvious. "You guys okay here?" and without waiting for an answer he offered Clare his hand. Rising, she turned and through some telepathic connection spoke wordlessly to Sue, also seeming to get the answer she needed.

"Good night, then" she said, looking back at us knowingly as she followed Jim into the bedroom. For once he'd gone ahead of his girl and was tugging her enthusiastically through the door.

I made a slow show of deliberately pouring each of us another big drink, playing for time in the room's fresh quiet. From behind the bedroom door the slightly muffled sound of Bryan Ferry's 'Bette Noir' weaved itself into our silence, and the various other muffled sounds that had stirred from within now faded, lost beneath the artistic strains of the delicately yearning music. From somewhere inside my head, juxtaposing with this haunting refrain, a stranger's voice took up a blunt, nasty triptych, ugly and brutal, but as surprising as it was it almost felt expected, and I watched it from the corners feeling strangely detached. Being alone now with Sue was making me nervous, never mind having to ignore that lewd clamour in my mind, and it wasn't made easier by a blossoming reality of what this situation could actually lead to.

"Well then Milo," she said, and I was glad that she'd taken the initiative; relieved to be distracted from the pressure of the moment, the buzzing pause that had been growing between us. "How come that's your chosen tipple then?" she asked, nodding her head at the square bottle with the iconic black and white label that I was just setting back down. "Isn't it a little bit random?" I stared at it as I thought for a moment, thinking back to where it began.

"My dad's got a menswear shop," I started, "and I used to work there with him on Saturdays, and a while back he got the idea for an 'old time' window display. He wrote off to the Jack Daniel's distillery asking if they'd be interested in him promoting their drink over here, and whether or not they had any props he could use to do so. He didn't hear anything back for a couple of months and had pretty much forgotten about it when a big dirty van drawing up on the street outside his door blocked out the daylight. He wasn't sure what was going on, or even if he should be concerned: there'd been a spate of robberies in the High street, but next thing a guy comes walking into the shop carrying a big old cart wheel in one arm and a small bale of straw in the other. At first Dad was bemused, looking at him without making the connection, but then the man introduced himself and explained who'd sent him, adding that they'd want the cartwheel back. There was something else in the van however, he told him, something he could keep, and returning made him a gift of a six bottle case plus a letter from the distillery thanking him for his interest.

"Once I'd heard the story and seen the cool-looking bottles I kept nagging him for my share. Eventually, though I was too young to drink, he let me have one, so I kept it like treasure instead. You know how it is; once you first notice a thing, afterwards you see it everywhere: people drinking it in old movies; the name popping up in books I've read. The brand's got something, you know? Like '501' jeans or the Porsche 911. I've been getting into a band called 'The Doors'. They did 'Light my fire' and 'Riders on the storm'; you must have heard of them?" She shook her head, smiling but saying nothing. "No? Well, I saw this film about them; 'No one here gets out alive'. It was on 'A Midsummer Night's Tube' and anyway, it got me listening to the music. Seems like Jim Morrison, the lead singer, was a Jack Daniel's fan and I guess I thought, 'if the black whiskey's good enough for him...'"

I realised that I'd been rambling, but at least my nerves had settled down, and I handed over the vodka and orange. I was taking my drink from the table and just about to sit back down against the cushions on the far side of the couch when she reached out, finding me half way between sitting and standing, and lifted the glass from my hand. She took a big sip from it and made a face like she didn't much like it, before putting both glasses back down on the table beside us. Turning back she looked at me and smiled. Still frozen above the sofa I reached out for my glass, and bringing it up to my mouth poured about half of it down my neck, gulping sharp and hard, before falling back seated beside her with our legs now touching. She leaned into me, and rubbing her nose against my cheek she whispered;

"So tell me, Milo. What was it that first attracted you to me this evening?"

"Those trousers," I replied without pausing, "I just had to have those trousers." The nasty little voice in my head had grown silent now, relaxed and assured it would get what it wanted.

Hanging on a string

We had no special plans apart from just turning up and finding a nice field somewhere to pitch our tent, but Jim assured me that the best outcomes developed from exactly that kind of planning. Off we set with such vital equipment as sleeping bags and pans etcetera, all stuffed in the boot of my knackered Ford Escort. We also brought with us a bag of provisions that Jim's mum had sent containing eggs and bacon, milk and some biscuits, instant coffee, cheese, ham and chocolate.

The roads were clear, and full of the joys of our friendship we played our music too loud, and drove a little too fast, egging each other on excitedly. We hit Hawkhurst and Jim started telling me of a girl he once dated from around our old village; her name sounded familiar to me though I couldn't quite place her. He said that she'd been away at school here at Hawkhurst, continuing wistfully how he'd once thought her the love of his life. One day it had just ended, he said, and he was never really sure why. In the silence that followed this confession I felt a deep ache and kind of wanted to share my pain about Rachael but in the end I didn't, the two of us just going along quietly instead, lost in our thoughts. Like the scenery that was passing by, pretty soon this reflective mood was left behind and before we knew it we'd hurdled Rye and were making our way out towards Camber, once again chatting and laughing as I listened to Jim recounting more of his tales; of places, and girls, and even of cling film.

Arrived at our beach destination, we were suddenly uncertain of what to do next. We drove along the sea front where the little fishing boats were moored bobbing, before deciding that we should probably head inland a little and find a place to stay. We stopped in a lay-by on the way and I got some water and plugged in the travel kettle to make some coffee: the very reason I'd fiddled about installing a 'cigar lighter' plug a week earlier. Jim delved into his mum's bag of wonders and brought out a little picnic packet with ham, cheese and biscuits, plus another packet of cheese unlike any I'd seen before: a multi-layered strata with a herby, light yellow one and a plain orange one sandwiched together. I couldn't help making fun of it at first, perhaps using humour to hide my fear of this brave new cheese world. I was surprised how extremely tasty it actually was, and felt very sorry when we'd eaten the last.

By early afternoon we'd located a suitable campsite and had pitched our tent near the top of the hill there. The very taste of salt in the air had been teasing us before we'd even reached the sea, and now all set up, we were more than ready to head off for some proper seaside action, especially as it was a nice warm sunny day. On our way out of the campsite we purchased the white disc that denoted our stay until Saturday. Setting off for the beach, we talked about what our ideas were and how our trip was starting to take shape, planning to head for home early on Sunday morning to get the best of the quiet roads. Parking up by the dunes at the far end of the beach we had it in mind to head for the surf but the amusement arcade there proved irresistible. Reasoning that it might be too early to put ourselves immediately at the mercy of the sun, we made a bee-line instead for the slot machines, having a round of crazy golf after that by way of secondary protection.

The golf was indeed crazy, with some shots pinging from the holes entirely, while others ricocheted back off assorted objects for the most unlikely hole-in-ones. As usual, Jim seemed to have more than his fair share of luck, but a titanic, chaotic struggle ended up with me as the victor. Walking back to get our beach stuff that we'd locked in the car I was feeling pretty full of it; throwing the keys up high and then catching them in unspoken, gloating triumph, until missing a catch, and bending down to pick them up from where they'd landed, I found instead to my horror a drain cover and saw that the keys had fallen straight through it. I stared at the floor, and then at Jim who was looking at me speechless, shaking his head. We had no spare keys, and all of our stuff was in the car; no way even of getting back to the campsite.

After a while spent lying on our chests in the sandy road trying without success to prise up the metal grate, a small crowd of holiday-makers had gathered. They were enjoying our impromptu spectacle and even offering up assorted suggestions, though it was clear from the nature of these that they were contrived for their added enjoyment rather than to be helpful. At least we did have one thing going for us: we could see the keys themselves, still sitting where they'd landed on a ledge just beneath the grill. Eventually, after watching from afar and enjoying our man-vs.-metal struggle, a stall-holder with a hook on a pole came to our assistance, fishing the keys out for us as the assembled spectators 'oohed' and 'aahed', finally eliciting a happy round of applause as we were hooked and lifted carefully from our dilemma. Suitably chastened by my carelessness, and effusive with thanks for our cheerful saviour, we got into the car and collected our stuff. The day was back on track and we headed over the top of the high dunes to the beach.

A great expanse comes into view for anyone willing to toil to the top of the dunes: the sea pulled far back into itself to reveal leagues of wet sand; little pockets of glistening water where shells and hermit crabs reside, while on both sides the sandy coastline stretches away without end. Long grasses wave and blow in the wind at the top, but as you climb down the steps to the beach on the other side the wind disappears and all that is left is the gentle hand of the sun on your body, warm and relaxing: exactly what we were there for. For a little while after we got changed we sat cross-legged by our stuff, acclimatising ourselves to the scene as we looked out to the sea and the odd tanker that was there moored, enormous on the horizon, until eventually we began to speculate how far out the sea might actually be.

"Two hundred metres," was James's best guess.

"Rubbish!" I informed him, "At least half a mile: it has to be."

"Well, let's take a look shall we? And however far it is, I'll beat you there. It'll be just like the old days," he laughed. An elderly couple were sitting on deckchairs behind us, and asking them to keep an eye on our stuff we started to walk out carefully past sunbathers supine and kids with buckets and fancy hats on.

"Let me know when you're ready," he mocked.

"Okay. On the count of three, if you're sure you can take losing."

"Whatever!"

"One, two, three, GO!" Off we burst; our legs and arms pumping like pistons and straining to push ourselves ahead as we tore out over the sand towards the sea. Jim had got a better start than me but I caught back up and now we were neck and neck, as fine an example of boyish competition as you could hope to see, running flat out against each other. Looking across to my right I could see there was nothing in it and he looked over at me, seeing the same, both of us putting our noses ahead and willing ourselves faster. Suddenly I was lying stretched out and face down in the sand, thwarted, not sure where the track had gone but knowing it meant the end of my race. I blew the wet sand from my mouth and looked over to where Jim had been, and there he still was, prostrate just as I. Getting up, and wiping the sand off our bodies, we shook hands laughing, conceding that this one was a draw.

We spent the rest of that afternoon on our towels, never actually reaching any meaningful depth of sea, which seemed only to retreat further the more we approached it. We'd ceased our quest at one of the far out channels and splashed the salty water over our sand covered fronts, scooping handfuls of the refreshing stuff onto our heads and into our hair; running cool down our backs and all over our bodies, before walking back dripping and heroic.

Reading our books and listening to music we lay in the sun, and before the day was done Jim had got us into a conversation with a small group; a lad called Gary with two girls, Charlotte and Diane, noticing as they were leaving that Gary's rugby top marked him as belonging to a club fairly local to what had once been our village. As we got chatting, Gary told us they were staying in Rye, the three of them wangling a room for two somehow, saying that they had come down this time last year too for an annual party that was due to be held here on the beach tomorrow.

"You don't want to miss it," he said, "a shindig that will stretch for miles," and he also told us that the following night they planned to go to 'Saturdays', a club along the seafront in Hastings, where they'd rounded off last year's trip. By the time they left we'd agreed to meet both on the beach the next night, and at the club, thinking it would well fit our plans to leave the campsite all packed up beforehand and head straight for home in the early hours, after a visit to 'Saturdays' with them.

It was already bright with sunshine the next morning when we awoke, which surprised us as sleeping in the tent wasn't the most comfortable: just a sleeping bag and a ground sheet between us and the hard earth. We put it down to the sea air, and the soporific bleats that came from the sheep in the adjacent field. Sitting in a sheltered passage between the tent and the car, we set up the little camping stove. Jim fried bacon and eggs, flavoured inadvertently with some stray blades of grass. I made coffee and we sat eating and feeling pleased with ourselves in the warm morning sunshine. We talked about the old days at school; some of the mates we'd known who Jim stayed in touch with. Monkey was one, Jim sometimes playing Rugby with him when he was home for a weekend, and he recounted a preposterous tale that he'd told him a few months earlier. His Dad had been grilling him about mysterious noises in the night when Monkey's girlfriend was sleeping over; noises he'd imaginatively passed off as the rumblings of a chest freezer in the room next to his. This somehow became associated in our minds with the occasional bleating that came from the field next door, and as foolish as it seems, we spent the next hour laughing at each prompt from our ovine neighbours.

By the time we'd lazily cleared off our plates and washed up our breakfast stuff the air was closing in; the atmosphere pregnant with the sense of a summer storm which turned the sky above us to an ominous grey. We took this as our cue to hide under the canvas, in time listening to the patter of the telegraphed downfall as big rain clouds moved in from the sea. The slow morning theme persisted and we fell into it easily, half reading, half dozing, until the little spate of bad weather was passed, and our minds once more turned inevitably to sustenance. We took what we needed with the evening's party in mind, and headed back in the direction of the beach, coming upon a quiet country pub just on the outskirts of Rye which was having its black hoarding, out by the road, freshly anointed with chalk. We pulled into the car park and walking from the car saw that a 'ploughman's lunch' was the newly writ offering, and striking us both as serendipitous we went on inside and ordered one, washing the country lunch down with a couple of pints of the local bitter. Outside in the car park the afternoon sun was back with a vengeance and the heat, or the beer, made me suddenly tired, wobbly even, so we found the side door into a little playground annex. It was really just a longish garden with little swings down at one end and benches with tables at the other, and lying down on either side of one of these tables, the sun's little pin rays on our faces and necks, we dozed.

Parking up once again at the beach it looked no different from yesterday, nor in fact any different from all the other times I'd been brought down here, starting from the very first holiday I remember as a five year old child. The parking area on this side of the dunes was so vast that the instantly wind-swept cars that were parked here seemed pretty sparse, while the ever-changing dunes themselves seemed immutable, so high and unadulterated: a natural barrier whose beauty was ever preserved in their intrinsic barrenness. Families with children were still arriving to catch some late afternoon seaside, picking assorted things out of their car boots: deck chairs, wind cheaters, picnic bags, little camping stoves, frisbees and lilos; each member packed up and heading off loaded for the foot of the steps like a Tibetan expedition. Looking up from the base to the top of the dunes a solitary green kite was darting in and out of view, teasing us from above as it dipped amongst the grassy outcrops of the peak.

Once up and over the top of the brow, the two of us skipping past our fellow climbers along the way with nothing but our sleeping bags and a few cans of 'Special Brew' to carry, the scenery below bore activity that was markedly different from that sleepy, sandy canvas I was used to. Large groups of party-goers were dotted almost uniformly apart along a portion of the beach, already formed up around heaped piles of wood, made ready for the fires that would keep them warm tonight. Sound stations were being set up sporadically along a length of the strand. Once descended, we sat ourselves on top of our unrolled sleeping bags, close to where we'd seen the others yesterday in the hope that we might meet up again. We each opened a can of beer and supped on it as we watched the comings and goings around us, drinking and talking rubbish, wondering how we might be able to join in the festivities.

"You 'ere for the party lads?" An accent I thought might be Liverpudlian or maybe Glaswegian broke our spell. Looking around, we found a tall skinny fellow standing above us, a big faded spider's web tattooed over one side of his gaunt face.

"Yup," said Jim nodding slowly, looking slightly unsure of how much to commit to this unlovely apparition.

"Sorted. Glad to meet yer," he said putting out his hand. "It's a 'fiver' each, includes your drinks and a place round our little fire over there. Won't be so little actually," he laughed. "Music will be starting up pretty soon so come on, let's get you involved," and so saying he headed back towards the group he'd indicated. We looked at each other; somewhat dubious but shrugging, and got up to follow him.

"There you go," he said as he seated us in a newly cleared part of the circle. "What yer names?"

"Milo."

"Jim."

"Welcome boys," he smiled. "You can call me Spider. Now, what do you want to drink?"

I don't remember too much about the night, only that some time beyond midnight I decided on a plan to search for those magical others; that little group we'd met yesterday and grown so fond of. I trudged for what seemed like miles along the beach, my thighs heavy with each sandy step and my head lolling about on drunken shoulders, making my way between each party point. The music of each one faded before growing louder again at the next, the sound system lights shining reds, yellows and oranges out from the black total night beyond. I lingered by each bright lit fire, storing up the flames' warm embrace, before tearing away and struggling on again into the cooler, darker air, sure of my futile mission and drawn to the next group, and the next. All the time, I muttered reassuring inanities to myself; pieces of wisdom that I'd learnt from the lines of songs that suddenly made perfect sense, totally solving and neatly wrapping up for me all of life's mysteries. Along the way I passed lights that became people, themselves straying from the orbit of their own fire, and having gone further and further, fighting the fog in my head and the desire to fall and sleep where I lay, I relented and made my way backwards counting again each fire that I'd passed. I lost myself to the numbers, rechecking around each group that I came upon with my head fixed on sideways; staggering so much that even the other drunks became wary of me; glad to see me moving on, and only then sure that my intention was not to give grief. Finally, just stopping and sinking, everything went blank.

When I woke in the morning, my headache was not the first thing I noticed. Consciousness came upon me only slowly, but as it did I felt pleasantly warm, finding myself lying straight and neat on my back, with my feet facing out towards the sea, comfortably tucked up with my sleeping bag right up to my chin. The sun's heat was just beginning to rise. I had no memory of being so neatly parcelled, but it was very nice to wake so nice and cosy, and for a moment I lay still, pleased to be there listening in the quiet around me. Various sounds were coming from near and far on the beach; sounds of people moving about, rolling up mats and sleeping bags, and laying there I watched as the birds circled above me, hearing their squawks from the dunes behind. I heard James's voice, and lifting my head to look about me I became immediately aware of the pain behind my eyes. My mouth was dry, and my tongue felt pitted and swollen. Jim was sitting about ten metres away, chatting to a girl as he sat around what was our fire, and catching sight of me moving he approached.

"You're awake are you?" he enquired.

"Uhhhhhh."

"Here, have some of this water Milo," he said, coming at me with a large Pepsi bottle in his hands, apparently full of water.

"What am I doing over here?" I asked him.

"I found you here," he said shaking his head. "You were murmuring something about wanting to sleep in the sea. The heat from the fire was drying out your essence, apparently," he grinned.

"How come...you're alright?"

"I'm always alright," he laughed, "but I haven't slept at all and I'm knackered, and we've got a date tonight, remember? Come on, drink this, let's go and get ourselves a bit of breakfast and then we'll go back to the campsite. I want to get some shuteye."

He virtually carried me off the beach and back up the stairs which ascended the dunes, but once there I was getting back the communication with my legs and was able to shuffle slowly down the other side, all on my own. First, we drove to a cafe that we'd seen in a tiny side road back in Rye, and with my head out of the window on the way, the numbing blow of cool fresh air rushing by my face felt good. We sat at one of the tables outside with its plastic table cloth, and though I had no appetite Jim insisted I shovel down a fry up as best I could. "The perfect antidote," he said, and I think he was right: by the time he'd driven us back to the campsite I did feel a whole lot better, just tiredness now afflicting me, arriving as most other folks there seemed about to be setting off to begin their day.

"Perfect," he said smiling, "nice and quiet, just as we like it," and shut up in the tent, the warm sun shining through on top of us and the netting keeping us safe from any flies, we didn't wake until late afternoon.

Once showered, we got dressed and started to pack all our equipment away: somehow the tent had become a whole lot bigger than it was when we'd taken it from the boot just two days earlier. Luckily, we weren't in a rush. In fact, reasoning that it would probably turn out to be a late one, we hung about a bit longer, the plan being to head out for Hastings at around eight pm and get a 'MacDonald's there, before hopefully meeting up with the others. Whether I was just being careless, or perhaps still bore some of the numbness that last night's excess had brought to my head, I learned a valuable lesson about country driving. Coming up to a hairpin, I remember seeing the sign and dismissing it as not much of a problem, but it really did turn out to be a hundred and eighty degree bend: one which I was going much too quickly to negotiate. I found myself on the wrong side of the road, hard braking and stationary, staring at the driver of a

Mercedes who had also stopped, luckily for all I guess as he was coming from the other direction on the correct, left side. The driver was not at all pleased with me, and I had nothing to give but apologies, but I've never forgotten that bend and I'd like to think that from then on I've always been a little more cautious when driving in unfamiliar territory.

Despite my efforts, we arrived in one piece at the Hastings seafront, and finding MacDonald's just a few doors down from the club that the others had mentioned, we parked up and jumped in. As we entered we saw Gary and the girls, who must also have had the same idea, and shuffling up to make spaces they beckoned us to join them. They'd also been at the beach last night, but had come along later and gone a different way, so we sat swapping our stories and lining our stomachs anew with thick creamy milkshakes. Gary and Diane it turned out were almost an item, but not quite, and something of her slight aloofness with him reminded me somehow of Maddie. I also recognised, from bitter experience, his 'puppy-dog' desire to please; the combination of factors telling me that he had more of a thing for her than she had for him. I had to admit she was a good looking girl; tall and slender with long blond hair. We all got distracted by her legs when she got up to go the toilet, ultra-elongated as they were by the short club skirt she was wearing. Charlotte was quite the opposite. Petite and pretty, she had dark hair and eyes, as well as a cute little smile. Of the two girls, Charlotte was the much more outgoing and, as we sat chatting around the table, surprisingly witty. I could see Jim was taken.

We queued up outside 'Saturdays' in single file, Gary and the girls in front and then Jim behind me at the rear. The bouncers let the three of them through ahead of me, and naturally thinking I'd be rejected it was a relief to be waved on after them. As I exhaled my breath of relief I turned to see Jim looking confused, held up by a fat-fingered hand in his face.

"You eighteen mate?" the guy asked, and Jim was aghast. Standing head and shoulders above me, and with a face full of bristle, I don't think he'd ever been challenged before, and the fact that I was already accepted made the bouncer's question surreal.

"Are you joking?" he asked seriously, and then, without waiting for an answer, "Why are you stopping me?"

"It's my job," replied the bouncer, not showing any of the amusement that surely was the whole point of this contrivance. "Do you have proof of your age or not?"

Jim looked about him for inspiration, momentarily stunned blank from this humiliating indignity, as the four of us stood awkwardly looking on from the foyer. Remembering that he had his university pass with his date of birth on in the car, and shaking his head in disbelief, he asked me for the keys through gritted teeth. He was still muttering, as agitated as I've ever seen him, when he'd satisfied his besuited tormentor and we all traipsed together through to the hall.

The place wasn't busy and we got our bearings huddled into a blue velvet horseshoe on a raised section just off to the side of the dance floor, around the corner from the long bar. Having all put into a whip, I offered to go and get the first round. Returning with the drinks on a round bass tray, I found Gary and Diane close in conversation: he looking as if all his prayers had been answered, while Jim had adopted the polite, attentive pose that I knew so well, listening and nodding to Charlotte as she leaned in trying to make herself heard above the disco sounds of Sharon Brown. Walking up the few steps through a set of thin, golden spindled railings,

I placed the tray with the drinks on in the middle of the table and then sat down there on the outer side opposite the two couples. We each took up our drinks and met in the middle of our circle with the chinking of glasses and salutes of 'cheers', then drinking our drinks as we exchanged short shouted sentences at one another, accompanied by lots of miming and gesticulation.

"Which one of you is the dancer?" asked Charlotte, like she already knew the answer, and looking at each other we both instinctively shook our heads. "Diane, come on; let's go and have a dance," she said, turning to her right, "the boys need a little bit of warming up yet." Going off she looked back from the top of the steps and winked at me. "You'd better get another round in!"

We watched them disappear into the crowd, and leaning over Gary put his elbows on the table in front of him.

"What's the plan then boys?" he asked. "Which one of you likes Charlie?"

"I'll take her for dance in a while, if that's okay?" said James, looking at me.

"Sure," I smiled, gracious defeat being one of my specialties.

"I'll let you know how the land lies when I come back," he said as I carried on nodding my acceptance.

When Diane and Charlotte returned with cheeks newly flushed they saw that another couple of drinks were waiting for each of them and they laughed, and we all sat again for a while. It wasn't long though before Gary, who had been itching, took Diane for a dance and Jim took the cue to offer Charlotte the same.

"Are you alright here on your own?" she said to me as they were about to go, and I nodded smiling, quite pleased that she'd thought to ask.

I sat sipping my coke, now switched to non-alcohol as I still felt some after-effect of last night's headache, and I didn't want to be unfit for our long drive home. I was trying to convince myself, and anyone who might see me, that I was happily lost in the music. 'Hanging on a string' was playing, its refrain of 'You never told me you were waiting, contemplating,' striking me as ironic as that was exactly what I was doing, feeling perhaps that if I acted happy then true happiness might follow. As it happened though, I did have much to be happy about. For me, these few days with Jim had been spectacular, and since we'd got reacquainted my life had pretty much taken off in a way I could hardly have dared hope for. The weekend I'd spent at his, not to mention Sue, was amazing. Though I felt a bit grubby when I woke up on the Sunday morning, moving around each other in the little flat now as awkward strangers not knowing what to say; getting washed and dressed, and leaving as quickly as I could to put an end to the morning's torment, still it was the most wonderful of awkward torments. At last to be party to a drag I'd for so long only imagined; this air so full of discomfort that it felt almost sweet, it was such a weight as I couldn't have been happier to bear, right up to the moment that I'd pulled closed the flat door behind me. And now here I was again; away from home, at last like a grown-up feeding and fending for myself. If I couldn't have the girl, at least I was out where I should be, and I knew there'd be others. Maybe it was time for me to take the next step and find myself somewhere to live; somewhere I could begin making my own life.

Reflecting on all this I ended up gazing into space and nursing an empty glass. Then Jim and Charlotte were walking back, but not really together. My searching look was met with James's shake of his head as he took his seat. After a few more songs Gary and Diane returned, and off the girls went to the toilets again.

"I reckon you've got a chance there mate," said James, indicating toward the girls as they departed.

"Really; you don't like her?" I said surprised but interested.

"Yeah but...just no spark, y'know? And anyway, Claire's still on the scene, and it wouldn't feel right." We got more drinks, and the girls came back with their make-up freshly applied; heavy blue around Charlotte's eyes and lips shining with gloss.

"Are you going to dance with me then?" she said without sitting down, and nodding, with a gulp, I rose and set off behind her.

The little enough drink in my body mixed with the music in the air, plus the excitement I felt now dancing with Charlie, and I threw myself around like I'd never done before. I felt so free; arms out wide, chest puffed and chin high, spinning around and holding her and then letting her go, and her perfume in my nose and around my face, she full of laughter at my euphoric exhibition, but seeming to like it nevertheless. We stayed out on the floor for ages, hungrily latching on to each new beat as a different song took over and setting off again crazily, all smiles and gusto. I caught a glimpse of Jim at one point downing a pint; half pissed, half bored, as the music played on. When a slow dance started, we moved in close, and I slipped my hands down off Charlotte's back to her rounded behind in the way that Monty's big brother had once told us, saying it was how you found out what a girl was really thinking. As I did so she lifted her face and kissed me, and pressing my hips against her for a moment I lost the rhythm of the dance, feeling dizzy at the touch of her lips.

We went back to the others hand in hand, and James's indulgent smile made me feel happily self-conscious. Gary pointed out the time; it was nearly two am, and he said they'd have to be leaving in fifteen minutes. Charlie and I went out to the car, saying that we needed to get a bit of fresh air, and we sat there kissing with the sounds of our breathing amplified a hundred times, talking a bit and starting to get to know one another. Too soon the other three came out and were tapping on the windows, Jim giving the car a bit of a rock for good measure. Charlotte gave me her number and I promised to call. Feeling totally elated, I wished that the night didn't have to end. Hastings's parting shot, and the picture that stays with me, was Charlie waving through the rear window of Gary's Vauxhall as they drove off past us. I was still trying to sort out my route, finding myself giddy and almost too drunk with happiness to make sense of the map. We set off shortly afterwards, back on our long way home to normality, with Jim already asleep on the seat beside me.

My Old Man

I had been away for only the shortest period of days, but coming back my sights were fundamentally shifted, and at last they were set beyond those listless and anaemic horizons that for so long had defined my miserable existence. I wouldn't continue to live the same way: I couldn't. The very limits of my bedroom and of family life itself now felt outgrown and mean, a cloying lack of space oppressing me like some obstructing phantom, ever present and keeping me from a desperately needed exit which I could sense but not find. Suddenly my anguish had an urgency; was a fiercer thing than anything I'd felt for years. The status quo of gloomily depressed ennui I'd lived with, since even before we'd moved here, was replaced by a fever that lifted exponentially the tension in the air: I was clanking around in my skin like I needed to shed it. My parents, knowing before I did that this change was the vital catalyst, the crucial ingredient for reforming my life, patiently accepted my ranting and injustice, watching from places withdrawn as at last I started to become a man.

Thanks to the introduction from James's father I was soon commuting to Old Street in very heart of London itself: to me a distant part of the universe and a huge world away from the provincial supermarket of my earlier despair. I found myself now surrounded by suits and shiny shoes; people with real ties that didn't clip on, and who treated me, colleagues and bosses alike, with an office civility which would have seemed alien just a couple of weeks earlier.

I couldn't wait for those half-hour phone calls with Charlie, filled with tacit grins and not a lot more, as I twiddled the flex at the bottom of the stairs with a stupid look on my face. Now bashful, now trying bravado, those chats had to keep us going because I couldn't bear to let her visit the suburban home I was sick of; where the man-child was desperate to spread his wings but didn't know how. At last I'd found in myself a little pride, and it made for a quandary. Neither of us knew what to say but we knew that we didn't want to let go: thinking about a way to move on from here consumed me.

"You know the answer Bruv. You've got to get your own space," was Tommy's matter-of-fact assertion, as I sat at his kitchen table digging my nail down a 'Budvar' label, whinging round in circles like a child. "Somewhere in town; maybe a flat-share near the new job. Won't be too expensive round there, and you'll be right close to all the action; right nice and cushty-la."

"I don't know anyone," I retorted. "How the hell am I going to find a share if I don't know anyone to share with?"

"Ain't there no-one at work?"

"No. Well, there's a girl called Louise, but she lives in a squat. I don't think I really want to go there!"

"If Louise wants to squat you should let her," he replied, and we both laughed. "You're just too picky!"

"I wish I knew someone though," I continued, and he fell into a thoughtful silence.

"Hold up!" he said at last. "Of course, you don't need to know anyone. Get hold of the 'Evening Standard' and take a look in the rentals section there. It's always full of people looking to let out spare rooms. That way you'll get to know 'em plenty soon enough. Come on Milo, don't look like that. It will be brilliant, trust me: no time at all to the office and you'll be on my hunting manor too. We'll go out and have a right time of it and you'll be able to get your girlie up, eh? 'Bout time you started moving things along; don't you think so?"

When I moved into the little box room in the house share off York Way Tommy was as good as his word (as if that was ever in doubt), my very first visitor and a familiar face as I adjusted to a new orbit. I remember him gunning his oversized Chieftain Jeep up Royal College Street that night as high above the road we made a tour of the area, me sitting thrilled beside him. Though I knew I was to properly find myself, at least I'd found my place for now. By standing on my own two feet I felt like I was finally making it; that everything really was going to be okay. Listening to Tommy's trademark deep rumbling laugh that filled the cabin and harmonised with the throaty sound of the engine as we shot up the road, it almost felt like we owned the place.

As the two of us sat around the dinner table later on with my new house mates, I felt that Tommy was my accreditation; a show of association of which I was rightly proud. My thinking ran that if he was my mate then it was a given that I wasn't just some freak loner; someone that others ought to scrutinise and be wary around. As the night went on we all chatted and laughed and got to know each other, and it felt like a little bridge was being built; an imperceptible movement into a whole new community. When I look back and recall simple times shared like these, no matter how much time passes; no matter how far apart the people may grow, that long gone innocence and friendship still seems to shine as a beacon and burn warm in my memory. I'll never forget how Tommy was aghast later on when Chloe, the longest standing member of this ever-evolving household, expressed her first-impression of him that he wasn't 'boyfriend material'; nor that shard of guiltiest pleasure I felt when I heard her say so, even though I couldn't possibly have disagreed more.

Truth can come to us by osmosis, and if we grow up in a traditional environment with our family and friends around us, our very lives speak of where we've come from and teach us much about ourselves. It was different for me. My parents' move to our village had been a clean slate and a blatant rejection of the old. As far as tradition was concerned, it was like growing up in a vacuum, and my journey of self-discovery therefore was a much slower one. Eventually I found that the situations that could teach me about myself, about who I was and where I really wanted to go, were those where I could totally let go; immerse myself in unknown seas, and see myself as I truly was, out there swimming with strangers. Tom got me started down this fertile stream of consciousness because of the belief that his presence gave me. With him there I felt I could trust myself enough to leap through the darkness with my eyes closed, finally free to be who I was instead of wondering who on earth I should be, now invested of a self-belief that I had always lacked before.

Finding myself back in the town of my birth, I found myself ready; hungry even, for the manifold diversions that were everywhere on offer. It was inevitable that the old iron stadium would once again raise a call. I went along the first time almost bashfully, out of pure curiosity; walking up in the East Stand shadow one weekday evening when the place was asleep. It wasn't a match night and the entire complex seemed a dormant, sleeping giant; the silent echo of a memory from long years ago. That ordinary living street with its terraced houses and its wide pavement road, what an incredible disguise it was for what really dwells and rattles around the old marble halls, there at the pit of the hill where the crowd will throng thickest. Before long I was properly back, standing for the matches on the North Bank terrace. My presence at this populous hub seemed at first a bizarre juxtaposition, and I found it hard to believe that it was me amongst these very different animals, but as I returned again and again the experience seemed to normalise. The sights and sounds of these matches became my sights and sounds, and pretty soon Tom and I had taken up almost like regulars with the East Lower crew.

I still hadn't been to a game with Dad since I was five years old. Since our first outing together he had spent virtually all his time chained to the high street, branching away from the West End to establish his own suburban chain. Although this move took away the stricture of human bosses, the cruel master of self-survival only took their place. By the time I moved to London, however, Dad had retired, and my returning to the area: in London terms just around the corner from Highbury, made natural a belated homecoming for the two of us. It was a joint visit back to this most enduring of temples that had waited nearly twenty years, and by my finally moving out of the family home we also found that the love and the friendship between us, stifled and obscured by proximity and competition, came back into focus. Now going forward; being carried along on such awkwardly rusty trips as these at first were, a natural oil was dripped and worked into the parts of our relationship, and though at first creaky and stiff, they became gently easier. A new rapport at last could grow between us.

I remember one of those earliest games that Dad and I spent at the ground together. It was in the time before I'd found the 'me' that was really at home in this brave new environment, and Liverpool football team, the eternal champions at that time, were coming to town. High in the West stand I sat polite and controlled beside my father, perhaps showing a little bit of my new found 'passion' for the game; baring to him just a fragment of the rougher edge that I was comfortable our fledgling adult relationship could take. Warmly dressed in his thick grey knitwear and wearing his red rimmed glasses, those ninety minutes with Dad were a 'hundred miles walked' for how the two of us were together. We both looked on nervously disbelieving as Arsenal scored three goals without reply on that perfect afternoon; an afternoon of victory against a seemingly undefeatable Liverpool team which provided an inestimable prize for us, far beyond the three league points.

I ask myself this: what other melting pot is there which could have brought together, with such an intense common cause, my life's polar opposites; my best friend and my father? The 'fuck you' non-conformist that was Tom; challenging and daring; scarily over the edge and leering right back, and then Dad with his rules and his certainties; living by the clock and liking it that way, with no room it seemed for doubts and no truck with errors. The love of football seems to create a parallel universe so that wherever we are in our lives; whatever we represent in our homes and our offices, it has the ability to unearth in all of us a child and a warrior; to raise up the meek and the measured; bring voice to the mute, and join them in fellowship to the rowdy who too often in their passion feel themselves alone. Each of us recognises, and is recognised by, those who too are drawn to this fierce primal gathering.

The very first time that the three orbits collided, Dad's tie and Tom's Maori necklace surreally met for a mid-week cup game. Tommy brought the chieftain and at the wheel is holding sway down the Caledonian Road. Dad's sitting huffily stiff in the passenger seat, only just now appraised of the measure of our party as I hadn't dared to pre-warn him. Tom's pick up was late: never a great start. I had stood outside the tube station in silence with Dad counting the minutes; waiting for his belated appearance. Now in the car, the clock's running down and we're getting later and later, lost in a web of one-ways and the newly fashioned dead ends that conspired to frustrate my best efforts at navigation. The atmosphere is loaded with neither extreme seeming likely to meet; this first for our triumvirate seeming likely a last. Dad's sitting upright in his three-piece, muttering irritably. Tom is throwing the Jeep this way and that, searching out a way while in the back my face is feeling red as I pray silently for a release of the tension that's building. Dead ends block our every turn but Tommy knows, and doesn't he always, with a touch of smug bravado; that confident 'just watch this' mug; 'have Chieftain will travel', he's up on the pavement and driving over a bumpy path that looks impassable; down by a brick wall bumping and over the grid. Dad's having kittens, spluttering and about to eject but look, the magic man's done it, we're over and on the main road and suddenly making good time. The mood has changed like a spell; the old man's relieved and laughing and so am I, so am I, and Tommy's ear to ear grin is saying it all.

Of all those first visits when Tommy and I would sit there together at the stadium there's one memory which will never, ever fade. There we were in our East Lower seats with the stands on either side of us calling their names; the North Bank raising voice to the clock end, and the Clock End back again; chants that endured until the stadium itself had died, to be raised again like ghosts from time to time when the new place might fondly remember. The play has already begun and the usual suspects are all in their places around me; the funny looking strangers that lately are the boys I hug or groan with as occasion demands. A spectator, I'm watching as wave after wave of emotion crashes around the stand, some of the more sensitive among us taking it full on, spinning head over heels, while on others the merest spray is observed: some swimming and others drowning as wave breaks and wave forms. On the pitch it's now us, and now them, now us, and now them, with all the attendant hope and anxiety that is consequent from such a spectacle; such a binary contest as this one. A friction is starting to build in the clash of emotions.

In a deep, crazy way it reminds me of a dream I often had when I was a young kid, even before I went off to pre-school. An awful, desperate nightmare that repeated night after night and left me grateful to wake; to lie shattered a while, wracked with the feelings of dread still upon me, lifted too slow by fresh consciousness which yet felt the weight of my sub-conscious pain and sullied for a while the mood of the morning. My blanket, or rather the satin strip that had once been there attached; my comfort which I'd rub for hours between my forefingers while sucking my thumb, would be drifting inexorably away from my reach, getting closer to a dark sense of evil which was personified by my paternal uncle. In the dream, he faced me across a wicked carousel as he sneered and radiated meanness. Perhaps for this dark relative 'wicked' is a bit harsh, but all I felt from him as a toddler was a spiteful, ugly enmity. I never had the opportunity to re-evaluate my childhood opinion, denied by that uncle himself when Dad tried in vain for reconciliation, many years later. In my dream, I would watch in growing horror, feeling utterly desperate and hopeless, as my uncle prepared to snatch and take away my life's greatest jewel, only to see my blanket at the very last, impossibly, pass him by. He'd missed and now my blanket continued on a path back towards me, bringing with it such a feeling of relief; of hope and life itself re-born, that I was completely overwhelmed. Preparing again to catch it I'd be just too late! Again it was gone; I had missed it. I would watch as the satin strip went around all over again on this treacherous cycle between my uncle and I, my heart leaden and certain that this time my most treasured prize was his, and life would be over.

The play on the pitch goes on, and around it a tempest of emotion continues to gather louder and louder as appeals are made to justice or to some greater power. As the volume swells it fills me, lifting me higher with its very particular freedom. I begin to hear a sound so deep, a growl that's blended with the noise and clamour, ugly and base and fearsome, as if coming from a forgotten time. The growl rings out with passion distilled, devoid of manners and pretence to leave only fear, pure threat and confusion. As if I have been sleeping, slowly I wake to this primeval alarm around me, just knowing it at first without question. As the fury whips higher, I'm lost somehow in its din to those around me and, filling my ears, my nose, my head, I turn and see to my horror, bared vicious teeth, neck taut and temples pumping, the cries are mine, like nothing I've even dreamt before, a shameless apology for everything I've been and all the adrenalin I've run from.

Because deep down in all of us lies a late, desperate energy to fight and survive. This energy in me had lain hidden, dormant and unknown, and was only uncovered by this returning here; coaxed out in the same arena where I was once overawed as a child, where the noises of the crowd had before washed around me. Back then, the promise of this terrible power could not have been explained or understood, but survival was ever our task, and our mission ensures that the tools to do so are located within us. In these late days of ours we're more than likely to turn from what is deemed the ugliness of our deeper animal towards an ideal of a gentler, better mannered mask, but this is a luxury that hunger and fear conquered has allowed us to adopt as we shun the original provider. I would have known this terrible power which had always lurked within me had I not been made a little too polite; a little too inhibited, but from that time on I have known this energy as my constant companion, a deepest hum and mine to summon if ever such strength; such emotional brutality, should be what's required.

A strange realisation inside of me clicks, and suddenly back to myself I slump in my chair in a state of dazed wonder. 'Who I am?' are the unformed thoughts that I'm thinking, or rather 'who am I now?' Totally and beautifully calm I feel suddenly so complete; so balanced with the chorus about me that's a perfect refrain, a balm for my emotions, as the noise from the crowd affirms and absorbs me. Looking blankly ahead I slowly become aware of the rows of head that stretch to the pitch just below me; of the flow in the game, and I see Ray on his right jinking past me down the outside and... No! He's hit it and it's in and the place goes mental. Bouncing men are in other men's arms in open mouthed, disbelieving celebration all about me. Polo is disappearing down the row in his ecstatic victory charge, to be lost in a yielding, happy pile, and looking up I see Tom standing there looking down at me, a question in his eyes. Suddenly I'm exhausted; overwhelmed by what I've just witnessed, experienced, right here in the middle of it, gazing out at the backs and the coats that obscure the on-pitch celebrations with a massive smile on my face.

Part 2

Whirls, and vapid swirls
of fragment frames do rise in plume,
then eddy on the winds that years huff,
puff they dance about my room.

Bright-lit globes for my mind's viewing
gaily glittered, steeped in time,
the hours starred,
the moment daring,
my perfect love,
oh test sublime.

At colours bright I stare in wonder,
scan fiery lights to show me more,
let whirls yet dance,
their pirouettes do thrill me,
but I've said before,
no mind now but for sparkling globes
to pass and hold my gaze in awe.

The Soldier Stood Alone

Getting to *The Barn* ahead of the main throng, you'll find it a half-country, half-town sort of place – a civilized one where you can quietly sip a pint and imagine that same quiet ascendant on the streets in the world outside, just the right number of cars easily passing on roads that are spacious, clean, and open like the inside of the salon itself, not yet packed wall to bar with drinkers. The presence on the door, though, of those gatekeeping Goliaths gives away that a quiet night is not what is reckoned on; but for anyone lacking a bit of self-confidence – acceptance and authority issues their baggage wherever they go – the barely perceptible nod of permission returned to a half-hesitant, tacit entreaty right at the threshold is the best you can get. That final barrier opened is invariably the sweetest, and no matter how many times I've breached the same, it's always a relief when my allegiance to order and to the right flag has been accepted, when membership of the club has been taken as given.

Swing in through the second set of doors, and the red-checked carpet arrests your eyes: only later will a surfeit of patrons overrun it, so its gaudy pattern for now remains unobscured. This wide tartan path weaves from the entrance before appearing among the oaken legs of the tables and chairs which run along the windows – these glass eyes to the world which gaze upon the courtyard outside – then spans its dominion through the salon and around the wooden bar to the room at the back. The columns that stand floor to ceiling with their shelves clean wiped are devoid of the foam-stained tankards that will come on later, as yet unadorned by crumpled and discarded shells once packed full of crisps. These icons of convenience stand proud from their freshly vacuumed foundation, neat little islands in the deep red sea where the bar is a shoreline, and vessels there stand ready and stacked with the nuts and the nibbles replenished. The staff lazily enjoys the ticking down of a casual afternoon, aware of the shadow that will gradually overtake the hours before kick-off.

Passing around the corner under the wall-mounted screens, we come to the back room, a larger cabin and meeting place with yet more sturdy-looking tables and chairs, also set out in orderly groups but interspersed with settees and other eclectic seating. Here, within the confines of the wooden wainscoting and the peeling wallpaper, small groups are starting to form – a melting pot of sorts where suits fresh from the city mingle with the more casual clientele. Some of these characters have come here just as they are, dressed up or down; others have disguised themselves with a costume change along the way in order that they might play, or perhaps even be, for the night, someone different. They wear a variety of apparel but are almost all of a sex, and though ages are spread, there is something about this microcosm that makes young the old; and aping them makes old the young. All are here to watch and to play the same game. In the air, a mood is starting to build, at first taking hold very gently but stoked and stroked by the mute, talking heads and the noiseless headlines on the televisions: a clip of someone at training, of a tackle, or – better still – of the flash of a goal with all its emotional associations, a regurgitated aperitif to this evening's action. Gentle billows of excitement already start slowly to fan the bodies of those here assembled.

This is no men-only environment, of course, but you need something of the man about you even to want to attend on a night like this, engaging in the latest football banter, or at least knowing your offside rule, to be an honorary boy. The older girls, who've burnished their credentials in years of attendance, are quietly confident they know their game as well as, or better than, their male counterparts; the younger ones more noisily take the game to their masculine companions, ready to fight for their place with words should their commitment be scorned. And let us not forget the part-timers, the candy here and there, the pretty and not-so-pretty ones just along for the ride, happy to dwell in this ball-crazed crew and be set apart – or upon, even – by dint of their sex, enjoying that extra attention which scarcity affords.

The tables are starting to fill now, empty chairs sought from those nearby to accommodate another addition, seats becoming premium as the clock's hand, moving closer to tonight's kick-off, swells demand. Groups that met early for a leisurely transition are shedding the day, welcoming together the night's entertainment of friends and beer, the tribes settling in for a football call to arms. There are couples unromantic and trios and quartets and more, some all in it together with a singular focus, beating their point from all sides to the centre, and other, looser groups with multiple points of focus, multiple personalities too strong to submerge and form themselves gently into one happy whole. These habitually splinter to a variety of simultaneous conversations, and taking the room in its entirety, I see all different heads, many rapt without distraction but others too that flit just above or float like a bee from one bud to the next, dipping momentarily to some nectar here and some nectar there, never fully at rest.

Commanding the back room from his usual spot in the corner of this growing hubbub sits Polo, a veritable sore thumb holding court from another world as only he can. This is always my first point of call: a duty to pay my respects if I'm early enough on any given match night. Though ours is a typical acquaintance of the terraces, our relationship based on a single theme and our time together an accident of this singular pastime, there's nothing typical about Polo, a character amongst characters. The first time I laid eyes on him was quite some years ago. An intrepid few of us, having shrugged off inertia to split from a larger block, upgrading from the restricted-view stalls which previously we'd felt honoured to call our own, were picking our way unfamiliarly to new seats in the stadium. Stepping carefully down the concrete levels one grade at a time, excitedly getting closer and closer to the summer green turf with each descending row, we spied our little block, empty and waiting next to a vision. He was very black, or rather had skin of deepest brown, and his age was indeterminate – I found out later he was a good ten years older than me – with dry black dreads and white eyeballs shot through with red and a face deeply ridged with crags. It was one of those moments: middle-class liberal brought shockingly face to face with his own white prejudice, but making bold as our near-petrified little party hesitated, I strode in first across the row to the seat beside him, taking a place and my fate at his left hand as if I weren't scared he'd eat me. He didn't. As it turned out, I lapped him up, staying there with him and indeed looking forward to the way his wit and personality would enliven my Saturday-afternoon experience right up until they turned the old stadium into high-ticket housing.

That first encroachment on to his territory seemed to spark a definite challenge, and he came on to the newbies as if the stand were his own, but maybe that was just how our fear translated it. Perhaps he was just being defensive, and maybe it was his way of making sure that we were safe, marking out to us who he was, in my face as I received his hand and, leaning backwards a little, cautiously shook it. The boys shuffling in behind me got off lightly with a nod, and quietly flushed, we sat ourselves down feeling self-conscious and exposed, trying to banish from our minds the thought of that secure comfort we'd enjoyed just a few months earlier behind those blind pillars at the other end. The game began and the minutes passed, but the next time he turned my way, his foray was kinder, and pretty soon we were exchanging the basics of name and how long a season ticket holder; and before I knew it, we were sparring over our latest Dutch signing, already acquainted and beginning a beautiful relationship.

Polo was a great showman: his hands with their own mind each constantly moved high and wide, illustrating this or expanding on that, and his head never sat still on his shoulders. His voice he always used to augment these wild gestures in a range of different tones that increased his dramatic emphasis. Even when he wasn't talking to me, I wanted to be part of his admiring audience, chuckling away to myself at the gems I picked up on, always keeping an ear free for the dirty poetry that his well-chosen words inevitably became. His cadence was captivating; this filthiest of mouths was full of humour, and his body too was always active, seeming never to spend a whole game fixed to his appointed chair. I'd turn around to find him moved to a spare seat down the row, chatting with someone or else to a few rows down or right by the pitch to catch up with another, knowing everyone around us and everyone knowing him. Wherever he might be found, however, he was all over the place when a goal went in, the late all-seater code futile when occasion required that overspilling emotions be given their flight, and the rows below us were well used to bearing his weight, the spontaneous crush of celebration.

When that moment would come, my instinctive response was a swing to the left, my face suddenly bulging with happiness, for a bear hug with Tommy. After that, it was PJ beyond, who, with his little brother, made up our original band of pioneers. Somewhat relieved now and all squeezed-out, I'd let go and turn away to Rusty behind me, joining with him for a sober acknowledgement of the happiness we shared; and then lastly to my right, where more often than not I'd find a row half vacated. Polo's exuberant tsunami once again would have cut out its swathe, sweeping all before him. Helped back now upright by his long-suffering neighbours, half irritated but half honoured to be included in his destructive excess, he would stagger back towards me in the still-joyous afterglow as helping hands continued to make sure of his way, lest without their support he should spontaneously fire off again. Reaching me, we'd enjoy a more refined clasp, and little as I am, I was always grateful that what was left of his celebration was its gentler coda.

The enthusiasm of terrace behaviour is only suitable in situ, but we all know the score: to be a part of this action can be truly inspiring, and I'm sure that none of us would want it any other way. Nevertheless, patterns of behaviour are insidious; they get right inside you, and like it or not, they will come to shape the person you turn out to be. A case in point was the Manchester United game the year following our move. I recall Anelka banging in his first for the club, a near-post screamer as unexpected as it was spectacular, and suddenly PJ's little brother was the one going maddest. This taciturn, shy little boy let out a war cry, his first one ever and learned from his fellows, a high-pitched roar from somewhere within, his jaw so wide in the flare of his passion I wondered if he'd ever be able to close it again.

Over the many years, Polo and I have shared a lot of time there together. Despite the unfulfilled but never fading sense of threat, he is always a most pleasant companion for an afternoon or an evening and nearly always provides a perfectly timed entrance which, just as the teams came out on to the pitch, finds him descending the steps and acknowledging the standing masses with regal nods, bowing and smiling like Louis the Fifteenth as if we all are standing in his honour. This perennial little theatre, this prelude of his for those of us about to be entertained, brings from us, his hangers-on, appreciative laughter without tire. Customs like these and the sharing of these simple, uncomplicated times, both joyous and painful but always banging the drum for the same cause regardless, have translated naturally in me into affection – as gratitude also, and not only for his excellent company, the witty commentary which makes me chuckle and lifts my heart. It is also for the simple fact that he always has accepted me there, has let me belong. It's impossible to describe how much it means to feel like "one of them", whoever they are, and even if away from that place, despite all those fine hours, there is no common ground between us – even if away from the red and white we don't exist at all – what we have is more than nothing, and I guess that's just how it is meant to be.

It's the same with Rusty, the guy who, for years, has sat behind me. We are more alike than Polo and I are, and we actually share some interests beyond the remit of this theatre. He is also a city worker, based not far from me somewhere in the square mile, and in particular, we share a keen interest in food and the latest restaurants. As the game goes on before us, we often risk the ire of our more focused brethren by talking about nothing very relevant: what we were cooking that night, what restaurants we've been to during the week, rapping with each other in fact about anything and everything, always trying to be the quicker and the funnier and always enjoying the challenge as we play the part of the lads we've chosen to be here. However, we know with certainty that we can't take this thing beyond the exits – that the requisite magic will vanish once the final whistle blows. Indeed, when we did bump into each other one time quite by chance when leaving an open-air concert with our respective girlfriends, we found ourselves stumped with lines on our foreheads as each tried to place the other's familiar face. At last the penny did drop, and after the gushing relief of realization and introductions and pleasantries few enough to lead our conversation, within a few mutterings, to a stall, we were glad to part quickly, scuttling away to our separate paths and not to think more on the curious embarrassment.

Picking my way around the chairs towards Polo, around the legs that will soon be trekking off to the stadium, I think of how often I make this same pilgrimage, this prematch tradition which I hope means something to him too. I could just get to the ground and be there waiting in my seat – he'd come along anyway – so I hope he gets it that this going out of my way to pay some respect means I think something of him. As I approach, I can see that he's just finishing up a prematch tradition of his own, and as he looks up from the three roll-ups that he's building on the table, he grins at me with his big, gold-tooth smile.

"How you doin', Po?" I start, my habitual opener, smiling at the two fellow gooners that he always meets here before the games, a man and a woman who I guess have known him forever, though I've no reason really for thinking this.

"All right, Milo, all right; not bad, I reckon, not too bad. Right fired up for this one though. Little something here to keep it real," he says, looking down at the smokes as he slides them into a Silk Cut packet before putting it safely away. "In case of nerves, know what I mean?" The packet disappears into his green army-type jacket, whose various pockets could provide enough storage to fuel a campaign. He pats it approvingly.

"Should be all right tonight though, shouldn't we?" I continue. "The boys are playing well at the moment."

"Hmmm," he muses. "I don't like this lot though: Bad, bad bunch, they are, I'm telling you; nasty business up there I had one time," and he seems lost in his thoughts as he talks ten to the dozen, pausing for an intake of breath through nearly gritted teeth. "Worst little incident I've known; caught me trying to get away and did me proper, oh yes, nasty bastards. Wouldn't give 'em the steam off my piss. Know what I'd like to give 'em though – know what I mean?"

"I hear ya, mate," I counter, affecting to know what he is talking about. In truth, I have no experience at all of the kind of tribal violence that was endemic in the eighties and before to which I assume he is referring. The nearest I got to that unacceptable ugliness was a few seasons back when some Chelsea Neanderthals graced our row and I had to endure a running commentary laced with anti-Semitism. Aside from that trip with my dad when I was five years old, I didn't become a regular until already well into my twenties, but "I hear you, mate" was what I always said when I didn't what to show my ignorance, when I didn't quite understand what I was hearing but didn't need to hear any more. In Polo's case, this was invariably some clash he'd been on the right or wrong side of somewhere or other up or down the country.

Away from the ground and without the comfort of the game going on before us, our interaction has an awkwardness that is inexplicable when compared to our pitch-side ease. The conversation often runs empty, and I find the short silence before I make my excuses slightly embarrassing, as if it has found us out. I feel sorry for that, because I always find him fascinating: he is so different from me, with the things he's experienced and witnessed, and I have always suspected he is wise like a plain-clothed preacher. "What time you going down there?" I ask fatuously, my signal that I am taking my leave. "Perhaps you'd better watch your step and get down early, eh?"

"Nah, mate, not on my manor. I'd like to see 'em try it here! Don't worry; I'll be down regular. Stand for me at kick-off as usual: whole ground rises for Polo's entrance," he says with a satisfied certainty, and as he does so, he sweeps his arms wide as if embracing the thousands that will rise as his welcoming party.

"Nice one." I grin at him and then in turn at his silent partners. "See you at the barricades, then. Laters."

Making my way back to the other side, a way now grown more and more like a jungle impenetrable, I see Tom sitting down in a group of the lads and chatting with Banks. The nice untouched pint beside him is obviously mine, and squeezing through the crowd, I sit next to him on the chair that he's kept.

"Ta, mate." I smile, lifting the glass for a touch against his.

"My pleasure, bruv." He smiles back, putting his arm around my neck and giving it a gentle squeeze. Momentarily captive, my head hangs there helpless as I wait for him to release me. When he does, I salute the table with my drink before bringing the glass to my lips and taking a few slow gulps and then placing it back down. Proudly, from deep within, I release a burp and then wipe my mouth with the sleeve of my hoody.

Banks, as always, is the smartest dressed of our group in a collared shirt, and even in jeans, it's clear where his Mrs' iron has pressed its point. The long coat that hangs on the hook of the nearest column completes his rigging, its perfect nap his symbol in big-C Conservative navy, equally at home in the solicitors' office where he is a partner or at the bar of his golf club where the members' rules are perfectly in tune with his own. With him are his two sons, Peter and Jamie, both grinning and already into the excitement. The younger of them is handing his phone around to show his latest choice download; he answers my reticence with a characteristic leer that indicates I won't be disappointed; and all the while, Banks, as usual, keeps his attention carefully distracted, engaging with Tom on a matter more suitable, a matter which wouldn't so easily entertain the ensemble. He's long since accepted the truth that, with his offspring, he can lead a horse to water, but it might be spat in his face.

As the older of the two brothers, Peter holds himself back appropriately, though he doesn't distain a quick peek at his sibling's venal offering, distinguishing himself through immediate disassociation rather than enduring to ignore it completely. He has the inestimable benefit of a good woman, she who straightens his path; and due somewhat to his appearance, he is much brighter than he looks: the enormous green parker and bald shaved head paint in caricature a mindless, violent thug, an image which his little, piggy eyes and tombstone teeth, alternately white and gold, do nothing to dispel. His voice is a surprise each time he speaks: the soft, lisping product so incongruous to the mute image, and you'd never guess what an accomplished designer he is, his greatest creation possibly this most misleading Uncle Fester exterior. I still have a few of his creations, T-shirt keepsakes that so well recall the special mood of some football times that we have spent together, celebrations of things we once had in common.

Now the phone has moved on, and Ray is enjoying a rerun of Jamie's show, nodding his rapt appreciation down at the other end in that annoyingly obsequious manner of his, one that I'll never get used to. We came back from Cardiff together one time, missing the last direct train home and enduring a long night of grief because he insisted on a last-minute stop for a packet of mints despite my protestations as I saw the clock ticking down. Due to an overly developed sense of loyalty, I waited with him, but I've never been able to let it drop; and since that time, I've had the suspicion that under the veneer of quasi-normality, there's something about him that's seriously amiss.

Next to him sits Wolfie, initially my introduction to this circle. His toothy perma-chuckle spills out to the table around him as it always does; his jocund eyes always seem to smile more at a thing inside him than at anything in particular without. Taking me in with the sweep of his gaze, polite as ever, he bends me a nod by way of a greeting. I don't know what it is that so entices me about him – maybe that sense of having all that he needs right there contained, wanting nobody and nothing else – but something of the ease he exudes always has seemed so attractive that I never have quite been able to abandon the hope that we'll become better friends. Even if lately I've perceived him moving gently and inevitably away from the others, the guys he grew up with as a classmate of Peter, it is those deep, lasting roots I am secretly jealous of, imagining a closeness that now I begin to understand might be more a projection of my own insecurities than something really there.

"Off for a leak, bruv," announces Tommy, getting up and heading in the direction of the toilets. Leaning forward on my elbows, I lazily rest the bottom of the pint in the cup of my hands, the lower lip of the nearly horizontal glass resting on my teeth. Sitting here at the table, I'm separate from the others, lost in my thoughts, apart from them as I look over my nose to a clear orange lake. The sleepy mass of liquid seeps slowly past my teeth and into the cavern of my open mouth; the warm beer drifts past the sides of my tongue and down my throat in little swallows. About me, the table is caught up in a variety of miniplays, chats about this and that, and it's wonderful that we achieve regularly such an easy equilibrium here despite such diversity, all because of a love of football. Sometimes I have wondered if the lads feel as shallow in their relationships with one another as I feel in my relationships with them. Even for those born in the same family, football holds famously as a glue and an ever ready ground for conversation, a pitch for words to be kicked about on, practice for people who might otherwise have nothing to say. What would happen, I wonder, if suddenly this smooth field we rely on, this happy pastime, should just disappear?

My very first meeting with Wolfie was a night out in town; the two of us, thrown together by our association through work and ascertaining that we shared the fundamental allegiance, were further surprised to discover how near we sat at the home of our heroes. It was only natural that we should look out for each other, and even more so as, independently, we both used this pub as a prematch base. For whatever reason, though, no matter how much I tried to work myself in his way or how many times I flashed him bits of me that were usually enough to impress, to make a favourable mark, it just wasn't to be; and with an invisible cap on our intimacy, we remain friendly but not much closer than that to this day. Thinking too much is a skill I was born with, and as I look up and over at him now sitting lost in his own content, a bemused question suggests itself, one that I always find thrown up by my bafflement – the one that asks, "Is it me?" My obsession with objectivity, if that is truly what it is, rather than just being too insecure, almost demands a positive answer, but equally why can't it be, "Is it him?" The question that follows from this rhetorical standoff is this: "What the hell is it that I'm looking for anyway?"

I get it that if everyone is your best mate then you don't have one at all, and I understand too that the world has many different types and that all of us being what we need to be makes for one big, happier place. Of course we have to let people be who they are and not try to make them who we want them to be, and I also get, belatedly, that if you know it's just not going to work, then having the strength to let go ultimately determines whether you will find happiness. When all is said and done, though, a question of justice remains. The way we interact with others defines not only ourselves but the world as a whole, and failure to render to someone his or her due, whether in friendship or in life or just out there in the street, is the height of toxicity. Acquaintances like Wolfie have no debt to pay: he has never owed me more than he has given, and if I wanted more, well, that was my look out. There are others, however, and you know who you are: the calculators and conspirators who take without giving and do not feel shame or compunction or soul, the treacherous and inconsistent who leave their erstwhile friends scratching their heads with their innocence lost, the liars, those twisted by their misguided envy. The list grows long, and though the passing of time is both teacher and nurse, it's those who hurt the people we love that hurt us the most: this is a pain that burns with the hottest of flames, and for them we reserve our deepest thoughts of vengeance.

The Changeling

Such ugly realisations as the one preceding, such conclusions that I'd one day draw to help understand a certain type of 'friend' around me, were still out of my reach as I stood waiting for Charlotte at Kings Cross Station, nervously shifting my weight from one foot to the other. It takes a back catalogue of life experiences, not to mention a plethora of grown-up relationships, before you even start to learn some of the really useful truths; so it's hardly surprising that I didn't have the meanest shadow of the tiniest perception of such things as I stood there expectant under the huge domed roof, which, looking up, would have seemed just as filthy a hundred years earlier. I was wondering instead if I could really remember what the hell she looked like, if in her absence I'd exaggerated her looks, if I'd even recognize her when she'd got off the train and was walking towards me. Attending by those old brick columns there on platform five, it seemed like ages since we'd danced together in *Saturdays*.

I still have a snapshot in my mind of the first time I passed through the door of my new single bedroom, taking a look to survey the four walls as I closed the door behind me; and from that moment, I wanted her there. First impressions are important, however, and when finally I got her here, all to myself, I wanted to be sure that she'd find something I could be proud of. To achieve that, I needed a few bits and pieces: a poster, maybe, or a natty throw of the like I might find at Camden's world-famous market, plus some idea of the place and a plan for what we could do. As part of my exodus, Dad had driven me here on Sunday afternoon, notionally to help me find my way on the other side of the tunnel, but I think that for both of us it was a sentimental journey. A couple of cardboard boxes were on the back seat behind us filled with the things that I thought I most needed: my stereo, some records, my trusty clock radio, and a couple of recent diaries; also a baseball bat and a catcher's mitt that I'd had since a family trip to New York when I was fifteen. Once we had brought these items up the stairs and placed them on what was to be my new bed, we returned to the family home for a final night as man and boy. That evening, we had a celebratory goodbye dinner, and Mum, Dad, and my sister mock solemnly presented me with one of those boxed mugs you used to find on the shelves at Clinton Cards. In my favourite red and white colours, it bore a motif declaring "The Exceptional Man" with a cheeky "You're Sensational" on the inside of the lip. I'd cherish this kitsch little trinket for the next thirty years.

Waking on Monday morning, I took my leave as the rest of them slept, quietly closing the front door behind me and noting the metallic tap as the letterbox flap swung into place a fraction of a second behind the door. The sound was the faintest knell on a time that was passing. Pausing for a moment, I looked up to the second-floor windows and was reminded of another time I had come home in the morning light from a nightshift and had looked up this way, on what I was about to discover was the morning after the night when my Nana died. Carrying my bag, I walked full of purpose to the station and got the train to work, and when five o'clock came and I went back down to the Underground, like a traitor, for the very first time, I headed north excitedly to my new Camden abode.

Outside the station, the well-meaning campaigners had their anti-apartheid plaques bobbing in the air, and walking to my garret, I passed the space-age Sainsbury's, a carbuncle to some, looking like an alien landing on Camden Road. Crossing over, I went down the diagonal Lime Street and, in a couple of minutes, had reached the Constitution Pub; the gatekeeper to the estate where my roots would be taking was there standing tall and proud, a white edifice looming its long shadow out over the railings and on to the canal. I didn't know it yet, but this little corner would prove a perfect place to retreat to, somewhere relatively peaceful yet just ten minutes along the towpath from Camden's beating heart. It was a place I'd fall in love with for its uniqueness of spirit, and I'd look back to this forever as the time when I really came home.

The next weekend was the first in my new lodgings, and I planned on poking around a bit – investigating what the whole Camden thing was about and getting for myself some local flavour. Chloe had allocated a shelf in the fridge for me as well as a bit of cupboard space by the kitchen door, and wanting to stock up with some goodies, I set off on Friday night to the supermarket, planning to grab my first few essentials.

In a way that I now recognize as a particular weakness, by the time I'd covered each aisle selecting the things that I couldn't do without and had then paid up and packed the bags, I found myself at the end of the checkout in possession of far too much shopping to easily carry. Despite it being only a short trip back, it was going to be a tough one. I tried to make it in quick marching spurts, stopping every ten paces or so, but even with this short duration, the heavy plastic bags cut deep, fleshy lines into the skin on my fingers. By the time I'd made it almost halfway, I was starting to feel that the weight of the bags was pulling my arms from my shoulders, and then, to make matters worse, it started to rain. From out of nowhere, there were sheets of water dumping from the heavens, in the murky direction of which I could only glare in disbelief. Relentless, it poured down on me from above, even bouncing back off the pavements to get me from below, drenching me through to the bone.

I reached the front door and lowered the bags to my feet for the umpteenth time, my clothes feeling like nothing but wet, sodden rags that hung from me as the water poured off my hair and cascaded down my forehead all over my face. It was almost blinding, and all I could do was stand there, too exhausted and washed out from the ordeal even to reach into my pocket to search for the key.

As I stood dejected at the front door about to gather myself and the shopping, it was suddenly open, and there was Chloe's broadly smiling face, an amused witness to my impressive drowned rat impersonation. Before I knew it, she'd reached out and taken up all the bags that were sitting on the path around me. Whether it was due entirely to the rain, or to the dawning reality of my new life, or perhaps even the excitement of the past week, suddenly I felt totally exhausted and submitted without resistance to being ushered to the head of the table in the lounge, where my housemates were waiting. Chloe found a towel to dry me as well as a dressing gown to replace my now useless clothes, before disappearing to the kitchen to put my shopping away.

My extreme appearance had caused quite a bit of hilarity, and I couldn't help feeling a bit isolated at first, doing my best to go along with the banter, but then slowly it dawned on me that this was a prearranged welcome-to-the-house fondue. Such a gesture, coming out of the blue, completely changed the dynamic. In no time at all, I actually felt comfortable, happy to be there amongst what felt like new friends, and the evening was a sweet one. It also had a memorable end: I got a fireman's lift to bed from our housemother, Chloe, I think because she wanted to prove another of her talents rather than because my physical condition actually precluding me from walking up the stairs. I felt it was a little undignified, exiting stage right and waving to the others as

I hung upside down off the back of her shoulders, especially at this early stage of our acquaintance, but by the time she'd laid me down on my bed and tucked my as yet bare duvet neatly under my chin, tired and drunk and happy, I wasn't complaining.

Our house was a newly built three bedroom on a mixed estate just off St Pancras Way on the north side of Kings Cross. Nowadays, it's a neighbour to the newly developed station and a renascent environment that reaches up beyond Goods Way with bridges, lights, and fountains, part of a new built infrastructure. Back then, the area was a foggy haunt for wraith-like prostitutes that loitered toothless by the old gas storage vessels, nightmare visions that regeneration will never brush away. In the house, the mixture of people seemed to work really well.

The girls that shared the largest room, Chloe and Elsie, had found the place like me from an advert in the London paper, Chloe having been here for a couple of years with a succession of itinerant room-mates. She was a beautiful spirit, one of those people whose goodness is immediately apparent and, as the indisputable angel, would make sure that we maintained an affable harmony by checking us others if we didn't take care of the things we were meant to. She was sporty, always trekking out for the weekend to scale one peak or another, replete in Lycra pants and a huge rucksack fully loaded, with her blonde ponytail neatly tied and swinging behind her. During the week, she was as likely to be playing squash at the courts where she worked not far from the house as canoeing along our local stretch of canal – at one time in training for the Devizes to Westminster trip, which pretty much says everything about her. It also explains how she always kept her body so fit and so strong: her hard shell was the perfect case for the soft, gentle heart of a caring mother.

Within a few weeks of moving in, I got to see her in action. A space came up on the ski trip she'd booked, and though I'd never ventured to the mountains before, she persuaded me I'd love it. She even convinced me to buy my very own rucksack to carry my goggles and the ski suit I borrowed from James's mum, insisting that no youth with any self-respect would be seen dead pulling a suitcase. Had she already seen me sporting James's mum's lime-green one piece, she'd have known that self-respect was not one of my strengths. It was an amazing first experience, the place in France set high in the mountains in a purpose-built resort with plenty of snow, and she cut an admirable figure in her luminous yellow salopettes and straight blue jacket, disappearing in a whoosh down seemingly impossible slopes as I watched in awe.

"Milo, see the highest peak, way up there?" she said to me on our first morning out, pointing into the mountains that ranged above the nursery slope where she'd brought me, wanting to get me my ski legs before my first official lesson that was scheduled for the afternoon.

"Yes," I said slowly, following her hand up to the top of the misty mountain.

"You'll be coming down from there by the end of the week." I didn't exactly disbelieve her, but it seemed unlikely; but sure enough, she was right. She coaxed me sympathetically over the next few days as I returned from my lessons with new sob stories: how they'd left me as I fell behind; how I'd made my way to the bottom of the chair lift and then found myself all alone at the top, fighting back the tears as I stood trying to make sense of the map she'd insisted I carry, convinced that my destiny was to freeze alone up there as a tragic monument to French antipathy. She listened and nodded, then massaged my aching back and gave me hot chocolate, convincing me to keep going. I have my love of the sport today thanks mostly to her.

Though also a good person, Elsie was a different fish and, compared to Chloe, was much more guarded. She didn't have her room-mate's ease of engagement, and her demeanour was mouse-like, remaining somehow wary of those around her. We always managed to rub each other the wrong way, and in the main, our relationship was always on the edge of contentious. From Ireland, with a head of dark black curly hair, she was average in size for a girl, which made her about my height, and it was her constant fussing about things which seemed irrelevant, the whining about one or another of her pointless obsessions, that marked my card against her. Maybe it was just that she wasn't Chloe, who was so protective and big-hearted, that Elsie would always suffer by comparison; but between the two of them, the relationship was perfect, and it was really that which was most important for the practical working of the household.

Billy, a West Country boy who'd lost his accent after living in town for a few years, occupied the third and largest of the bedrooms. He was always getting out and about, always to be found somewhere around Camden or further south in the West End. If he was home, he was getting ready to go out with his mates, sometimes bringing them back for a late-night "wind-down session", as he called it, after midnight in the lounge. I got used to coming in and seeing a few of them waiting for him, engaging in a holding pattern with drinks and sometimes all sorts of other diversions at hand, before he appeared downstairs all ready to go, and they'd then head off, moving in formation to attack another London evening. He seemed to me the archetypal city boy, a market maker at one of the home-grown firms, full of confidence and bravura and a master of life's happy wave, which he bestrode with a proud, upright arrogance.

At first I felt a little uneasy around him. The impression he gave off was one of confident superiority, and due to the goings-on I'd seen in the lounge, I was more than a little wary, not to mention surprised, at how candid it all was. Surmising that Billy saw himself as above the rules made for ordinary people, I worried that he might be unpredictable. Funny how patterns emerge after a little while where initially there seemed only chaos. If he came in from work on a weekday evening, he always looked knackered, dark rings pronounced around heavy, sunken eyes; and unapologetically, with a coffee and a couple of biscuits, he'd take over the television as if by right before sloping off to his bedroom. A few hours later, sometimes when the rest of us were going to bed, he'd stir either spontaneously or prompted by a call or a visitor, but either way he'd head out again, disappearing until deep in the early hours to a club down by the stables or a restaurant for a meal, sometimes venturing down to the West End, where he might have a business dinner. But whatever he did, by the time I woke in the morning, he'd already have gone off to work, and I couldn't imagine how he managed to get by on so little sleep.

He was a compelling character who could be quite charming when he wanted to be. After a few weeks had passed and I'd got used to his brash, direct style of communication, especially to the language he used, I actually found him very friendly. As in any person who gives off such a knowing air of confidence, I believed in him wholeheartedly, respecting him in the way that his projected status demanded, and accordingly he took me under his wing. In a little while, we became mates, and I started to tag along on his late-night forays, taking part inevitably in those esoteric games he played more and more often with remarkably little encouragement. I didn't have his appetite and capacity for such things, however, and my participation invariably ended abruptly, and early, with my crashing out somewhere – the corner of a club or under a table – and then, sleeping balled up, I'd lay where I fell until roused and returned to my bed, Billy all the while pushing on with the partying banner flying high.

All that was to come, but having slept well indeed the night after the fondue, I woke in the morning to Billy hard at work hoovering the stairs. I emerged bleary eyed, and he greeted me with more of his good-natured banter. Going downstairs, I found Chloe clearing up in the kitchen. I helped her with the mess from the previous evening, wiping the table and standing with her doing the drying up, and soon everything was shipshape and the house was looking good again after its weekly purge. Now each of us was ready to move on with our weekend plans, and this was to be my market day. Having been instructed to drop down on to the canal by the ramp opposite the Constitution at the entrance of the estate and then to walk along the towpath towards Regent's Park, I soon found myself right at its heart. In Camden terms, it was still fairly early; and walking along the quiet towpath, it seemed steeped in another time, sleepy and tranquil and not at all like the world above where the cars were perpetually darting about and the people stopped or went on at their mercy, slaves to red and green lights at the lip of each junction. At the lock itself, I found a barge being lowered for its journey's next leg, and fascinated, I couldn't help but sit down there and watch. I was captivated by the sights and the sounds of the sluicing waters, by the power as it burst between the gates, and by a little dog on board that ran from the bow to the stern and back again yelping as the vessel gently descended.

Bikes passed me wide at the edge of the roomy banks, and on the other side, as I lifted my gaze, I spied the yellow eggs and blue egg cups set along the roof of the TV-am building. They formed a breakfast rampart, each one of nine or ten marking an anniversary of transmission: familiarity in this setting an unexpectedly pleasant surprise, a reminder of the years of morning broadcasts that I'd absently watched on the television at home. At the gates to the busying flea market before the Camden road bridge, I could sense an energy, a buzzing just beyond the old brick wall; and looking into the muddled bazaar, I could see the little stalls crammed close together, everything on sale from food to clothes to records and trinkets. The canal's still syrup water stood between the two sides, keeping this warren distinct from the opposing shore which, draped in tranquil beauty, looked calmly on from the sanctuary of its separation. There was a weeping willow over there with perfect, impressionist fronds that I could hardly believe were not brush strokes, and a glass-walled restaurant which overhung the lock, a tea room for visitors who required a dignified perch, come here to witness the bohemian displays beneath them at some comfortable distance, girt with china. The scene made a sharp juxtaposition with this other, grungy side that one step further would make all mine.

I could not have imagined the wondrous things that would be there to greet me, the astounding sights, when I'd travelled those few minutes from home to the eponymous market along the canal. Nor did I have any premonition of how coming into this other-worldly ghetto would affect my soul so profoundly and immediately. It wasn't just the stallholders so used to their environment, knowing masters of the diverse treasures they peddled from islands to the seas of people that eddied around them. Nor was it merely those creatures with piercings and trappings from a multitude of styles all mingled together and making the place a universe of curiosity, moving around secure in the knowledge that this place here was for them, of them, and because of them. Nor was it, on its own, the music that vibrated the air, the sounds which came from here and there and everywhere – from atop the ramp on the road where a busker busied himself with a guitar and a recorded electronic soundtrack, bringing about him a crowd to watch his sincerity play; from the chimes and the whistles and the drums and the tongues from every corner of the Earth. These noises mingled with the smells of the burning joss sticks, the sweet essence of marijuana, the boldness of leather, and the endless complexity of food aromas – the crêpes, the daal, the candy floss. Nor was it merely the ornaments, the ancient Eastern incense burners, the Buddhas and gourds and hanging metal gongs all set among the old sheets that delineated the stalls, casting the lot with different colours and tricks for the eye. Rather, it was all of it together overwhelming the senses, all of it forming conduits to other areas which led the wide-eyed entrant deeper and deeper into the catacombs, which in turn lead to others and others still, no way back but to go on ahead. This little universe combined to create a whole which left a timeless, new-age impact deep and lasting.

Of course, I already knew the area's reputation, even if I didn't understand quite what people meant by it, but I came away that afternoon with a whole different mindset. My fixed ideas of life, of what was possible, even of myself were completely refuted. I understood now that my place at this party was booked and that everything on offer, much more than I could ever find space for in a single lifetime, was mine for the taking. The next few years of my life were very much a celebration of Camden, a skip with the spirit that thrived hereabouts, and for once I could feel glad of the depths that I'd come from, as the shock of this new was all the more vigorous, all the more a revelation, for having been blind to it before.

Hovering an inch above the concrete path as I went back along the canal that evening, I saw every twinkle of sunlight that reflected in the pool, each rush that waved to me of the oneness in the wind, and each ripple that spread away soundlessly in the wake of the ducks to the walls at the edge. I had my bounty: a *Wild at Heart* poster; a multicoloured duvet cover; and a beautiful candle, thick and tall with a simplicity of coloured wax blocks, somehow epitomizing this very place where I'd found it. I took the rising slope that came off the towpath and brought me gently back up to the village above, and walking by the little green strip, I cruised around the corner until the door of number twenty-two was in sight. Sitting alone in the lounge, waiting for the others and wanting for nothing all at the same time, I marvelled transfixed at the burning wick which now lit up the table, the clear wax pool that showcased the marble-like bowl of candle that lay still and solid beneath, and I knew that life would never be the same again. Truly, it was a different Milo who sat there with the television off, silent, at home in the empty house.

Hard Headed Woman

The following Friday night, a time long awaited, was now right upon me, but what a week it had been. With last weekend's awakening in the mystery of the market, I had a sense that finally I'd begun what would be my life's journey, one which felt long overdue; but the week that followed had been so filled with crazy ups and downs that, had I not gained such heart from the visions and possibilities that I'd taken on board there – had my foundations not been so fortified and boosted – it would simply have proved too much to bear, and I think I'd have cracked. There's no doubt that it was my focus on this long-hoped-for visit, to my mind, a glittering prize for the battles that were now mine to win, that got me through with my new found optimism just about intact.

After coming home sick from work on Wednesday morning, I'd slept right through to Thursday afternoon and, feeling considerably better, had enjoyed just mooching around on my own downstairs in my pyjamas, venturing out later as far as the newsagent to get a copy of *Time Out* and do some more research for the coming weekend. I could easily have gone back to work that afternoon, but I knew there'd be no questions asked, and the temptation to skive was much too strong. The trouble with taking such liberties is that just a sip gives one a taste for it, so when Friday morning dawned, the lure of my laziness was too great to resist, and I earned another day of leisure with a faint call to the office for sympathy and permission. To be fair, the way they'd last seen me meant I didn't have to try too hard to be convincing.

I'd arranged to meet Charlotte at the station at half past six, so at five o'clock, I got myself showered and only then changed out of my pyjamas after a very lazy day. I was standing in the kitchen thirty minutes later not really knowing what to do with myself, certainly too anxious just to sit down and while away the forty minutes before I'd have to head off.

"Tonight's the night, is it?" said Billy as he walked past me on his way to the fridge. "Bit nervous, are we?"

"Nah," I lied transparently, "just … excited. Can't wait to see her." By now I was almost convinced that I'd got it all wrong, that she'd be a shocking embarrassment, and that I was about to endure a complete disaster that I'd never live down.

"What's it like then – this delightful addition to our weekend? Will I be impressed?"

"Yes," I told him earnestly, "she's really nice. Funny and intelligent."

"Nice aris?"

"What?"

"Aris. Aristotle. Sounds like Bottle. Bottle and Glass?" he said, seemingly expecting me to pick up his meaning at each subsequent point of his explanation. "Her arse!" he said, exasperated. "Does it 'ave a nice arse!"

"You're disgusting!" said Chloe, walking into the kitchen, smiling, and shaking her head at me in sympathy.

"You love it!" he replied, buckling under the shocks of his laughter.

"I'm sure she's very nice, and Milo is much too sweet to be thinking of judging a girl in such chauvinistic terms. Don't you be corrupting him – you'll have me to answer to."

"Mate," he continued, still laughing, "don't forget: if you can't handle it, just send her next door; I'll see her all right for you."

Walking down to the rendezvous, the same questions kept popping into my mind. Would I recognize her? Was she nice looking, or had I been deluding myself? Where did she plan to sleep? Standing there a few minutes early and waiting as patiently as I could, I tried to keep my mind blank and push away my anxieties. I couldn't remember exactly where she'd be coming from, and I furiously scanned the swelling multitude of passers-by with my eyes darting around hopefully, looking for a face I could remember as each train arrived with its crowd temporarily overrunning the concourse. My heart leapt into my mouth whenever I saw someone that I thought resembled Charlotte – some head of thick dark hair with a body just a few inches shorter than mine – only to settle back down and reset momentarily as the doppelgängers continued briskly by on their way to who knew where. At last I saw her, already close to me smiling and pulling a small case on wheels behind. What a relief! I'd have known her anywhere, her hair cut in a wavy bob and her toothy smile that I suddenly remembered so well. She looked great. She wore oversize jeans belted tight to her waist and a black, short-sleeved top with a multicoloured scarf, a blaze of reds and yellows tied in a knot around her neck. I didn't move when I saw her, just smiled back, relieved and vindicated, and stopping a foot in front of me, she shook a silent ta-da before giving up her face to be kissed.

Walking up behind the station, we slipped from the road and on to the canal that I was so proud of, into that different world of the soul where the evening sun still hung high and shed its deep orange light on the surface of the water. I didn't want to tell her I'd been unwell, so I regurgitated details of last Friday at work, inventing trivia about the people I worked with just to try to make her laugh. She told me what had been happening down her way since we'd last spoken and that Gary had been coaching her ahead of her visit.

"I should be on my guard," she said in a tone that was either serious or mock serious. "He's been warning me about boys in general: only after one thing!"

I couldn't tell what she was really trying to say, and confused, I replied reflexively, "You know my intentions are honourable."

"Drat!" she replied, and the pendulum in my head swung back again to maybe.

I could see that the girls were waiting in the lounge for us as I cracked open the front door, and leading her dutifully in there to meet them was awkward: like taking her to meet my parents. I needn't have worried; they were really sweet and welcoming and made the atmosphere easy, though Chloe telling her I was a lovely boy and a great housemate was pretty embarrassing. Billy had already made himself scarce: another blessing, as I didn't need him teasing me, but still I couldn't help wondering how this special night might end. After all, she'd come here to stay for the whole weekend, and she knew I only had a small single room. Perhaps I'd be sleeping on the floor or maybe even down here on the sofa, but one thing at a time, I decided; I'd worry about that when we got there. Charlie had grabbed a sandwich to eat on the train and said she wasn't hungry, so the four of us sat down in the lounge together, chatting and watching whatever thing came on the television. The two of us on the sofa were together at last, quietly comfortable as I waited for 10 p.m., when I planned to set off on what I hoped would be a game changer.

The credits rolled on the programme we were half watching, and Chloe got up with a polite, accommodating stretch, saying that she needed to head up, as she planned to set out early tomorrow on a train to Birmingham for a climbing exhibition with her soldier boyfriend. I looked over at Charlie with a smile.

"Come on then. Let's you and I go out," I said. "Let me show you just what old London Town has to offer."

"Out?" she said. "Now?" To my delight, she sounded genuinely surprised. I really felt as if I were playing a joker, a card that the old Milo wouldn't even have held in his fan; and as we made our way to the tube station through an evening that was just about losing the last remnants of daylight, I could feel her pull closer as she strode into the unknown by my side. This change of pace had endowed the evening with a new energy, a different flavour, and feeling the empowerment of control, I noticed myself getting a bit cocky, mimicking a little the way I'd seen Billy with his cool and his swagger, gently teasing her by refusing to reveal where we were going and just telling her to trust me. Once out on to Camden Road, we found the street alive; there was a buzz in the air and much activity as we passed by the bars and the restaurants and the clubs. The atmosphere all around was incredible: it was a whole different place now that the curtain of night was drawn and its creatures were out. This was a world away from the quiet streets I walked along on my way to work and back, and though I tried to maintain my attitude of blasé indifference, this was a first for both of us, and going in silence, we were fascinated and excited in equal proportions.

Weaving up against an opposing tide that streamed down on us as we climbed the steps to the street exit at Leicester Square station, we emerged as if to the centre of the world.

The swarm of people and static jam of cars made a mockery of the hour; there were many more than I expected at this time of night. The air itself seemed charged, and the pavements, the buildings, and the lights all bustled with what seemed a defiance, an unspoken ambition to rage until dawn. The whole place was awash in the nascent weekend's excitement: artists on stools by their pictures, which hung from the railings in the middle by the park; brightly lit sex shops where wary groups loitered, afraid and undecided; and sugary couples licking Häagen-Dazs from tiny plastic spoons as bright and colourful as the ice cream itself on little chrome chairs at little chrome tables.

We bought tickets for the midnight show at the Comedy Store, Charlie insisting she pay her own way, and with a half-hour to spare, we sat upstairs by the big glass window in Burger King that commanded the part of the square below it. Cradling our coffees in our hands, we observed the randomly conceived spontaneity that flowed there before us, the characters that came and went and then came again in a spectacle like a movie reel on speed, speculating in a light-hearted pleasure game what the people we followed were saying to each other, her accents far better than mine. We passed the time happily, aloof as we stared down on the square, full of the sense that we'd only have to dip into the multicoloured waters to swim among these fish, to be the very same as them; and it felt as if just being here made us part of a scene, members of a midnight elite and a far-out clique – a feeling unique and priceless.

The dream just got better, and what a call the Comedy Store turned out to be! A few minutes after twelve, and there we were, sitting in the seedy little club at the epicentre of the West End, a room tight and edgy and filled with smoke. The lighting was low and intimate, and thin black curtains dressed up but did not obscure the raw brick walls. As we waited for the show to begin, we sat there unsure of the people around us, quietly overawed and a little breathless but somehow braver for it. Facing the stage at our little table, we made up a vibrant foursome with Miss Vodka and Mr Jack Daniel's; and when it came, the two-hour set was genius. The highlight for me was a pre-Edinburgh famous Lee Evans whose name I'd seen on the bill but not recognized, jerking about the stage while we fell together laughing and almost crashing our heads, careless faces shining as if we were kids in the sea.

Our relationship, so long on hold, was now set free and we ran with it, each little turbo blast of joy magnified by the relief we felt boosting us on our way. There's no need for words when the heart's meaning is bright in the eyes, and the two of us were now travelling together atop the same happy wave. Streaming out with the crowd at two in the morning, coming down in the cooler, fresher air of the Leicester Square night, our stretched-from-smiling faces were glad of relief. It all seemed so natural, so ordinary now, with her arm around my waist and her head on my shoulder, and it made me feel inches taller. Looking down from above, and suddenly there I was: out and about in the night where only the cognoscenti dared venture, playing in the big league with my girl by my side, smiling and joking as if I belonged, loving each moment and knowing so was she.

We almost jumped in a cab on the corner at Charing Cross Road, but when it came to it, we just weren't ready to tear ourselves from this place of such happiness, so we headed north on foot, grabbing a cappuccino and hanging for a bit with the regulars at Bar Italia. From there we ambled slowly up Dean Street, both of us merry and feeding off the life still thriving around, comfortable with each other as if we'd been there for years as we carried on walking in the pleasant night air. At Goodge Street, we nearly took a cab, and at Euston

Road too we almost succumbed, but the walking was easy, and anyway there was something about the night, about the stars in the sky, that refused to release us. As the clock came around to four in the morning, we found ourselves coming upon the estate's entrance on St Pancras Way. The sky was growing lighter behind the Constitution Pub, that proud white monument which stood framed by the dawn and its weak hint of morning.

In the kitchen, I quietly made us a couple of instants, and we tip-toed with them through to the lounge, where we sat apart, chatting in polite, hushed tones, sharing what an amazing evening it had been and how good it all felt. The cups were empty, and still moments passed, the conversation now feeling formal and pointless as I stalled in the face of the inevitable question, balking at my fear that I might break the spell. With a deep breath to steady me and calm my heart, I lifted my eyes to the floor above and put it out there with a more resigned than hopeful "Shall we?" She nodded, smiling, and I could hardly believe it. Something oddly grown up struck me about the scene when she left me waiting for her, sitting excitedly on my new patterned duvet facing the door in my shorts and my T-shirt, disappearing to the bathroom to take out her lenses. She came into the room and into my arms, and we fell away kissing. I'll never forget that sense of disbelief as I held her, that sense of us being together, and the ecstatic realization that she was giving herself to me; the fleshy sensation of her body hard and soft; her hands pulling my T-shirt, wanting me like I wanted her; my hands at her knickers; that strange, slide-fitting feeling as she took me with her arms around my shoulders and on my back at that final acceptance; and the swirl in my head and the burst in my heart like I'd just entered heaven.

Movin' On Up

There was an ease about the next morning as I made us coffee and eggs, bringing out from my cupboard the croissants I'd bought especially for this occasion. It was a simplicity that reminded me of the best times in the village, when the day wanted for nothing and everything about seemed pleased just to add to the overall harmony. Billy was on his best behaviour. He had risen late as we had, and I felt secure enough to leave him chatting politely with Charlie in the lounge: the deed now done, I was confident that he couldn't blow it for me. I could hear the two of them getting on famously. She really was as lovely as I'd described, and when I entered, I could see that he was impressed – that I'd grown a little in his estimation. Apart from taking her to see the market and maybe going for a meal later, I hadn't given much thought beyond last night's itinerary, and our schedule from here on was fairly open; but Billy mentioned as we were preparing to head out that he and a couple of the guys at work had a bus party sorted, a farewell to a colleague who was moving back to Oz.

"Charlie's definitely welcome," he said, "and if she must bring you along too, then I suppose that would be OK." Enjoying the backhanded compliment, I told him it sounded like a plan; and after giving us the details of where we should meet him, he waved us off, leaning by the front door with a fag hanging from the corner of his benevolently smiling mouth.

Back on the towpath, it was another beautiful day, and we sat for a while on a bench with the warm sun on our faces, eyes closed and bare arms touching, relaxed in skimpy and light summer clothes. A raft of ducks was paddling and quacking, and we watched as they made about for little pieces of bread that a bunch of kids threw into the water. Once at the market, I took us straight up the ramp and on to the road bridge, moving along in our own silence through the sounds and the stalls with awed glances occasionally exchanged. She seemed as blown away as I'd been – as I actually still was. There was just so much going on here: the sheer volume of people, either moving distractedly like us among the multifarious offerings or just hanging in the peaceful realm by the edge of the canal, picking at picnics, swinging their feet through the railings, rolling cigarettes, or tipping back drinks and enjoying the sunshine, painting themselves on the rich local tapestry.

Charlie started looking at garments on the various stalls that reached out half over the pavement outside the shops on the high road, so I slipped into the record shop on the opposite side. It was already by then a curious throwback in a world of CDs. As they always used to, the second-hand sleeves quickly had me captivated, reminding me of and taking me back to that much earlier time. Once again, my mind boggled at the artwork, the imagination and incredible diversity, and I loved the order of the neatly boxed sections categorized by an endless list of styles and then further indexed by the alphabet. I didn't recognize the sounds that were playing, but of course they were perfect, wafting over the dark wooden rows from behind the counter where a middle-aged DJ stood like some John Peel lookalike, a beard and a self-satisfied, smug look on his face. This high-street guru had his Saturday crowd about him: adoring girls and hipster guys who no doubt gathered here to pay their respects, to self-validate by inclusion. It was just like those Saturday afternoons when I strayed from my dad's shop – those dudes that hung about seeming so much more clued up than I'd ever be. I wished I could emulate and was so much in awe of them: the rightful in a place where knowing the score was your password and where my ignorant, interloper presence was suffered with neither acknowledgement nor regard. Now here I was again, rummaging through the various pieces and still not quite sure what the different genres really signified, feeling self-conscious, as if everyone were watching me, and still a little ashamed of my ignorance. But now I was starting to get it: that this was a melting pot of many and a place you could be exactly who and what you were; and whatever that was really didn't matter, because the next guy was not like you or the next guy like him, and the one after that was like no one before, and so it went on. If you were not happy being who you were here, you could be someone different: no one cared anyway.

I was lost in the archives when Charlie eventually came to find me, and before we left, I chose an old copy of *Rumours* to take back with us. It was a record I wanted but had never got around to buying before, one I felt had a cachet which would make its own statement. From there we ambled in the direction of Camden Underground, passing the poster shops and the head stalls but then taking a right on to Inverness Street and threading up through the fruit market. Continuing along here, we passed through the quieter streets, drinking in the back-street locality as our wanderings encroached upon a gentrified extreme of Primrose Hill, so quiet that even the birdsong seemed boisterous, finding our way from there back on to Parkway and hooking over the top near the railway until we stopped in a cafe at the bottom of Delancey Street. Here, back again by the high street, we had a badly needed drink and a bite to revive us before returning to the house exhausted from the sights and scenes of our journey. The magic of the area was such that even a little stroll like this one, a meander with nothing better to do, would always wrap itself into an adventure of some kind, an assault on some locked-away, forgotten part of the mind through the things that you saw, or the strangest looking people, or whatever it was that you found going down. A place like this one, where there was always so much going on, so much to be inspired by, to choose from – it really was the perfect place for me to grow and develop.

The house was empty. Billy had already headed out and was probably working his way around town through a list of last-minute essentials before going straight on to the meeting point tonight, and he'd left behind on the table in the lounge a couple of his signature marks: an ashtray he'd been using and a crumb-scattered plate. At least he'd remembered to turn off the television. Elsie was still not around, and though I'd assumed she was sleeping in this morning, she must also have gone away for the weekend – might even have headed out early with Chloe. I came to realize that she was pretty coy about her private life and was always bizarrely elusive if, trying to be friendly, I asked what she'd been up to. Consequently, our relationship was probably just the way she liked it. I thought maybe it was me, but I later found out that she could be like this even with her room-mate; I guess it's just the way that some people are.

Anyhow, this meant that we were all by ourselves, and we threw open the patio doors and let Fleetwood Mac's West Coast offering carry out to the sunbathed garden. It seemed a stroke of genius to bring the sofa outside too, and once we'd done so, we lay next to each other with the clinking ice in our drinks melting down in the sun, the two of us growing sillier and ever more familiar as the heat and the alcohol combined. Next thing I remember, I was chasing her around the garden – she was just beyond my reach – and then tripping up the stairs behind her for a repeat performance of last night's climax.

We roused each other blearily just before seven thirty, and realizing that we were short on time, we made a break to the bathroom and jumped into the shower. We'd just woken naked together wound in the duvet, and though there hadn't been much in the way of shyness before we fell sleeping, it struck me now as we stood there unclothed and dry, waiting for the water to heat up, as an overly intimate situation. Perhaps it was some kind of predictable post-coital shame, or maybe one due to the fug in my brain – I was slightly hung-over and about to go drinking again – but whatever it was, the moment jarred, awkward and strangely vulnerable, until the water worked its magic: the soapy stream that ran rivers through her fine hair; our bodies glancing; and her wet, silky softness. The remnants of self-consciousness quickly washed away, and we came out on to the mat still laughing and poking each other, still mucking around, and drying quickly, we got ourselves dressed.

I was mightily impressed that she was ready as soon as I was: even before she'd put on some make-up, she looked great in a simple white sweater dress, still with its label on, and a thick leather belt that she'd bought at the market. I loved it too that she seemed happy to make a dash for the tube with her hair barely dry. Nine o'clock was the pickup time for the bus, and the bar we had to get to was in South Kensington, so we changed at Kings Cross and shot a diagonal on the Piccadilly line. We found Billy and some mates exactly at the place he'd described, over the road from the station on a busy corner. The party was already in full swing, and even though we made it in good time and the bus had yet to arrive, it was obvious that my housemate had long been off the platform.

Open to the sky and pumping sounds from a tape that someone had brought for the journey, the old red double-decker blundered along London's streets. Holding the rail as we stood on the top deck, on top of the world, we waved down at the tourists who turned to see where the Paul Oakenfold soundtrack was coming from, loving the outside-in looks on their faces and knowing absolutely that we were part of this city attraction, one of the floats that passed in London's carnival. Going over the marvel that is Tower Bridge, Charlie and I fell to our backs on the soft padded bench and reached up our hands like we might touch the Victorian ironwork above us. Sounds like a riot came up from the deck below – noises of stamping and leaping about like something from a Prodigy video as our fellow travellers gave themselves to the party freaks of their alter egos, the lights of our indulgent city blurring above and around us. Tippling fearlessly from spirit bottles, we also dashed down the steps at stops at various selected pubs en route, passing each time through the lower deck's pungent haze and accepting cautiously in tiny draws the proffered stubs, feeling ourselves a little dangerous, a little daring as we barely inhaled.

At Farringdon, the bus parked, and off we all rolled, spilling into a bar by Cowcross Street and, following the others down a twisting flight of stairs, danced our way into a party at the basement level. Our own rave on wheels had enflamed us, so our arrival injected the room with energy and lifted the tempo as we spun out on to the floor with our arms pumping in the air above us. The heavy beat was a perfect pattern to set on my limbs, and I copied what I saw of Billy as he moved dizzyingly on his toes with his knees bent, mouth and eyes wide open. Breathing heavily but balanced and wonderful, I exulted in the crowd of smiling revellers and found myself suddenly alone in the middle of the floor, my reticence gone AWOL. I popped here and corkscrewed through to there, not still for a moment, not caring at all but loving the looks as I danced on and on in the maelstrom of noise and the flashing lights.

Stopping back by the stairs to catch my breath I looked around for the others, for Charlie, but the room was too packed to see. I half imagined my name was floating softly in the air above the banging rhythm. As if in a dream, I lost the sound – perhaps a trick, I thought, that my mind was playing on me with my ears too full of my beating heart. But then, above me at the bend halfway up the staircase, I caught sight of her: Charlie laughing and waving, then turning away as she made off into the bar above. I was behind her in a trice, pulling on the handrail and leaping the steps in twos, keeping pursuit as she fled the building, darting right as she exited the door and running straight past the bus that was parked outside. Another right turn took her out of sight up the road beyond, and reaching the corner just seconds behind, I found no one there: not a soul up the hill and no movement on the little patch of grass bordered by railings on the left, perhaps an old graveyard. Listening intently, I took a few slow steps up the hill.

The beat of music came from around a turn just ahead of me, and following the sound, I entered a narrow alleyway which opened slightly into a small, dingy yard behind the shops we'd just passed, their metal back doors raised up on a service ledge which ran along the side of the yard at about chest height. Broken blue pallets and the metal roll cages I recognized from my time in the supermarket lay like props on a film set, and as I scanned the darkness, the scrap-metal sheets and the bars, broken and bent, seemed contrived for an ambience of grimy neglect. That's when I saw her sitting on the concrete ledge with her hands over her face, still as a statue with her bare legs dangling. Quickly I was upon her, my knee up on the ledge, and even as she shrieked to be caught, our mouths came together, kissing deeply. My hands went up her dress and pulled at her knickers, the right side coming off her hips and halfway down her thigh and then out from beneath her. Her hands tugged my belt, still caught, pulled at the buttons of my jeans as I pushed them down before they were even undone, forcing them away, and then she was up and on me like a flower on a pin. I was inside of her, staggering for balance as the music pumped beneath us, my hands cupped beneath her; suddenly unsteady and together we crashed down on my arse with an almighty bang, and I groaned in pain. On top of me laughing, I was all inside her.

As the fires inside cool down and the midnight hours pass, the night comes upon you. Lying there in the quiet with Charlie's head at my neck and a throbbing pain growing beneath me, we were almost too peaceful to move; but after a little while, she got off of me carefully, searching around for her knickers as I gingerly bent my knees to lift my hips from the freezing concrete and pulled my jeans back over my aching rump. Spent and heroic, we strode from the alley with my arm over her shoulder, keeping her close; and we didn't mind when we found on the road that the bus was long gone. We picked up a cab easily on Farringdon Road and kissed in the back all the way home.

In the morning, we lay awake for a long time, talking about the night before and then moving on to our hopes and our dreams, side by side in the single bed. She spoke of her family, her grandparents and her father, and I was happy to listen, let in to a special place and respectfully glad to be there, revelling in our happy closeness. She couldn't believe the mark I now wore at the top of my leg, an enormous blue badge ringed in black, big enough to be proud of and worth every inch as she covered it in kisses; and we laughed at the state of her white sweater dress which had seen its first and last wear. We still had the house to ourselves – Billy was probably still going somewhere – but we went out anyway, walking along the canal to the market and then up Chalk Farm Road, continuing up Haverstock Hill when neither of us wanted to stop walking.

She'd planned to get an early-afternoon train. I didn't want her to go, so we sat and had coffee and waited for a film to start at the cinema, a happy couple among the patisseries and dry cleaners of the Belsize set. It was early evening when we came out, and we headed back to mine for a bit of pasta and a last goodbye; and then I walked her down to the station, down the back way via Camley Street, past the wildlife reserve and the big old gas cylinders. Once there, we didn't linger, kissing like we meant it and promising to speak soon before she stepped up on to the train and was out of sight. I turned on my heel and headed off as if I wanted to go somewhere, but once around the corner, my walk home was slow, full of wistful emotion that could hardly be put into words.

When I got back, I found Billy's bedroom door closed, and anxious for someone to unload my excitement on, I peeped into the darkness. Soundly asleep, he looked like a corpse, so I just let him lie. It wasn't long before the girls returned, and sitting together in the lounge after Chloe had made some tea, they asked how the weekend had gone.

"She seemed lovely," said Elsie, and I agreed, and I told them about the bus and the party and even gave them a glimpse of the bruise that caused me to wince whenever I sat on it.

"I fell over," I said, adding cryptically, "I had my hands full at the time."

Chloe looked at me quizzically but thought better of inquiring further.

"It's just nice to see you so happy, Milo," she said. "You're positively glowing!"

I loved her for knowing it.

The Chain

Funny isn't it? You get to that magical target in life where your dreams have always led you, and suddenly the destination of your truest wishes becomes your new starting point, the things that you imagined as the ultimate luxuries now just inalienable basics, and a hunger with an ache that's insatiable has grown there inside you. I wonder how little we'd actually need if we truly valued what we had, but it seems unlikely that we'll ever find out. Western society simply does not encourage us to think that way, but our ever reaching desire for more, whether materially or in our relationships, is no recipe for long-lasting happiness. Ultimate happiness can only come about when we understand that here is the only place worth arriving, that now is the only prize worth striving for, that what we have in the here and now is our only chance of salvation.

We were certainly on a roll, Charlie and I, the relationship going forward just as it had started: if not love itself then love's young dream. Mostly, those weekends when we were together, the ones we seemed to spend all the time we were apart looking forward to, would start with her arrival at Kings Cross Station. First stop would be the house to drop off her stuff and have a breathless catch up, and from there we'd head out to kick about in Camden down by the lock at one of our favourite pubs or bars or a laid-back Tex-Mex place that we loved down by Mornington Crescent. We'd either come back to the house later or head on to a gig, or a party, or just go on a wander, never tiring of the kind of stuff that was always going on in the high street and the roads there about, the place always throwing up some kind of surprise, an eruption of energy.

When in town, we increasingly joined up with Billy, our 24–7 party man, whose crowd was becoming my own; but on a few blissful occasions we went away for the weekend, meeting at a lonely lane cottage that we rented in the Cotswolds. The location was only about forty miles from where Charlie lived, so whenever we met there, she'd drive up. This allowed her to stay later at work and make up for those times when she rushed out early for the southbound train. She'd let the traffic subside before setting off, and always getting there before her, I'd have got my head down early, practicing Billy's trick, so that I could be all the livelier later on. Memories endure of those country weekends, and I've still got photos of hired bikes and long country lanes as well as pictures in my mind of where we horsed about on the cycles and sometimes came off. But more it's those autumn evenings that are embedded within me: deeply snug in the cloud-like duvet, I'd be half roused from my padded sleep by a click of the latch at the bedroom door and stir to see her there smiling. From under the covers, I'd watch her carefully taking off her clothes and then brace as she jumped in beside me with fast, freezing hands.

I was so happy with what I had on that it didn't seem possible that life could get any better – little did I know. A job was going in the small orders department at Billy's place, and without even an interview, he ushered me in. Life was to be stood on its head. I was now working for a market-making firm in the City of London; I had officially arrived – but where? What a weird environment! I don't think anything could have prepared me for this new normality. I was now caged with a group of wild animals who all competed furiously and unceasingly to be the most alpha of males, a game that took me quite a while to get used to. Without Billy looking out for me, I'd never have managed at all, and even with his help, it took a while to really get the taste for it.

We were glorified phone operators, sitting there side by side with our headsets on, a long line of us going all the way down the desk, which had a conveyor belt running its length. Poised almost itching to be first to strike a phone-line light as soon as it flashed and thus win the call, over the day we'd grab as many calls as we could on this first-hit-wins basis, taking the order and writing out the ticket as appropriate – buy or sell, share name, and quantity – and signing our name before placing it on the belt before us to be taken down the line for collection by the position keepers. It was they who would honour these trades by taking the reverse position, eventually trading a block with the main book upstairs to keep their exposure light. The number of trade slips would be tallied at the end of the day, and each one was a point for the trader who'd written it. To be that day's winner meant walking tall from the office, the grudging respect of your peers a cloud around you like heady cologne. I came to love the competition, and I hungered to come first – made sure that I did save for the off day when I didn't have my mojo – but hardly six months had passed when Billy surprised me one night by telling me that it was time to move on again. One of the juniors upstairs was leaving to become a full-time model, and his place was up for grabs; in fact, the vacated seat was on Billy's desk, and it was mine. This news was as exciting as it was unbelievable but absolutely terrifying as well. I had no idea how they did what they did up there. All I knew was taking orders and writing them on a bit of paper; my biggest challenge thus far had been to hit a button first, and now suddenly I was to be a desk assistant. I felt sure that I'd be instantly found out, that they'd smell my fear.

A few years later, I learned that it wasn't just Billy who was pushing for me. A senior in the firm, an older man with soft grey hair and a name from the Bible who always had a smile on his face and deep lines in his skin which seemed to have been cut there by his kindly disposition, had also taken up my cause. I'd been lucky enough to come to his notice when asked to run some simple errands, so when Billy had a word with his boss, the way was already clear for me.

Coming into the firm through Billy, I hadn't realized it, but quite by chance I was now something of an insider in one of the only predominantly Jewish firms left in the city – among my own for what must have been the first time in my life. This wouldn't even have crossed my mind, as it was something that I'd never before had to take into account, yet here it was a real factor and of real substance. Of course, the whole notion of identity can be very superficial, and as I got to know the rest of my brothers, it was the differences – forged of my exiled upbringing – rather than the similarities that were most apparent to me. However, that notwithstanding, instead of automatically being at a disadvantage, my heritage here gave me some favour. What a rich feeling it was suddenly to belong, and an odd one too when I realized I was being taken to the bosom purely because of the part of me that had always before been a source of mistrust and suspicion. It might have been odd, but it certainly wasn't the worse for that, to be safe on the inside. I also discovered by identifying with others like me who, as insiders, were slightly at odds with the mainstream, the realization that each one of us is so infinitely complex, so ultimately unique, that we are never in fact quite on our own.

I remember that Monday morning entering the dealing room on my own and half expecting to be set upon or, if not, then at least beset by howls and boos and calls of "Stranger!" from the guys, who were like those I'd got used to battling with downstairs but ten times more so. I felt a fake – didn't feel worthy of setting foot upon this place of the gods, coming up as I was from the stagnant air of the office world below straight into the financial world's heart of darkness. As I self-consciously kept my face lifted and moved across the huge dealing room feeling awkward and small, I saw Billy beaming with an empty seat beside him: my new seat! I can still recall that boost, that pin dropped on my blind journey through the unknown, and I'm sure he sensed or maybe even remembered from his own time the deep fear I was pushing myself through. I'd been so nervous all morning that I'd barely been able to get myself off the toilet, but seeing him there and reaching what felt like a kind of sanctuary, it was all I could do not to throw my arms around him and grimly hold on.

A few weeks of keeping my head down and my mouth shut, and still very much in awe of my new surroundings, I somehow found myself commandeered to play in a five-a-side football competition even though I swore honestly that I was useless. For whatever reason, those that had been able to slide out of this extracurricular event, Billy included, had done so, but with my pitch boss, Hardy, particularly enthusiastic, I had been firmly committed. At least it was for charity, I told myself, and the fact that it was taking place at that famous red stadium, my very own, meant it could have been worse. I figured that my attendance would at least help the work cause – if my lack of ability didn't prove fatal, that is. As it turned out, the day would became a factory of some of my happiest memories, just part of the collection that would soon be stacking up from that beautiful place, though these were quite distinct from the many others born there.

By the time Friday lunchtime came around on the day before the tournament, our squad was just five. There was Hardy and his teenage son plus another couple of the dealers and me. Needing a few more bodies, I suggested that I call up some mates. It was going to be all of them, actually, but I didn't elaborate, and speaking to Tommy and Jim, I begged both to join us. It wasn't just that we needed the numbers, I told them. I was desperate for their support, and had they owed me any favours, I'd have called them in. Jim had seen me play football, so he understood immediately; and even Tommy, who hadn't, didn't need an explanation. The boys came right through for me, and what a lifesaver that was for a nervous Friday evening – knowing that I'd have my friends right there beside me.

It was a funny thing, arriving to play rather than to watch. Denuded of the match-day masses – the crowd with all its assorted paraphernalia – the stadium and surrounding area was like a giant found sleeping. Walking in through the carpeted corridors on the way to the pitches and the changing rooms, a totally different aspect of the place was laid bare; but excitement and trepidation made sure that our actual entrance was a blur, and I remember almost nothing at all of that.

My earliest memory of the day, probably my favourite, was an ice-breaking cameo of Tommy doing something amazing right out of nowhere and marking his turf. We'd formed up outside in a little circle for a prematch warm-up in the car park, which was the only suitable place that we could find, and there were the seven of us out back after registration, hesitantly getting to know one another. We still had a little time before the games upstairs were due to begin, so we started passing the ball around between us; I tried to, anyway, asking myself how my two left feet and I had been talked into coming along. When I'd insisted again to Hardy that morning that I'd not really played much before, he had said he was certain I'd do a brilliant job as goalie.

I did at least think that I looked the part sporting the various bits of kit that I'd borrowed: hooped red-and-white socks and an Arsenal short sleeve, a plain cotton one with the white cannon like I'd had as a kid. Bouncing about on my toes, I was ready to relive the glorious sporting career I'd never actually had; but when Jim kicked the ball to me,

I failed to control it, and hitting my foot, it bounced up and away off the underside of my knee. Jeremy, one of the market makers from the European desk, stretched out a leg to arrest it, killing it dead as he snorted at my utter ineptness and swiftly moved it on to Hardy. Though twenty years our senior, the boss was as fit as a whippet, still master of the squash courts and playing vets football on more than the odd weekend. From his sudden look of intensity as he received the ball, I could tell he'd decided it was time to impress the troops, and there it was: a step over and then a little flick off his standing leg and then another; but this last one was much too strong, and to our amazement, the ball sailed up into the air and clean over the wall. It was built fit for a penitentiary, so this was no mean feat. Anyway, there we all stood, incredulous, looking at each other, with our brand-new football, bought only this morning, now over and gone. We didn't have another, and the little group was lost entirely for words.

Of course, Tommy knew what to do: unconstrained by the boundaries that inform most people's perception of the world they live in, he knew no fear. I can still see him standing over there by the wall with his chin cradled on his hand and a searching look on his face, and it flashed across my mind to wonder momentarily what he might be up to, but in a moment I knew he'd been searching for purchase as he inspected that thick old tree. Its solitary branch disappeared across the top of the wall, all of fifteen feet high, stretched out from the car park over to the garden of the terraced house beyond. Before anyone could speak a word of advice or caution, he was suddenly up on the other side of the wall, hanging from the branch with one arm. With a dull thud, he was gone from sight, and still none of us knew what to say. Literally nothing – only baffled looks of disbelief as the sounds of rustling undergrowth from the other side indicated the drop hadn't been fatal.

"Found it!" proclaimed his triumphant voice, sounding far away as the ball came sailing back over, bouncing high as it landed on the tarmac with a whack. There was a scrambling sound as rubber scuffed brick, and then Tommy's head poked over the top, beaming down on us with that enormous grin. Then he was back and a hero, and I was bursting with pride, loving the reflected glory and sure that I could feel a little elevated in my new colleagues' estimation.

Upstairs, a minute for half-time after the first half of the first game – a five-minute baptism by fire – and we were all in the huddle with our hearts beating and nerves gasping for rest. We'd only just held during the opening storm our opponents unleashed right from the whistle. Clearly used to playing as a team together, they'd caught us flat-footed and had seemed almost irresistibly strong; but once we'd got a rhythm, we'd found our way back, and the game was still scoreless. The tide had definitely turned, and we were holding our own now, looking like we would push on; and indeed we did, getting stronger in the tournament from there on in. If we'd had a larger squad like those we were competing against, we'd quite possibly have got among the honours. Back in the clinch, Hardy exhorted and the boys nodded, but it was Tom who reminded them all how the keeper had kept us in it, my early double save denying an immediate breakthrough and keeping morale intact. The boys around me took it up, and then came pats on the back, and I was so full of gratitude to my dear friend I could have cried.

I even scored a goal later on! Ushered out of goal and on to the pitch for a final minute with one of the guys having taken a knock, I found the ball at my feet, and as bidden, I carried it forward. The air seemed to grow thin, and though in reality the other team were backing off and the pitch had opened up, it seemed to be closing in around me. I felt a sudden overwhelming exhaustion – too tense, I guess, in this unfamiliar situation – and in a fit of desperation, I kicked the ball away towards their goal. How it eluded their keeper, I'll never know, but it dribbled into the net; and turning away in disbelief, I felt at that moment as if it were the high point of my life.

That night found me lying stiff and exhausted on the sofa in the lounge, aches all over my body but each one another reminder of happy satisfaction. Charlie sat at my feet watching the television, just arrived and settling in for a necessarily quiet evening, while Billy sat across from us making ready his water pipe. I hadn't felt this knackered in years; the day's excitement had been mental as well as physical, and it all seemed like a dream as I looked back on it: I could hardly believe it. The tournament hall had been thick with celebrities: cast members from *EastEnders* and various semi-familiar sportsmen who together made up a celebrity team – one we narrowly failed to win the prize of a match against. In a lull between games, I'd gone downstairs to fetch something from my locker, and entering the changing room, I'd seen Jim down there fixing his shin pads and minding his business, and my eyes scanning beside him fell upon the colossal sight of big Frank Bruno. "All right, Jim. All right, Frank," I'd uttered in one wide-eyed breath of amazement, carrying along on my way too shocked to stop and say anything more than this to my boyhood hero. I did catch up with him again later on, back in the arena and better prepared, approaching him this time with my hand outstretched.

"All right, Frank?" I repeated. "Sorry to bother you, but I'm such a big fan, and I just wanted to say hi, let you know what a big fan I am, how much I admire you." My prepared speech spoken, I just stood there, and the big gentleman took my little hand and shook it, nodding in time with our handshake as he looked into my eyes.

"Nice one," he told me, making me feel like a million dollars.

So there I lay, a day like this one unimaginable such a short time ago: my own place, my own life, and Charlie gorgeous there at my feet. She didn't notice me staring at her; watching her quietly in a kind of reverence, my eyes hopping over the pretty features of her face, taking her all in as she sat following intently whatever it was on the television with her soft lips slightly pursed and a serious little frown on her forehead.

"All right, Milo!" Billy's exclamation was like a trumpet blow, jolting us from our respective reveries, and looking over at him, I could see from his clown-like grin that he'd caught me and knew what I'd been thinking. For an instant, his moment of triumph hung in the air, and then the next moment he had his head over the pipe, sucking up bubbles like a smoky Shakespearean witch.

My life was beginning to change very quickly, and very quickly so did I. One of the biggest changes was that Tommy wasn't much about, unusually, though I'm sure it wasn't due to any kind of planning. I think he just sensed that I was trying to break from my shell, and perhaps he just stepped back to give me the space to do so. Anyway, it shames me to admit it, but things at home had become so crazy that I hardly noticed. The weekends were spilling on to the weeks as one big party, and there was no time for peace. I'd awake exhausted on a Monday morning begrudging my job, resenting it for cutting short the sleep that I needed, for curtailing my social life; and when the long day was over, though rest was precisely what I needed, it was the last thing I went looking for.

Around this time, I could almost sense my personality beginning to harden, some of the softer edges I'd carried through with me rubbing themselves flat, and between Charlie and me, things irretrievably started to change. The novelty of my playing at being someone else had begun in jest, but pretty soon I liked this brash alter ego too much; the joke just got too funny, and in my mirth, I was no longer able or willing to retrace my steps to the line where this play bordered truth. I started to adopt an air of arrogance, the trait of high-handedness that I admired in some of the seniors around me at work, and soon this morphed into plain irritability. Charlie tried to pull me up on it, but I felt it was my right, and I rebelled at the thought that she was cramping my style. I resented feeling guilty when I wanted a lie-in on a Saturday morning when she wanted to go out – when I hadn't wanted to be brought home early from drinks after work on Friday night. I blamed her too for that nagging inside when I went off to the ground with my new football mates instead of staying with her. In truth, she was as easy-going as she'd always been; the guilt that I felt was all coming from me, but that didn't stop me from blaming her for it. Even when we were out together, we seemed more apart. I was too quick to lose myself in the crowd at a party, not caring to notice or admit that I wasn't treating her right.

It would be easy now to blame myself completely, and it wouldn't be too far from the truth, but what really happened is that the world around me changed so much that I grew far from that boy she'd met in Camber. Events were pulling me in a whole new direction, but I couldn't go there with the anchor of this relationship; and though she had filled my heart, mark 2 Milo cared only for himself. I managed to stoke my irritation, my impatience, and my sense of injustice by convincing myself that she was to blame for the tension I'd created within, and whatever she would have done, whatever we could have said, unconcerned and unrepentant, our demise was just a matter of time.

It all blew up one Sunday. I got it into my head the night before when we were out in a pub by the Thames where the marketing girls had arranged a big bonding party for us and our partners that she was sulking with me, and it was winding me up. There were hundreds of us there: most of the dealers and some senior partners too and plenty of the auxiliary staff – lots of pretty girls who made up the bulk of the back office and didn't mind dressing up and making great company of themselves. I was a little nervous, still feeling very much a junior in this exulted company and all the more desperate to make my way in, and I knocked back the drinks a bit too enthusiastically. I could feel I was annoying her, always there right at my arm with a look that I read as disapproving. It exasperated me that she didn't seem to want to join in – didn't even seem capable of making the effort to look like she was having fun. While I was desperate to look the part for the dealers, Billy's mates whom I was starting to get in with, all she did was remind me of where I'd come from, the saddo that I didn't want to be any more. Frankly, I was finding her an embarrassment.

"Milo, can't we go home?" she whispered to me, the wrong side of eleven o'clock, just as things were starting to rev up a little, and I couldn't contain myself.

"I know," I said spitefully, "why don't you go home? You're obviously not enjoying it here. I'll see you later." With that, I turned sharply away but not before registering her look of surprised disappointment. I almost cracked as I saw the sadness in her eyes as her heart fell wounded by my outburst, but I had no mind for remorse, brushing away its tendrils as it reached out towards me. Sad to say, the City's party life had already got its claws in, and it's much easier to flee, cloaked by that perfect shield of anger, than to stand and admit an uncomfortable truth. Striding away, looking to detach myself and get lost among the revelry, I could feel her looking after me as the distance between us grew further and further.

I didn't get back until after it was light, but I was priding myself how virtuous I was in returning at all. As the party was winding down, I'd found myself chatting at the bar to a little brunette I'd been dancing with. She wasn't someone I recognized from the office: indeed, her little group was not in our party but had been in the bar next door and had been drawn to the noise. Being all female, they'd been allowed to join in. She'd obviously taken me for one of the dealers, and I'd got her and her mates intoxicated by the drinks I was handing out from the free bar. She'd fluttered her eyelashes at me, and I'd stayed with her even after Billy had gone on, finally pulling myself away only when the last window of moral opportunity presented itself. As I stumbled out of the taxi, I couldn't help but remember her tiny little skirt, how it had lifted as she'd danced, and the fingers she'd pressed down on my arm when I had told her that I had to go. Once inside the front door, I stood for a few moments muttering to myself at the bottom of the stairs, deciding whether to go on up or not. Weighing that I was the injured party, I decided to teach her a lesson and crashed out on the sofa in the lounge.

When, late in the afternoon, I finally surfaced, Charlie had gone. Chloe gave me some time to wake up and to let my head clear and then tried to talk to me about the tearful heart to heart the two girls had had as I lay snoring oblivious downstairs; but way too full of myself to take any notice – to listen to truths she might help me to see – I just gave her a piece of my mind, rebutting her presumption of involvement in my affairs. By now I was getting lost to myself, and even with this kindest and most patient friend, my relationship was starting to fracture.

Imagination Limitation

A bottle of beer is suddenly thrust into my line of vision and brings with it awakening, the realization that I've been lost momentarily to all things around me as I stared inadvertently at the table while nursing my empty pint glass. Turning my head to look along the arm that's holding out this attraction, I see Wolfie's face smiling, all teeth and glasses, an infectious grin of friendship that lights up my own. His hands combine, and after cracking the metal top from the bottle with the key shaped bottle-opener that is one of my favourite marvels of engineering, lager refills my glass without a word spoken; he just smiles and keeps nodding at me, his chuckle silent and a twinkle in his eye. The bar is filled to capacity now, so rammed that our little refuelling won't be easily spotted by the staff or the bouncers, and though this shop-bought intervention is a cheeky move, it's quicker to fetch the drinks in from down the road than try to fight a narrow pathway to the bar when the place is heaving like this, only to end up standing there and waiting for service, endlessly expectant.

What a scene, what a mix is this bar full of ill-fitting strangers, some sitting, some standing, and some in between; and were it not for the accident of the love that we share, the institution that brings together this bizarre marriage of equals, these faces familiar as our own wouldn't be a feature in the fabric of our lives. Nor would there exist that warm recognition, the special stranger status that flares rich and warm in its shared associations. Whether or not our fortnightly reunion is really as substantial as the noise it generates, still it endures as one of our greatest traditions: that easy air of bonhomie, the nods and smiles we give out like flowers to people with whom we've barely exchanged a word yet for whom we feel the deepest unspoken affinity – for the remembrance of times we've shared in this bar, for being part of the buzz that we always find building about us in the air as well as in our hearts, a buzz fuelled by the collective identity which is as comforting to us, as easy and welcoming, as gentle immersion in a warm lapping bath.

The subtle burr of engines starting adds an electricity to the feverish ambience – tapping toes and restless legs which take up dancing as the appointed time approaches. The tide that comes to carry us away to the ground soon will empty this saloon, and accordingly, we deal out the last of our surreptitious bottles and cans to be disposed of in bite-size gulps along the way. The spent cases here also need to be accounted for and secreted, removed in one of the backpacks for dumping outside lest our detritus cause exception, bring to management's note the informal BYO policy that we prefer, direct their attention to us when next our circus comes to town.

"Now I gotta take a leak," I tell Tom, who's just returned. "Boys," I say to the table and to no one in particular, "I'll see you outside." Getting up, I make my halting way against the little traffic that's now trickling like meltwater off the bigger block, and reach the little cupboard in the corner that passes for a toilet. The familiarity in this room is too close for comfort – the passing without room – and all for a pass that's supremely comfortable. I join the tail once I've made it inside the door, shuffling the increments towards the front of an obedient, almost childlike queue. We're all patient in our ordeal as we concentrate on this stinging need that grows ever more acute the closer we get. The lucky men going about their business before us are always too slow, and the long wait continues until each one's completed and turning away, squeezing back along the line and out past the men that stack there behind them. Oversized bellies are held and sucked in, but even with breath held tight there's not an inch to spare – the lack of space exacerbated as we guard our own positions, hovering there not daring to yield more than we must in case another takes advantage. Finally, we slip with gratitude into the prized gap our predecessors have left behind, filling their space and a relief thus releasing. There's no privacy here, so instinctively we make our own, and others', virtually, planting our eyes and looking conspicuously away, asserting the decorum of our sight, knowing that a look at Medusa might turn us to stone.

In this last room of truth, there's no room for swagger. We are all befittingly humble as we go about our basest business in this vital place of truce; our metaphorical swords left on the other side of the door so we can draw out in safety sword business inside. What a pleasure it is when the waiting is done! I hardly even wanted to go until I stood one behind, but now all my cares are over, my stresses expelled, and the next leg of the trip is assured. Standing back on the outside of the toilet door, I finish adjusting myself and make the final fastenings of the buttons on my jeans. Looking up, I spy a new place: carpets strewn and beer glasses abandoned, the recently vacated hall yawning satisfaction with its own sense of relief. All set and reborn, I fix on my path and head out through the exit.

Cantaloupe (Flip Fantasia)

Outside the pub, the summer's evening feels like midday, the air light and fresh and the sky an innocent blue still celebrated by the chattering of birds. Stopping in the little porch just beyond the arc of the door closing behind me, I think to myself, *one step at a time,* as I look across the corner of the pavement and over the road. A single white cloud hangs above, fluffy and perfect and hardly moving; and a car heading down to Old Street passes slowly by, navigating smoothly the humps that help to keep some local peace less ruffled. The street lights that line up before me with a few cars parked at the meters beneath them are redundant, at this early time, here on the near side of the pitch where we play on Thursdays. Beyond it lies the old pub in that long-dead corner where, as young men, we stood nursing our pints of orange juice and lemonade, drinking and laughing after that seminal tournament, now long since just a wood-shuttered shell. That was a lifetime ago, and almost all of the originals are faded from memory, but nevertheless there remains a handful of guys, veterans now but at one time the latest new recruits, who've made it down the decades and still form part of the current squad. Their earliest participation has passed beyond the grasp of my recollection as I gaze back through the mists of time, staring in baffled wonder at the changes I recall.

Back when it all began, this whole area was something other, and the short distance from the City was an ocean unbridged. Never venturing beyond our territory of suits and chrome bars, we only discovered these pitches by dint of the firm's move to a new Farringdon office, a move that was at the vanguard of the area's wider conversion. Still, what a happy chance it was that we did find them and that despite my lack of prowess I was again cajoled into coming along. From the very beginning, and then deepening with my continuing association with the games that go on here, my life garnered for itself a very different facet from any I'd previously worn – a mask, of sorts, which I could be comfortable with and which, amalgamating into the complex of the person I am, would amplify my happiness.

For that original tournament, the teams were roughly cut along desk lines, with each to include one mandatory female. Even that somehow seems the stamp of a different time, a different way of thinking. Coming out of his soccer semi-retirement especially for these games, Hardy claimed Penny as our own, and she certainly was the sporty type, if you know what I mean: always around in the gym downstairs or swimming in the swimming pool. Her function at work was to support our desk, and we did work fairly closely together, yet I'd never noticed her in any kind of romantic way before. Now, for some reason, I couldn't help myself: those long legs of hers in her too-short shorts running up and down the wing like some helpless Bambi, her big trainers with their repellent action which denied her the ball whenever it got close. She was even worse than me, but it didn't stop me trying to include her. It seemed only fair, and taking the knowing derision of my other teammates – even braving Hardy's stare as I passed her the ball whenever I could – little did I know I was reaching out to the love of my life. Maybe it was because she was there with us that day that finally I developed a taste for the game, one that before had always eluded me; but it inspired a twenty-year tradition: this twice-weekly game unbroken from then until now with its magical alchemy that makes friends of base strangers.

What changes there have been in that time, without and within. In front of me, the shell of a soon-to-be-opened Tesco local holds the ground where from time immemorial the zip factory stood – smart new flats needing smart new shops if the smart new people are to come here. This hinterland between the City and Islington is now all filling anew with johnny-come-latelys, displacing those who've dwelled here since the rebuild of the sixties and seventies as modern Britain trades ever forward without looking so much as sideways. The baths round the corner, which at one time were precisely that, before the advent of cosy modern plumbing, are now a place for City dwellers to don scuba for dive courses. Even the old car park across the way – where someone relieved my comfort jacket from my unlocked Alfa as our game went on oblivious, fresh from Penny's shoulders on our first night together – now has given way for a neighbourhood generation plant, a truly modern miracle that stops me to wonder and makes me feel old.

What a feeling was that sense of inclusion in those first few months, and even if I was only running about there because I owned the game, nevertheless the joy felt boundless. I was hopeless back then, and no serious knockabout would have had me – just too gauche and clumsy, I'd have stretched the patience of the most forgiving – but here was a step change, and as captain, I wouldn't even have to stand around embarrassed as alternate fingers picked the players around me, passing me by. Once I'd paid the block booking and rounded up the teams, I found that those of us who made up the first football evenings were in a flash transformed into more than mere colleagues. A new spirit was born. These nights soon became a fixture we looked forward to, and though of course the City doesn't stand still – people moved between firms and many things changed – still they came back for our games on those precious weekday evenings, bringing new recruits from their new places while keeping alive those older acquaintances too easily lost. As the personnel revolved and renewed and the player lists grew broader, perceptions changed too: I left behind my useless and too-apologetic persona after those earliest years as a little experience and plenty of guidance helped carry me on, the regular practice ensuring that a modicum of skill and even some savvy would soon be my own.

Today I find that this game has vested me with an authority – and affection even – seen as I am as the father of this child that gives so much to so many and no less to myself. What specifically I've gained is an appreciation of something that was so much lacking in me before, a *savoir faire* of the company of men – an education as only times like these can bestow. Over the many long years of these football evenings, these meetings of overgrown kids in our multicoloured costumes with sometimes even our names on our backs, taking a breather in goal, I've gazed up at the clock on St Luke's crooked spire to see it watching down on us as always, allowing my mind to wander across the thousand nights it has watched us play here before. Revisiting the joy of those evenings and the sheer happiness the game brings to all of us boys here and now and here and then, I let it infuse and wash once more all over me, exhaling as quiet tribute to the history and satisfaction that belongs to these moments a long, private sigh.

It's lucky that the act of remembrance pleases me so much, for I'm awfully slow to forget. Whatever star heralded my birth, whatever the constellations were when I arrived, a love of comparing the present with the past is very much a part of who I am, and especially my fascination with my own development as a person: where I am now versus who I was then. Finding myself at last on relatively dry land, I rail at my time in the sea – at the waves that used to bully me and that I found much too strong, at the fears that had got me so weak – and I wonder if we're all made the same. Do we all, having such fundamental frailty, so beset by doubt, make so little effort to hide these fault lines from others?

The door behind me suddenly swings and starting, we both apologize; and now reconnected, I watch him go off down the street. Warm summer air breezes against my face, and I can still feel the faint glow inside, the residue of tonight's exertion; and I think about the boys I've left behind in the pub. On average, I've been playing variously with or against this crop, depending on how I've picked the teams, for pretty much ten years. A few are very good footballers, and most are good men, but it's the good hearts who confirm this fixture as the special thing that I feel it is – those unafraid to show their deeper feelings, their true appreciation of what our coming together has meant. They are the ones who give it what love it has, without which I know we'd be swimming in a void. It's to them that I'm truly grateful.

We had our annual prize giving this evening, a tradition instigated a few years ago by the big man to provide expression for his untamed heart. The process is exacting: we vote on a variety of esoteric classifications which change every year, and the awards go to the winners after an opaque, highly subjective, and completely secretive totting up. Chopper received the coveted Fouler of the Year Award – my fierce, feisty friend always a worthy winner – while Captain of the Year went again to the man who's gone by the nickname "Captain" nearly as long as some of our younger players have been alive. To my not-so-secret delight, with a *Total Goal* DVD to prove it, Goal of the Year, for a second time, went to me, this year's award more worthy than the last, as it was given more for the goal than merely to commemorate a celebration inspired by my goal-scoring tourettes. The most unpredictable award and the hardest one to call is Man of the Year, and this year it went to the Jackal, who probably won by a nose due to his recent wedding, which was taken to mark a step up from his already embedded "thoroughly good chap" status. Those of us around the table, many previously honoured by the non-recurring appellation, as well as

Wobbles, a dead cert man of the year in waiting, banged down our genteel fists as rowdily as we dared, reminding this year's man that he must get the next round in.

Unusually, I'm not set to any kind of deadline tonight. I didn't know how things would pan out, but in the event, most of the boys scattered soon after the official business was over. One made his apologies as he dashed off for a dinner appointment, another was meeting his girlfriend to see a film, and one was heard muttering about catching the birth of his firstborn as he gathered up various bags – that or some other equally lame excuse. But by and by, only the tiny core remained. I'd thought that perhaps the night could be a big one and so had prepared myself accordingly, and had the boys dug themselves in, then I too would have stayed, the match due for an 8 p.m. screening making a most suitable attraction and a football double header with our own. The evening would have progressed smoothly as our smiles for the pretty barmaid got wider and each drink made us merrier, and at some point later I'd have slipped off with my white beads to round off the perfect night. Alas, such madness as I'd planned required the cover of a crowd or, failing that, anonymity; so with the ranks growing thin, I took my cue when the adverts came on, taking up my bag and rising to my feet.

"Thank you, Charles, you legend," I said, "and to you too, boys, for your kind recognition of my shooting prowess. I shall treasure this forever," holding up my DVD award and bowing my goodbye to the small party still assembled. To various good wishes and the gracious, seated bow of our giant orchestrator, I stepped outside to the Finsbury evening; and looking about me now for some inspiration of which way I should go, I pause one final time to dwell in the sad pit of departure, reflecting on the hour or so that we just spent chatting. A very different game begins once the

6.15 booking is rattling our door with their not-so-gentle reminder, informing us that our time has gone. No longer running and shouting, some of the players are quite different men away from their pitch: the maniacs now calmer with their mad passion spent; the generals much quicker now to cover the ground as they review each part, each incident of the play, and each special goal; the exacting now much more forgiving with their pint-easy smiles. The battle is past, and each and every one of us shares in the victory.

It's time to move on now, so where should I go? The unresolved plan once more at the forefront of my mind, I had a place to locate; an itch needed scratching. Normally I just dash from here not really looking, game over and the race on for the 6.25 in a *Groundhog's Day* loop each Tuesday and Thursday, so out of habit I cross the road on the way towards the station and walk past the edge of the pitches. Now, however, somewhat self-consciously I find myself dawdling, furtively eyeing the little nooks and the crannies as I go, the gaps in the hedging that are usually concealed by the blur of my haste, looking for a sanctuary with the walkways of the high-stacked flats looking down from above me. From somewhere up there I can hear a radio, tinny and far, mingling with the birdsong in a universe of silence. As I reach the park opposite the church, it's clearly a no go – too full of youths, some walking with dogs and others huddled in menacing groups – so I keep walking on, my hand dipping into the pocket of my jeans and my fingers searching out the case with its familiar, steely pattern, cold to the touch but the trigger for countless warm memories.

Rounding the corner, I fancy that the street at the top might be clear, and indeed, as I reach the junction there's just a couple hand in hand, already far down at the end and walking away from me. The near side is also vacant, and I spy my chance. Getting up to sit on the low wall, I lean slightly into the hedging that borders the park with my two feet dangling, and the little case is out and in my hand, the water bottle drawn from my bag and placed at the ready by my side. I squeeze the catch on the case and it pops open, a silvery butterfly again flat in my palm; and pausing for an instant, I inspect its happy contents: the little sachet that's like a stick of sugar but much, much sweeter, and lifting it out, already I'm smiling. With the case secreted back in my pocket, I take one final precautionary glance around me, but I'm not even kidding myself: the engines are running, and it's gone much too far to stop. But it's all good anyway – all clear as I tear open the packet top and tip the shiny pearls greedily on to my tongue. They fizz there on contact, and lifting the water to my mouth, I take one enormous gulp after another, washing everything away as I drain the plastic bottle of its watery dregs just to make sure.

A pause, and the very next moment it is upon me: warm blood careers through my body, and electricity shoots along my limbs and into my fingers and toes. It's like a crazy ride now – like a magical roller coaster. I see my face is all a big smile as my head bucks and rolls, struggling to keep up, to hang on with the buzzing surge that waves right through me and then back again, that first course which never fails and never fails to thrill. Right out to the teetering edge of destruction it pulls me, almost over but not ever beyond, sucking me back to my very centre right before it takes me too far – back to that deep calm which pervades my core, where that marked feeling of eternal rest contrasts so starkly with the previous intensity. In this space of perfect order, I regain myself and take a moment to taste this newborn tranquillity with my eyes newly opened. Looking about, everything that I see is simply a part of me, and tiny part of it that I am, what a peaceful feeling it is – a wonderful sense of belonging and of history shared. For am I not home? Is this not that little corner of the world that first beckoned to me, that fed me and bred me and lifted me up? Am I not a favoured son of these trees, these walls, and this very sky? What a thing it is now to feel so loved and wanted; but more: are these not the very streets that found me my Penny? Are these not the roads and pathways that kept my future reward safe as she went skipping on her young legs from the City road to the Golden Square chip shop for her Friday-night treat? Transfixed, I stare as she traverses my disbelieving gaze, not knowing or noticing me as, all lost in her past, she dances a jig and pushes her washing-filled buggy, disappearing up the street as her future beholds and fading from view as she melts once again to the mists of her youth.

A half-jump, half-slip from the wall, and I'm back on my feet and taking a couple of seconds to find some balance, boosting my mind back to conscious control. Now walking assuredly, I make my way out of the shadows and back towards the more quickly flowing stream, heading down the path that I came by with the tube station a goal vaguely pinned on my mind. The bag on my shoulder seems to grow heavier and heavier with each stride. I push my legs out purposefully for each slow, steady step as I continue towards the main run of shops. Stopping for just a second at the barriers, I realize that the spent paper sachet is still balled in my hand; pausing to concentrate, I find the earth at the base of the bush with a flick. For such well-aimed mischief, I afford myself a wry little smile, walking on then around the barriers and through the estate.

At the exit corner by the road, I see her again, thick with the crowd at her thirtieth birthday. The party seems to stretch on endlessly around her; she has a vodka in hand and is beset by the fun of the moment. As I catch her eye, she mimics Lisa Kudrow's flash dance in the opening sequence of *Friends*, raising her free arm above her head and radiating waves of happiness; her love for me seems to span the room. I smile back, but it's getting harder now: the cloudiness is growing, and the darkness of the world is closing in. I need to get to the bench by the shop, sit myself down. I almost buckle as I round that final corner, and she's older now, patient hands in her lap as she sits on the bench waiting silently for me, soft eyes smiling and habitually kind. Slumping beside her, my head falls back to its rest against the trunk of the central tree, gazing up to the leaves that reach out on the branches above. The bag's half hung on my shoulder and half balancing on the wooden slats, and as she leans inevitably against me, I nest her head gratefully with mine, forever joined and our comfort made.

Don't Let It Pass You By

Life continues on this street at a tempo of its own. It's a flow best described as slow and dragging and is very much like the locals themselves, who continue about their business oblivious, inured to the various dramas which sometimes occur but never distract. Whatever the minute brings, the flow here seems to remain at a constant, life continuing at its lacklustre pace despite those momentary flare-ups which add a flash of colour to the mundane and grey default, whether the drunkards and users who gather at the corner and from time to time will put on their show; or the wild-eyed crazy man who screams forth the jumble of his mind; or the kids out nicking on their pushbikes, weaving between the pedestrians who, like everyone else around here, have seen it all before. This non-City sector just beyond the grasp of the beast has even managed to keep faith with its decidedly working-class retail outlets: Superdrug, Argos, even a Co-op; and despite the refurb, there's not a chain coffee shop to boast of – unless, that is, you count the Rainforest Cafe proclaimed by the Shell garage on the opposite side.

I'd known well this street from the landmark roundabout for years before the football again made my visits here regular: my first town job was at the original British Telecom building at its north-west exit. Like so many others, it's been razed and rebuilt since then. James's dad, a big cheese at head office, shoed me in on a temporary contract, and I worked in the tenders department just when the company had become quasi-private. The commute and office environment were a big change for me; and not only did the job get me out of my retail cul-de-sac, but it also served as a kind of professional halfway house, a decompression chamber for the lighter, more refined air of the City, that wondrous square mile which snorts and breathes just a few hundred yards to the south, where my association with Billy would soon hatch me a place. A few years ago, more than seems possible but certainly long after I first emerged blinking from the Underground station, this whole street was redone as a sort of urban oasis, the pavements levelled and relaid in large grey stone with seats and benches set around some fine, tall trees, all neatly spaced with their roots neatly planted. Despite this gentrification, the natives still cling on stubbornly, blissfully unaware of their deprivation, their lack of shiny cocktail bars and high-end designer stores. They still go about their way as they always have, and in this workaday environment, the half-conscious body lolling about on the bench is barely worth notice.

Lost in a maze of dreams as consciousness briefly eludes him (though all the while keeping a tight grip on the strap of his bag), our hero lies slumped on the bench at the far end of the street. But wait – look down here, and you'll see him appearing from the rising walkway. It's just one of the multiplicity of exits that snake from the subterranean ticket office, a tourist's nightmare and a nightmare of tourists and other passers-by, and he's just as I remember, eternally dogged and wracked as I pass him by. Every time our paths cross when I enter from the street or when I ride up behind him on the escalator from the Northern line, it's the same apparition, the same ghost of a September morning, desperate and close to exhaustion as I pulled myself to the office, my breath growing heavier and my skin turning grey, grimly keeping on in the hope that I'd find my inhaler waiting in my drawer. Mr Morris, the manager who had been granted the dubious benefit of my inexperienced enthusiasm and who had taken me somewhat under his wing, had stood over my chair with solicitous concern; and after seeing me right, he had sent me off home. Mostly relieved now with the medicine applied, I shuffled off with my chest still raw but a hundred times lighter, the blue-pump angel held tight in my fist; and though the days that followed were all about recovery at home on the sofa, I was finally unburdened, prepared at last and ready to move on.

The day before this important watershed had been a long one and a long time in coming. I'd not seen or heard from Maddie in ages: life's course drifts naturally on, and our respective ships, it seemed, were moving further and further apart. Just a week into a house share and with all sorts of exciting changes finally starting to add flavour to my life, I can honestly say that for the first time since we'd met, I'd actually stopped listening to hear from her. Of course, if I did chance upon something that brought her to mind, I still wondered about what might have been: those old diaries, for instance, the ones I'd lived by, that I'd packed and moved up to Camden with me – those old dated sheets in their leather cages where I'd meant only to keep safe my thoughts, locking up there instead my hopes and my dreams. I knew that she was a few years into an arts degree or an MA or something, living in a northern part of London I'd only vaguely heard of and doubtlessly loving her student lifestyle; but if pain did remain, it was now dull. I had now processed and accepted my failure. It is no mere platitude that time is a great healer, and I'd never thought as little about her.

Just a week into my new, grown-up existence and out of the blue as I headed off to work on a bright Tuesday morning, my very first letter at this new address was sitting conspicuously there on the mat, forwarded by my parents, who'd failed to warn me. Just seeing the envelope inside the Jiffy bag made my heart skip a beat: unmistakable and a real piece of work, one of her signature handmade missives with "Come" in big, black letters on the cover. Inside, the hand written message declared, "The time is now," and there was a phone number at the bottom. She wanted to see me!

As soon as I got to work, I called Maddie's number, and it rang and rang; and when eventually she did answer, her bleary voice seemed at first unlike one I recognized. It took some moments before I discerned it was indeed Maddie grunting and a few more again before she realized it was me. I wondered if maybe it was a little early for her – she sounded as if I'd woken her prematurely – or if the previous evening had, perhaps, been a big one. When my name finally did register with her, she was fulsome with apologies, and straight away, we arranged to meet the following evening. That night, lying in my bed and quite unable to sleep, I hardly dared to believe that this could really be happening; but hadn't we always said that our time would come? Now that it had, I couldn't help shaking my head at the irony of the timing: Charlie's visit was just days away, and it struck me as too bizarre that things should work out like this. Then again, hadn't I just made the biggest move of my life? Living here was a huge leap out towards adulthood, and our mantra had been that when we were older, and the time found us right, the people we were destined to be would come together again as lovers – that our names from long ago had been written in the stars. I reminded myself that I shouldn't be getting my hopes up despite what her card said: Maddie had let me down before. It even crossed my mind that I might be better off not going there at all, but what could I do? She was an old friend, and anyway, I really couldn't help myself. I was overcome by curiosity and the slimmest hope that maybe, finally, dreams can come true.

I could hardly wait for the next day to pass. I helped my boss carry boxes of prospectuses to the reprographics studio down the road – the same place I'd pass years later on my journey from a different office to the football pitches – and throwing myself into the work for all I was worth, I collated and stapled with abandon, but the clock still wouldn't budge for me. When lunchtime finally arrived, I walked down to

Golden Lane with Louise, a many-ringed co-worker who lived with her dreadlocks in a squat at the Elephant, rattling off my thoughts ten to the dozen about the upcoming evening and mercilessly boring her with all sorts of silly details – the minutiae of our previous and all my silly hopes and desires – as my excitement completely got the better of me. The poor girl barely got a word in. Back in the office, the workload was minimal, as we'd just completed a tender, so I spent the afternoon compulsively rearranging my drawers again and again. At long last, it was time to head off.

I'd imagined that the journey would take longer than it did, and getting to the meeting place even earlier than I usually would have, I took up a position outside the tube station and surveyed the very different landscape I now found around me. In itself, it wasn't so distinct from the bricks and concrete of Old Street, but stacked piles of refuse bags glistened wet with the rain that had just stopped falling, and the litter-strewn street was so full of mess and discarded vegetable waste that it was hard to see where the road ended and the pavement began. Aside from all the dirt and the rubbish, there was a decidedly alien air about the place. In an ethnic dress shop, worlds away from the boutique that Mum had co-owned, multicoloured sari-type garments hung from rails across the width of the window, tightly packed together in a squashed Eastern collage. Next to it on the stall outside, the greengrocer offered the strangest selection of fruits I'd ever seen the like of. On the corner opposite, there was a spartan kind of barber; black and white pictures that looked as if they'd been torn from magazines and Sellotaped to the window displayed a selection of what looked like the same short cuts, while the cluster of dark young men inside gathered like a conspiracy, with no one apparently cutting. Time went by; true to form, Maddie was keeping me waiting. As I endured the suspense feeling more and more conspicuous,

I grew edgier, hanging around like a spare part in the day's fading light.

Then I saw her, and the evening lit up. A lovelier vision and more womanly than I remembered, she had a big smile on her face, and it looked like she knew it. She feigned a tiz as she came gliding along the pavement, and as she reached me, we hugged and I was instantly conquered, that Christian Dior smell that was always her own carrying me back to those old village dreams, enveloping me once again like a child in her cloud. Nothing else was happening, nothing else mattered – nothing but those deep, warm feelings – and I wished I could stay here like this forever. I felt her release a little, and giving a last squeeze, I let go before stepping back and just gazing at her, taking in the subtle changes that the few years had made, changes that before my eyes were already starting to disappear, to normalize, replaced by that old familiarity. Like an old friend, I remembered that slight assumption of superiority that she wore so subtly in her smile and her look of poise, of control. She started apologizing for her timekeeping – unnecessarily, as suddenly I could hardly remember the wait – and I batted away her whirlwind of excuses, which were accompanied by that forgive-me smile that was another of the keepsakes I'd unconsciously treasured for years. When she was done, we stood silent again regarding each other.

"So, how are you?" I said at last. "Where have you ... what have you been doing?"

"Oh, Milo! Look at you. You haven't changed at all, and still so many questions. Later there's time for that, but it's so good to see you!"

"Do you want to eat? What do you want to do?" I smiled, asking questions again.

"Actually, we're hooking up with a few of my course mates. I was sure you wouldn't mind. They're all dying to meet you," she said, and though I felt the sting of disappointment that I wasn't immediately to have her all for myself, it thrilled me too that she'd actually told them about me. "Come along then," she said in mock reprimand. "We'll be late!"

We made our way through this unlikely district as dusk slowly choked off the light, and though I was in the company of my queen, it nonetheless felt more and more dangerous and unwelcoming the further we went. She was taking me again from my comfort zone as we headed to this favourite restaurant of hers to meet her friends. I kept looking around nervously as we passed broken windows in boarded-up flats; street lights that stared down coldly on metal mesh railings; and cars, battered and burnt, awaiting repair that never would come – all bringing back and magnifying the feelings of discomfort I'd had as I stood at the tube station. Fear began to surface as we went further, morphing the shadows before me into mean little monsters that lay scarcely hidden among the blackened brickwork and the flickering of lamp light on the sides of the buildings as my feelings of dread swelled to deepest foreboding. As if it were some kind of sanctuary, almost wistfully I recalled the tube station that we'd left behind us – as if it were some refuge at the beginning of this *Mad Max* odyssey, a last portal and my only chance of escape that got further away with each reckless step.

As she prattled away, Maddie seemed totally at her ease, however: to her, these streets were home, and she was oblivious to my anxiety as she kept up her endless narrative. Listening to and losing myself in her voice, I kept a lid on my mutinous feelings of panic, letting her words and her sounds soothe me as she described the people who were waiting for us; and when we'd stepped safely through the flimsy restaurant door and it had closed behind us, when the tiny bells that lay entwined in the bead chain that hung from the ceiling there had heralded our arrival to her friends, the relief was intense.

She led me behind her to the table and presented me to the waiting group. "This is my Milo," she said, and I fancied that those faces looking back at me, though outwardly friendly and smiling, bore here and there hints of pity, even perhaps some of scorn. I told myself it was just a product of my battered perception, twisted by the ghastly walk here; but clearly, for better or worse, they knew my name. Whatever they were thinking, I was only interested in Maddie, and boy, now that I could relax again, what a sight she was. I'd sat in the seat offered on the side of the long table, withering submissively again into the minor part I was used to playing when in her entourage, and had then watched as she proceeded to the head, where a space was opened up for her easily to slip into. She greeted her newly parted praetorian guard with extravagant air kisses. As I watched her, I marvelled at the woman she'd turned into: her dark hair now longer than I recalled, her face slimmer, and her manner so assured, with such an enigmatic guile she seemed like something from a book or from a painting like the ones she now spent her time studying – a woman that, to the girl I'd known, was a promise made good. Over the dinner, she was the very centre of attention, and I shook my head admiringly at the way she spun her magic, holding court over those around her like the wiliest ringmaster.

I didn't eat much that evening. In truth, I couldn't really stomach the Ethiopian fare that was the restaurant's speciality. The others seemed to revel in it and also in my ignorance, and they were quite sniffy when I admitted that Chinese and Indian were the extent of my dining adventures, but I didn't care. I was just happy to be sitting and watching her, receiving every now and then one of those brilliantly directed smiles that came as if from the sun. More and more certain that the night would be ours, I cared nothing if I never ate again. When we all said our goodbyes and parted company, the two of us headed for her place. My silence this time had nothing to do with the streets we were walking: I no longer noticed the squalid surroundings or the odour of threat in the air. I was too proud, too excited in my frozen enjoyment: the short walk back was a biblical pathway to a long-promised land.

A Forest

Her room was a pigsty. Entering ahead of me, she turned the light on and swept a pile of clothes and assorted art paraphernalia from the bed, inviting me to sit where a crust of pizza had just been – it fell to the floor to join the takeaway containers that already there littered. The chest on the side was a mess of books and cups and coffee rings and even a couple of unwashed plates still sporting their cutlery, and the cracked turntable cover was smeared with something that I hoped was ketchup. On the opposite wall, a thick, painted gloss fixed shut the two uncurtained sash windows, tinged with a weak glow that seeped in from the street light outside, accentuating their frigid white finish. Entering the room, it all seemed so chilly – somehow colder than the night we'd just come in from – that I gave an involuntary shudder. It felt much too cold to think of shedding any of my layers. Looking around and seeing the thick dust on the windowsills gave me a start, and I felt a tingling itch in my chin – a sometime early warning that my asthma was coming, and patting my empty coat pocket, I suddenly wished that I'd brought an inhaler.

Maddie went over to the little sink in the corner which, with a fridge and a kettle, served as her kitchen, and after flicking the switch to boil some water, she turned to the record player, bending with her bum in the air as she picked the Cure's *Seventeen Seconds,* which stood on the floor next to its cover. As the music came on, the eerie sound of the opening bars filled the room with a sense of disquiet that seemed perfectly matched to my memories, transporting me back through time and space to her wooden kitchen table in the village. She sat down, smiling at me on the two-seater sofa opposite the bed.

"It's so good to see you," she said. "I'm so glad you came up. Sorry about those guys in the restaurant. They're lovely, you know, but they can be a bit up themselves sometimes. Anyway, we can have a proper catch-up now. Tell me everything. How's your new job?"

"It's OK," I said, nodding. "Not terribly exciting, but it beats stacking shelves, and I've moved now. I'm up in town; got a room in –"

"You have to see these," she interrupted. "We're studying *l'age d'or* at the moment. I know you'll love them," and so saying, she came over to the bed and pulled up a huge volume she'd previously moved for me, setting it open on my lap. "Isn't it amazing?" I looked at the image of a withered pocket watch hanging over the dry branch of a tree, studying it dutifully and postponing my revelations until later.

"How's the art going then?" I asked as she handed me a coffee. "Still enjoying it, I guess?"

"Oh yes, it's amazing! We've been focusing on the impressionists this term. We went to an exhibition at the National just last week. The history can be a bit dull, but the way they painted – the achievement of their original thought and the way they expressed so much of themselves in their work – is just inspiring. Do you know what I mean?" I had no idea what she meant. All that I wanted was to hold her in my arms and worship her at last as the goddess I'd always seen her to be. The longer she talked, the more I thought about those early dreams and how much I'd longed for this moment.

"Now tell me all about your little girlfriend," she demanded. "Candy, is it?" Her question came like a bolt to the heart.

"How ... what ... she's not really my girlfriend," I protested.

"I ran into James in the village. He told me you'd had quite the time on your camping trip. She does sound very sweet. I'd so love to meet her, and Ian was saying that my design show would be a perfect evening to rally all my old friends. I'll be flat out, of course, but it will be such fun."

"Ian?" I asked when she'd stopped talking and my thoughts started to clear. "Who's Ian?"

"My boyfriend, Ian. Do keep up!" she laughed. "Haven't I told you?" I was speechless. "He's great; you'll love him. I can't wait for you guys to meet. He's away this week, but we'll definitely get together. He really is quite wonderful."

"But you said ... I thought you said ... 'our time' ..."

She smiled her happy, friendly smile at me. "It really is so good to see you," she asserted.

Slowly, and without giving respite from the pain that my outrushing hopes had left behind in the vacuum where my heart should have been, the rest of the evening passed in flat resignation – that feeling again, like her very own mug. Once I was certain that she lay in that large bed asleep, lost with an impossible distance between us, I gave myself to tears as I shivered for warmth on her frosty two-seater with my knees hugged to my chest, wrapping and rewrapping myself in my coat and the thin sleeping bag as I quietly deflated, shrivelling to nought. I don't know which part of it was worse: that she'd done it again, raising my perennial hopes just to dash them with that blithe innocence she tacitly proclaimed; or that I, after I'd sworn I wouldn't again be her patsy, had mugged myself off the first time she'd come calling, half-betraying by the yearning in my heart a relationship that was hardly yet born. I thought of the times back in the village when I'd first seen her at the bus stop and been caught by her eyes, of all those kitchen-table courts where I'd struggled for king and come up with jester. Then I thought of Rachael, the last look that she had shot me as she closed her front door, of our love never known. Without the comfort of anger to shield me from my own pathetic grief, feeling wretched with my quiet blubbing and cold to the core, eventually I fell asleep, and my wet eyes were dried.

I didn't know exactly what time it was when I awoke for a second in the night, but everything inside and out was still and silent. Everything, that is, apart from a humming – a low wheezing from my lungs as they wrestled the air. I realized that my asthma was starting. I closed my tired eyes and hoped that sleep might put this breathlessness behind me, but when again I opened them to the darkness, my chest was still heaving and tight. For a while I lay half-awake as I regarded this halting strain, listening to the old-man wheeze as if it were coming from somewhere else; and after skimming sleep for what seemed an eternity, when I at last opened my eyes, frozen and exhausted, the light from the window had something of day.

I knew that I had to reach the office. I prayed that I'd find my inhaler in the drawer of my desk, sure I could recall moving it about yesterday and hoping it wasn't just some fanciful mirage. Sitting up, I tried to pull on my boots quietly so I could leave without any goodbye: I just wanted to get out. But as I scratched around in the half-light, she must have heard my stunted breathing, and opening one eye, she asked if I was OK. I told her I was and that I had to go, and kissing her cheek, I left, pulling the door behind me. Following her sleepy instructions, I dragged myself all hunched around my chest slowly back to the tube station. As it was early, the carriage was empty and there were plenty of seats, and feeling spent from the exertion of getting this far, I let myself collapse exhausted over two places, the warm, subterranean air a relief like the final wish of a man condemned. As the train's rumbling journey carried me, I slipped in and out of sleep, dreaming I was bobbing on the waves of a perfect green-blue sea, afloat in the water and blessed from above by the sun.

As I rode the Old Street escalator back up to street level with my hands tightly gripping the black rubber rail, I couldn't help but notice how out of sync it was with the grooved metal steps. Periodically, I had to force myself back upright to counter the handrail running ahead. Slowly I came through the ticket barriers in the hall and emerged at last to the weak morning light on the ramp in the shadow of my building. Faces of concern all around me paused as they registered the grim picture of my struggle, a harsh rasping my only reply as I battled, near doubled, for air. Despite the distractions and the embarrassment that being the centre of attention usually would have inspired in me, I remained singularly focused on the relief that I was sure – that I prayed desperately I was sure – waited in my desk. Trying to manage through my increasing tightness, every step, every movement, and every breath took effort; but somehow my overwhelming weariness lightened my anxiety, and I didn't have the energy left for panic. I concentrated on one step at a time until finally I reached my desk and opened my drawer, finding my inhaler.

After a dozen or so puffs had my chest at last feeling better and no longer my enemy, I was so slumped and relaxed that I almost hung from my chair, bizarrely reminiscent of the pocket-watch picture I'd seen last night. I still felt broken but also inexpressibly happy; I still felt wracked, but the ordeal was over. My boss looked a mixture of shock and relief: shocked by the vision of my entry and relieved that the nightmare had passed, and he bid me to rest for a while until we were sure. When I said that I felt OK to go home, he asked if I needed an escort. It was a question I almost couldn't comprehend: all my focus was on savouring each easy breath, and with the weight now lifted, it slowly began to creep over me that it wasn't just my lungs that had been released. Maddie had been my inexplicable madness for so long, and almost shockingly, it occurred to me that I no longer knew why. The very idea that I'd built of her as some kind of ideal had been a poison that had cast its deadly shadow over my life and had kept me held in a self-indulgent spell; but now it was broken, and life had moved on.

I thought about the previous weekend: the totally unexpected awakening I'd experienced when exploring my new neighbourhood and the inspiration that had completely overtaken me. I could now look ahead to this very weekend with its promise of real excitement and an optimism unburdened by the past. Wasn't Charlie worth ten of her anyway? Never again would I feel like I'd missed out on something because I'd missed out on her. Later that morning, as I reached the empty house and fell under the warmth of my welcoming covers, the sensation I had was beyond that of mere survival. Flush with the thoughts of my new housemates and Charlie's impending arrival, I felt reborn and utterly liberated. The moment before my head blurred into unconsciousness was one of the sweetest, most reassuring moments of my life.

In the Waiting Line

As I come to on the bench, my head is nice and light, and the feeling of sickness is gone, though I'm immediately aware that my mouth feels very dry. Reaching down, I find that the bottle in the carrier pocket on the side of my bag is disappointingly empty. I look up, and of course there's the Co-op just a few steps away. Standing, I find I'm pretty steady, much more in control of those currents that run lighter and more gently now around my head, and securing the bag over my shoulder, I'm present enough even to take a quick look around, making sure I'm forgetting nothing. With a few short paces, my gait achieves a certain rhythm, and gathering momentum, I enter the store and skip down the three steps to the body of the shop like a pro. I'm a master! People are running around everywhere on their own special missions, and there I see the guard, eagle-eyed and static amid this euripus, conspicuous in his blue-capped uniform as he regards me for an instant. Spotting nothing out of the ordinary, he moves his gaze on.

Finding the fridge where the chilled water's kept, I take the first one I see, reflecting that I must still be quite altered if I can be so spontaneous, not comparing the offers and prices and the yellow flash labels that advertise this week's value combo. Upon joining the wiggly queue with my item in hand, I spy a packet of pistachio nuts and select them too, as I know how they fill a hole. Rehearsing my checkout moves as I edge closer, I think that I don't want to slip up, don't want to spoil this sweet charade by a sudden absentmindedness at the crucial last moment, that single point of actual human interaction – for instance, by letting my mind wander and forgetting to pay. But there's no time to fret in this efficient establishment, as my number is up, and accordingly I proceed, smiling as I do at the cashier behind till number eight. I wonder if my smile is right – if I'm grinning like a maniac or if I'm smiling at all – but my card slides in, the PIN is a good 'un, and I'm back on the street.

Looking each way to measure the flow, I put this new plastic bag into my bigger one and look down at my phone. There's eight minutes to make the train. The whole deal's like clockwork, and I can't help but think how clever I am – like a junkie in disguise with my head in a cloud but my legs good and grounded and taking charge of me with one step and then another, both in the right direction, carrying me along as the rest of my consciousness enjoys the journey, the distraction of the local diversity, and the wealth of characters that always exists here. I can't help wondering at the separation that makes all of us so utterly distinct, at what sort of lives those paths might lead back to once they have crossed here with mine. Where do these people come from? Does our being here mean anything? I feel my eyes scorching holes in their faces as I watch them pass by. I feel them burn with my stare.

As I start to descend the ingress, I stumble a little, and my bag swings off my shoulder as I look up behind me to that old building which gradually disappears from view as I continue below. We both know, of course, but we remain silent about the time that has passed, each disbelieving how the years have continued to stack up since our distant beginning. In the ticket hall, the crowd is a mass that oozes to the gates. It slows to a bottleneck, and I carefully withdraw my pass, my movements deliberate as if underwater; I pass through to the other side, freed from the squeeze, and slip it back safe in its place as I take the sharp right through the exiting herd and head for the stairway. I do not adopt my usual chasing style this time – the twisting of my body into the spiral bend to speed up my passage – but instead am sure-footed and careful, cautious now, my hand hovering by the rail all the way to the bottom.

On the platform, my fellow travellers and I gaze waiting in our own worlds, a single class made common by the journey we share, our timetable set by the electronic board that hangs above. Invited by the metal bench, I sit down and begin fiddling with my ear buds, at first confused by the tangled wires, but I overcome and dopily attach my phone to the jack, checking what there is by way of entertainment: *30 Rock.* I've seen this one already, but so what, I think, and laugh to myself, happy to be seated here easy and safe on my way. *It'll be like seeing it fresh in this state anyway. Gotta love that intro; gotta love those faces!* The first train's arriving, and the tunnel fills impossibly with noise. This one's not mine, but it bursts in with a whoosh, so close to the platform that for a moment of panic I feel that it might suck me in. *As if,* I think, newly brave as that feeling passes. At least its departure won't be as vexing, sitting here at this end of the platform. *Be calm,* I tell myself as off it goes. *Next one's the one. Don't forget. Don't want to miss it – disaster!* The show fills a few minutes that pass like seconds, and again a train rushes in, my train, this one somehow arriving with a sound less perturbing. Holding the show on my phone, I pull myself up, sidle over to a door, and then stand off like a great citizen who's mindful of others, giving the world a bit of love, my own bit of space.

Next thing I'm on; and my favourite, most comfortable seat is free; and I'm set, my bag down between my feet before me. Getting my bearings, I see the guy opposite is staring into a device. An elderly but active floral-shirted *Guardian* reader with wide rims is sitting down next to him; and there are some folk with brollies, neat and to the ready. One lady's got a patterned Hermès scarf tied over her blonde, once-young hair, and we've even got some wearing shorts and a couple of too-fresh haircuts. Having shot my glances and got the measure, I can now dip back into my own world; the train moves off, and I slip back inside.

Every now and again, I'm roused by my own laughter, and I have to check that the masterful cracks that are roaring mirth in my head are not disrupting the sobriety of the otherwise-peaceful carriage. No, it's OK, and like a baby stirring half-awake with a yelp and then falling back into its own mysterious dreams just for a pat and some murmur of reassurance, I'm glad to be back in my tiny world of three colour inches, where the funnies are practised and the writing is smart. At Emirates Park, the glare of the evening sun brings our window alive, splashing its picture of summertime glory, and for an instant I'm reminded where I am and where I am going. As the station fades away so does the journey, and I close back within, wrapped warm in that sunshine and sealed with a smile, and I'm lost in a special place; the pearly destination at last has arrived, and I've nothing more to do, nothing left to think. There's nothing left but bliss.

Torch

Around the courtyard outside the pub, the various retail offerings are fighting hard to ride a peaking wave of consumption. The chippy's churning out its great trade in hake and fries and battered saveloy, burgers and buns and other assorted dainties, and discarded sauce and condiment sachets already pepper the pavement like confetti post the nuptials. Fast hands in blue plastic gloves frantically feed the snaking line that hums with impatience. The punters coil in an orderly file around the glass counters and right through the door. Should there be any whiff of disorder – the suggestion of a queue jumper or a glint that the chips well might be dangerously low – you just know that the whole place would go off like a powder keg. The 24–7 over the road is on match-day high alert as chancers mingle in their shoppers' disguises to surreptitiously take up, just for the thrill, the odd can or an illicit bit of something that later can be chewed on – those toxic packs of processed meat which taste all the better when you've nicked one: they'd have to. Meanwhile, the deli next door is altogether less burdened in its exclusivity, loosing off a gourmet pastry here or an artisan cheese roll there, the happy smiles of the serving staff so much more than mere teeth, dressed in neat white half-aprons befitting the visit of each genuine gourmand. This is some rarefied world, and its subtle, crusty air is divorced from the chaos that reigns outside, marked out as separate by the bright ping of the bell which sounds on each and every opening, casting away as it does so those rebellious football demons.

Back in the courtyard, each group that's separately formed of much the same parts begins now to congeal with its neighbours as the mass grows with each latecomer's joining, each fresh arrival boosting further the numbers as we get closer to the moment at hand. Now packed with its assembled throng, the square's close to saturation, and each subgroup has grown beyond itself, losing its lines in the singular crowd, shoulders rubbing expectant shoulders in a friendly jostle and the area so filled with bodies that re-entering the pub is escape into peace. The final moment is upon us, and like departure-lounge passengers awaiting the call to board, everyone is up on their toes; and then, as if a whistle has blown, all of a sudden the crowd is off and rolling, the surge well and truly begun as it spills over on to the pavement and forges the road. Cars, no longer masters of their tarmac, wait motionless and fuming, hostages helplessly regarding the blithe human river that passes the width of their windscreens with faces drunk on anticipation, or trepidation, or alcohol, sauntering and skipping and sprinting as they're drawn towards the heart. These many diverse currents, having burst through the containing banks, now rush to join with their brothers, those kin who also now pour from all of the corners to the same swelling sea.

Quickly scanning about, I see no sign of the lads; but Tommy's above the others, and I catch sight of him with the chips in his hand as his prematch tradition dictates, standing out from the melee to wait as he watches from the distance of the road that divides. Already with an eye on me, seeing me seeing him, he flicks his head in a nod from over the way, and we're off, keeping our separate sides as I try to dart ahead of the pack to cross over at the end of the street and meet at his corner. I keep half an eye out for his bobbing head, which I see and then don't among the torrent around him, as we both make our way along with the crowd; but it doesn't matter how quickly I might want to get there, how much darting and gap-taking I achieve. The huge mass finds and imposes its own speed of passage, and any brief getting ahead is but an illusion, a trick designed by one's own anxiety to keep up one's efforts.

Pausing at the top of the hill, I step out of the fray and on to a flat-topped brick wall that borders the pavement. The bricks are burnt black with dirt and years, mottled relics completed by a tubular railing that runs across the top, identical to the one in my memory outside those black-and-white flats of Everlyn Court: both of them hewn from the same ragged era and monuments of a time long gone. Despite my vantage point, I can no longer see my brother, seeing instead the crowd moving as one physically and emotionally as it funnels off down the hill. Turning my gaze to follow its path, I'm struck by the wonder of this sight. There is always something magical in this meeting of so many, always something sublime about the mass of red that seethes and breathes like a giant serpent, a dragon rich with fire caged in by the buildings and the famous east stand that waits down below.

With all of his flat caps, Lowry painted this scene years ago, but we see the same heads today, the same church, and the same creed. And just as those he depicted were then channelled, so we are now, lest the Devil be permitted to jump upon what otherwise is our idle time, time that's ripe for reflection and apt to reveal. All too briefly, in a flash of detachment, I catch a glimpse of what truly we are, gathered here morphed into passion's plaything, this animal, living and breathing, which, were we not united together and bound in our servitude, would be too vast to contain – both for them and for us. Intoxicated and intoxicating, the irresistible spirit of the crowd is everywhere about me; and taken by the heart, I plunge amid my heaving cohorts, all of us going down together in the same joyous fashion, lost and staggering in songs and chants and grins and bravado, past towering blocks and cars left abandoned at least until kick-off, past burger vans and black-wearing constables who bear separate witness to all of this turbulence, hoping for early relief. Stretching away down the hill in our tens of thousands, we flow to where Saturday-afternoon rules apply; and thus, by the rule of the beast we're set free: free to shout, free to snarl, free to forget.

In a Rut

What a slope it was that I set myself to that Sunday afternoon, laid out unconscious on the sofa as Charlie slipped away in tears. I woke just in time to see the weekend retire but went on out anyway, not just allowing but willing Billy's pipe to lead me further and further off into the darkness. Flattered by the shallow hearts around me, I allowed the vanity of my self-importance to carry me away, telling myself and all who would listen that she was the problem; and it didn't cross my mind that I should call her. I don't think it even reached quite through to me that I'd really hurt her, so focused was I on my own forging ahead, on driving beyond the next staging post, up another rung of some illusory ladder.

I was so distracted over the next few days that when I got home from work on Wednesday to find her pink stationery waiting in the form of a letter, it came as if from the blue – a missive from some long-gone acquaintance, from a shadowy dream that I barely recalled. My surprise and curiosity on first reading her reproaches quickly turned to indignation, the very expression of such misguided and deluded feelings as she unloaded on me seeming a damned imposition. I couldn't understand it: instead of entreating me and apologizing, accepting how things had gone between us and how she'd failed to keep up, she had the gall to call me selfish – to throw neglect in my face despite all the allowances I'd made, all the times I'd stayed my own enjoyment just to accommodate her. She even asked me where the good guy had gone! Her unjust slights burned, and I was now on a crusade, calling immediately with my righteous anger peaking. Into her answer machine, which allowed me the convenience of venting without interruption, I poured my scorn, letting her know in the most certain terms how much fun she'd been spoiling and what a drag the relationship had turned into. I said that I'd only come back at all on Saturday through some false sense of loyalty, and now, I went on, I felt like a fool. I ended my cruel rant by taunting her arrogantly, saying that if once her friendship had been something nice, it was that no longer, and the time had quite obviously come for us both to move on. I advised her to bloody well grow up and accept it, finishing my tirade by ripping her letter up over the mouthpiece. Thus having relieved myself to a point of satisfaction, I put the phone down.

The following week, I got a final message from her, another handwritten piece like the one before on the same girlish paper complete with a matching pink envelope. It was a lot shorter than her previous one, and having calmed down a bit, allowing myself to realize that I'd over-reacted and wasn't perhaps being altogether fair, I couldn't help feeling a quiet respect for the dignity and the measure of her tone. She said she hadn't realized what an encumbrance she'd been, apologizing for her own lack of sensitivity with a sincerity that left me quite humbled. She went on to say that she'd loved the time we had spent together, but she understood things were not always as they seem, and anyway, clearly that was over and done. Better to fondly remember what we had than to keep on crying as it got further and further away. She finished up, "If you ever find yourself wanting to give me a call, Milo, I'll always be pleased to hear from you. Who knows – perhaps this isn't the end? For now, at least, goodbye; thanks for all the happiness."

I still have this letter neatly stapled in my diary alongside various other bits of memorabilia that I couldn't let go of, each of them like so many curious butterflies, beautiful and dead in a faded collection. As I look over it now, it truly puts flesh upon one of the keenest regrets of my life: namely, the way that I ended my relationship with this kind and gentle girl, to whom I owed something far more than this. It couldn't be helped that I just wasn't that boy anymore, as much as I might wish for both our sakes that I could have been; it couldn't be helped that the life that had sprung up around me was changing me deep down inside. She had been instrumental in my salvation; her promise had catalysed me and pushed me to take ownership of my life, to make a start on my journey. But now, consciously or not, I knew that I wouldn't get to the places I still needed to see, learn the important lessons that my development required, with the easy comfort that she was beside me. It's no use regretting that this happened – that would be like regretting that night must come before a new day – but what I do regret is that it ended like this. Had I been less wilfully callous, less enrapt with this new life circus of crazy, I would have called her there and then and begged her to forgive me; but of course, I did not. Instead, I puffed myself up and convinced myself that I was casting her away with the bad old days, shedding her with the skin of that tired old Milo. Losing myself in arrogance and ambition, I just let her slide.

Life then went on at a hectic pace, and as Billy and I got closer and rode more and more in tandem, the balance in the house started to shift. Maybe because of the greater friction that our boisterousness caused, or perhaps just because he could, Billy decided we would strike out on our own, get the kind of pad that was more befitting of his true player status, and he started to look at alternative properties. I'd been really happy living here, but deep down, it rankled that Chloe knew where I'd come from: she looked at me sometimes as if she saw right through me and took my brash, spoilt behaviour for just what it was. Though I had in truth outgrown the single-bed box room, mostly it was the fact I'd got so deep into Billy's lifestyle – so caught up in the glitter and the whirl – that if he was jumping, then it was only natural that I wanted to follow.

One evening, almost as if we were acting out some long-sought revenge, we just dropped it on the girls that we would be off, right there and then. Thinking it would be a wheeze that would leaven the moment, we merrily threw handfuls of cash up into the air – cash to the tune of our month's share of rent – but even as we watched with stupid grins on our faces as it cascaded down on to the settee and settled over the lounge carpet, our gag itself fell flat. The girls' shock and disappointment was plain to see, but we just ignored it, telling ourselves as we left that we'd fulfilled all our obligations and giving no thought to the problem of replacing us as we moved ourselves and our few packed boxes into a taxi waiting outside. As for Elsie, I suppose I really didn't care: she was always going to live her life at arm's length from the people around her; but the raw sting of Chloe's pain was not so easily denied. It seems incredible that I hadn't at all expected this – had thought that a betrayal of this order could have had any other result. I guess that's the measure of my self-centred ignorance. Though she tried to cover her feelings by adopting a mask of defiance, the hurt and disappointment were easily visible on her face, her expression devoid of her usual happy calm and so strangely incongruous. Hanging back from our leaving in the doorway, she didn't even come forward to say goodbye, and along with a chapter of our lives, the front door slammed in our faces.

I loved what I considered the grandeur of our new place, even if it was a dilapidated grandeur – a fact that, naive as I was, I managed subconsciously to ignore. My room, for instance, had an en suite bathroom, but as the year rolled on, it became freezing: it was actually a badly converted outside toilet. The proportions were good though, and I especially liked the feel of space that we got from the unusually high ceilings. Billy chose a room with a view that spanned right across the communal gardens. Our rooms both opened on to the lounge, which he equipped with the latest TV and hi-fi bought especially for the occasion. Picked for our parties, the place was an open house, and just stepping outside our bedroom doors meant taking a piece of twenty-four-hour chaos. There was always a crowd there, whether large or small; there were always candles burning, among other things, and music playing. Though I loved the idea that I was living life like some kind of party soldier, I quickly fell in love with my indispensable earplugs.

As the weeks and months wore on, I found that more and more I longed for respite – for the sanctuary of Chloe's maternal consideration – and I started running, taking myself away from the mayhem for an escape into peaceful bliss, where the tapping of my trainers on the tarmac became, for my mind, like the lullaby of the road. I lost myself to the thoughts of that old place, thinking of Camden and wondering at how impossibly long ago the short months since then seemed. Inevitably, when I got back from my fresh-air excursions, I felt quite virtuous, my body invigorated, with its exercise dues paid and the cobwebs well and truly blown away. Buoyed by the pheromones, I'd jump in with whoever was in situ, whatever was going down, all the while telling myself how good it was I was keeping the right kind of balance. By my standards, the drinking was getting pretty savage: it seemed that no sooner had I carried a bag of fresh ice up the rickety wooden stairs from the chest freezer in the basement, we needed another to serve as clinking accompaniment in the tumblers we quaffed. Bottles of that old black whiskey stacked up on the lounge windowsill at an alarming rate, each one a design classic and a misguided badge of honour.

More often than not, the mass evenings culminated with us slumped in a drunken stupor, a state which my co-host and I took no little part in engineering; liberal measures both of encouragement and alcohol poured until a blanketing fog of unknowing rested upon the crew that remained. By this stage, we probably spilled more than we drank, but we kept our feet down right through to oblivion. Not everyone wanted to go all the way at first, and not everyone came with restraint all abandoned; but the call from the other side was too strong, and no matter how resolute the abstemious, we rarely failed to win them around – too great the temptation on offer and too easy to find a rich vein of pleasure. As soon as we'd sparked up each little party, any doubts that lingered would be suddenly forgotten, the genius suggestion accepted as the brilliant idea it now seemed – at least till the morning. The nights were our focus, and we pushed them to carry us as far as they could. What did it matter if our beds didn't see too much of us? What concern was it whether we managed to stir ourselves from the sofa or the living-room floor? We took these thoughts with us in the not-so-early hours as we crawled wasted under our covers, searching for the comfort of one final reverie, one final slip to a place with some rest before the shock of the alarm clock rang the time for a drag to the office.

These marathon evenings were starting to catch up with me at work, and it was a good thing that as a lowly junior I didn't have much responsibility: I couldn't have handled it. Sometimes, and not always due to my state of rest, I had but a thin grasp of what was going on around me, even finding the explanations quite baffling. However, I got on well with the others and was extremely happy to be right there in the thick of things, whatever that meant – whether running out for the lunches, reparking the bosses' cars, getting the coffees, or whatever else was needed on the desk at the time.

The mates I'd made in my brief spell downstairs thought I was living the life fantastic, and they puffed me up for my so-called legendary lifestyle; but when it came down to it, I really wasn't doing myself any favours. I almost always managed to get in to my seat on time, but quite often I was still in a mess. At my best, I was never as awake as I should have been. If I got stuck on a problem that I couldn't easily resolve – a checking query or a position that just wouldn't balance – I'd get moody and bitter, and I hardly gave the impression of an aspirant for junior dealer. I got caught sleeping in an empty office a couple of times after especially ferocious all-nighters, and this had the beginnings of a bad reputation, if not with Billy's dealer mates then with partners at the firm who really did matter. Once I even got caught dozing under a table in a meeting room. I got myself a warning for pretending, blearily and unconvincingly, that I'd been there looking for something at the boss's behest. I was lucky to get off as lightly as I did. The truth is I was totally caught up in the flow. The two-hour "power naps" and the late nights that followed became a self-perpetuating cycle, one of deathly fatigue or light-headed elation, one I found too strong to break from and was too weak to want to, too much in thrall of the pack running ahead of me, behind me, and all around me.

Thus passed the dark winter, and it was now early spring, a Saturday morning about six months after we'd first moved into the apartment. Awareness came with Billy crashing through my bedroom door to wake me in the way that he'd grown accustomed: gripping my shoulders with pumping hands and shaking my head on the pillow. It wasn't the best way to wake up, but he just didn't seem to get it. He was still wired, as usual, from his antics the previous evening, but there was no time for pause as he continued seamlessly to link more nights and days. It was slowly dawning on me that we no longer communicated on any substantial level, and though our relationship was an easy one, I was starting to understand that we subsisted on superficiality and innuendo. There had always been down periods of relative normality with Billy before, but they seemed seldom now. Having eased off the party thing a little, I regarded our habitual goings-on through somewhat more sober eyes and realized with a kind of astonishment that his weekend was pretty much a sixty-hour party roll. I accepted that no matter how hard I tried, I couldn't keep on going the way he did, and if only to myself, I was ready to admit that I didn't even want to. I naturally was drawn towards Billy from that first time we met. I was ripe for some new influence on my person that would lead me further away from the old, discredited Milo of my adolescence, and everything that he stood for completely fit the bill – not least that cast-iron confidence he so effortlessly wore and his boundless, heroic appetite for party-time chaos. But after having spent all this time immersed properly in his world, having really drunk in the water, so to speak, the insider's view had turned claustrophobic.

At least a few times a week, our local office haunt would end up properly heaving, and at closing time, the crowd would often break out to a club or a disco, and though some of the seniors could be a bit sniffy with juniors like me hanging on – those of us that were male, anyway – Billy was my pass, and the association with him made things a lot easier. Knowing my place in the scheme of things also helped, but I didn't mind: with the company credit cards always behind the bar, limitless in their liberality, it was a great place to unwind.

Friday nights here always seemed a little slower than the other ones, the dealers coming over the road from the office in their twos and threes for just one or two and maybe another; but this particular Friday night, it didn't seem to be slowing down. By about 8 p.m., I felt I'd had enough, despite the urgings of Billy's intensive training programme, but even as I slipped away before things got too messy, part of me didn't really want to go at all, and I remember turning on the steps and looking back wistfully through the doorway as the dying rebel in me nearly stayed my stride. There I saw Billy standing on a stool right in the middle of the brouhaha with the crowd all around him, his arms outstretched like a crazed conductor and his face a picture of supercharged mania. I turned away and left with a fresh sense of resignation, and indeed my body must have been craving some real sleep, as I crashed out as soon as I got home.

Here I was now, waking blearily compliant under my flatmate's vigorous urgings and feeling much better rested for the swim I'd just had in sleep's deep oasis, stretching and taking in the welcoming glow shining through the window from the morning outside.

"You are one lucky fella," he told me, and I grinned, nodding agreement. "Stop!" he exclaimed. "Fool, I haven't told you why yet." I awaited further explanation as he paused for effect. "Tonight," he went on dramatically, "you shall accompany me to an elite dinner party where we shall have wine, women, and spliff, but not necessarily in that order: Tracy has invited some of the boys back to her place." I frowned as I searched my mind for an idea of whom he was referring to, recalling after a few seconds that Tracy was one of the girls who was often in the bar where we drank – a really striking one too. Seeing from my smile that I'd got the association, he went on to say that he'd kindly accepted for me.

Despite the semi-restorative evening I'd just enjoyed, there was something in the anticipation of another big one that didn't thrill me. At least a dinner party sounded a bit more subdued and a bit more appealing, but even so, I couldn't help letting my head sink back into the pillow with a sigh.

Billy feigned a look of disappointment and shook his head at my apparent lack of enthusiasm. "Mate," he chided, "work hard, play hard. You know the score. You know it makes sense." So saying, he went to pass back out through the door but turned as he did so to poke his head back round at me. "Taxi comes at seven thirty," he said, "and dress smart, Leonard – bon vest and all that." With a wink, he was gone.

We'd already had a couple of drinks as we sat waiting for the taxi in the lounge, Billy waxing lyrical about the previous evening and assuring me that tonight was going to be mental, when the sound of the buzzer announced that our transport was here. Calling into the entry phone that we were on our way out, I couldn't help but notice how particularly unkempt was the driver's appearance: the distended picture's black-and-grey face beadily stared out at us through the video entry phone that we passed in the hall, a vision with dead, hollow eyes and his chin all covered with untidy tufts of little grey hairs. Billy kept up a constant dialogue on the brick of a work mobile as he sat slouched beside me in the back of the cab, his right leg crossed awkwardly over his left, reminding me of a Count Dracula on stilts with his long dress coat hanging unbuttoned around him. As the taxi moved on, the noise of his chatting faded into the background, and speeding up the hill to Highgate, I noticed the little alcohol buzz playing its games in my head. My eyes were fascinated by the unfamiliarity of East Finchley's provincial scenery once we'd crossed the A1 – the local boutique cinema whose showings I'd seen advertised in the *Time Out* listings, the Stag pub on the corner where I thought I must have gone once before, probably the furthest into North London before this evening I'd yet ventured as an adult – and all of it passing me by in a blur of lighting and windows. I started again to feel tired, and it got me to wondering what on earth I was doing here. Make no mistake – the life I was living was close to one that I'd always dreamt of, but something about it did not feel right. Deep down, I knew there was something discordant. Some little part of me I'd somehow left behind and forgotten was fighting back and telling me that I'd never be entirely happy this way. Perhaps the tension this created, the constant background hum of resistance, was gradually wearing me low.

Now we were crossing above the iconic North Circular which, as a child, I'd always heard referenced. To my ears then, it had seemed like some legendary road in a far-distant land, and reaching it now felt strangely unsettling. Clearly, it was a blessing that we were looking down on that dismal river of stationary cars spewing their murky exhaust as we travelled freely above, albeit held temporarily for a red light. At least it wasn't ours to be held prisoner by that awful, stagnant line, but the air was now heavier and so was my mood. I didn't know how much further we were heading, and I still wasn't really up for tonight. I certainly didn't feel the gratitude that I knew Billy thought was his due. Actually, I felt peeved, as if it were me doing him the favour just by being here, and at the same time I was troubled by a sense that seemed to be steaming up from the cars below, a sense that somehow by coming so far from my comfort zone I was exposing myself to unspecified danger.

"Fuck," I said. "What am I doing here?" I was speaking more or less to myself, but Billy shot me an eye, and picking up on my resentment, he gestured with a finger and an angry frown that he'd be taking this up with me in a moment. I breathed a long sigh.

"Got to go ... Yeah, sort out the troops," he laughed. "Yeah, see you later," and with that he ended the call and fixed me with a glare. "What is up with you, Mo? Get a grip on yourself. You look like someone just ran over your dog."

"What's it all about, Billy?" I complained. "We go out, we get messed up; we go home, we get messed up. I'm tired! I don't know what I'm doing anymore. Surely there is something more than this?"

He shook his head, but he wasn't laughing. "Mate, get a grip. This is the dream you're living. The parties, the drinks – drinks that someone else is paying for, mind, just like these company cabs. Were we not sent here precisely for this?"

He was into a sermon and getting quite animated, and it wasn't a big car. I suppose I did feel a bit guilty at my lack of *joie de vivre*. He seemed so pissed off with me that I started to wonder if he might contrive to teach me a lesson and see my prayers answered, and when it came to it, I didn't want the very things I was complaining about suddenly to come to an end. Unnervingly, I noticed throughout Billy's torrent that the driver was eyeing me in the mirror, a silent, frozen chuckle fixed there upon his grim face. "You think there is something more?" Billy went on. "Like what? Relationships? Don't make me laugh. We've both been there. Look at those saddos in the office with their fiancées and wives and whatever. Before you know it, you can't even go out and have a laugh with your mates. First it's the week nights and then the weekend. Next you've got kids who bleed what little life there is left out of you." I stayed silent, and he started to calm down a bit. "Maybe later, maybe when we're fifty years old and we've done all our living, but for now you better get this straight and start enjoying the ride. There is nothing better. A truly rational mind can conceive nothing greater than this," he said, now with a smile and putting his hand on my shoulder. "If you can't enjoy all of this," he said, widening his arms as if to embrace our entire lifestyle, "there must really be something wrong with you."

88 Lines About 44 Women

We arrived in the cab at almost exactly eight o'clock, as smartly punctual as we were dressed. Just as we were stepping out on to the pavement, I saw Andy and Dave alighting from their taxi on the other side of the road. Like Billy, they were market makers at our place, authentic animals of the trading floor, though in Andy's case the description was not merely figurative. He was genuinely one of the barrow-boy crop from Essex, and as colourful as he was with his words, legend had it that he could be just as creative with his fists, with a famously short fuse to boot. Here was one person you really did not want to mess with, and I always liked to give him the widest possible berth. If you didn't know him, you could think that he was just very funny. Indeed, he had a quick sense of humour and, like Billy, was always up for a laugh; but even at his best, there was a darker side lurking, and he was ominously unpredictable, snorting and scraping like a restless beast. Having actually seen him lose it a couple of times had inspired in me a well-founded terror. He was highly regarded at the firm, as he made good money. Consequently, when he had a few too many and ended up straying a little over the line or, more often than not, completely ignoring it, a designated hush-hush team swung into action to help make those little misunderstandings somehow go away. Catching sight of him, I let out a quiet groan which Billy chose to ignore: clearly he'd not mentioned that Andy might be coming on purpose, knowing I'd most likely have declined.

"You boys actually made it then," said Billy, puffing up large as they came bowling over the road towards us. "Up for the crack tonight then, are we? After last night, I didn't think you'd still be up for it." The boys clasped hands and slapped each other on the back as I stayed off a deferential couple of metres, looking about me to see if there might be anything

I recognized in the area. The closed up Kwik-Fit opposite with its blue and yellow sign was the only mark that was vaguely familiar.

"Don't you worry, Bill, my son," said Andy. "We'll be leaving the crack all for you. Just thought we'd come along and watch you harpoon it," he laughed, before glancing over at me with a little nod that seemed friendly enough. "I see you brought along your wing man," he said, again addressing Billy. "He'll be holding your slacks for you, will he?" he laughed again, giving me a wink which seemed to indicate that I should be laughing too. "But you better stop fucking about tonight and put it to the sword, eh? Else word will be that you ain't got one."

"Not wrong, Andy," said Dave, joining the fun. "Longest mating dance I've ever witnessed. You must be losing your touch, mate!" he quipped. Dave too was very much a part of the senior set, but he was one who always came over as approachable, even if he was somehow a little more so when Andy wasn't about.

"Yeah, well, we'll see," said Billy. "We shall see," and passing off the banter with a shrug that was the very epitome of cool disinterest, he made his way through the hedge that marked the property's border, going down the path to the big front door. "We certainly shouldn't abandon hope," he added enigmatically over his shoulder.

Following behind him, I looked up at the brick building before us and noted how the unusual circular structure was unlike anything else around here. Actually, it was unlike any structure I was familiar with, seeming to give no clue as to when it might have been established. Simultaneously it appeared both contemporary and aged, and apart from a little bit of ivy that crept around from behind it, the impression it made was plain and nondescript. Billy's hand hovered over a buzzer labelled "Basement Flat" in red biro letters, and after pausing for a moment, turning his head again to see the other two following down the path behind us, he firmly pressed the bell. After a couple of moments, a girl's voice called out from the intercom, "Come on down, boys. Go to the right and then follow the stairs."

We pushed ourselves in as the buzzer sounded and found a reconstructed entrance hall, the smell of new carpet there mingling with an odour of freshly collected mud. An upturned mountain bike was leaning against a wooden radiator cabinet, its seat and handlebars standing amid a scattering of free newspapers which, along with some shiny coloured fliers, littered the floor, the latter extolling the delights of a local takeaway. Four grey letter boxes hung up on the wall beside the entrance to the basement stairway. The front door drew closed behind us with a heavy metal click.

Coming last down the stairs, I saw Tracy looking out from her flat and holding open her in-swinging door. I'd seen her often around the bar by our office, and though we'd only spoken on the odd occasion, you didn't need much prompting to emblazon her on your memory: she was close to six feet tall and absolutely stunning. Usually she wore jeans and a T-shirt – a ripped pair of high cut-off denim shorts that she had worn on one very hot day last summer I remembered especially well – but tonight she had really dressed up. She was sporting a dress, red and sleeveless, and hardly very much of it: the cut-down back which showed off the slimness of her body was so low that it literally took my breath away. Her light-tanned skin looked smooth and perfect, and her black, shiny hair reminded me of that Uma Thurman bob in *Pulp Fiction,* only a little longer.

Billy might have set his cap at her, but to me she was about as accessible as a picture in a magazine, so totally out of my league that I couldn't imagine her as the quarry of mortals. It wouldn't have dawned on me that I could possibly have anything that a girl like that would be interested in. As the boys mucked around making their entrance, I waited behind and, lost in admiration, was immediately absorbed, staring at the rose tint of her cheeks and the sparkle in her eyes, which were dark like her hair.

Suddenly, I realized they'd already gone in and she was standing there waiting for me, still holding the door. Whenever I'd seen her before, I'd always been protected from the full force of her charisma, hidden in the company of my colleagues – in the noise and the testosterone and the fury of the bar – but caught cold in her gaze now, there was no place to hide. I froze in the headlights of her presence undiluted. She smiled with a faint hint of laughter on her face, a look of amused curiosity, and I stood there winded and mute as if my powers of speech had all gone, managing only to utter a grunt as eventually I staggered awkwardly towards her, bending like a minor under her outstretched arm that was still keeping open the door. She went to kiss my cheek as I did so but caught me instead on the side of my head, and she let out a laugh. The cloud of her perfume set my head spinning, and moving beyond her into the flat, I didn't look back, chased inside by the burn of her stare I imagined upon me.

Turning in from the hallway, I was amazed by the size of the dining room. In fact, the whole interior completely belied how dull the place looked from outside, everything the opposite of what subconsciously I'd been expecting. It was much larger than our place, and the decoration was opulent. The colour scheme was a spectrum of reds that ranged from terracotta in the hallway to light, watery pink in the dining room I'd just entered. A grand wooden table was laid for ten with matching sets of silver candelabra, place mats, every conceivable piece of cutlery, and exquisite matching glasses. I looked about the yawning gallery, and my eyes were drawn to the fireplace in the corner, alight and throwing out considerable heat. Billy and the others were already rapping together, swanning about the room nonchalantly and playing it cool, but I couldn't have even if I'd wanted to: I'd never been anywhere that looked this good before, like a grand hotel or the very best restaurant. The quality of everything and the attention to detail struck me as remarkable, and I gazed about from one sight to another, trying to take it all in.

Tracy lived here with three other girls, two of whom she'd been at university with. Caroline and Nancy were sisters whom I also recognized, having seen them occasionally with Tracy in our bar, and the fourth introduced herself to me as Alison as she went about offering drinks from a big silver tray. The four of them busied themselves coming in and out of the dining room, splitting their time between here and the kitchen. Having taken a glass of something pale and bubbly, I'd allowed myself to be drawn for a moment away from the others, leaving them to their banter as my curiosity got the better of me and going across the room for a closer look at the little *objets d'art* that I'd spied upon a low wooden cabinet. The ornamental figurines were quaint, but what really caught my imagination as I approached was a framed set of black-and-white pencil drawings which decorated the wall above the antique sideboard. These pictures were strange and foreboding, barren and hopeless, and they weren't at all the kind of thing that I'd have chosen to live with. The first depiction was of a kind of forest, but the tree limbs twisted from the wood into anguished human forms, with representations of angels and demons rising from the trunks beneath. The next seemed at first like a landscape, but on closer inspection I realized it was a sea of heads. The bodies, out of sight, were submerged under a waveless pool, with the water level at different points up the various faces: some showed from just under the chin, while others, excruciatingly, were almost overwhelmed past the base of the nose. The third and final scene was an expanse of desolation: naked bodies of women and men strewn listless about the ground as far as the eye could see, abject and yet resigned in an eternity of waiting.

The sound of the buzzer drew me back above, and turning away from the wall, I saw Alison setting off with a look of childish delight on her face. "Mark's here," she announced as she cantered to the door, and observing her, it struck me how adorned she was, in contrast to Tracy, with a matching necklace and bracelet set, her diamond earrings sparkling and looking expensive. Though probably only an inch or so shorter than me, she was the littlest of the four girls who shared the flat, and her most obvious feature was a fine head of wavy ginger hair, the few freckles above her nose completing a complimentary caricature. She disappeared into the corridor, and for a few moments, I could hear her giddy noises of welcome from the hallway. Shortly after, a tallish guy entered the room and stood before us dressed in a black dinner jacket, a white dress shirt, and a black bow tie. His hair was the exact same shade as Alison's, and it was immediately obvious that he was her brother. Andy was the closest as he entered, and he fronted up to him in an embarrassingly alpha way.

"Where's the wedding?" he snarled, betraying not a hint of humour. For what seemed like a long few seconds, they regarded each other with no further words exchanged, the whole room suddenly static and soundless as time stood still, the air's electricity at once running dark. Appearing at the doorway, with the briefest flicker of alarm, Alison paused and registered them before breaking the impasse.

"Andy," she said tentatively, "you've not met my brother, Mark, I think?"

"Ali said the company was exclusive," Mark responded warmly, taking her cue, "so we thought it best to play it safe. One can't ever be too smart, don't you think?" So saying, he looked over his shoulder to the girl who had entered with Alison – as it turned out, his girlfriend, Yvonne, who was dressed as formally as he was – before looking back and offering Andy his hand. There was a momentary hiatus.

"Any brother of Alison's ..." said Andy, now grinning or at least showing his teeth though without evident warmth as he accepted Mark's hand. Grateful, the room again stood at ease.

"Tracy, darling," said Mark as she now approached him, taking the opportunity which the armistice presented of moving herself between the newly resolved foes. "You look absolutely wonderful," he said as he kissed her in greeting, "just as you always do. Now, you must introduce me properly to these lovely friends."

Seated around the long table, we nibbled on olives and munched crostini sticks, talking among ourselves as the girls continued to bustle in and out, sitting down with us for a moment, or refilling glasses, or generally tending to their various duties. It was hard to keep track of them as they buzzed about, appearing from the kitchen now tied with an apron that hadn't been there before, a wooden spoon or a spatula in hand which had just been making itself useful. Billy and I sat opposite each other at the end of the table furthest from that busy door, with Tracy, when she wasn't engaged and absent in the kitchen, between us at the end. Opposite her at the head of the table sat Andy, his immense ego thus well catered for. Alison sat on his left, and he had Dave, appropriately, on his right, with Mark's girlfriend Yvonne next to Dave and Mark opposite her and next to his sister. Caroline and Nancy took the two remaining places next to me and Billy respectively. My flatmate seemed very well pleased with himself and satisfied with his position among the female company, but for my part, the little measure of isolation from our colleague at the other end was the biggest bonus. That man monopolized the conversation at his end, but we could pretty much keep out of it and chat quietly to each other; we were quite unaware of the atmosphere that was brewing between Andy and Mark.

The girls proved great company, and the two sisters seemed, outwardly at least, very different from each other. Caroline, beside me, was the quieter of the two, self-contained and almost demur. She was a painter, having studied fine art at university and coming away with a first. Finding this out about her surprised me, as I thought I could spot that type and she hadn't struck me at all in the way I would have expected. Rather than being flamboyant and full of herself and her artistry and treating me to a detailed account of the evolution of her gift, it was only when I pressed her that she told me of her time at St Martins, of her having lived and studied in Florence, and of her boyfriend there and how she'd taken her Italian competency to quite a high level. She was hardly effusive, but once she did start talking about painting, a sparkle lit up in her eye, and she told me how she liked to run before beginning work on any new project, how she went deep into her mind as the world travelled past her and life's noisy distractions just fell away. She didn't think of her distance or speed but just scanned and rescanned the beauty around her, cross-referencing the things she saw with her favourite pieces, which she kept in her memory in infinite detail, connecting herself with some fresh inspiration. She wasn't as tall as Tracy, but even without the heels she wore, she'd have been taller than me; and she wore her long blonde hair hanging straight down. She told me about her parents and all their good deeds, and I felt jealous of the admiration that she had for them. Her skin was pale, and her features were gentle, just like her demeanour, and through and through, she just seemed so kind, with an inner beauty that shone brighter the more we got talking, that I could easily tell she was a very special soul – the kind of woman you'd be lucky to love.

Nancy was the sportier of the two: it was she that had introduced Caroline to running, and she was also the more naturally outgoing. Studying with Alison at university, she had majored in biology, and meeting up there with Tracy, the three of them had shared digs together from the second year. Incongruously, her real passion was as a performance artist, and currently she was a troupe dancer working in a show in the West End. Billy was very much enjoying the banter with her, chiding her about what he described as "prancing about doing no good for no one" while she took it all in good humour and gave as good as she got.

I already knew from the few words that we had exchanged in the bar that Tracy was a student of some kind, and when I asked her now, re-presenting myself as something other than the blithering idiot she'd let into the flat, she elaborated that she'd majored in Computer Science and was continuing her studies with an M.A. in Advanced Computing at the University of London. I thanked her for the invite, and she said it was about time they repaid us for all the drinks we'd bought for them after work in the bar. It occurred to me then that being both beautiful and smart, she'd probably never had to buy herself a drink in any of the places she went to. As familiarity grew, the extreme effect she'd had on me earlier was wearing away: it's amazing how quickly we can recover from even the most stultifying situations, and she was so kind and friendly I found myself chatting to her easily and completely forgetting myself. I had to admit that I was starting to enjoy the evening.

Tracy got up to go to the kitchen for the umpteenth time to help her flatmates, who were now getting ready to bring out a starter. Slightly narrowing his eyes and raising his eyebrows, Billy fixed me with one of his knowing stares. "I see you're warming up to this now, eh, Mo?" he goaded me, smiling, alluding to my gaze, which had followed our host from the room.

With that incredible dress hanging in little spaghetti straps and exposing the entire length of her naked back – her shoulder blades and the little bumps that ran under her perfect skin right down her spine – I couldn't seem to help myself, staring each time at the bottom of the flat V where the back of the dress came together just below her hips, where it floated above the roundness of her buttocks. Trying to work out whether she was wearing any knickers was killing me. Again and again, I watched her leave, and I found myself obsessing over whether it was her back I was looking at or the flesh just below it. I was hopelessly drawn, and it wasn't only her leaving that brought consternation: the dress hung loosely and was just as revealing at the sides, and sitting beside me, each time she moved it revealed the soft flank of her breast. Each illicit glimpse excited me, startled me like a jolt of electricity; but having been brought up to act the gentleman, I really was trying to ignore my basest desires and avoid taking these cheap peeks at her. I didn't want to give way to my crudest desires, but though my nagging conscience was on heightened alert, trying to lift me from her thrall was a losing battle. Checked now by Billy's accusation, I could only admit my predicament, and

I laughed with him guiltily. Sharing this with him seemed to make it all right. Maybe I was getting more and more obvious, but it was beyond my control.

"You can think about me ploughing that later," he said under his breath, leering, "when you're knocking one out in front of the mirror." The crudeness of his words stunned me, and I looked around quickly, relieved to confirm that the girls were still absent. It was as if his unapologetic baseness managed to spike a bit of conscience into me, and suddenly the depths of my voyeuristic depravity felt shameful.

"Don't look at me like that! Don't even try to tell me that you don't know what this is all about; I can smell it on you. The whole point of living is to get what you want and not make excuses – to eat from the best tables and smash the plates afterwards. Tell me you can ever get enough of this," he said, looking around at the table and the glasses of wine, nodding with a wink at the girls' seats that were still empty around us. There was too much truth in what he was saying to allow for any rebuttal. Having nothing to come back with, I remained silent, confounded and found out. "No," he said, "of course you can't. So better take all you can – as much and as often as possible – and don't try to tell me we're different. You'll see, Milo: you won't end up regretting the things you've done – only the birds that you haven't!"

As if on cue, the girls appeared in procession, each bearing a tray of steaming hot bowls. The cauliflower soup was exquisitely spiced with pepper and garlic and other things that I couldn't put my finger on, the smell quite unlike that of the mundane vegetable I'd been expecting. We ate from white china bowls decorated with a grey rim and a light and dark blue pattern with a flower and a spear of diamonds at each of the four corners, and these our hosts placed down gently upon dinner plates of the same design, which were in turn on matching chargers; thus the set was complete. Once Tracy sat, we started to apply ourselves, paying the chef for such a subtle and warming delight the compliment of our silence, engrossed in our starter as we sipped the hot liquid from beautifully rounded spoons.

Up at the other end of the table, a conversation was picking up between Mark and Andy, and we listened as we supped. Mark had begun by asking how we'd come to be acquainted with his sister. Alison told him that her flatmates had met us in the bar that we frequented and added that we worked nearby as investment bankers. Mark responded to this information by turning to Andy and asking what this actually entailed.

"You mean, like, what do we do, Mark?" was Andy's rather unfriendly retort, seemingly uninterested in the soup but falling upon Mark's question with something like real hunger. "Tell me, what do you do, mate?" he shot back.

"I run an art gallery called Lucien's just off the King's Road. Perhaps you've heard of it?"

"Nah, I don't think so. Not really my thing, art and all that."

"Well, quite," said Mark. "I'm afraid that I know as much about what you do as you know about what I do, but I hear so much about investment banking nowadays, and it would be great to learn about it from the horse's mouth, so to speak."

Andy held his gaze for a moment as if he thought Mark was taking the mickey, and then, looking around almost theatrically at the others who were looking up at him from their soup, he said, "You want to tell him what we do, Dave? Do you, Bill? No? All right, I'll tell you what we do, Mark. We do what real men do." He paused here pointedly. We'd all had quite a lot to drink by now, and Andy had been hitting the wine after necking his beers earlier. He'd also been in and out of the room almost as much as the girls had before dinner, and I could easily guess why. Not unusually, he was quite animated and exuding aggression, and though I admired Mark for keeping his composure in the seat which he must have felt was too near to Andy, even if he did have Alison as a break between them, it crossed my mind that he might not know what he was getting himself into. "We take what we want, Mark," Andy went on, "we give what we don't want, and we always tell it straight. Now there ain't much of that about today, is there?"

Mark looked perplexed. I couldn't tell whether he was aware that Andy's hackles were rising, though it would have been pretty hard not to be. I was grateful to be a mere spectator of this tête-à-tête, but it was an unnerving thing even to watch.

"Andy, sorry, I really don't catch your drift. Can you elaborate?" he asked. "What is it that you actually do?"

Unpredictable as ever, Andy seemed to soften, and he slipped into a textbook explanation that I found surprisingly enlightening. "We are market makers. Market makers make a market in things, providing a two-way price to facilitate either buying or selling for assets like gold or oil – or anything. In our case, it's equities – specifically shares of listed UK companies. The price or valuation that we apply is generally relative to a previous price and factors in such elements as the price of similar investments and changes in news flow and general market sentiment. On enquiry by a broker, we state at what price a particular stock can be purchased or sold, standing by our price for the duration of the enquiry. When we give out our price, we don't know whether we are talking to a buyer or a seller, and that's the tricky bit. If we buy right, we sell at a profit. If we sell right, we buy back at a profit. But if we get it wrong, we can lose millions, and you don't get to be in the business as long as I have, and Dave here, if you get it wrong too often. Ain't that right, boys?" he said, looking around.

Billy and Dave joined in, the conversation continuing along the lines of what a difficult and undervalued service they were providing, applying their above-average intellect and courage for the good of the free market and democracy – a treatise on machismo played to the table by the irresistible buccaneers they undoubtedly thought that they were.

While the boys were enjoying their self-congratulations, Tracy turned towards me and, to my embarrassment, caught me looking at her from the corner of my eye.

"Quite something, eh?" She smiled knowingly, and at first I assumed she was referring to what I'd been looking at, until she indicated Andy in full flow again down at the other end of the table. "He's such a gent," she went on, her tone neutral enough that I wasn't really sure where she was coming from. "In the bar, he's there for everyone's gratification – wants everyone to have a good time – but up close, he can be kind of scary."

I agreed and mumbled something about not being very like the others.

"Oh really?" she said, sounding dubious. "You're somehow better, are you?"

"No," I said, shaking my head, "I don't mean it like that, but you said it yourself. I wouldn't go around making people feel uncomfortable the way some seem to thrive on. Look, I'm just not used to all this; maybe that's the difference. But what an evening you girls have laid on, what a show. I feel really privileged to be invited, by the way – thank you again – but the last thing I'd want to do to repay such kindness would be to create a bad atmosphere. Your flatmates, Ali's brother – they all seem so nice, and it's always great to meet new people, different people, but I feel embarrassed tonight to be associated with ... you know ... it's just bad manners."

"What about all this macho stuff then? I thought all you guys had to be the same just to get the job done."

"Well, we don't all buy into that," I lied, not wanting to admit that I was a long way from reaching the kind of status that the other boys had achieved, that the risk, the shouting, and the cojones were ambitions that I could still only dream of. Perish the thought of her finding out how lowly my role really was – a glorified booking clerk with coffee responsibilities. She'd probably take away my soup! "But when the markets close," I continued, "we're all here just trying to get on with our lives, aren't we? The least we owe each other is a bit of respect, a bit of civility." She smiled but said nothing, her brown eyes seeming to look right through me as she flashed her white teeth. I was unable to bear her silence, so I stuttered on. "I ... isn't that what we all want?" I protested a bit too strongly. "You have a beautiful place here, by the way. I've said that already, I guess." Again she stayed mute, still hitting me with that smile which made me feel I was shrinking before her. Starting to feel my earlier sense of panic reawakening, I pointed to the drawings on the wall behind. "Whose are they?" I almost croaked. For a moment, she looked beyond me to where I had pointed, and then she looked back.

"You like them?" she asked, again inscrutable.

"Um, they're interesting but a bit scary – a bit dark, no? I don't know much about art," I apologized.

"They're mine," she said, looking back over at them. "Illustrations from *The Inferno* which was one of the texts we did for A level. My parents gave them to me when I moved in here." The smile on her face was gone, and now she looked serious, almost sad. It was the first time I'd seen something other than a reflection of inner control in her features. "They always puts things into perspective, I think – remind me where we really are and how the different levels of sin are always within us and around us. All this talk of some other place, of there being something more than this, is just a distraction, a way of forgetting that this is it and there is nothing more, that there's nothing truly beautiful in this world that doesn't have a measure of ugliness behind it."

"Rubbish!" I blurted. "How can you say that? Just looking at you, I know there must be a God somewhere." My eagerness had run away with itself, and I blushed to have heard myself let out something so crass; but instead of scorning me, she gave a happy laugh and put her hand on my arm, and I felt a little squeeze which ran like a shock through the parts of my body.

"You're funny," she said. "I like you. Maybe you are different from the others."

Cocaine

I can still remember her telling me that she liked me and that I wasn't like the others, and I remember too how odd her words sounded at the moment when I heard them – how out of place was the calm, matter-of-fact look with which she returned my questioning gaze, seemingly insistent on some strange premonition. It crossed my mind that perhaps I'd misunderstood her intention and that she'd meant it rather as a prelude to some cheap joke that was now brewing, but she did not laugh or retract what she'd said and her words grew between us. Their meaning overtook me, and the world seemed infused for the moment with this newly surreal notion, one that confounded my idea of a neat current order with its undertone that hinted that maybe, somehow, I could really be a part of it.

I love gazing back wistfully at my life's favourite memories, and there are special times of the year when I always find myself lured by the temptation. New Year's Eve always is one of them, along with my birthday, nights that are so steeped with inherent meaning, coming like starred annual signposts, that they're perfect for the narcissistic ritual of wandering back through the files in my mind to dwell upon them. I always find her amid my highlighted memories in the scene of that evening that became so precious because of where it would take me. With a great deal of satisfaction, I recall her magical words, attended now by the glory of what was to come, in just the same way that watching an Arsenal victory replayed on the television comes wrapped in the comfort of knowing the result.

For longer than we can remember, we live our lives to find the very sentiment that she expressed to me there, the unparalleled prize of acceptance – to hear that we're valued and to find that we're safe. Perhaps it's because that night was an exception that it sticks out so in my mind: things are not always the way that we read them. Sometimes our hopes and desires mislead us, and more and more, I realize how others beguile. The more innocent we are, the more naive, and the more plainly we speak, the more easily the petty intrigues of others can deceive us. Those of us who give vent unguarded to our true emotions are most likely to be played for fools.

It was the earliest hours of a happy New Year, and I was just making my way back home from the Professor's house. A few of us had gone round there together to join the celebration. Penny and I were there, along with another couple, we with our two boys though for the first year without A.J., as she had her own plans, they with their two littler sons. I mustn't forget Mum, of course, who was always up for a party. With the New Year rung, a last heady nightcap with the host delayed my leave taking, and finding as I said my goodbyes that the rest of our party had gone on before me, I got it in mind to make up ground on them. Full to the top of this evening's cheer, I was on quite a buzz and figured that it would be a wheeze to head them off by taking the railway crossing that was further down the line, so I walked beyond the one I would usually take and which I knew my quarry would have used minutes earlier. Though it may not have looked that way, I felt steady enough within myself; and when, after a minute or so, I came upon a couple who seemed to be hanging out on the pavement, a girl and a boy in their late teens or maybe early twenties, I was careful in going around them so as not to cause any concern. Pleased that I'd successfully negotiated my legs and my body through this physical challenge, I went just a few steps further before the boy's voice rang out behind me.

"Oi, mate," I heard him call, "can you just hold on a moment?"

With the mission at the forefront of my mind, I wasn't thrilled about the prospect of any delay, but I didn't feel I could politely refuse. Pulling up, I turned to look over my shoulder, wondering what he wanted. The pair of them were now a small distance apart, ambling slowly towards me. He was the first to speak.

"Didn't you beat me up about twenty minutes ago?" he enquired as they halted about five feet away.

Dark memories of a singular adolescent nightmare began to pervade my mind and spread their tendrils around me through the still night air. It was a lifetime since I'd even recalled the incident, so many years having elapsed that I furrowed my brow to accept that the memory as prompted was really my own, yet the evil stirrings came nonetheless in echoes of menace through the tunnel of time. What could have persuaded me, I wondered, that it might be a good idea to return to my old comprehensive school for a disco – to that miserable place of torment which I'd left only a few months earlier when I'd moved up to the grammar school? Perhaps it was that Christine had asked me to go along there with her. Though we were still only children, there was some kind of mysterious subplot between us which, despite the confusion it brought, was excitement and lure. In the back of my mind, I might have had misgivings about going, but ultimately I suppose I just thought my shadowy fears were unfounded and convinced myself that it would be just like those childish affairs I was used to at home: a disco like the annual ones I'd been to with the local children, who all came together with the music on their minds, living in the protected bubble of rural village innocence as we did. Somehow, despite all the unhappiness I'd experienced for being around them during the two school years previous, I failed to take into account that those rougher kids I'd tried hard to avoid, that prosaic breed with their mean agendas, might be in attendance. This seems to me now a clear example of a particular feature of my personality, one I wasn't even aware of until someone else pleased with my weakness pointed it out to me, whereby my natural hope and optimism can trump my experience, leaving my expectations much higher than the harsh reality for which I should be prepared.

Details of that evening are mostly long lost, and the dark fragments that do remain are like the pieces of some broken and jagged collage: even back then, I think much of what passed came quickly to be hidden by the crash of events, the unfolding whirlwind that would blow to my core. I'm sure the night began as unremarkably as these nights do, and I do remember being in the hall and enjoying what felt like a prodigal return as the music started up, smiling and happy and enjoying being there as I basked in the attention that my presence was creating in a room filled mainly with girls. I enjoyed the sense of achievement and triumph that came from having moved on – feelings that during the time I spent there would have been strangers to me. I think I danced a bit and felt secretly proud of how I was able to let myself go. Then, a little while into the evening, in a momentary lull when for some reason I was standing on my own, a boy I didn't know approached me with a message: I was wanted outside. Imagining to myself that this must be the beginning of some sort of romantic adventure, I followed him willingly. I didn't for a second perceive that this was something far darker. As I say, despite the lessons that I should have gleaned from those terms that I had spent here, malice and evil were far from my mind.

Out through the doors and around the side of the building we went giddily along the path at the top of the bank until we came upon a large crowd that had assembled. A sense of anticipation was in the air, an unspoken suggestion as people parted that they'd been waiting for me. *Wow,*

I thought to myself, *what a return tonight is going to be. There's even a crowd here to witness whatever it is,* but as I looked around to see if I could recognize anyone, a rough-looking boy whose face was vaguely familiar kept getting in my way. Now, as I continued to scan the faces around me for a friendlier one, he kept his hand on my shoulder. *What craziness is this?* I thought to myself, still somewhat excited even as my confusion grew deeper.

"You beat up my little brother," I heard him tell me, but I hardly bothered to take any notice of such a ludicrous statement, continuing to look around for a clue that would give the game away. Having been taught from a young age that fighting was never an answer to anything and that I should rather remove myself than be caught up in some kind of physical confrontation, I'd never so much as lifted my fists.

"You beat up my little brother, didn't you?" he insisted, and absently I tried to dismiss him again, still not getting it and still wondering when I'd find out who had called for me here. Next thing the little brother himself was presented, a boy I'd never seen before, perhaps a year or two younger than me, whom the crowd had pushed forward – somewhat hesitantly, it seemed, from the look on his face.

"You're going to let him hit you," the senior said to me, "and you better not hit him back." I didn't understand, but things seemed to be taking a nightmarish turn, the night transformed into darkness and strangers and threat. He had my full attention at last.

"You've made a mistake," I told him. "I haven't beaten up anyone. I didn't beat you up, did I?" I said to the littler one, imploring, looking from him to his brother and then back again. Suddenly a blow struck the side of my head, and turning around in dull surprise, I saw that the older boy's face looked twisted and terrible. He looked out of control.

"You've got the wrong person," I pleaded, hearing my voice now higher and not quite my own, yet still I was convinced that this was just an honest mistake and that if only I could reach him with the truth, the misunderstanding could be made to go away. The next punch came from the younger one, and I remember that it felt so weak compared to his brother's that it hardly registered. But then their blows came again and again, and staggering between the two of them, I still persisted in trying to disabuse them, trying to save them from the error they were making without even thinking of raising my arms for protection. Again and again, I got up from the ground as the night spun around me, the massed crowd making way as I fell and then lifting me up to push me back to my twin crazed aggressors. I remember that as I got up from the grass for the umpteenth time, I did finally see someone I knew, a girl I'd been at school with since we were infants.

"That's it, Milo," I heard her saying, her face seemingly beaming admiration and encouragement, "don't fight them back."

"I'm not going to!" I remember snapping back at her in anger – some words like that anyway, as if my retort could somehow vindicate and explain the horror and confusion I felt. I didn't understand anything of what was going on as the disorientating blows kept on coming. Eventually a teacher was there, and the crowd had disbursed, and someone was telling me off for fighting. My parents were somehow called and came from a party they were at to pick me up. I still didn't get it, mumbling how they'd got the wrong person as the blood was being dabbed from my cut, puffy mouth. We were told that I should be taken to hospital for a tetanus shot in case I got lockjaw, but we went straight home instead: the fear of this mortal infection would stay with me for the next twenty-four hours. Once Dad got a lid on his anger and remonstrated with the organizers, we drove away in silence as I sat licking my wounds in the back of the car, suddenly raw to something dark and malevolent in the world, too pressed by shame and humiliation to understand or even guess at the feelings of helpless disappointment I'd brought down on all of us.

The trauma of this night was kept from my conscious mind for a long, long time, and the useful growing that it could have inspired – the processing and internal development which would have taught me I had to stand up for myself and face life's challenges – would come only much later, once I'd been awakened to the secret that things very often are not as they seem. I walked with my head down after my disco humbling, but I think I was naturally timid even before. I remember how comforting it was to hear my older relatives tell me that roughness and fighting should not be for me: such things just didn't belong in my idea of my world, and on the odd occasion when violence did rear its head, I always was afflicted by disabling fear. We don't have to spend our lives fighting, but it's certainly true that any day can bring challenges, in all shapes and forms, and if we don't have the strength to do what is right – a strength born of confidence and hewn from experience and the lessons we've learned – we hardly deserve our place in society. Failure to accept our responsibilities, failure to prepare ourselves to stand up and face our challenges with courage and conviction, is the most debilitating path we can possibly take: we can't seek our honest path without it, and the life we end up with is merely a life that others allow.

I wasn't a coward in everything. One of my earliest memories is quite flush with pride: little more than a toddler, I pushed off from the side of a hotel swimming pool, bidden by Mum, who was trying to encourage a few of us – a buoyed group of infants clinging to the side in the warm-water pool – to trust the rubber rings we were wearing.

"Go on," she exhorted, but it seemed impossible to dare until some spark inspired me to launch myself just when she looked to have given up and was turning her attention to another among us. Pushing across the pool's corner, I surprised us both by being the first to make the leap on my own, and I remember that feeling of pride and revelation when my aid kept me afloat as I whooshed through the water towards the onrushing side. Pushing through our fears is the only remedy, but it's easier said than done. Whatever it is that ails us – whether it's a fear that keeps us from standing up for ourselves, or whether we're just afraid of admitting the truth that's right there before us, or whether it's a fear that inhibits the expression of those precious feelings that we bear in our hearts – courage is vital. "Faint heart never won fair lady" goes the saying, and there's nothing more true. What could be more intimidating than putting oneself out on a limb at the risk of rejection – risking the crushing of one's hopes and dreams and all that one is? This particular conquest of fear is literally the fight of our lives, and each of us is the living product of the self-same battle successfully fought going back through the ages.

Now here I was again. This insane sequel had been so long in coming that it was hardly even possible to believe it was what it seemed.

Is this really happening? I heard a voice ask in my head, but I did know the answer, and I took a good look at my would-be assailants as they stood there before me. He was about my height, perhaps, as was the girl, though both much younger and leaner. She looked excited, while he was confident and calm. Something about the way he stood convinced me this was indeed what I thought it was. Needless to say, despite his introductory question, he didn't have a mark on him – nothing at all that could indicate he'd been in any fight.

"You don't look very beaten up to me," I responded, somehow feeling a little pleasure that at least this time I wasn't a clueless innocent – that neither confused nor bewildered, I was able to call the lie, however unpleasant the consequences. They were close to me now and were closing yet further. Even though I knew what was occurring, I felt trapped in some insane dance, unsure of what to do next. Then suddenly I heard footsteps approaching, and another nightwalker was nearing the three of us from the direction I'd been travelling towards. Hearing him also, the boy and girl withdrew to a less obvious distance, and I spied my chance.

"Hold on, can you, mate?" I said, the very act of asking for help making me feel a little embarrassed. "There seems to be some funny business going on here." He looked up at us sideways as he passed, and without slowing, he put his head back down and gave it a shake, mumbling some excuse as he continued on his way.

Then he was gone, and the still night's silence once more descended. They were closing on me again and were too close for me to run. Any hope I'd had of avoiding this had left along with that passing stranger, and I knew that whether I liked it or not, it was about to happen. My thinking was indistinct and a blur of emotion, but I did know that I wasn't just going to be passive this time. If I was to be a victim, then at least I wouldn't be complicit. They were just a car's width away when suddenly I raised myself towards them and let out a growl.

"Come on then," I said, locking my jaw and showing them my teeth. "Bring it on!" As if executing some kind of visual joke, the girl shot back across road, and from the other side, I could hear as she started complaining.

"No need to be so aggressive," she whined. "It was only a question." She sounded genuinely offended, and her voice struck such a plaintive tone that I shook my head in wonder as I noted how confused I'd have been if I didn't have a firm handle on what this really was. Her partner, meanwhile, had not much retreated, but at least he'd stopped and possibly had taken a step away from me. Regathering himself, he again stood before me, but I could tell that my reaction had not been part of the plan.

We were sizing each other up, and I knew it was going to be just the two of us. As we stood there, I found myself in uncharted territory. He still looked very composed and calm, but though fit and hungry, he certainly wasn't any bigger than I. In fact, as I continued to take his measure, it occurred to me that his build looked comparatively light. He looked very confident, but I reasoned that if I hit him, I'd hurt him. As we stood there facing off, my own appearance came to mind: I'd worn my lenses tonight, and I knew that without my glasses I looked younger and probably more physical. I was wearing a sleeveless puffer jacket which, leaving my arms free, even made me feel stronger, and the same was true of my jeans and heavy boots, not to mention the red tea-cosy hat pulled down on my head which hid the receding hairline that might have given away my age. I was probably close to thirty years this yob's senior, but I must have looked the least frail I conceivably could. The realization was a funny one, and deep down I could almost feel myself starting to chuckle. I knew that I was starting to smile.

"Really though?" he was saying as he looked into my eyes. "You actually think you can handle it, do you?" For the first time in my life, confronted by the threat of violence, I wasn't falling apart. Something had changed. I was becoming aware of my own influence on this situation, and it struck me as almost unbelievable. As he stood there still stopped in his tracks before me, I could feel that my confidence was growing. I could feel the smile on my mouth stretching by the second.

"Reckon I can," I told him, with an incredulous lilt in my tone, as if I were sharing this fact with a friend or a confidante; I felt almost grateful to him that I had someone to experience with me this magical moment.

"But do you really?" he went on, though his presence seemed to be shrinking before my eyes. "Isn't there some little bit of doubt in your mind? It's not something you want to get wrong now, is it?" He had kept on talking, but his words rang of weakness.

"'Undred percent," I said, raising my chin and consciously dropping the *h* so I could better sneer at him. As I watched him take first one step away and then a next, a leering smile rose up from inside me and broke out all over my face.

"Jog on then," he told me from where he'd retreated halfway across the road, "be on your way," and turning with a feeling of disbelief and victory, I laughed.

"Yeah, right," I chuckled back at him, and making my way home filled with a true feeling of contentment, I reflected on what an amazing night this had been, what a way it was to start a new year – what a distance I truly had come.

Six Underground

It's true that generally, I was settling down a bit and starting to find my game in this kind of company, but up at this level, it was a different matter. I couldn't imagine ever taking someone like Tracy for granted: being close to her made me feel clumsy and self-conscious, and even with her compliments and the compliment of her attention, I felt impossibly inferior. She was like a statue breathed into life, a magic key for any door the world could put before you, and the first prize for any contest. Something about her seemed quietly sublime: of course I was in awe of her! As much as I had learned about how to play the game – about not really showing yourself but rather showing what was required for a given situation – now and again I found myself just watching as she spoke, and all that was forgotten. Thoughts of her filled my mind, and I wasn't able to prise my eyes from her; the room around faded into the background. Coming to myself now, I realized I'd been doing just that – missing a chunk of the conversation as she said something to Billy while jabbing a playful finger at him. The two of them were laughing, and despite not knowing what they had said, having learned well enough how to slide myself easily into the merriment around me, I joined in their joke. As I did so, it flashed across my mind that I must have come on some in the last twelve months and also that I must have been pretty drunk to feel quite this relaxed in the shadow of such exalted company. How good it felt to be sitting here sharing her air! Now I was smiling; now I was flashing my teeth.

Down at the other end of the table, the conversation had been continuing in a vaguely polite but adversarial strain, and when Tracy switched her attention for a moment to what they were talking about down there, I managed to look away from her so that I could do the same. Mark was still probing Andy about the machinations of the financial world, now saying something about having read lots of stuff about City goings-on recently.

"I'm sure these things are a bit of an exaggeration," he went on, "but one of the articles said that bankers are all greedy buggers who collude to fix prices and swindle their clients. It said that's how they can afford to drive up and down the King's Road honking the horns in their Lamborghinis, drinking their flaming Ferrari cocktails that cost twenty pounds a pop. What do you think about that, Andy?"

I wondered what Mark thought he was doing: was he trying to start a fire? I could almost sense Tracy holding her breath beside me, and for a split second, the room seemed to resonate with the sound of a glove thrown down until, moments later, Andy actually slammed his fist upon the table. His cutlery leapt from its setting; the rest of us did the same. His still-full bowl of soup spilled out over the plates and on to the table's dark wooden surface.

"I am sick and tired of listening to wankers who know fuck all," he virtually belted out into Mark's face, "whining and moaning about everyone else because they don't have the bollocks to go out and get it for themselves, stuck in their pissy office jobs regurgitating crap they have no fucking idea about," he added, his hand heavy with anger as he replaced the bowl on his plate. "I didn't nonce about doing worthless A levels, or go swanning off to some poxy university aged eighteen to do a fucking history of art course, or some other shit on taxpayers' money – my fucking money – so I could then piss off around the world finding myself on my gap year while shagging the natives in some mud hut and telling everyone about all the charity work I was doing for Africa."

Mark's expression clearly showed that he didn't really want to have pushed Andy's button. "Calm down, mate," he said. "I only meant –"

"Don't tell me to fucking calm down! And I ain't your mate." His voice was tangled with violence, and Mark shrank back quickly. "I was running errands and paying housekeeping at sixteen years of age while giving it 'yes sir, no sir' at work. It was proper work and a proper slog, and these fucking whiners ... I don't want to have to listen to any more whining from you, Mark!"

Having been stunned frozen like the rest of us, Alison suddenly came to her senses as Andy paused, and she stood between the two of them, ostensibly to clear his place so she could mop up the soup that was spilled. She looked at Andy. "He's just saying, Andy ... aren't you, Mark?" she said, turning this way and that between her brother and Andy. "Tell him. You're not trying to be offensive."

"Come on now, boys," said Tracy, also rising and moving towards Alison as the rest of us continued to look awkwardly on, "this is meant to be a party. We're all friends here, aren't we? Come on. Kiss and make up."

"I'll clean up this mess for you, Andy," said Alison as she continued to juggle his crockery. "No harm done." Andy took a deep breath and looked up at the ceiling, bringing his gaze back down with a mischievous sparkle in his eye.

"OK, honey, you do that," he said, eyeballing Mark and then looking back again to Alison, "but I will have that kiss from you, dear, just to seal it." There was a moment's hesitation before Alison bent her head down and kissed him on the lips. The thunder had passed.

Alison left the room with the plates and the mat that had been drenched, reappearing with replacements and a cloth to fix the table. The girls then cleared the remaining bowls and were off to their posts in the kitchen once again. Mark and Yvonne moved away from the table together and stood chatting by the fireplace. She looked shaken, and from what I could see, he seemed to be reassuring her. Andy and Dave got up and took the few paces down to our end, sitting at the still-warm seats that Caroline and Tracy had vacated.

"All right, lads? What do you think of that prat then? Might have to teach him a lesson if he doesn't get out of my face."

"Would be a shame to spoil the evening, Andy," Dave piped up. "The girls have gone to a lot of effort."

"Yeah, well. It will go the way it goes, and I know that you know exactly what I expect of each of you, whatever way that happens to be. I'm sure that's understood," he said, looking especially at Billy and then me. We both gave the requisite nod, and though I wasn't sure how Billy felt about it, I knew it made me far from happy. The thought of physical conflict filled my belly with dread, with a type of adrenalin that I must have been allergic to and that sense of misdirection I'd felt earlier. The feeling that I was going the wrong way on the wrong road began to grow again, but this time it felt immediate and even more nauseating. The girls returned before too long with the main course – a stew of beef with a mash of potatoes and bowls of creamed spinach – and we all retook our places, but I couldn't feel hungry anymore.

As we sat, I noticed Tracy lifting a weather eye to Andy, who was now engaged in being his most charming self to Alison. Outwardly, things seemed to have normalized, but his little speech kept sounding in sickening echo around my head and it was clear that his belatedly congenial exterior was just a hollow deception.

"So, you two share a place, don't you?" said Tracy. "Did you meet at uni?"

"Nah. Milo's not been to uni," Billy replied with mock dismissiveness.

"Neither have you!" I countered instinctively, though I felt immediately how badly I'd fare if we continued making comparisons between us.

Billy just laughed. "He moved into the little box room in a house I used to share. That was how we met. You should have seen him: up from the country and right wet behind the ears, he was," he went on, teasing me with a big grin from the other side of the table, "a right little sweetheart, and he hasn't really changed much. Anyway, I took him under my wing – took pity on him, I suppose – and I got him his start. Look at him now, eh? Almost passes as one of us. You'd hardly know what a muppet he is," and finishing this pleasing little summary, he broke into guffaws.

I knew he meant it all in good sport, and I also knew that he'd never drop me in it on purpose, but I'd made a conscious decision to let Tracy believe that I was a fully fledged dealer, and the prospect of my being found out a liar added to my sense of anxiety. That the ensuing conversation would unravel my deception seemed inevitable; then she'd know me for what I was: a charlatan and imposter. I don't know why I felt so grimly desperate that she not think badly of me, but the fear gripped me nonetheless. Various disparate strands of discomfort seemed now to be in competition inside me, all the while supported by a very real sense that there was more truth to what Billy had said than he'd meant or even realized.

That old friend of mine, that gnawing sense of rejection and disassociation, was back once again with a grip round my throat, and the hint of alienation was poisoning me. My senses were blurring, and it was as if I now sat watching the scene with myself no longer quite present, taunted by the sneer of some chastening commentary which was judging me harshly from inside my mind.

Desperate to master my mind's gurgling morass without being too obvious, I started taking slow, deep breaths; but then, on top of everything else, I had an oblique but growing awareness that Tracy's leg was brushing my own. The contact was too irregular and much too improbable, surely, to be anything other than accidental, but feeling her linger, I wondered again, and the very thought that there might be something to it began to obsess me. Her touch each time shot me a jolt of sheer excitement, too soon passing and leaving me hostage for the next and the next. It was harbinger to feelings of guilt and disloyalty and sheer mad confusion all mixing queasily with the deepest sense of misgiving about everything my life seemed to stand for. As it began to overwhelm me, the room shifted from its moorings, and I had the sense that my dizzying head was rolling a little on my shoulders. I could feel all that white wine I'd been throwing down my neck turning rebellious in my stomach with everything else there, so setting down the knife and fork for one final effort, I shut tightly my eyes, focusing on my breathing and trying to get ahead. Tracy's voice sounded genuinely concerned as she asked if I was OK.

"I'm all right, thanks," I moaned as bravely as I could, opening my eyes a fraction to look at her through a deep frown before shutting them once again. "I'll be all right in a minute." I knew that wasn't true, and I had to get to the bathroom. Across the table, I could just sense Billy looking on in that incredulous way of his, always judging others by his own heroic standards. I felt Tracy's hand on my shoulder.

"But you do look pale," I heard her say. "Do you want to have a lie down? It's not a problem." Opening my eyes, I started to rise.

"I'll just ... go and splash a bit of water, I think. Where's the toilet?" She pointed to the door where Andy was sitting, and I stood for a moment with my hand on the chair, suddenly feeling light-headed, as if my blood hadn't yet been able to follow me up. I remained there unsteadily as I searched for some semblance of balance.

"You sure you'll be OK?" she asked. "Do you want a hand?"

"Boys, we've got a whitey," broadcast Billy as he sat back in his chair laughing, his arms folded across his chest and his head shaking theatrically.

"I'm OK," I said to her, smiling weakly. Absently, I wished that I could shoot my flatmate a look of distain, but instead I pushed off, drawing up my strength for the herculean task of making it to the bathroom as the boys' laughter rang me from the room.

The corridor ran endlessly, its terracotta walls now deeper and hotter as I bore along the path that Tracy had shown me. My limbs felt heavy, and my head spun with the unremitting waves of giddy sickness that rose from my gut. As I struggled on, I used the corridor walls for support when my balance deserted me, pausing there for moments before pushing myself on again like some blank automaton. At last, I made it to the refuge of the bathroom door, behind which I knew I could hide with my disease from the others – where I could close my eyes and slowly repair. Reaching out for the handle, I held it and stopped, letting it take my weight momentarily as I leant on it in relief before it turned and the latch disengaged, the door swinging slowly open and bringing me, still attached to the handle, stumbling across the threshold to the salvation I sought.

On my knees now, I strained to concentrate, to push the door shut behind me and lock it up fast. Managing this, I shuffled to the red sink with the sickness in my throat and my head still rolling, and with an exertion that was almost more than I could achieve, I reached up to the golden taps and turned them all the way on. I stared entranced as water gushed like twin sculpted jets riven from ice in endless white shafts. With my forearms still up on the sink and my head now hanging from my shoulders, I listened to the call of the fresh, flowing water, and regaining my feet with a final lease of strength, albeit still bent over and with my heavy eyes closing, I twisted myself around to slump on to the toilet seat, the water singing its whistling song to the side of my head, which came to rest on the sink beside me. Secure at last, I slumped forward with my neck and arms relaxed and just hanging there lifeless, and closing my eyes, I let go as the unearthly spinning grew beyond my comprehension. The pounding water continued a song full of life, filling the room with gurgling, timeless patterns that repeated in nature's infinite loop as the water overspilled the sink, flowed on to the floor, seeped under the door and out to the corridor: a river relentlessly drawn to the sea.

Summer's Almost Gone

Found by the water's edge, we sit on a log pressed into the wet sand, our hosts' grand white villa where the morning had passed, looking out to the sea from the high cliff above. They threw us the keys to the clunky old jeep, which made easy our jaunt to the beach down below, and open-topped, it stands now beneath one of a few knotty old trees, hiding under the sparse cover of its dry, twisted branches and the deep green leaves as best it can from the afternoon's glare. Already the sun is well beyond its peak, but like the air itself, we are warm – with drink, with the food we had at the barbecue earlier, with our new dream of friendship. Lazily happy, spontaneously we start to swap bits of songs with each other by way of intimate offerings: our songs of the sea. First, Billy offers his impressive original "River Man", an other-worldly melody and a song for his love and for my tormentor. I follow in response with my own harmonious refrain: "Yes, the River Knows" by the Doors – as it turns out, a heretic augury, appealing, innocent, and final, as our light, trusting voices, unashamed but unaware, carry from us gently. Maddie and Charlotte sit engrossed together nattering in their costumes and sharing their secrets, while Tommy busies himself behind us on a makeshift dam – a construction to divert the trickle that flows down over the silt. He puts to work the pieces of driftwood he's gathered, branches long fallen, and stones large enough to divert the stream that runs shallow on its delicate bed of lightly ribbed sand.

Suddenly, we are running. Billy, Tommy, and I race each other out into the sea, feet splashing down into the shallows and pushing on further as they hurdle the oncoming ripples, legs crashing down like pistons upon the soft bed that lies sloped beneath our toes. We are three athletes together as fine as you'll see, half-cloaked by the freshly churned spray, a white curtain fizzing with surf. The sea is above our waists now, and we hold our upper bodies erect, shoulders urging stiffly the legs below to a slow-motion surge restrained by the ocean. Our straight line of three impeded, each strains sinews to be furthest, and then, as if it were preordained, as one we're launched into a long, stretching dive that casts each of us into the water before us, the power of desire exploding in our shoulders and arms to claw it, to grasp it, to drag ourselves through it. Dipping now to dive beneath a peak that's upon us, we shoot straight out the other side with hard swimming for a few fevered strokes until suddenly, again with that unspoken synchronicity, we draw up, the game a tie. Our bodies are set now facing to the shore in a slightly crooked line, with Billy a few feet advanced. Bobbing in the sea, gazing far out over a shoulder, we wait, looking to the lines of waves that stack up approaching from beyond the horizon, watching for a beauty, the prize, a wave fit to ride on and carry us home.

This one? No, it doesn't look quite enough. That next one? The one behind it, perhaps? We scour the surface of the water, looking hard, hopeful as each prospect glimmers but then, getting closer, just fails to shine; but here she comes – now, how's this? Our arms are poised to pump and capture the ride, but once again no, not quite. This one? Yes! Just ahead of the swell, we try to hook ourselves on with a couple of powerful strokes, but it passes straight through, too weak to carry. Let down, we reclaim those few metres tried and lost, gliding back gracefully to the exact position again where lazy, imperious legs can kick us afloat, bobbing and waiting.

Almost imperceptibly, I feel some half-hidden darkness from nowhere, and it brings me a shiver: it's something that troubles. *What is this?* I think. Surely it's nothing, or a stray shade, perhaps, spiky with menace, that just happened to pass and disturb me by chance. But no, it's here again: an uneasy sound blows with the wind. Though it's only the barest hint, the meanest suggestion, the air is now darker and pregnant with treason, and the water too feels less like it did. There's something wilful about it, and it hangs round my ankles, something no longer complaisant, a kind of ... wait! This wave that comes – here! Here she is, yes – quick, go! Powerful, masterful strokes. I've got it! Yes!

Man and water. In the sea and the roar, I am lost to the others, bumping along as the water foams all around me, beneath my chest and under my legs, blinding me with bubbles about my face, this all-powerful, all-thrilling, all-bucking ride as the sea holds me fast. Look at me! The wave breaks as it draws to the shore and tips me lower. Helplessly, I slide down its face until it catches me again for one final adventure as I'm tumbled and wrapped in its churn of watery turmoil, half thrown on the soft velvet bed that rises to meet me. Dragged across the sand, I plant my palms and lift up my knees to right myself, springing from the padded floor and turning around to look over the sea.

Beautifully wet and panting, I stand catching my breath, refreshed and exhilarated as my eyes start to clear and my vision's restored. I push the long hair off my face, and behind me, I see a couple of dots way out in the water: the other guys weren't on the wave in. The girls are playing in the sea just to my right, and moving to reach them with the water around my ankles, I run a couple of paces but then stop. What is this? Something feels wrong again, yet the girls are all right, their happily laughing voices carrying to me from there in the water. It's still a beautiful day, the sun shining in a clear sky, and it's warm, and there's hardly a breeze, and the sand is soft; it's idyllic. Dismissing my doubts with a shake of the head, I make to run in again. After another step, again I must stop. What is it? Is it me? Maddie is waving out to the boys, laughing as I watch her confused, shrieking as she tumbles in the waves. Is she playing? She's screaming just there in front of me, and I make to run and help her but I can't. I just can't get another step closer. *Run!* I scream in silence. *Quick, run!* But fear grips my legs. Now Charlie's screaming too, and mangled shouts rise from the different points before me, the air filled with horror and alarm, the water turned black as I stand disbelieving.

Near to the parked jeep, a group of local kids has gathered at the inlet, and I run towards them for help. But again, indecisive, I stop and then run right back again: two paces here, two paces there, into the sea and out again, but there's no more confusion. A nightmare's really happening. "Help me," screams the day, and all doubt is gone.

"Help, please, something in the water, people drowning, please," I cry out as I rush wide-eyed to them, their eyes staring back at me at me doubtfully, suspicious, before one of the lads jumps up and comes forward from his friends.

"Come on, quickly," he urges them, and following as they run together to the shore, I'm already leaden with shame, a spectator laid low by the guilt of my cowardice. I watch as they bring logs to send out over the water for floats towards Billy and Tom, impossibly far and no longer together. Right here, as if in an adjacent room, they're fishing for Maddie with a branch that's not quite long enough and she's losing her fight with the water. I can't see the others as the sea's frenzy whips up and my own miserable world is closing around me. I'm too pathetic, too far beneath my own contempt, just standing there with my jaw hanging down, not quite believing.

Far to my left, I see Charlotte cast out fortunate upon the sand, spat from the waves by a contemptuous sea. Her green bikini's twisted and pulled, and her hair's all plastered about her face and neck. She sobs quietly on her hands and knees where she has landed with her head down. Frozen, I stare at her. Somewhere far off, I wish I could go there, but I no longer dare: it's out of my hands. Eventually, she rises, and steadying herself, she kind of ambles stunned down the beach towards me, reaching me in her shocked zombie state and clasping my torso, leaning herself into me while I stand upright and mortified, abject and silent. I no longer feel worthy of returning her embrace. I am an unspeakable coward, and there's an ocean between us. Time passes standing still, and behind us, Maddie's limp frame is lifted from the sea by her shoulders and knees, bedraggled and lifeless.

Charlie looks up to my face without expression, and releasing herself, she pauses as if to make some comment but draws slowly away, moving towards where Maddie lies. My useless arms are still down at my side, my dead eyes still blank, and I notice that Tommy too has now landed, further still up the beach than where Charlie came out. Closer and closer, he's walking beyond me now in a daze of exhaustion, and as he passes, I turn for my eyes to follow him and hear a deep, gurgling cough and then another, a rasping from the depths of Maddie's water-filled lungs. She's alive, no thanks to me. She's barely conscious but can't stop heaving and coughing, and the shock's still completely overwhelming, but Billy – where is Billy? Still I don't see him, and Tommy comes back to me, puts his hand on my shoulder.

"Where's Billy?" I keep on repeating, and Tommy's shaking his head, and the drum is banging and banging, and I can't see Billy, and the banging goes on, and the banging on the door wakes me, and Andy is shouting behind it.

"Milo, Milo, what the fuck are you doing? Get out here!"

"Just give me a sec," I slurred, coming to my senses.

"Fuck's sake, mate, get a shove on."

I sat up straight and took stock around the room, noticing the water that was still running hard into the sink, and letting out a deep sigh, I found that my head felt pretty clear. Standing up, I turned to the sink and passed my hands into the still-crashing flow, splashing water over my face and all through my hair. It felt sharp and refreshing, and I mussed up the fringe that was now stuck wet to my forehead. There was still some grogginess, but I was definitely on the mend, and turning off the taps, I looked up at the mirror and into my face. Holding my gaze for a while, I tried to work out what it was that my reflection wanted to ask me, the two of us locked in a telepathic hold without word or meaning. Deep down, I could sense that we had much to tell each other, much to share, if only the words would come, but there was still so much wisdom lacking. Opening the door, Andy pushed straight past me, his angry face speaking volumes, but feeling OK as I made my way back along the corridor, I couldn't help wondering about the deep sense of unease that seemed to persist, somehow related to Billy: a lingering dread from the dream I had just had.

Rival Tribal Rebel Revel

"Were you having a wank in there?" said Dave, looking up jovially as I entered the room, despite seemingly being embedded in a cosy chat with Nancy. I was shaking my head in disbelief, rather than denial, as I made my way back to my chair, still unable to get used to the depths that my colleagues would sink to – the level we habitually operated at in the name of banter regardless of the company we were keeping. Coffee had been served, and reaching my chair, I found a demitasse and the coffee pot awaiting me, both from the same blue-and-grey patterned set that had been used for the earlier courses, and sitting down, I poured myself a black one, throwing back a big gulp of the reassuringly gritty and bitter stimulant. Caroline asked me if I was feeling better now and whether I'd like some dessert or not, and I passed on her offer, feigning with a face some lingering sickness. From the other side of the table, Alison started to clear away the plates, the bordered white pools of fine china scraped with the remnants of a rich chocolate cake interwoven in patterns with traces of cream.

"Good – you're all right now," Billy informed me. "You, me, and the lads are going on, and I'm telling Tracy here that they're coming with us. It's the least we can do to repay their kind hospitality." He spoke with his enchanting mix of teasing and assurance, and though she hadn't yet been entirely convinced, I'd heard his music and seen this dance many times over.

"It's a tempting offer Billy, but I'm not sure what the others will want to do," she countered. "It's been a long day already, and I imagine they'll probably want to clean up and then get some rest."

"You can convince them," he insisted. "Come on – you know you want to! This new club in Smithfield's is the absolute nuts. You'll love it." He wasn't leaving any room for refusal. His powers of persuasion were hard to resist, and so used was he to getting his way that I don't think the possibility of a knock-back even entered his mind. "There's a lovely little cafe just around the corner from our place where I'll take you in the morning for a revitalising breakfast, if you know what I mean."

Where usually I'd have gone right along with his inevitable patter, at that moment, a little piece of me was repulsed by it; and I could feel the deep niggle that it nurtured being wound tighter by twin fears now encircling me, rising up against me like poisonous snakes. I knew that I did not want to get dragged into spending the rest of this night, not any more of it, in Andy's dangerously brutal company, no matter how nice the entourage, but aside from that, the thought of Tracy being run over and flattened like some sordid scalp just struck me as too cheap to contemplate, too awful to bear. Of course, if I had been in the driving seat, there would have been altogether different emotions, but I told myself that would have been a whole different story: at least I would have treasured her; at least she would have meant something to me.

As my momentary introspection cleared, I found Tracy observing me with a big smile on her face, her eyebrow raised like she'd been reading my mind. I felt myself blush as the possibility struck me I'd been thinking out loud. My face burning, I was just about to mumble my way into further embarrassment when Andy suddenly burst back through the doorway bellowing, "Oi, oi," as if he were on a mission and grabbing Alison round the waist as she stood clearing the table with her back to him. He spun her off balance, and sitting down, he pulled her on to his lap, the plates she'd been holding flying from her grasp. One of them shot over the other side of table and smashed as it landed on the wooden floor. Much to her obvious consternation, the two of them were suddenly very cosy.

"How about another of those kisses then," he said, puckering licentiously like a slimmed-down Henry the Eighth, oblivious to the accident and her squirming reluctance. "Come on, girl," he slobbered. "I'm right in the mood for some more of that reconciliation."

Mark sprang to his feet. "Let her go!" he shouted as Alison struggled, red-faced, to loosen herself, her free hand slapping Andy's cheek as hard as she could; but he pulled her in tighter and then caught a hold on the treasonous limb.

"I mean it!" roared Mark as he moved in closer. "Let her go now!" Suddenly, all in a blur, Andy pushed Alison from his lap and caught Mark's face a vicious blow with his forehead. An awful crack cut through the air. Alison let out a pained cry as she collided with the wall, taking a hefty knock on the arm. Mark took a couple of staggering steps backwards holding his nose and then fell on his backside as he tripped over the foot that Dave had stuck out behind him.

"Stay down!" Dave snarled into Mark's already swelling face.

"Stop it, now!" Tracy shouted towards Andy as she jumped from her seat before holding her distance behind Dave's shoulder.

I sometimes wonder how it must feel to be one of those who can revel in the sights and sounds of violence – who can hear in the clash of fist upon skin or bone upon bone the trumpet call of some glorious, manly elation. How different things would be if I were not impaled on a peak of fear whenever adrenalin rushed in, if my head did not fill with nauseous thoughts of my own vulnerability, of my own mortality. Now I felt unmanned and embarrassed and sick as I'd not felt before, much too scared of Andy to behave like a man and filled with shame for my snivelling reaction. I just wanted to crawl away and hide and get some space between us, and so it was decided: let the evening melt down from here if it must; it could do so without me.

For that horrid moment, time seemed to freeze, and we were like unmoving actors who held themselves paused and waiting for a curtain to fall. This was no West End climax, however. The lights did not dim, and applause did not start up to ring out the scene. Rather, in this room struck horrified by violence, from our different points of view, each one of us was drawn awfully to the picture now framed: Alison grimacing and holding her elbow; Tracy blinking, not knowing which sibling to attend; Mark on the floor with his nose dripping blood down on to his hands, guarded as Dave hovered above him. Andy was the key, stopped in the air, and he seemed slightly to waver. It was he who broke the spell, turning and making a move towards Alison, who cowered at his advance; but immediately it was clear that everything had changed: Andy's expression looked as if he had just awakened to find this unexpected mess all about him, caught by surprise and unacquainted with the perpetrator of this unholy disturbance. Whatever the cause, quite surreally, the ugly brute had disappeared. Alison looked as confounded by his implausible reversal as he did, and forgetting for a moment the throbbing in her arm, she allowed his gentlemanly proffered hand to lift and reseat her. Once he'd done so, Andy disappeared to the kitchen and returned with a fresh glass of water to further demonstrate his concern; and while this strange denial was playing out before us, his cheek still glowed with its livid reminder, the witness to where she had landed, and a testament in red to what had just passed.

After Alison, it was Mark's turn to be regaled with kindness, allowed up from the floor and led by the girls to the bathroom. And there was another change in the air: Andy now was contrite, full of apologies and abundant with toilet paper, effusive in his attentions. Had the change in the atmosphere been less bewildering, Mark might have been less willing to accept Andy's attempt at reconciliation, but as soon as the blood from his nose was staunched and he straightened up, almost as good as new, the boys were shaking hands. Andy announcing to the room that he was "sorry that things had gone a bit Pete Tong", observing Yvonne picking up the broken crockery with what seemed like genuine surprise, as if he were unable to recall how the plate had broken and scattered in pieces on the floor. Tracy told Billy that she wouldn't be able to come now even if she wanted to, and though it wasn't what he wanted to hear and he pushed on a bit with his attempts to try at least to prise her away, I think he realized that it had become a lost cause.

A taxi was ordered, and the noose was tightening around my neck. Billy and the boys were starting to get high again on their bravado, revving each other up in advance of yet another after party, but I wasn't going there. I was resolved on a way out, and I had to act quickly.

"Tracy," I said, turning to her quietly, "I don't feel well again. Do you mind if I do take that lie down? I don't want to be a pain."

"Of course," she said, continuing in a curiously matter-of-fact manner, "you can sleep in my bed if you like." There was something so markedly neutral in her tone of voice and in the blank look with which she cast her offer, as if it were the most natural thing in the world, that I paused, and doing a double take like I'd missed something obvious, I almost forgot the ruse I was playing out. Had I heard her correctly?

"It's just one room past the bathroom," she went on, "the very last."

"Bill," I said, looking over to him, making a great show of weakness and exhaustion as I rose from my seat, "you guys go on ahead. I won't make the journey like this, so I'm going to get my head down. Catch you up when it stops spinning."

I'd spoken quietly to play up how badly I felt and because I didn't really want to involve Andy and Dave in the conversation, but the three of them were all together, and the other two heard. Andy said nothing at first, just looking from Tracy to Billy to me and back again with his eyebrows raised, but then as I started to make my way from the room, he piped up, drooling.

"You 'ave a nice rest, Milo," he said. "I think you're gonna need it."

As wearily as I could, I flashed a dismissive shake of my head towards my flatmate, repudiating the insinuation, and without stopping, I continued away from them gratefully towards escape and salvation, hearing as a parting shot a guttural "best of luck" as I reached the door. Going through it, I couldn't help but take a last look behind me, and catching Billy's staring eyes, I half-thought I saw there a look of something like mute panic. He looked like a man who was falling or drowning – a look that reminded me eerily of the dream I'd just had.

Supersonic

Her bedroom was warm. A heavy curtain hung over one wall covering what I imagined could be a window, the drapes deep red like everything else: the carpet, the wallpaper, the duvet cover, and the pillows on the mattress which sat without a base on the floor in the centre of the room. A solitary flame flickered on the chest of drawers, a stout candle of rough chunks of red wax burning bright in a silvery ashtray. I stripped to my shorts and my T-shirt and, clambering on to unfamiliar territory, I got down on the bed. The clean cotton sheet felt like silk beneath me as I lay listening to murmurs and the sounds of clearing up that came from the kitchen: a song of china, of glass, and of steel. Purposefully, I tried to empty my head, to think nothing but to let the experience of lying in this strange bed in this strange place grasp me – a strange place so infinitely more desirable than the one I'd grown used to. Tracy slipped in, solicitous, and kneeling over me, she asked if I felt OK. Still feigning weariness, I nodded without speaking.

"Do you want me to take your top off?" she asked, and I nodded again, and helping me take it over my head, her hand seemed to linger on my stomach and on my chest. Before leaving the room, she put the covers back over me and kissed me on my forehead.

The sounds that seeped from along the corridor grew softer with the passing of time, warping the images that sprung from my subconscious, and I realized I was starting to doze. Falling sound asleep, in my dream I was lying tangled with a woman, kissing and caressing a long, slender leg as I cradled her smooth calf in my hands, my eyes closed and my face at her knee. Planting mysterious kisses, I traced slowly higher as my lips teased along her thigh and then higher still to the top, where I wallowed in the excitement of her sweet, sticky flesh and the aroma of lust that swirled all around me. Opening my eyes, still dreaming, I realized with a start that a model of a leg was all that I had: there was no woman, and all I was wrapped in was this pointless plaything which hadn't any meaning. Suddenly everything I was doing felt foolish and full of shame.

A gradual awareness of the sweet smell of incense that now filled the room slowly formed as I came to, lifting me from the ignominy of my dream, even if its empty hangover still burdened the pit of my stomach. The florid smell of Eastern dusk reminded me of Tommy, and I wondered about him as I watched the smoke fronds as they spread winding through the air to the ceiling from beside the candle. Aware of something behind me, I turned slowly to find Tracy lying asleep on her side facing towards me, her breathing gentle and her closed eyes completely still. Perfect in sleep, she looked like a figurine made large with not a hair out of place, her dark fringe splayed neatly on her forehead and the rest of her mane tied into a ponytail. I was transfixed. Being there in the bed beside such a creature, the very one I'd been admiring in the filthiest of ways all evening, was a privilege electrified, and being this close, I felt that anything was possible – that this night could go anywhere. Late or early, it was that stillest of times, and everything was peaceful as I listened to the easy rhythm of her breath.

If being here has only gained me a bit of space, I thought to myself as I lay watching her, *a bit of time to take stock and get my thoughts together, I can consider myself lucky.* The fact that I was sure I'd avoided further trouble by stopping here this evening was a relief, but as I continued to drink in her sleeping form with my eyes and my heart rate began to increase accordingly with the thoughts in my head, I had to remind myself that I couldn't jump to conclusions. *Hold on,* I told that part of my body that was busy planning its immediate future. All Tracy had done was be kind enough to let me have somewhere to lie, and it was only through lies that I'd got myself into this most intimate of situations. *Would it really be me lying here if she did have something other in mind?* And yet here she was, and here so was I, and what if? As the night's conundrum continued to vex me, added to my silent musing came thoughts of Billy. I remembered that this was meant to be his night, his trophy. What if the impossible really did occur? How then would we reconcile it between us? The margins of my mind weighed up these onerous considerations, the pros and cons and sheer unlikeliness and improbability, but there was nothing equivocal about that other, more single-minded part of me, full steam ahead, and so much so I could feel it hurting, a devilish nagging growing louder and louder until it was impossible to ignore.

Watching as she slept quietly beside me with her red mouth gently closed, I couldn't take my eyes off her – off her dark hair that shone smooth and bright and her long, black eyelashes. To the side of her neck my eyes were drawn, where a tiny pulse beat an uneven rhythm, and then to the rise and fall of her breast – to her naked flesh that teased through the sagging neck of the old T-shirt she was wearing. Taking care not to disturb her, slowly I lifted myself on to my elbow, lifting along with me the duvet we were sharing. As more of her body was revealed, I stopped, hardly chancing a breath, gazing upon the swell of her belly which rose and fell beneath the sheath of the T-shirt; at her arms crossed on the bed between us; at her long, slender fingers. Like a thief, of its own resolve my hand reached carefully over and took the duvet at her hip, peeling it down guiltily beyond the bottom of the T-shirt and over her knees that were bent in towards me. She had no knickers on! The bare skin of her hip, of her thigh, of her flank was unbroken and bare, and she was lovely from her head to her toe. All I could do was keep staring, my breathing now deeper through my mouth, which hung open, the pressure grown worse.

"This the best you can do, is it, Milo?" she said mockingly. "This is your seduction technique?" Her eyes, now open, again took on that controlled, amused aspect and looked challengingly into mine. As she unfolded her body before me, I caught sight of a tiny devil tattoo like the cheeky motif of my keenest football rivals, Manchester United, at the top of her thigh. Blind from seeing, I stared, not knowing whether I was looking at the devil itself or at the thin spray of hair revealed beside it. Lest this dream stop, I dared not even blink.

"Come here," she said, reaching for my hand. I held it towards her and watched for a moment while she took it and paused with it held in her own, my head too full to wonder where this tantalisingly slow dance was heading, until she pulled my arm closer and pressed my fingers into the soft flesh between her legs. As they stole up inside her, she flicked back her head with the tiniest gasp and closed her eyes, her legs locking tight on my wrist.

I couldn't breathe. My whole body felt tight, and my heartbeat was racing; I was tingling all over, infected by this filthiest sensation as, struck disbelieving, I held rigid beside her, hungry like a savage. My outstretched arm was beginning to ache.

"Kiss me," she said, a moan that tumbled like a threat through gritted teeth as she reached her hand to the back of my head. Shuffling closer, I placed my cheek on the sheet beside hers. Our faces apart by the length of our lips, I was lost entranced in the warmth of her breath and the smell of her skin. Finding each other, our mouths closed together, our tongues prying gently, shallow and polite for a couple of seconds but then harder and deeper, barging and yielding, lock-twisted between us. As I gulped back the lungfuls of air that passion's flame demanded, the dizzying sensation of flesh grew sharper and more intense as our faces rubbed and our bodies bumped with our eyes shut fast.

Between her legs, I felt a hand grip my wrist, and I opened my eyes. Bringing up my fingers with a glint of proud challenge, she wiped them across my cheek while, like an impassive plaything, I just gazed back at her. She brushed them on my nose and my chin and then on my teeth as her eyes drilled into mine to see if I'd flinch, to see if I'd crack. Convinced, she drew them on to her own tongue and flashed it between them, asking something of me. Sucking on them, she continued to stare until something inside me burst and I couldn't any longer hold myself from falling upon her mouth, freeing as I did so my hand for her cheek, for her neck, wanting to rip away that loose-rimmed T-shirt but running a clawed hand instead down the side of her body and back up again inside it along her soft length of skin to her full-falling breast, her tight little nipple, touching her, holding it, stretching against her, my hips in an agony.

"Wait," she commanded, pushing me on to my back with a frown modelled on something stern, "just wait." I lay there in a sinner's world of bliss as she undid her hair, and as she straddled me, brushed it across my face and my eyes. I watched her, keeping hard to the sight of her breasts that jiggled as she shook her head and then her body, as slowly she made her way over mine. Now her mouth was on my chest, now on my stomach, her tongue in my belly button, and then sitting back astride my knees, her hands went into my shorts. She held me and wiggled me about.

"What are we going to do about this then?" she asked, and both of us laughed at so happy a thing. As she pulled at the waistband of my shorts, I lifted my hips to help her to undress me, and casting them away with a dismissive flick, she returned her attentions to the uncovered region, keeping me down with an arm up my chest. I watched from above as, down there, she lingered and shocked me with nips here and there.

When the surf is up and the music's playing, you just have to dance: how we danced for those hours of darkness in that rocking and rolling sea. Hand in hand, we chased one another along the shore with the water kicking around us, riding the waves that we fashioned with our bodies, exploring the coast and far, far inland as we forged up that friendly river. Sometimes laughing, sometimes bearing bravely the sting of passion's mindless intensity, we savoured both the delights and the trials, and music we made of our carnal communion. There was a fire, our very own inferno, tendons taut and tangled flesh grown hot enough for the Devil herself. Now running and now resting, stopping and then starting, again we kept true to the path until, at last, the morning was sneaking in on us and the light outside was pricking the deep red shade. Having played ourselves dry, we lay there together, just about touching in the fading warmth of our sun, passing our ember time in slumber until, waking again, we were cool and strangers.

I remember that Northern Line carriage on my way back home the next morning: a lovely relaxed one, satisfied as I was, and more than a little wiser, watching the landscape of flats and allotments that passed beside the over ground stretch of track to East Finchley. I was heading back to face the music, but a few disparate strands of thought kept running through my mind. Apart from feeling like a non-leaguer who'd just scored at Wembley – a baffled crowd turning about to ask if anyone knew the guy with the birthmark on his bum – what struck me immediately were the logistics: the amount of ground I'd actually had to cover, like working different jobs on different parts of a building site or spinning plates and hardly having time to enjoy the patterns. Another memory that endures, a real anomaly and the reason it turned into something of a marathon, was that when it came to it, I couldn't quite get over the line. Maybe it was because I was occupied by multifarious misgivings: perhaps the leg dream had freaked me, or a deeper shadow that was weighing on my subconscious. But even I knew that once the Devil had got me, there was only ever going to be one outcome, and as we dipped and rolled and ravaged, it wasn't thoughts of Billy that were holding me back. Whatever the impediment, in the end it took something really nimble; her facility of reach which was marvellous, and shifting her weight on to one shoulder before me, her mountain trick came quite the surprise, allowing me, as I gazed out over the back lands with the flag firmly in place, finally to ring that bell.

Dressed in the morning, I'd observed her blankly from the bedroom doorway as she pulled that T-shirt back down over her body, covering her breasts and then, as she rose, putting her treasure again out of sight to see me from the flat. Even at that moment, it intrigued me that instead of elation – instead of the sense of victory that surely should have been mine – I felt almost nothing. Having experienced something I'd have given my teeth for – just for a taste – my emotions were quite numb, and the glory achieved seemed of little worth.

As worthy a conclusion as that is, it's not quite the whole story, ignoring as it does the thing of true value my time here had won, even if I wouldn't realize it until much later on. Before this night that, answering my prayers, had been filled with those hours of magic, knowing that my confidence and my ambitions were unnaturally low, I'd never wholly trusted my own judgement, never wholly accepted the integrity of my assertions. I made allowance by discounting the conclusions I came to, acting rather on what I thought my real desire would be if only I dared admit it. Now that I'd come down a hero from such an unlikely peak, however – now that I'd achieved something which before I might have thought impossibly beyond me – it gave me new parameters and a whole new perspective, and I wouldn't any longer feel infected by inferiority. With the memory of this night to boost me, to build me back up whenever I fell into doubt, I was able to feel that I could actually take myself at my word. I could be sure that I wasn't merely kidding myself in my desire to settle for some tawdry second best. Because of this, when the time came when I would insist to myself that really I was happy, that really I was with someone that I wanted to be with, at last I would have the confidence of my convictions.

The Sea

Down with the flock at the bottom of the hill beyond the Clock End stand, I'm lost in the mass of my fellow supporters. Buried here among the many where the view of the self is so easily hidden, the mark of the crowd is the measure by which we are reckoned, but up close, the more intimate details bely the overview. The mass of oneness is actually an infinity of individual particulars seamlessly combined in this buzzing people-scape; bodies entering and exiting the fray confound what appeared to be one steady flow to a mutual destination. The space down here is another surprise: there are gaps that were hidden previously in what seemed a constant sea surrounding bobbing islands of policemen on horseback. In fact, it's a multiplicity of layers that's at work here, a sub-stratum moving beneath the heads of the tallest pedestrians, less seen than those seniors and seeing less too, and still further beneath are the flying sedentary in the wheelchairs, focused on plying an assertive egress from the legs all around them. Bewildered children there are too at this height, kept close in hand and guided swiftly from packed, crowded dangers by the pull of their elders, who see more.

At the VIP entrance, select guests gain marble comfort, arriving for a welcome by Herbert's bust. Some linger atop the steps to be seen while others wait there for their party to build or to survey with a farewell scan this moveable feast as those of us about to worship in the people's stands keep moving along the way. At our own turnstiles, the ruly mass waits, and joining its edges, we're sealed by those that come behind us, adopted by a more or less orderly prequeue that begins its final approach, making its way towards the crude spartan turnstiles that are painted in everyone's favourite colour. Polite, shuffled feet make their claim for the spot left by those who've pressed forward, pigeon steps seeking the place with movements that everyone recognizes until the crowd diverges into single files and the way ahead's clear. At this point, the privilege of singular relief is achieved, the fear of displacement allayed at last by this gaining of place. The crowd bestows a responsibility too to keep such a place for those behind, and those behind them.

Solemnly, we pass the bearers, who flank us like accompanying angels, observing them pleasantly lest they take our avoidance of them for shame at an empty-handed pass. This is the way we make our peace with the noise of their buckets, which shake as if involuntarily, the coins therein ringing their appeal for more. Finally, under the auspices of the guardian whose hand protrudes from the all-knowing tollbooth to relieve us of our ready torn stubs, at last we can enter, expectant and humbled, through these shadowing gates, not twin but many, approved now to pass for the coming adventure with our memories intact. Not long behind us, those others will follow who'll soon know our footsteps and make them their own.

Part 3

Just blowing.
And whichever way,
The wind does choose,
Is chose for me.

No hand on tiller firm to guide my path.
Nor bright lit sky.
Not mine a star to follow.

Just fancy free,
And weak,
My fate is shrugged.

What's coming come.
I'll fear ye not.
But lead me, gently,
Not astray.

Days Go By (Acoustic)

From singular funnels, the mass quickly reforms on this other side, and again we begin. In the concrete bar where poured pints stand lined up on the counter, ready to be drunk, I spy Tommy waiting with his pint in hand and another on the ground between his feet.

"Where'd you get to, bro?" he asks with that look as I approach.

He shakes his head when I tell him, "I was waiting for you."

"Got to keep close, Milo," he admonishes patiently. "Can't have life getting between us – there's no telling where you'd end up," and laughing, he passes the latest in a series of liquid tokens of our mutual esteem, a token I gratefully accept.

Standing here supping quietly, the reserve of true togetherness, looking around, it's like watching the latest episode of a play all around you: the people you see once again in their spots, week in and week out, all of the comings and the goings. One of the guys has a new girl in tow: you always notice the new girls, especially the pretty ones. Sometimes it's an acquaintance or a friend from work that pops out to surprise you with a cameo guest appearance right where you'd least expect it: that being almost everywhere, of course. Our drinks done, I fetch the plastic pint glasses back to the bar, and returning through the sticky crowd, we turn and take the stairs together to that climatic surge of excitement waiting inside at the top. Swelling at the brow's approach where the arena for our main event comes into view, we burst out on this sight of glory, this pitch fit for passing. Still observing the grass, we make our last little way across the row to the plastic pew seats where the others sit ready and waiting – though not Polo, of course – drinking in the deep sense of calm that presages the coming action: an empty grass carpet all peaceful and green, all colour and perfection. A scene is set.

It's funny, but I tend to watch the players as they come on to the pitch more intently than I do sometimes when the game is actually in full swing, perhaps because it's before the overwhelming stimulus has blunted my senses. On they come, running and swinging their arms in their colours as we all stand clapping and cheering for their entrance to the field. They line up for the photo with their mascot miniatures in hand before passing their opposite numbers with handshakes and a show of respect that can be so very wanting once the game is underway. The Arsenal captain wins the toss, and kick-off, as usual, goes from right to left, thus giving our block the habitual prospect of a special second half should the boys in red and white finish as strongly as they usually do. At the end of this preamble, with the crowd still up on its feet, comes Polo. His head switches from side to side as he gurns all the way down the upper steps to harvest the cheers, reminding me somehow of a black Dr John whose appreciation in *The Last Waltz* is no less sincere, caught up as my Saturday-afternoon partner seems in his pantomime maintained. Shuffling in at the very last moment, he graces each one he passes with that personal nod, that knowing smile that seems just for us, as if we're in on the ruse; and as he takes his place at my side with a last graceful flourish, the kick-off is taken, and the game's underway.

The Needle and the Damage Done

Returning home on the morning after the dinner party, I resolved to face the Tracy issue head on and to be as contrite as possible: I knew it would be an issue, but I hoped we'd be able to sort it out. After all, it was Billy who always said you had to take what you could – no room for feelings in love and war, etc. – and I hoped that he'd be a man about it. Coming in, I went straight to his bedroom. I wasn't especially surprised to find no one there and his bed not slept in, and I assumed that he must still be out. The lounge was shrouded in darkness by the heavy curtains as I passed back through on my way to the kitchen, and though I registered the tell-tale marks of some recent playfulness – a scattering of videos, the ashtrays, and the half-drunk drinks – I didn't notice the bundle on the floor by our record player. I made myself a brew, raiding what I could from the fridge and the cupboards to fill my cavernous hunger; and it was only when I returned to the lounge to eat in front of the television, putting my tray down to draw the curtains and open the window to refresh the fetid air, that I noticed his hunched-up figure on the floor by the records, his back against the wall and his knees bent foetal with his head in his hands.

I didn't know what I was seeing at first, and the sight made me start, but as the realization dawned on me, the shock only solidified. It was as if an eerie darkness descended as I watched him speechless. He lay there shaking, still dressed as he'd been the night before though without the tie. Moving closer, almost too quiet to make out, I could hear whispered mutters that didn't sound like the voice I knew, but kneeling by his side with my ear close to his mouth I realized he was repeating something like "the best of luck, the best of luck, mate" again and again. He didn't respond when I tried to communicate with him, and he looked so pallid – even more so than usual – that I should have known things weren't right. But brushing off the dread hand of the obvious, I thought, or hoped maybe, that it would pass – that he might be having a bad but temporary reaction to some exotic he'd taken – so I pulled him up from the floor and got him into bed. He didn't exactly help, but he didn't resist either, and leaving him there, I figured he just needed a chance to shake it off and later I'd find him better again. I lay on the lounge sofa, trying not to think about what might really be happening, watching the box without choosing anything of interest, and before long I'd drifted off.

It was already dark when I awoke, and in those too-brief seconds before my memory properly returned, flash recollections of the night before pricked me with delight. The ominous realization that I'd still heard nothing from the room next door almost immediately dispelled my lightness. My heart in my mouth, I went in to find Billy out of the bed and down on the floor again by the doors that led to the garden. He was back in the position I'd found him in earlier. Going close to him and putting my hands on his shoulders, I panicked, shouting his name in his face, but still he seemed not to hear me, unmoving but for the incessant shaking and the low, worried muttering.

Not knowing what else to do, I rang Chloe. I hadn't spoken to her since we'd left, and though I'd often thought of her and had always meant to get back in touch, the shame I felt at how we'd departed, the memory of her unhappy face as she looked out after us, and the guilt she brought back to me at the way I'd treated Charlotte seemed always enough to postpone actually doing it. Now, holding the ringing phone, I dreaded what she'd say to me, but more than that I dreaded that she might no longer be on this number, as there wasn't anyone else close at hand I could try. After what seemed like a very long wait, she picked up the phone, and it was the same old Chloe. She actually sounded so pleased to hear from me that I started to cry.

She pulled up outside in a taxi some twenty minutes later. I opened the door to find her just as I remembered, her ponytail in a plait and dressed as if ready for some strenuous pursuit, and we hugged in the hallway. Like a long-lost sibling, I can't describe what a relief it was to be held by her. I took her straight through to see Billy, who was still in a heap on his bedroom floor, and switching the light on, she went over to him carefully, putting her head close to his and whispering to him as I stood watching from the doorway, upright and worried as the awful trembling continued. Still he was muttering those words that seemed to come from a mind far, far away. Holding his hand, she tried to find a way through to him but could get no closer than I'd been able to. Then, looking round at me and shaking her head, she said we should call an ambulance. Quickly we cleared the flat of the most obvious contraband before the crew arrived, and they asked us a long list of questions that I barely had answers for: I didn't even have an address or an idea of who to call as his next of kin. After they'd gone, we sat in the quiet of the kitchen, and I told her again the little I knew. Now that the story was furnished with an ending, all that had preceded seemed blindingly obvious.

Leaning over our mugs that evening, it was as if we'd never been apart, and for the first time in ages, I felt truly comfortable with who I was, no longer straining to be something different, though I guess the shock of what had occurred had probably tranquillized me. I was glad to tell her how sorry I'd always felt about the way things had happened and how I'd behaved, and though we didn't mention Charlotte by name, something unspoken passed between us that we both understood. To me it felt like absolution. Before I realized how long we'd been talking, it was already late, and exhaustion catching up with me, it was time for her to go. She rang for a taxi and waited while I showered. She stopped to tuck the duvet under my chin in bed as she had in the old days in Camden and left me with a kiss on my forehead. I was already fast asleep as she let herself out.

Slide Away

I was so freaked out and anxious when I awoke the next morning that I hardly knew what I should do: whether I should go in to work and make a clean breast of it or, feeling more than a little implicated in something that had now come horribly unstuck, just take my passport and head for the coast. Ideas of flight were fancy, of course, and just going in and ignoring Billy's absence and expecting that no one would notice was clearly impossible. Also, having some small idea of the severity of what had occurred, it seemed a total dead end to go with a lie and pretend for some small delay that everything was OK. Thinking about it, no matter how nervous I was, if I wanted to continue with my city education, then really I did need to face the music. I definitely needed the help of someone I could trust, and thinking about that, I resolved to see the man who surely must know what had to be done.

Nervously, I went up to the dealing room and to Hardy, who was there as usual on the pitch before me, and red-faced and awkward, I asked if we could have a word. In one of the empty offices at the side, I told him what had happened to Billy, telling him also that I didn't think his condition was one that would pass. A little ashamed, I confided to him that I was worried about the repercussions for me, saying how I thought it would be better to come in and be totally honest, to throw myself on his mercy – at least then I couldn't be blamed for evasion. To my mighty relief in the event I didn't even have to go into much detail. It turned out that he was ahead of me, taking it in and nodding like he'd seen it before.

"You've done the right thing in coming to me," he said, and assuring me not to worry, he sent me straight to personnel, patting me on the shoulder and telling me to repeat exactly what I'd told him without being so candid about my own misdemeanours. After doing as instructed, I was kept alone in a soft-sofa office down there for what seemed like ages – so much so that I began to wonder if I was about to be given my cards or, worse still, if the police were being called. But when the manager eventually came back in to see me, Hardy was with her, and from the look on his face, I could see that for me, at least, it would all be all right. In the interview that followed, he let slip that he wasn't especially surprised by what had happened; the job was a high-pressure one, and Billy clearly wasn't cut out for it. Finishing, he turned to the personnel officer who'd been sitting in with us pretending not to listen, and this seeming to be her cue, she asked me there and then if I felt I was ready for the step up to trainee dealer.

When I went back up to the main dealing room and made my way to our desk on the other side of the vast floor, to the newly vacated seat on Hardy's right which was now my own, I sat myself down in a quiet state of shock. An array of emotions presented themselves, not least the realization that my impromptu promotion meant I'd no longer be able to continue playing the clown: it certainly wouldn't do to carry on in the way that I had been. I'd taken no notice beforehand of anything other than whatever task I'd been given, barely aware of the real work that went on around me, and what little I did observe, I didn't bother even trying to understand. Now, however, I felt that the clock was ticking; I'd been given my chance, and it would be up to me to show I was worth the investment. I made a sincere resolution that I'd give it a proper go, that I'd do whatever I had to and make whatever sacrifice, knowing instinctively that the chance I'd been given was too good to waste. Underlying all of this was a strong sense of guilt, a perverse feeling that once again I was profiting as my good mate's substitute, but as the enormity of my opportunity began to sink in, this guilt, I found, was displaced by fear. It would be quite a while before that enlivening emotion started to numb. When eventually it did so, the sensation that remained felt almost like excitement.

Later on that day, I got a message from a dealer on one of the other pitches that I was wanted in the Dragon room. Making my way up in the lift, I stared at my reflection, wondering anxiously if personnel had realized that I hadn't really told them everything and wanted to question me further on some of the details before they'd let it drop, but I was surprised instead, after knocking and entering, to find Andy and Dave in there waiting for me. Andy was not looking best pleased. In the collision of events, I'd hardly given the two of them a thought, but inevitably they'd got wind of the situation and they wanted me to fill them both in. Andy was bristling, but when I told him that I had not mentioned their names, the atmosphere quickly relaxed and they went on to tell me how they'd come in for a swift couple with Billy before leaving on their way fairly sharpish and that when they'd said their goodbyes, he had seemed fine.

"There was nothing wrong with him when we left on Sunday morning," Dave told me, muttering his amazement and shaking his head. He seemed genuinely moved at what had occurred.

"You sure he's not just blagging a few days' holiday?" was Andy's contribution, and though he may have been joking, he looked straight at me, apparently intensely serious, and I wasn't sure. Either way, with the air cleared and the issue sorted, the boys were happy to let me go.

"What about you?" asked Dave as an afterthought as we headed back down in the lift. "How did things go down after we left?"

"I had a little sleep is all," I told them. "I got a cab back a few hours later, and that's when I found Billy. You know the rest." I'm not sure they believed me, but it gave me some sense of satisfaction to hide what really had happened. I knew if I had told them the truth I'd have gone up in their estimation, despite what could be seen as my disloyalty, but this way at least I wouldn't be further betraying the guy who had done so much for me.

The mental affliction that had befallen Billy passed in time, and it was a great relief that he made it back to the land of the living. Never again did he return to the flat, however, going from his place of recovery to live with his mother in her home somewhere near Woking. That itself was bizarre: as far as family was concerned, I'd had him tagged as an orphan, but I met her one evening when she turned up in a Volvo to collect his stuff: a gentle Home Counties woman in a floral dress who chatted to me politely without asking any questions as I carried the bags I'd packed to the boot of her car. She shook my hand before driving away. I did go down there to see him on a few occasions after that, but as much as he looked and sounded like the Billy I'd known, there was a wariness about him now, a caution for life which stood like a wall between the friends that we'd been. Though of course in some ways it was good to know that never again would he return to being the man he had been, knowing him the way that I did, it was impossible to ignore the suspicion that perhaps it wasn't actually his illness that had got in the way of a fresh reconnection. I suspected instead that secretly he hated me for taking what he'd considered his own and that our failure to renew our closeness was the product of his holding this against me and taking tacit revenge. I knew that partly that was my guilt talking, but if truth be told, I never got the thought quite out of my mind. It was as if a fundamental part of his makeup required that his true self remain locked away, protected – as if that place inside where he kept his inner counsel either couldn't be or didn't want to be breached by my pleas and entreaties. Thinking back over all those months in the flat, those times that seemed now like a crescendo of craziness, it was obvious to me this had long been the case.

It's not always easy to tell what a person's actual personality is and what is rather the manifestation of the life he or she leads, but without the effect of those self-destructive ways in which Billy had previously coped with life's stresses, the difference in him now was startlingly clear. I really hoped that we'd be able to develop a more appropriate relationship, partly because of what I felt was my own culpability in his downfall, but it wasn't to be. Maybe it wasn't the fault of a darker motivation, and perhaps I really was too entwined with what had turned into a traumatic past – reminded him too much of a time that was still too raw to deal with. Whatever the case, he now had to turn his back on our friendship. When eventually I stopped making the phone calls, gave up pushing for his evidently reluctant companionship, he dropped from my life.

Finding myself now alone in a ridiculously expensive flat was a problem that I had to deal with quickly. Because of the generous split that Billy and I had agreed on, even if I could have found someone to share with, the rent would still have been too high, so I had no choice but to give notice. I moved out at the end of the month. It wasn't as if I was sorry to leave. The decadent lustre which had so impressed me when, in a bustle of excitement, we'd first moved in was now well and truly tarnished, but because my search for somewhere less bling and a whole lot cheaper took longer than I'd hoped, there ensued a nomadic few months. I found myself sleeping for a couple of nights at a friend's from work here or moving in at another's for a night or two there, and for quite a while I was hopping about, unable to settle down anywhere. I stored the stuff I'd accumulated in a Kings Cross lock-up, keeping only the few bits and pieces I really needed close by me at all times in a black leather rucksack: a clock radio which provided for the early mornings; a signature bottle of Jack Daniels which provided equally well for the late nights, though these were more seldom than they had been; and a book I dragged around which proved more for carriage than for actual reading. I also kept my toothbrush, toiletries, and a change of underwear in that bag I lived out of, replenishing it from the stores I kept in my locker downstairs at work or the boot of my car. On occasions when the little bit of luck I needed didn't pan out, when sleeping plans I'd had in mind didn't come to fruition, I ended up finding a way back to the office and pitching underneath my desk, always to the amusement of the facilities department, who would discover me there on their early-morning floor walks, letting me lie with a wink and a nod. I was always careful, however, to make sure I was back up from the showers in time to escape the remark of my colleagues, ready in time for the day to begin. When such a ride as this starts rolling, you need to be ready and alert. I was on the edge of my chair, too nervous to squeak. I remember how overawing it was and how grateful I felt to be sharing that air, a junior dealer in nothing but title, gripping life's winning lottery ticket tight in my fist, watching those majestic seniors from the sidelines. They were all so assured, so confident, and so in control, walking the walk as if they were born to it.

It's the mystery that confounds you, a riddle whose answer, once revealed, is a thing of disbelief: that you could grow enough to be one of them. But then, with the passage of just a little time, the ride going only a little way along the tracks, patterns start to form from what seemed to be chaos – a hint of some order revealed as that blurring shroud of ignorance falls silently away. The original confusion gives way to some clarity which feels almost too good to be true. Little tricks and timetables become apparent, and confidence grows. The admiration of those kings around you, which once seemed limitless, becomes measured now with a somewhat lengthened yardstick. The view from this newly elevated vantage point tinges that earlier total deference with a shade of impatience as put-downs are rebuffed and repudiated more strongly as you dare to feel you might even make it, might even belong: why shouldn't you? Those erstwhile heroes are now the opposition, obstacles even or the enemy, and where three months' superiority was once a lifetime's achievement, an honour and a badge and a fine thing of awe, now a few years' head start can be waved off as nothing.

Once I'd got my lucky break, if luck can be divined among such an unfortunate set of circumstances, my career started to lift me higher, a dream-like escalator which slowly but surely would take me along the gold-paved path to becoming a fully fledged dealer. For the first few months, I just looked out and wondered, afraid I would reveal the full depth of my ignorance and confusion; but under Hardy's gradual tutelage, I was gently immersed, and by the following Easter, it was time for the stabilizers to come off. Albeit under pretty close supervision, I was ready to take the ride. This being before the days of electronic trading, the book, jobbing sheets and all, literally was mine, as were all price and trading decisions. I've never spent a week as tight with anxiety. It was impossible to eat when my heart was in my mouth, and I steeled myself each time the STX rang or a direct line with the Oppo lit up, making my price and being damned, living with the consequences. It felt at first like I was a kid playing out some ridiculous bluff that would be quickly called, but I actually got away with it, and in a haze of bravado, I made it out flat, taking pain early on but dishing out some of my own when I could, getting my own back on those ranged against me. When Hardy returned from a well-earned holiday with his wife and children and I still hadn't bankrupted the firm, my rite-of-passage week was rewarded with a raise and a bonus – only a little one, I would realize later, but conferring nonetheless an inordinate amount of pleasure. To management's amusement, I received it with a heartfelt, pumping handshake and hurriedly rounded up Chloe and even Elsie that night to treat them to a celebratory Chinese in Parkway.

A few more months passed, and the hot summer came around. My next solo stint was the whole month of August. These were the last days before they all mixed indistinguishably together, and I can almost recall each anxious session and how tremulous I felt. Going in, I would gather myself, full of nervous anticipation and as much courage as I could simulate. I spent distracted evenings sitting in a theatre or a bar, oblivious to the plays and the people around me, mentally revisiting exposures and my various book positions. I considered the various strategies I might employ for each putative scenario I could come up with, making sure that I anticipated everything and that nothing could surprise me. I had to entertain in the evenings, and of course I took my place with the others; but what I really wanted was an early night, remembering well that this was my chance and I didn't want to blow it.

As the days and the weeks gradually went by, I became more ensconced. I was always inclined towards keeping things tidy, not swinging the bat too heavily, and was a little quick, perhaps, in booking a profit; but you played the game as you saw it, always remembering that a loss was a loss and you didn't go hiding it. You worked the percentages and honoured your responsibilities, and only when a position was closed could you count up the cost. With a regularity starting to reveal itself, the days began to resemble each other, and as the sessions thus melded, my confidence grew. I still grappled with the jumble of numbers, but every day was fraught with the same kind of tension; and as the moves and the bluffs became more practiced and more assured, I slowly started to feel that I knew what to do. The sums of money involved seemed always to grow larger, but somehow even that became irrelevant as they too lost their power to shock.

When a sudden electric change occurred, a reverse or a break out that I hadn't predicted, the adrenalin transported me to my very own movie as principal actor enjoying the cameras. Oh, what a ride! What an incredible playground this was turning into for someone like me who was so into the excited atmosphere, truly thankful for the good fortune that had got me here, blessed as only the luckiest few can be. I went about my duties joyfully, half deadly serious and half in disbelieving jest, taking note of the markets – the ticks and the moves – trying to see the next wave before it appeared. I pored through the news in the overnight newspapers which could subtly change the market's mix, trying to glean the ramifications of a story from that morning's *Financial Times*, moving quickly to accommodate a headline that might arrive out of nowhere – one that would instantly unbalance what I had thought was a perfectly weighted book, all of a sudden losing a block of stock on a phone call and realizing immediate action was required – quick thinking and a steady voice or a powerfully strong conviction to brazen it out, to sit there tight and wait out the storm.

Sometimes, when all the stars aligned and purple rimmed the day, the dice couldn't help falling for me, and everything I touched was pure genius. Anyone foolhardy enough to stand in my way then was lost in my wake. At other times, my desolation was equally assured, as I would err to wait or jump too quick, covering a short at the top and lifted back out at the bottom, a confluence of confounding events so neat it seemed as if they'd been written precisely for my despair! As bad as that got, still I loved this place, and I really trusted in the general integrity: those few wrong 'uns I became aware of who twisted the rules I thought the exception, and I was sure that they couldn't prevail. Gradually, as things on the desk progressed for me and my target earnings and lifestyle got closer, the image that always recurred was of that late-eighties Halifax advert – that alluring yuppie with the bank account, the docklands garret, and the soft suede jacket strolling out easy on a Sunday morning for a cup of freshly ground somewhere exquisite, with that big smile all over his face broadcasting to the world how he'd conquered the dream.

On most nights during the week when we had properly accounted for all the trades and reconciled the positions, a group of us younger dealers would head out for drinks. There was great camaraderie as well as some figurative butting of heads, the guys constantly battling for their place in the pecking order. Sometimes on these forays, an older dealer or two would grace us with their company, perhaps newly divorced and looking to reconnect with the after-hours community they'd recently eschewed, finding themselves all of a sudden alone, stray, and bewildered as the reality of the fantasy crashed noisily about them – the addition of a child making it no easy path to recover the formerly comfortable habit of that long-remembered ease. It wasn't all disaster, and there were other veterans whose domestic accommodation provided an easier balance: husbands and fathers let out to blow off some steam and enjoy some after-hours gaiety with us, their pseudo children.

Always there was a flavour-of-the-month bar, a place we'd patronize noisily and expensively for a time, beginning our evenings there like a city swarm of locusts who, by our boisterous and unconducive behaviour, would eventually push out any who were not our own – behaviour which we would moderate only if the indigenous clientele suited some purpose. In time, as all seasons do, the season would change, and inevitably a new champion among the multitude of saloons would open. Taking its turn in temporary prominence, it would depose our most recent shebeen and leave it in peace – quite often too much peace to remain viable – slowly to build back with a new and quieter kind of clientele once our thundering herd had well and truly moved along.

When we'd had our fill of horsing around in bar number one, we'd have a head of steam built up, which would lead on to a break out, and we'd slide into a few of the waiting sherberts to set out on an evening raid to the West End – Covent Garden, maybe, or down to the King's Road for a pizza or some teppanyaki or another kind of meal. Whatever we chose, it would inevitably end too drunk for civility in a food fight. Never mind if our loud and unsubtle antics were disturbing for those unallied patrons around us, the killjoys. This was our town, and we were its heroes! It might sound pretty outrageous, childish even, to be flinging food around London's finest. Certainly it's a breach in spirit of the expected city behaviour, the age-old code of conduct made up of *dictum meum pactum* and a stiff upper lip, but bizarre as it seems, this was just a natural extension of what we were doing during the day. The I-win-you-lose mentality of direct confrontation, a showing-off game of who could go the furthest, fitted very neatly into a "work hard, play hard" philosophy unbounded by manners, a culture of excess unleashed in the Big Bang of a few years earlier. It was all part of "making a name for yourself". Bravado and drink formed a noxious cocktail that quite often and quite literally spilled over. Flicking a bit of chocolate mousse on the tablecloth or some other collateral damage was a thing of no consequence, and if you had happened to arrive into this world with a measure of reticence, this ubiquitous culture chipped at it slowly. Either you joined in as one of the boys, or you got out; it was as simple as that. Later on, at the end of the evening, we'd stumble back to our respective dwellings, or sometimes, all late and lucky and soft and hand in hand, back to someone else's.

If I didn't fall into a cab, barely able to mutter my address, on too many occasions to count, I found myself on the Tube, drunk and then sleeping, and often missed my stop, condemned to spend the evening riding up and then back down again the Northern Line like a narcoleptic on a mission. Finally arriving home, I'd stumble through the doorway and up the stairs, using my palms as extra feet, the mumbled incoherencies and impassioned monologues broken only by heaves of sickness as, doggedly, I drove to the sanctuary of my doorway. Collapsing safe within, I would often spreadeagle there in the hallway and sleep fully clothed with my laces still tied, the handle of the bedroom door above me a distant dream, with its comfort trappings behind it again out of reach.

It wasn't always about smashing it, but those times certainly took their share and were often memorable. One occasion that stands out in my mind as formative was my first – and, for many years, last – boozy business lunch, a thing I've almost never repeated. I was taken to a restaurant in Throgmorton Avenue by a youthful but more experienced interdealer broker who was a friend of our desk and the girlfriend of our "man in New York". I'd hadn't as yet actually met him, but we'd talked on the phone, mostly when Hardy was away, as then it would be my turn to take the 9.20 rundown once the US session had closed. Even on the phone he was quite a character, and I was hugely in awe of him. Feeling that his projected image was something that I should aspire to live up to, I spent the lunch drinking copiously and not even bothering to eat. By the time I went back to the office, itself a mistake, I was seriously slurring my words, and my vision was impaired to the level of monochrome. I was fit only to be sent home: Hardy's look of reprimand I'll never forget. When I awoke the next morning with a dizzying headache plus a feeling of dread in anticipation of the reception I'd get at the office, I vowed not to drink again during the day, to partake only once the market was closed. My daytime sobriety pledge stood me in good stead ever after. Were I the temperate sort, I could have been less strict in its application, but even though I took to heart the frightening lesson of Billy's fall, still there was something inside me that positively craved the excess. Perhaps it was just greed, that hungry twin of the City's driving siblings, but it's too easy to bite off too much when it's laid on a plate – to think you can handle it and get lost in the chewing.

Oh Bondage, Up Yours

Watching from our place in the middle, we shuffle gradually through stages of awareness, learning without realizing it. As children, our adults are all knowing and all caring. We perceive them as relevant only where they relate to us, but when, late in our morning, a new dawn comes, informing us that they are merely grown-up versions of ourselves and we therefore just younger versions of them, this new light is shocking. Innocence jarred by our realization, the games we play are now all invested with an adult hue; but games they remain nonetheless, for though we dress ourselves in grown-ups' clothes, they're not truly fitting. Real wisdom must wait for the passing of many more years, so as we continue to thrust out here and drive out there, these childish advances are merely training. We're not yet capable of determining our path and not yet equipped to attempt it.

Lucky to have a seat among those at the main table, to take a share of the action and be spoilt by the view, what a comfortable place we find ourselves in. How we love to watch the game from here: happiness itself to enjoy it with those enjoying it with us. The happier we are, the faster the hours seem to run, but what is there anyway but to live? What a slick path our lives glide along when desire and fate combine, leading us ignorant and acquiescent to a true destination. What a shock it is one day when, without warning, the mirror returns our stare with some newly distinguished little mark – a late splash of grey, perhaps, or something that redounds with a smidgeon less of the question we once lived by, a smudge of the stoic that lurks in the eye. Fast forward again, and when everything has been said and done, for all the sleek, passing beauty we knew in our youth – for all of that sheen and all of that hope – can there be anything more splendid and victorious than the briefest look that the luckiest of us will wear in the depths of our age when, with our learning complete, we at last can fully accept the truth? No longer fearful or greedily desperate for a little more time, this long-suspected view of the eternal brings with it a grace to bless our last living moments. True understanding and the peace that it brings are life's prize in the ultimate.

Unlike life and true knowledge, however, the financial world has a steep learning curve. Despite its contrived and self-serving appearance, the rules of the game are really quite simple. Run your profits, Cut your losses. The first cut is the cheapest. Our moulding elders would always repeat these as mantras to us, along with the classic, "Don't buy 'em, don't sell 'em, but don't miss it," a valedictory joke as they stood at the doorway, leaving us in temporary charge to head off for a lunchtime excursion. Inevitably, the hold they could keep on their hard-won places would grow increasingly tenuous and almost ceremonial as we continued to mature. Soon enough for them, at some unbidden time, a changing of the guard is inevitable.

Society must not underestimate the role of these parents and the making of room for those whom they've nurtured, who come to replace them. This is a test in itself and the ultimate sign of a job well done, but it never is easy to be reminded by some fresh impudence how we too were uncouth and unlearned, perhaps disrespectful, in times gone by. Remembering that different parts of the river flow with the same water is wisdom distilled, but giving way graciously takes a strength that's usually wrought of love – that or the surest position. Therefore it is only at all of our peril that we abandon the old, that we sentence the aged to dwell miserably in forests of autumn unlit by the respect that is their due, the very quality of which transforms into beauty the passing of time. Without such deserving grace, the old have no recourse other than to refuse to be so – to labour beyond their natural strength and to set thereby a much tougher path for the youth that follow, their way blocked and a fight in store for what should come free.

Penthouse and Pavement

Work was great and the firm was doing well, and somebody high up decided we needed new premises. It might have been just that our lease was up, but looking with fresh eyes at our offices, you could see that the building had become run-down and was really quite antiquated. Some of the floors I'd visited were a warren-like maze of Dickensian corridors, and it was clear that the decor all over had not been refreshed for decades – except in the top floor client dining rooms, that is, a pristine juxtaposition. For the few years I'd been there, and from what I guessed must have been quite a few years before that, the company had been situated opposite the Rothschild building in a lane between Cannon and Lombard Streets. The decision was to move slightly beyond the limits of the City – unusual for that time, I'd say, as it was before the Docklands revolution – and we ended up in a newly built office by the station at Farringdon. Those who lived in North London most welcomed the announcement, and the cohort of lads that came in from Essex most regretted it, as it meant leaving behind the Central Line's Bank Tube station which for them had been such a blessing. Though our new location was hardly more than a mile away, this new area boasted a distinctly different character from the one we'd grown used to. Some would say it had a special charm lent by the genuine shops, such as butchers and delis and the retail flavour of Cowcross Street and of Hatton Garden beyond it, not to mention the historic meat market, which, round the corner at Smithfield's, allowed for twenty-four-hour drinking and the buzz this quite literally entailed, unique at the time and a gift by way of royal charter dating all the way back to King Henry the Eighth.

The new building was nothing like the cramped old offices we'd been used to. A large marble reception area perfectly set off what I dubbed a *Masters of the Universe* escalator, which ascended to the dealing room, blowing smoke up the dealers where a lift might have served just as well. There was a canteen downstairs where we could get all manner of foods, invariably for takeaway to eat at the desk, and a whole floor devoted to fitness: weight and resistance rooms and studios and squash courts and even a swimming pool. An outside team was brought in to manage the sports facility, and to establish quickly a measure of corporate bonhomie, they organized a five-a-side soccer tournament, taking part in which would inspire me to organize my own game, one that would endure and would have an effect on my development as a person that I couldn't have dreamed of.

It makes me wonder, when I look back over all the years, when I think of all the opportunities and all of the friendships that have sprung from this most unlikely of accidents – the numerous post-match evening specials and those annual drinks around Christmas time. The first came a couple of years after our game began, a karaoke night in a North London Chinese with bring-your-own Jack Daniel's (a pregnant Penny would later have to bear the brunt of my over-indulgence). Much more recently, on an evening at a bowling alley in Brick Lane, a group of us comrades bowled, drank, and were merry: a celebration of friendship whose warmth was as deep an acknowledgement of our closeness as ever men are likely to admit to sharing. These two sandwiched so many more between. Once I even got a chance to run out on the professional pitch at Barnet's Underhill stadium in a stag party eleven-a-side game that one of the boys had arranged. Another occasion that stands out was when we took a team up to Luton. We distinguished ourselves by winning the wooden spoon, but I was nevertheless glowingly proud of my player-of-the-tournament performance, my four goals scored coming two from each leg!

If I were to tally up the hours I've spent at the pitches of my twice-weekly fixture, now twenty years on and still counting, the total would be something of note. The deeper legacy of the game, however, was the initiation that it gave me to an exclusively male environment, affording me an understanding of men's rubbing-along mores which beforehand I'd lived quite ignorant of. That and the wealth of the friendships that came from it, the quality and longevity of the relationships born of respect from the crucible of competition, cannot be overestimated. This very different aspect of my life, as much as my growing success and professional accomplishment at work, had an unquantifiable impact on me.

My parents were quick to notice the change. They'd gravitated back to their roots and, though still living on the wrong side of the river, had begun spending quite a bit of time up in town, catching up with the friends they'd left behind when they'd broken out all those years previously and even making new ones in the various groups they'd joined. One such group was the Hampstead Heath Hikers, in which they connected with similarly minded pensioners. Our relationship now was a good one, and they popped by on their way through occasionally, but they saw little enough of me to appreciate my subtle evolution. Things by now had gone full circle for me; I was living in a two-bedroom flat in Camden with one of the juniors from work, who rented the second room at quite a discount: I could afford it, and it was a good arrangement for both of us, as he provided me with pleasant companionship.

The folks were coming up to see this latest gaff and to meet my flatmate, and on the spur of the moment, we decided to head up to Kenwood in the hope of getting tickets for an open-air showing of the film *Casablanca,* a poster of which I'd purchased on one of my early forays along Camden High

Street. If you got the weather, these open-air evenings were wonderful; a lot of people dressed for the film in the smart attire of the actors themselves, ready to settle down and tuck into their picnics in the provided deckchairs. There was an air of occasion about the whole thing that might have been verging on snooty, but the cumulative impact of the location was breath-taking: the trees and the lake and the setting sun plus a *je ne sais quoi* that was hard to put your finger on. Just being there gave one the sense of being a London insider, a sense that felt priceless to me. Unfortunately, and not especially surprisingly, when we got there we found that the show was sold out. We were about to give up and go when a feeling of being so close overcame me. With a part of me desperate to get us involved, and keen also to make a show for my mum and dad of what their prodigal son had become, I started to ask some of the smart people who were still coming in whether they might be willing to sell any spares. Much to my surprise, after a few disdainful knock-backs, I acquired a ticket and, hugely encouraged, began to advertise in a louder voice that I was buying and selling. Having spent years trying to boost me beyond my reticent shell, Mum and Dad were dumbstruck, happily redundant and proud to see me come to life as a son they barely recognized. My behaviour was not appreciated by all of the attendees, those I might describe as the Glydenbourne set – the elite that came here to enjoy an exclusively refined evening – but eventually I had bartered and exchanged us to a set of three adjoining deckchairs, and the evening was one of the loveliest and most memorable that the three of us ever spent together.

I always think it's surprising how deep our long-held impressions lie, for despite this and other examples of my growing confidence, they always seemed to slip back to an earlier image of the man they thought me to be. As a good example of this, many years later, we were all on an extended family holiday that Dad had generously insisted on paying for, husbands and wives and children and mother-in-law all in tow. A rep one day cajoled me into taking part in that evening's cheesy entertainment, and I found myself singing and dressing up like a woman, generally making a fool of myself in front of a large audience. Enjoying the show and insisting that I should have been voted the winner instead of second place, they again expressed their utter shock that I should have been prepared to behave as I had. I just shook my head, thinking as I did that this behaviour, for me, was pretty much par for the course.

I Don't Want To (Go to Chelsea)

Down on the pitch below the game recommences as a sideshow to the main event, a sporting backdrop for the jests and idle banter that we content ourselves with as we sit up high on the concrete terraces. For those among us easily distracted, this brotherly repartee becomes the *raison d'être,* can come to replace our watching of the game, especially when the sport itself is not sufficiently gripping. But let there be just a flash of action or a ripple of excitement shooting through the crowd, and immediately our heads turn and we are drawn back again to the spectacle as the faithful we are, searching for the source with our fullest attention and reminded all at once what really we're here for. Somehow chastened for any previous lapse of respectful focus, we find that for a time that ensues we remain locked in a concerted spell of concentration as if it's mandatory to prove the argument for our continued attendance. Here comes Tommy, picking his way back along the row, having missed a couple of second-half minutes in seeing out to the bitter end the half-time refreshments queue. He bears carefully the spoils of his patience, the oversized cups which proclaim in our very own colours their sweet liquid contents, and we empty therein our hip flasks for the perfect mix to match the occasion.

Back on the pitch, refreshed after a fifteen-minute power nap and the exhortations of Le Professeur, the players are rejuvenated, and the game is now much more evenly balanced than after the earlier kick-off. Both sides begin this half probing, and both repel blunt launched long balls that hurtle in as the players alternately look to build up some dominance in the middle and forge from that something dangerous to be carried into the opponent's box and then made to count there. The anxious affair that jangled our nerves in those first forty-five minutes, when our Arsenal warriors seemed to be sinking hopelessly beneath the cosh and it looked as though each ensuing minute was ticking towards our ultimate undoing, now seems to have been ridden out. No killer blow landed, and that dangerous storm has turned instead to a glow of justified hope, a feeling inspired by the little battles that are going on all over the grass as we take the fight to our enemies. Where before we chased shadows all over the pitch, showing hardly appetite or invention, our passes now look sharper, our challenges stronger. For those of us who watch, who fret in our seats with our views from above, we're back in the game with a hope that we'll conquer.

A yellow free kick just out from the corner of our box is given, and the referee heeds the standard complaints. The assistant's flag indicates some few paces stolen and, as instructed, the ball is moved back a little only to be replaced with a spin and the yards again stolen as we've come to expect. The players mingle, innocent of intention, as the wall forms, a couple of our lads standing off with their hands on their hips, taking up their positions slowly, not seeming to look – a study of nonchalance. The chanting from the crowd rises, with a whole singing section to our left whooping its support, rising and falling and rising again, masking the sound of the whistle. The shot crashes in but goes only as far as the wall, which it bounces off high and wide, falling sweetly for an ambitious but well-taken volley. Looping, the keeper does well to get down to it, turning it out for a corner. The opposition are resplendent in their colours as they dart through the box, custard to our strawberries, and the ball again comes in and is punched right away. Someone shouts, "Out! Out, Arsenal!" from somewhere in the stands beside me, and another chimes in with "Come on, Arsenal!" as the break is on. Hope and excitement rise around us, but the break's broken down with a pass gone awry, and lofted back from halfway, the ball once again is headed back out and then back in again, only their striker is offside, and the flag goes up. We hear the whistle this time as the game stops for our free kick, the crowd spontaneously taking up a heartfelt round of "Oh Arsenal We Love You" – our gift to the players for the joy in our hearts.

Sing Our Own Song

You'll meet all sorts of different types of people on the terraces. There are the philosophers, calmly taking in the game and bearing with fortitude the injustices, the cynical fouling, the time wasting, and the goals not given, keeping their oath that karma in the end will all balance out. These are steady and peaceful inside, and they come here to enjoy, to make the most of the occasion with an old, weathered smile that's the truest reflection of their calm interior: a little celebration is allowed when occasion demands but none too high. Then there are the generals, those football managers who are lost to the bench and so direct their campaigns instead from the stands, constantly spewing advice and wisdom. As they inevitably go unheard by their objects on the pitch, the arrangement is a recipe for frustration; and when the pressure is on, they all too easily lose their measure, quickly becoming the loudest critics, grown vexed by their team. Another group among the myriad that sit around us are those whose trust in the world is pierced by too sharp a sense of indignity and who arrive at the ground too weighed down by this grim point of view. For them, the referee and the linesmen constitute a clear projection of some eternal conspiracy, and with their heightened sense of injustice on overdrive, they're quick to soak up any fresh disappointment, bloating to a bitter sponge which, too soon full, drips out its bile on all with an ear. Some, like me, are like the wind, now blowing this way and now blowing that, sometimes master and sometimes servant of the moods ascendant within. Away from those who know us better, on arrival at the game, we might choose for this different setting a different personality, far from the one we usually project. When all is said and done, the way people are always comes down to the same things, whether kindly or mean, whether honest or less so.

The characters are seen larger than life under that special magnifying glass of the City, and they stand out in memories that simply refuse to fade. Before I made it to the dealing room upstairs, my first boss at the firm seemed the embodiment of evil. He was excessive in his appetites and bloated accordingly, loving to torment and to bully. Heading up a department filled with pretty young boys hardly much younger than he, his each day was Christmas. There I was, a little older than the mean and even more incredulous than indignant at what I saw going on, but I certainly wasn't speechless. It was only by learning a lesson which seems to reek of disgrace – that I shouldn't try to fight other people's battles – that I was plucked back from the punishment of back-office isolation, my education enhanced by a hasty transfer further below, where a new set of monsters was waiting, another group of demons not worthy of the position of manager. At least I can take some credit for knowing I was beaten and for my pragmatic tenacity, which kept me hanging on, despite the indignities, long enough for Billy to lift me up higher.

Though market making is famously a male resort, or perhaps because of it, I'll always remember the female dealer I worked under for a time on the desk upstairs. She was a pastiche of the brash American, who exceeded the men around her in hoarse manliness and so was rarely taken for her sex when she answered the phone – the product, no doubt, of those copiously smoked St Moritz cigarettes I was constantly sent out for, piling up a heap in the ashtray between us. She was a true professional who lived and breathed the qualities that the game required, risen to her status through nothing but excellence; but though she was kindly in taking me under her wing, she liked it less when I wanted to find my own way – when I started to challenge her. The thing I remember most of all now was how she spoke up for me outside of the office when it really mattered: even if we didn't always get on when we sat side by side, hour by hour, because of what she did for me there, I'll always remember her as a friend.

Another of the circle of freaks with whom I like to think I share a deep fellowship is the clever Yorkshire man who I've mentioned before and will mention again. An eccentric as broad as the spectrum itself, the man nonetheless had a very big heart befitting of someone of his size, in accordance with his love of the pint. I felt humbled one day when he assured me that my example had taught him something of importance, but whatever that might have been, we loved one another as friends whose mutual regard facilitated a long lasting bond. Unlikely as it seemed at first, after much prodding, he became a stalwart of the twice-weekly football game and, as such, still stands, almost always present at the drinks that come after and the founder of our enigmatic prize-giving which, once a year, brings closer together our tight little group.

When self-interest is taxing the mind, there are too few among us truly capable of differentiating between truth and that shady alternative which, running more in line with our desire, can be used as truth's proxy. Perhaps honesty's intrinsic beauty is too little valued or the clarity of truth to the muddled mind is too opaque; maybe we perceive the journey to this worthy destination as too fraught. Whatever the cause, within the City and beyond, a majority around us goes through life more servant of desire than of integrity. On those rare occasions when we do bumble into a genuinely kindred spirit, it does not go unnoticed, as long as we are able to see what we find, and almost inevitably, an enduring friendship results. This is how it was with Luca. His dad had studied with one of our bosses, and barely old enough to be employed, he came more for some work experience than with a view to anything permanent, though it wasn't long before others noticed and sought after his qualities. He had an old soul that struck me as wise in a way that I knew I was not despite having many more years under my belt, and we hit it off immediately. I loved his gently challenging honesty and his fresh sense of fun, forgiving him that by a certain light he looked like a younger version of me and finding that being with him took me back to a time I realized I'd never experienced. As the months turned to years, I grew to think of him as a brother, one who, with Tommy, shares a special place in my heart.

When he first arrived in the country, he was sharing a Kilburn flat with some mates he knew from back home in North Bondi, other lads who also had taken some time here to stop from their travels, and I remember meeting a few of them when, in the early days of our friendship, I went back there one evening. The ease with which they all seemed to exist around one another struck me immediately. Like me, they were Jewish, but unlike me, they'd grown up in an environment where they could be who they were without having to apologize for that. Growing up in a place where being Jewish was not awkward and embarrassing seemed to me an impossible dream. I remember that night sitting on the couch as the boys who should naturally have been my kin sat like disciples around me, trying to understand how my experience with our religion had meant nothing but exile and humiliation. Hearing me express my reflections of negativity, they frowned and charged me with being self-loathing, a term of rebuke I'd not heard before, but I think as they got to know me a little better – to understand where I was coming from – they forgave this first impression and adjusted their views accordingly.

Despite this bumpy visit, I felt pleased with myself for having made the special effort of reaching out. Reflecting on it as I made my way home tipsy in a cab, I felt that going round to his place would be taken as a demonstration of goodwill – goodwill which I was sure would be welcome and repaid. It occurred to me again how even though my relationships were becoming more numerous and growing deeper with the passing of time, socially, an acute desire for the acceptance of others drove my actions and behaviours. This overwhelming emotion remained strangely potent even though the bleak loneliness of my early adulthood was long past, a person having only to smile at me to induce tear-choked gratitude. The lessons that are forged in youth really are the lessons best learned, but I couldn't have been more right about Luca. That night did turn out to be the first of many, and over the coming months and years, it happened more and more that we went out together, sometimes for work and sometimes just for fun. Whatever the occasion, it was always a pleasure.

An evening soon after that first one turned into a two-man team-build, a memorable laugh and one that fast-tracked our new friendship. As it was the season for it, we decided to get all the ingredients back at his and embark on a mojito adventure, repeatedly making and then drinking them as we crushed the leaves and muddled the sugar syrup before liberally applying the seven-year rum, convincing ourselves it was the education we were chasing rather than the alcohol. With expertise sufficiently enhanced, we decided we were hungry and headed outside for the spontaneous game of chicken involved in crossing the busy road. Under the influence, we laughed riotously with each other as the lights and the car horns swirled in a psychedelic collage until we pretty much fell into the Indian restaurant we had set our sights on and ordered some doubles. We played bombers with the laminated menus that we didn't need to open and destroyed the poppadoms as soon as they arrived. By the time we'd finished our curries, bloated and happy, the edge had lifted from our drunkenness, and we crossed back over the road in a much safer fashion. Ready now to take it easy, we sat in his lounge and put on the video I'd brought along especially for the occasion. Luca thus got his very first taste of The Comic Strip's *pièce de résistance,* "The Yob". A few hours later, I found myself waking blearily on the hard carpet floor, and gathering my senses and my bag, I made my way home.

The first time I had witnessed this masterpiece was all those years before when I was sharing the flat with Billy, and its profoundly strange influence has left me forever in its awe. A dealer mate of his who I knew only as "Handbag" had lent us the copy, and watching it was a truly eye-opening experience. It was on one of those hard-hitting nights in the first few weeks after we'd moved in together, and a crew had formed itself around us spontaneously. Though later this set-up became all too regular and something of a drag, at this time it still felt fresh and exciting. The party mood was already building nicely, but this special film turned the dial to eleven: it was the most unashamedly non-PC thing I had ever seen, even back then when political correctness was something I was hardly aware of. The satire was so incredibly crude – so sexist, so racist – it was like nothing I could have imagined, and I was totally gobsmacked. I wasn't a veteran of City humour by then, you see, and my soul was not yet infected by the irreverent brand that is currency for laughter all over the square mile. Naively, I assumed that certain topics were simply not in play, so seeing that contradicted on the screen before me in the name of entertainment shocked me intensely.

My reaction when the film started was one of horror. I was glued wide-eyed to the set, hardly believing what I was seeing, but with the mood of unbridled hilarity around me remaining unchecked, I continued to indulge my curiosity. What happened next was surprising: my feelings of discomfort began to ease, leaving just dumbfounded amazement, and with the guys watching with me whooping with laughter, I began to feel myself enjoying it, albeit guiltily: before I knew it, I was laughing along with them. I could almost feel the subversion creeping beneath my skin, and when the shock changed to something more like admiration as the film went on, it blew me away. It was astounding how it seemed to contradict directly the certainties, the rules, and the assumptions that my upbringing had so subtly ingrained in me. Not only did I find it absolutely hilarious, like a door to Funnyland kicked open where previously I'd known just a wall, it was edgy and challenging. If anything could profoundly reach me at this particular time, it was the suggestion that I'd stumbled upon something that I couldn't quite handle: I wasn't going to stand aside and let that pass me by.

That's my theory for why the short film so infected me, but whatever the reason, my obsession had begun. From then on, Billy and I took to communicating with each other by throwing about the flat favourites from our repertoire of "Yob" one-liners, epithets that we'd lifted from the film which we practiced and polished so we could "do the voice, blindin'". This never failed to amuse us, and we never missed an opportunity to use one where it seemed even remotely appropriate, progressing on with inventions of our own that bore the show's unmistakably chauvinistic hallmark until eventually it had infected my entire personality. Someone once told me that I could choose for myself a virtue and, with practice, make it my own. Instead, I had chosen for myself a vice, and practicing it in this way, it was as if a part of me, just like in the film, had become this thing, this Yob: a thing that I'd been distinct from and of which, quite perversely, I was now very proud.

Coming Down

Even before I knew first-hand this world of high-octane excitement, when, as a BT clerical assistant, I moved into the Camden house share and started going along with Billy to the clubs and the bars, it was clear how the industry's largesse opened for its members the doors of upper-echelon entertainment. London's finest restaurants may be dullish and overly familiar for the dwellers of Chelsea and Mayfair, and maybe it's nothing out of the ordinary for people like these to watch a Champions League final battled out for their pleasure from a pitch-side seat, but for me these new-found privileges were nothing less than a step change. I will never forget the first time I went with the other dealers on our pitch for dinner on the Knightsbridge green at a bare-brick restaurant. I sat rigidly proper beside Hardy, and I remember when he turned to me with a reassuringly paternal smile, knowing that I was sweating as I looked down the prices and telling me not to mind them but just to order what I wanted and be sure to enjoy it! It wasn't that I'd never been to a restaurant: I'd been going with Charlie and with others, but before this time, price was the first thing I looked at before ordering anything; of course it was. Here, therefore, was true liberation and something that felt amazing to me; I found myself in a place that by rights was beyond my reach. All these years later, I still observe a happy pause to remind myself as I sit surveying gratefully another such place, recalling that long-ago evening once more with a glass of something nice in my hand and appreciating the fact no less for the passing of time.

Occasions were not always as responsible and civilized as they should have been: too much rope, I've found, can make for a dangerous mess. A good example of this was one time when I headed out to Oxford for a client meeting on a lovely midsummer afternoon. Having spent multiple good times already with this guy and having even been invited along to his firm's Christmas party, I considered him a friend; and with Luca accompanying me, the evening promised to be supremely enjoyable. The two of us arrived at his sleepy country station with the afternoon sun still shining above us, and the first thing we did was to take a stroll full of relaxed anticipation to the local Waitrose. There we could collect certain things that we needed: a bag of ice and a bottle each of Jack Daniel's and Gin as well as some mixers. We made our way next to a meeting place on the bank of the river as prearranged.

Swinging our plastic bags, we hung around waiting for just a few minutes until along he came, breezing down the hill towards us with a big, toothy smile on his face. After preliminaries, we traipsed off down the path together in the balmy summer breeze, penetrating the genteel wilderness and finding a perfect spot to lay down a blanket beside the shining bright water. Along with the bottles and the ice and the colourful plastic cups we'd packed for the occasion, we set a phone dock and ourselves down on it on the grass and put on some music, spending the ensuing hour or so pouring and drinking and drinking and pouring until the bottles we'd brought were half to the bottom. I started dancing about, full with the fresh air's idyllic freedom, until I was unable to dance anymore and just lay on my back, smiling happily with my friends right there beside me. We were close together. When it came time for us to go off and eat, I tried to get up, but my legs seemed to fail me. My head wasn't too tricky either, spinning due to the liberty my old friend Jack and I had taken, and it occurred to me that the crash diet I'd been following for the last few days must have weakened me. A little time was all that I needed, I told the others, and they were happy to delay.

After patiently and amusedly watching several failed attempts to stay on my feet, they decided they'd have to help me to the restaurant. I remember postulating optimistically to myself that this walk through the fresh evening air might be just what I needed as the two of them carried on a conversation around me, responding to my sporadic mumbled incoherencies with my weight shared between them. They got me all the way into town and to the table, but sitting there, I found that my head still wouldn't stop spinning; it seemed to be getting worse rather than better. I couldn't sit up straight and was now feeling really sick, so they removed me to the entrance, where I might get some air. I couldn't have been the greatest advert for the place, propped up and slumping on a chair in the narrow flock hallway beneath the assorted hanging coats of bemused fellow patrons. Time went by, and in my stupor, it seemed that the same people entered and in their turn left to find me in the same sorry state. I managed to remove myself to the toilet, where I then remained, defiant to the banging and the pleading that alternately encroached from without, bringing me each time back to awareness. Though my memory at that point of the evening is a disconnected sequence of hazy images, I'm ever grateful to Luca, remembering it was he who rescued me from there unconscious, having slipped into total collapse.

Once they'd finished their meal and mine, untouched, had been cleared away, they carried me on through the town to a pub, where I was placed somewhere convenient, sitting obediently like a stuffed guy on Bonfire Night. Mostly I drifted in and out of consciousness with my drink unmolested before me, but I could manage a clipped word or two by now, both with the boys when they came over to check on me and with some locals whose curiosity I'd piqued. Finally, at the end of this country adventure, I was borne up again and laid at the station across the seats of the waiting train for a long journey home. The ceiling of the carriage rocked in my gaze as we made our excruciatingly slow progress back east, and I came back to myself equally slowly, until finally, at Paddington, I was able to take to my legs – about as steadily as a newborn foal. I held my own sufficiently to convince Luca he could leave me there, trusting me to make the remainder of my journey without his assistance.

It was rare for me so totally to mistime my approach, as I liked to call those little misjudgements, spoiling what would otherwise have been a most enjoyable excursion; and as you'd expect when almost anything within reason is available for your pleasure, these evenings tended to be as good as they should have been. On too many delightful occasions to count, I found myself enveloped in a sphere of pleasure that seemed a soft, puffy cloud, with the perfect company and the perfect mood. I knew these sweet times for the wonderful privilege they were, and as much as I'm aware how superfluous these spoiling treats are it still makes me shudder to imagine my life lived without them.

Another year and another time, early winter finds Luca and me out under the stars on the damp, shining roof of the A Bar. The skies have clearly opened earlier, and the cushions left out on the dark wooden deck are still glistening. The whole area is empty but for the two of us and the palm trees with their big, waxy leaves bent heavy from the rain. Here we are, among the lights and the darkness, looking over the rampart under the lately dry heavens, looking out to the top of the grand old buildings opposite which have surrounded Oxford Circus since the days of the horse. We are on top of the world and right at its centre, and that's how it feels – a bottle or two of champagne always make a good starter and a nice way to get a light foundation in the front of one's mind. After overlaying that with a couple of swift black ones, always too swift, I'm ready for the cherry on the cake. The beads are passed to me with that warm, knowing smile, and they're taken the same way – taken in deep, a rush like the first taste of coffee slowly putting down the very last piece of a head-tripping jigsaw.

The evening of smiles has passed short and sweet, and it's time to go home. Leaving Luca to stay with the trees, I head for the exit. I say farewell to our hosts with something witty and charming as I pass by on my way to the lift, darting just in time through the closing doors, which are forced to reopen, and I come to a stop with an apology to the lately retarded traveller already inside, flashing a smile to pay him his dues as he pays back the same.

"Where you going?" I blurt, making the most of a friendly mood towards my new best friend.

"I'm going down," he laughs, the two of us both leaving the rooftop. "What about you?" I take up his lead with a wittily self-deprecating response which further enhances our nascent bonhomie.

"Back home to baby sit now," I offer next. "The Mrs is off out tonight. You got kids?"

"No. Keep meaning to settle down one day, just haven't had the time."

"You've done well, mate," I assure him, smiling, and at the bottom we shake hands like brothers and part, taking opposite sides of the pavement as we both scurry towards the Underground. One shadows the other a few paces away as we round the corner to Regent Street, and then he's lost to the crowds the next time I look.

At the railings and the packed stairway which leads the descending masses to the Underground, there's a preacher in a long black robe with a white dog collar and a camel-coloured jumper, his stuttering message expounded to weary-faced passers-by with fire in his voice and a glare in the whites of his eyes. To all outward appearances, he's ignored, somehow unnaturally apart from those folk who must pass him on their way, as if he does not belong in and is despised by their real world of slow-moving procession. Watching him with interest, I get nearer, and still captivated, I listen to the things that he cries.

"God will not make the choice for you," he says. "The fight for life against the Devil and the tools of the Devil is yours to win. Choose the Lord. Turn from sin and God will save you, but the choice is your own. Choose for yourself the way of the Lord!"

Hearing his earnest delivery, I can't help but notice, albeit impassively, that it all seems strangely relevant to my own happy state as the drugs swimming around pleasingly inside of my head massage my senses. I wonder if it's just the coincidence that tugs at my guilt – at my sense of misadventure – or is it that I really am choosing darkness as I slip into the mouth of the flow at the railings, taking the stairs to the vaults down below?

Can't Stand Me Now

Becoming a member of this venerable profession gave me such a deep sense of pride and satisfaction, such a belief in what I was doing, that it was as if a badge of honour had been bestowed upon me. I loved that it made me feel like a lion of the City, like one of my generation's chosen few and a part of the latest elite line, fearless and worthy. This innate sense of superiority, together with my growing addiction to the daily adrenalin rush and the fact that I had more disposable income than I'd ever thought possible, proved a dangerous combination. We weren't Premier League footballers, but we did feel as if we were playing in our own big league, and like those icons, we felt untouchable, as if the rules that governed our behaviour were somehow more flexible than the ones that governed those around us living their more mundane, more humdrum existence.

It isn't difficult to lose track of one's humility when living that kind of life: we could have what we wanted, and we often did. If we fancied larging it up West, then we might be found sucking our way through Zuma's cocktail list amid our favourite Knightsbridge bar's opulent minimalism, laughing at the brass, who sat posing on their bar-stool perches and cast surreptitious eyes from behind the aloof sophistication that served to hide, but not very well, their evening purpose. Or we might huddle in a horseshoe together at the chef's table of some swanky Marylebone hotel with Marcus Waring working for our delectation on his '1-2-3 lamb', a signature dish that we congratulated ourselves was not for the sheep. Huge bulbs of the finest reds breathed on the table before us as we sat waiting for our Hawksmoor delivery, another in a long, cheery line of great slabs of meat. There was always time for another Jack Daniel's, and wherever we were, there was always a switch that could take us into overdrive, always another gear to slam up to in pursuit of the perfect. It is a truly dangerous thing to be given so much for so very little, for such unearned riches as these only impel us to take a step further just because we can. Driven crazy by a ravenous hunger for this unfulfilling charade, it's a rare person that's smart enough to pause for the briefest moment, to stop and enjoy the flowers in the garden.

Because I've been there and have a privileged perspective on what the taste of excess can do to you – the way it makes you see yourself and the way it makes you think – standing apart from them, I read a hungry leer on their faces that makes me shudder. It's a look which speaks nothing of sex but stinks instead of a crazed, angry thirst for possession in the ultimate of everything and anything, fuelled by the arrogant certainty of rightful dominion and a warped imagination which cruelly accepts that murder itself is theirs by right if so they desire. There's no point too fine, and meek single measures reek too much of water for these masters of the universe. Watch them full of smiles and on top of the world in their packs in the bars, holding sway in twos and threes, demolishing drinks and saluting each other's egos as they bask in glory in their own private land at the edge of endurance, mouths twisted with grins too broad for natural emotion or anything pure, revelling again in this hard-drinking proof of supreme self-control. At times less guarded, the faces on these latter-day princes can reveal the well-mannered menace that lurks just beneath. Perish the thought that you should rouse them, that you should find yourself between them and some momentary trifling plaything, because there you'd be nought, a worthless irritation for the mighty to deal with.

On the pavements of our darkening capital with their straight-armed salutes stand these grim-faced monster-masters; taxi-seeking commandants brimmed too full of a glorious spirit which makes so much sense at the time that they're blind to the fact that this unbounded arrogance is an ill-gotten high, a self-induced haze which will be so much spent tissue in the morning. On the roads, you can see them driving at the speed of cock; and on the trains they are wolves slumming with partied commuters as the cloud of the night's uber-convictions still hangs over them, lost to the carriage as their garishly coloured buds pipe in another angry tune and fend safely away the air too sterile for greats such as these. A pumping rhythm mixed with who knows what plays tricks with their minds, and their hearts beat too strong with the excess inside.

Their self-congratulatory emotions rise beyond the point of common empathy, intense superiority affirmed, moulded, and locked in their jaws with a barely containable anger. The world is suddenly theirs, and every object in it is just for their pleasure, buzzing with convenience for just them alone. In their own powerful minds, they can do what they want, do who they want, and their addled brains radiate waves of mastery and excellence like energy beams from crazed, staring eyes, pulsing down the carriage with a power irresistible to seduce or destroy, the force of their will washing relentlessly over these minions before them. How manly and heroic they are at the last, that under such self-inflicted weight they manage so comfortably to carry themselves home, making that clumsy final leg with a staggering walk which serves only to emphasize how herculean their achievement, another sign of greatness to be celebrated in the minds of these masters of nothing.

Father and Son

Becoming aware of the long frown that's buried its creases into my forehead, it occurs to me how lately I've grown increasingly troubled by this idea of the world we live in as a twin-lane model – by the suspicion that there still seems to operate a sort of class system very like the one which, growing up, I was assured beyond doubt had been buried in times behind us. Even only a few years ago when I heard what I took to be the cynical delusions of conspiracy theorists, those dark-dreamt hypotheses which brought forth the proposition of forces hidden behind a smooth veneer and from there pulling strings – I dismissed them out of hand, summarily branding anyone of such a mind as an irreconcilable nutter. That was until my own nagging doubts grew louder and louder: it seems that learning will find you if you only live long enough, however you run and wherever you hide. During the most recent global financial crisis, I remember picking over the news on the screens and in the papers and how the litany of misdemeanours that kept on cropping up began to suggest certain historical similarities. The secretive meetings and dubious payments alluded inescapably to a catalogue of cousins, relations to the way things have happened in the past which traced out for me the shadiest hierarchy where the rich get richer and the poor stay the same. It's impossible to ignore, as if everything's guided by some perverted version of noblesse oblige. One set of rules applies to us underlings, while for our overlords, those you'll rarely find on a packed Underground platform or travelling with the masses on a slow-moving train, entirely more fitting accommodation is arranged.

When periodically I stop to retest my evolving convictions, life constantly delivering its latest bundle of experiences to qualify and assimilate, I wonder about the conclusions I've come to regarding the group of people who, in the business world at least, are roughly my species. Am I misled by some singular madness that I attribute to all of us? Could standing too close for too long, I wonder, with too suspicious a mind, be responsible for my having become misguided? It could be that I only think that I see where a business like mine must invariably lead, with no real witness to account for my worst fears, but I don't think that is the case. As dramatic and extreme as my concerns are, as thoroughly paranoid and far from what I once would have held conceivable, that latest episode and the evidence must surely prove a contempt at the highest level for the order of the markets; I believe for justice too.

Having witnessed the rigging of capitalism itself, supposedly on behalf of the weak and needy yet serving best of all those who dwell at society's apex, I was wholeheartedly convinced if not exactly of how things really work then at least of how things really are and of exactly what type of society the vast majority of us live in. Through whatever means – for some, perhaps, via the illusion of the ballot box or the granting of their infantile desires – there can be no doubt that mostly we live thoroughly assured not only of our freedom but also of the strength and integrity of our time-honoured democracy. I've come to believe that, where it really matters, the status quo has not materially changed in a few hundred years. We are not much removed from those ill-fated and gullible boys who were sent from their trenches to die for their country, exhorted by the leaders of that country to make it sweet and becoming specifically for those leaders themselves.

It can't be helped that such disturbing musings as these enter my head, but as I have no mind now for chewing on them, they leave just as quietly as they came and time passes slowly. Looking out blankly I register without thought or comment the movements of the players, who make their little darts and runs around me, the practiced feints and skills that they've perfected, cameos of entertainment that always are there if we care to take notice as I sit here expectant in the Kings Cross 'Parcel Yard'. Automatically, I check my watch and wonder if Jim will be able to make it. That's the measure of insecurity I have in this longest of friendships, a relationship that's increasingly defined by the times that stretch between our meetings. I have forgotten, as I always do, how very close we really are and how complete will be our connection at the very instant we reconquer the distance between us.

I arrived at the station early and had one of those meandering wanders around the places downstairs, ultimately finding myself sucked into the bookshop for a wistful perusal of the tomes with their handwritten recommendations on the flavour-of-the-month shelf. Delighting as I marked off how many of these classics I'd already read, I tried not to be disheartened by those I had not; this habitual stocktaking left me about half pleased with myself as always it did. Almost subconsciously, I then allowed myself to be guided to the alphabetized fiction section, where I sought out the Ms, half-regarding my arrival there as some oddly fortunate accident, dwelling for a few minutes to grasp the opportunity of reconnecting with a recent favourite. A girl that I had first met at a dinner party years earlier had introduced me to the books of the Japanese author Murakami when we ran into each other after many years in the Hampstead Waterstones. Just catching sight of Caroline that day had brought back the instant impression of loveliness she always exuded, the bearing that belonged to the kindest of souls, and falling into conversation there among the volumes, we had ended up by going for a coffee. Before doing so, she'd pulled *The Wild Sheep Chase* from a shelf to tell me it was something I'd really enjoy.

Even as she said it, I knew it was true. Sure enough, I was to find that the subtlety with which he weaved the purest mundane with a golden strand of metaphysical fantasy would spin for my imagination a deeply thrilling mystery, an allusion I had to trust bore some deeper connection with the half-hidden truth which lies behind finite life's curtain, slightly beyond yet tantalisingly close to the edge of my understanding. The author's voice rang with a question revisited, one which reminds me of the very first such journey I undertook in Herman Hesse's care, *Steppenwolf* having been given to me as a parting gift from a friend of Gloria at the end of a small adventure. I must have let on that it was an ambition of mine to be master of the classics, and this unbidden kindness was what had set me to the path. Taking my first awkward steps with a fixed sense of purpose more akin to duty than enjoyment, I was soon to find myself beguiled and enchanted. This awakening marked the commencement of an unwitting search, an ongoing journey that has lasted for years. It always comforts me to revisit those places where books have been my guide, those "realms of gold" that touch us and whose marks we'll ever wear, breathing fresh colour into long-faded memories as we continue to search for those treasures that surely must exist somewhere within the realms of reality.

With due worship paid, soon enough it was time to move on. Making my way up the staircase to the place of our rendezvous, I passed through the doors by the variously assembled parties that sat like self-styled gatekeepers at the metal tables and chairs with their pretravel pints before them, looking out from high above the butterfly concourse. I found an empty table for myself in the middle of the central room and felt the pause of relaxation as I sat in one of its four chairs. Looking up, I took note of the clientele at the various tables and settees around me. These co-occupants of this high-windowed atrium filled from above with a clear winter's light, were not at all what you'd call City regulars, these travellers awaiting their trains for a short window in this constantly changing club. These businessmen and their colleagues presented rather as a more down-to-earth type, though they were many different types, in fact, an eclectic mix of real people both old and young who seemed happy to make the most of the waiting time here. Their dress was clearly not the standard City uniform. The styles were far more varied and much more what you might expect for casual utility: even those travellers heading to meetings looked just smart enough and not a stitch more, contrasting even so with the civilians in their truly informal garb, perfectly fit for a journey ahead.

A permanent queue for Platform Nine and Three-Quarters might attest that hereabouts is indeed a special place, but to enter a truly magical world, one altogether more interesting for its existence in reality, you've only to climb the glass staircase and pull open those Victorian-blue doors which part resplendent in their brass fittings. Something of a timeless beauty has been preserved in the wooden partitions and the time-worn bricks, in the light beams that flood the area from all angles above and show off the grim splendour of such archived treasures as the corridors wear proudly. These signs, once lost to the smoke and grime of an earlier era, directed countless pioneers to the Waiting Room or warned them from trespass. This whole project is the rarest of things, bringing to us in restored excellence the evocative legacy and wonder of times gone by, all the better for not being overwhelmed by those rowdy superiors who ply their trade just a couple of miles to the south.

The group at the standing table in the corner to my left start to gather up their bags and their miscellaneous belongings: a jumper and a book; a plastic supermarket bag with its packed lunch retrieved from the floor, the silver parcel of sandwiches disappearing from view as the handles are taken up. Three happy hoverers make ready their final approach by moving just close enough to stake their claim, politely deferring by holding back just enough for the departing incumbents to leave unmolested: manners in action. Out goes the gentleman with the thick white hair all over his head and his lip and his chin as well as his daughter (I hope) with her Ugg boots and her long blonde locks. The grateful newcomers, a group of white, middle-aged men, replace them. One of the fellows is bald, and his shaven head is marked with shadows. He wears wire-rimmed glasses and a gilet over a soft blue fleece: he looks like he's prepared for the slopes. The man next to him is taking off a sports jacket to reveal a short-sleeved T-shirt. He appears to share the same hairline as our snow monster, but his head is unshaved. I see a monk's line with hair both dark grey and light sprouting all around his fleshy crown as he turns to put the dark jacket over the chair that he's just commandeered. Their last member wears jeans and a red checked shirt. His full head of longish dark hair is the group's crowning glory.

I look again at my watch to check the time: two minutes have dawdled past five, and still there's no sign of James. I do hope he'll get here. It's a feature of our relationship that I'm left wondering right to the very last whether a plan we make will actually come to fruition – an echo, perhaps, of that inaugural trip when there really was a surprise in store. Sitting and wondering in the tantalizing run-up to one of our irregular meetings, I feel it most clearly, whereas with Tommy it's quite a different case. By nature, he's unpredictable, a man who plans only in outlines and whose details can often surprise you, but though he'll almost always be late and full of some sort of craziness when eventually he does make an appearance, at least you know that he'll get there. The one time he did let me down I later heard from his distraught mother that he'd actually been under a bus.

You have to forgive that. Of James, however, I can never feel fully confident, so I'm always a little uncertain, suspicious even, of what he really feels towards me. In the unease and paranoia that dominate my mind at these waiting times, I've built for myself a picture of spite, thinking that he's keeping me hanging just to have a little fun with me with a host of cancelled meetings and the plans he's put back. Perhaps it's because we've always been peers and therefore are naturally more competitive that a sense of rivalry is part of our dynamic, unlike in my relationship with Tommy, where a mutual respect has found a way to replace the distinction that used to define us.

With the tetchiness that this last-minute suspense brings starting to tip my calm equilibrium, I take the phone from my pocket and put in my ear buds. Double-clicking the solitary button, I find the last track I was listening to, "Father and Son", and hit rewind. It starts playing again, and the deliberately picked guitar's sound fills my ears, a universe of silence behind each chosen note. Cat Stevens's deep voice always reminds me of when I first made the choice to listen to him. For many years, I had done so vicariously when the music swam from my parents' stereo incomprehensibly, close chased by my childish complaining. Listening independently to the nostalgic strain without so much as a by your leave felt more than a tad cheeky, but from the time I picked up the CD in the little shop at the market, it came to represent the most wonderful comfort, its sound an unspoken repudiation and a tacit nod of respect that echoed from the depths of my youth to play a new part from a new stereo in a new lounge, filling sun-drenched afternoons in the boxy York way garden.

Listening to that mellifluous crooner, my heart is an island, emotion-charged rivers flowing strong deep inside me with eddies that stir to the sweet nip of pain. Such reminders there are, fond memories of trials overcome, and I think of that battle I thought I waged with my father when petulantly I craved for my own path and for some assurance that I could have a future all my own, not wanting always to resent his support, which my weakness made indispensable. The singer's words, the tone of his voice, and the music itself almost plead to be understood, beg to confirm that you are not the first and that your frustration and anger are in themselves building blocks, essential components to ultimate success. To my amazement, I see my own helpless love for the children who day by day grow closer to adulthood, who think just as I did, with the same rash impatience, and I pray I might yet be the man that I wished to be when still but a boy.

My mind drifts away as I listen, wondering if this subtle thing of beauty might perhaps be beyond perception without the medium of song – if it is a truth so deep that it couldn't be appreciated without the singer's carrying vehicle except by those most perceptive of souls, perhaps. Could it rather be that I am just too inhibited and too intensely focused in my day-to-day life, failing to observe this gem always around me and attributing precious obscurity to it now as it dawns on me when in fact the rarity is caused by my own blind ignorance? The phone's vibration suddenly breaks my train of thought and the song with it, and when I look down, relief appears in the form of James's picture on the screen. The musical diversion has successfully carried me across another anxious wait.

"Hello, mate," I say, cheerfully greeting his call in my habitual form.

"Where are you?" comes the response. Jim sounds irritated, like it's my fault, whatever it is, and I chuckle indulgently as I describe my location to him as if to a child. I spot him almost immediately coming around the corner of the long wooden bar. His smile as he sees me brings straight away the warm joy of connection, my friend and I as easy and friendly as we always are, the doubts and fears of my brooding imagination dispelled by the light of our happy reunion.

Bernadette

A portrait of aging, and even though gentle, the signs are stark enough as these erstwhile classmates do meet here. It's an aspect of the scene we don't much care to notice and likely won't acknowledge even when we do, but what a shock it'd be if we stood by our school-aged selves – if those fresher youths nursed adolescent pints at an adjacent table, looking over at their ancients to sneer and giggle with an elbow nudge. Hair can be the most obvious of time's markers: James's head has been mainly bald now for many a year, though my hair is still full, entreated and coaxed and nurtured to stay. Then there are the lines. Even if still slight, they are an unmistakably riven feature on what once was the smoothest of canvasses, and they can't all be excused by too much smiling – though I do register that he is smiling at me now, as if he too is surprised by the glow of a two-way familiarity that brightens sharply the moment we meet. I watch as, with bright eyes, he busies himself stripping away the many layers of protection from the cold air outside. Our skin seems to grow thinner as slowly we age, another of time's undoing agents, allowing winter's icy teeth to sink in more deeply.

"So you made it then?" I say, smiling as he continues to order his newly unloaded articles. "What can I get you?"

"I'll get them," he counters, already standing, raising an eyebrow as he points at the two spent glasses that clutter the table. "What were you drinking?" "Oh. OK, thanks. JD and Coke please," I tell him, and I wait as he goes over to the bar in front of me, the long wooden counter made, perhaps, from railway sleepers, with three pump stations hosting various beers and ales and the obligatory television screen fitted to the wall at its far end. He's attended almost immediately, the service here also part of the fantastic experience which fits easily with the other-worldliness of that proximate Harry Potter attraction.

Jim returns and, with a wink, places two glasses of my favourite liquid pastime down on the table along with his pint. Surprised by his generosity, I smile gratefully.

"Mate, I can't stay for long," he tells me. "Got to get back home. Ruby and I are going out tonight."

"That's cool – it's just good to see you," I assure him. "It's been a while, but I always thought this would make a great place for us to meet. It's right where we both need to be to get home, and it's a nice little drinking hole besides, don't you think?" As I say this, I look around at the light-filled chamber, appreciating afresh the central atrium with its half-window partitions and clear glass roof.

"Hmm," he mumbles, unwilling, perhaps, to accede too strongly to my observation, not yet as imbued as I am of its evident charm. "What have you been up to?" he asks as he takes his chair. "How's the family? How's that wife of yours that I set you up with," he adds with a smirk. He's joking, though you'd hardly know it from the smug look on his face, but there is something to what he says. Seeing each other so rarely, it's almost inevitable that some of our conversation will reach back into our distant shared past. Sometimes when we go back over the people and places from our various vantage points, this light refreshed can cast upon a scene a different colour, a curiously different aspect on what before might have seemed locked down and immutable, which can reset something fundamental that long since seemed stone. Avid collector of memories that I am, it truly surprises me that I should have let James's fateful call just slip from my mind, especially because so much of the life I've lived ever since has been intrinsically linked with the heart of its subject. It feels truly bizarre when he reminds me of it.

I was on the pitch at work in front of my shield of screens, my windows on the world, and ready for business, I snatched up the phone as quickly as I saw the light flash, answering gruffly before relaxing back into my chair as I recognized with pleasant surprise my mate's voice. I remember thinking how unusual it was that he should be calling me.

"Hello, mate," I replied a little lairily when he asked for me, not realizing we were already speaking. "To what do I owe the pleasure?"

A little more consciously than I liked to admit, I was pleased that he'd found me here. Speaking to him from my power seat, I felt a surge of pride that I had a chance to 'be the dealer' before him, even if it was only the element of it that I could carry in my voice that he would actually be aware of.

"Did you get De Beers in?" he asked, a long-worn running joke which he couldn't help but unshackle whenever we spoke to each other: he knew that I traded the South African diamond giant, and it pleased him that it sounded like a drinks order. I laughed as acquiescently as I could after having heard him say the same thing so many times, and all out of ripostes, I waited for him to continue. "Listen," he went on, "I've got a girl here for you. One of our temps is coming to work full-time at your place next Monday."

"Really? Wow, that's funny," I agreed.

"It is, and we'd not even spoken before this morning. We just had one of those smiling relationships where she'd come up here every day and drop a report on my desk, disappearing without saying a word. This morning as she passed by, she told me she was leaving – that today would be her last day. When I asked her where she was going, she told me that she is coming to your place. What about that? Her name's Penelope, and I told her to look out for you."

"Jim," I said patiently, "there's about two thousand people in this building. There's no way I'll even bump into her."

"Well, anyway, I just thought it was pretty amazing. I thought I'd let you know."

It was ironic, therefore, that when, about three weeks later, a new girl was brought up to meet the dealing team, she was the very same and would be responsible for making sure that our currency book positions were kept in line with our actual bank balances once she'd been brought up to speed. Coming on to the floor of a dealing room was always a bit intimidating – I remember how it was for me even after I'd been working at the firm for a bit – but it can be much more so for a woman, as their sex is such a rarity in the testosterone-soaked environment. Back in the day, it wasn't uncommon to hear a volley of well-directed wolf whistles at the very hint of a skirt. A few years later, Penny would tell me that she suspected I was the one who used to produce this flattering sound, and only because my whistling ability was demonstrably useless could I convince her otherwise and clear my name.

That first time I saw her, she'd trailed the long way through the dealing room behind her boss as if on show, and coming to a stop before us with her hands clasped tightly together, she looked quietly mortified. She stood stiffly upright on long, slender legs accentuated by a lime-green A-line miniskirt which lent a view of her knees and shiny brown brogues. Hardy always maintained a strong empathy with the settlement department, because that had been his background, and understanding how crucial the role was, he was quite genuine in the big show of welcome that he made to put her at ease. Penny did seem to relax a bit as he chatted to her easily, all the while maintaining her well-mannered exterior, but that was shattered when it came to be my turn to shake her hand. I sprang from my chair a tad overzealously, and she recoiled in surprise, double-taking at how much shorter I suddenly appeared as I stood there before her. A couple of my colleagues thought this slight was hilarious and made zero effort to soften their merriment, but I just sucked it up: I was used to the disadvantage that my height always gave me, and I was determined not to let them see the bit I was crushed by their derision. I remember some time later feeling like I'd got a little of my own back when I revealed to her which one of these supposed gentlemen used always to whistle behind her.

Over the next weeks and months, we spoke regularly on work-related issues, and gradually I got to know her more. She was always pleasant and cheerful, but she could also hold her own if I happened to get a bit overbearing when we were looking at something contentious, and it got so that I enjoyed it when we did have to communicate, as nearly always we'd have a laugh. She was pretty too, and that didn't hurt: light-coloured hair that she wore down long and a frame that was slender and lithe. Sometimes I ran into her in the canteen where I'd been sent to fetch Hardy's takeaway, and she was in the gym if I ever went down there – though I was more likely to head for the squash courts. I often saw her about with her colleagues in the bars after work too, and I have a vague, drunken memory of dancing with her one year at our Christmas party. I spied her on the dance floor we'd converted for the occasion on one of the unoccupied floors of our building and made a bee line towards her, thrashing about close by for a while under the dizzying spell of "Cotton-Eye Joe" or something equally dynamic.

We knew one another but purely as work acquaintances, and I'd not consciously thought any more of her than this. I don't know why this changed, but I do remember when. My eyes were opened for the first time when Hardy convinced her to take part as our mandatory female in a five-a-side football competition. There she was in her shorts and her trainers – but what was it about her? The defiant sense of pride she gave off and her easy awkwardness plus the willingness with which she quietly took part. I also was impressed by what I perceived as a lack of high maintenance, having already experienced others for whom this was decidedly not the case. Her looks and her personality and the naturalness of her manner seemed suddenly to combine, and the package struck me as sublimely special. I think it was then that I decided to ask her out.

Moondance

The main event is here, and with the two sides facing off, the game is about to begin. Each has a plan for where play should be heading; each looking to impose their own pattern, to bring respective strengths and weaknesses quickly to bear. They probe and test each other, hoping maybe to force an early goal: nothing builds confidence like banging one away. The fixtures before line up in their many in a fading history list, but there's something different tonight, this game having somehow a unique glow as we go head to head, readying for a feint here or a thrust there, faking this way and now that, the ultimate prize on offer in this fight for survival. Knowing how the fates enjoy teasing and toying with our hopes, we keep premature thoughts of victory and celebration far from mind – no arms will rise up in the air until the final whistle blows. But though this night has barely begun, already I'm feeling like a winner: a minor miracle just to have got her here. She tried almost everything to push me away, and overcoming that is success in itself, a measure of how far I have come and something I know too well would have been impossible just a short time ago, before I learned how to steel my nerves and hold on to my hopes. I now have the belief to bat away those stinging darts which probe at rejection, holding fast long enough to make good my reward.

She sounded genuinely shocked at the impudence I showed in trying to breach her weekend with my repeated calls, upbraiding me for intruding at this sacred time, when she could set away the familiar girl from around our office and be her true self for fifty-five hours, a freer soul, a girl that I barely knew and did not yet know how much I wanted to. I was already supine, saving myself subconsciously, perhaps, from the prospect of a fall as I set to this latest courageous attempt, gazing at Craig's hallway ceiling. Focusing on my breathing and on trying to sound cool, I wasn't thinking about rejection: one line at a time was the way to go at it, and with or without faith in my method, I wasn't looking far enough ahead to countenance defeat. This was my second attempt to reach her today. I had called earlier in the afternoon and had been confronted by an accent from another world, an unexpected encounter with her gatekeeper that threw me as she told me she was out. I hardly knew what I was thinking as I put down the receiver, but I was resolved to try later; and though I knew it was already getting late for what I wanted of the evening, at last I could hear what I took to be Penny's footsteps coming to the phone. The game would be on.

"What are you doing calling me at home!" her proud voice almost shouted at me, and I was slightly taken aback.

"I ... I ... you said that we should go for a drink," I blurted out.

"You," she said accusingly. "You said we should go for a drink. I only gave you my number because I didn't want to embarrass you. What were you doing outside the changing rooms anyway? Were you stalking me?"

"But a drink," I went on. "We should ... we should go for a drink."

"Yes – a drink after work, not at the weekend. Who are you? You're Milo from work! What the hell would I have to talk to you about?"

"That doesn't matter. We could go to the Comedy Store in Camden," I suggested, trying an old faithful. "We'd have a laugh there, and you wouldn't need to say anything." Her anger seemed gradually to dissipate, and we carried on talking for a while in a way that I was a bit more used to with her. We weren't saying anything, but I knew it was better than saying nothing, so I held on.

"Look," she said eventually, trying to be patient, "you're a nice guy, and I don't mind going out with you after work sometime, but tonight I'm tired. I've been in town shopping all day."

"What did you buy?" I asked.

She sighed. "I bought a chest of drawers."

"A chest of drawers? That's nice, but didn't you say you'd moved back home to save money?"

"Yes, but I'm going to get a place of my own when I've paid off my bills, and I'll need a nice chest of drawers."

"Big drawers or little drawers?"

"Big ones. Nice and wide, smooth maple wood." There was a pause.

"Look," I pleaded, "I like you. You know I do, and we've known each other for ages, and we both share a love for chests of drawers. Come out with me. Come on – where's the harm? We'll have a couple of drinks, and if you don't have a good time, then fair dos – no damage done. What do you say?"

With a sense of victory that couldn't have seemed any less likely when the conversation began about forty-five minutes earlier, I scrambled about the hallway for something to write on. I grabbed a pink Post-it note that belonged to Craig's flatmate Lauren and scratched down her address. An hour later, I parked up inside the estate just off the Archway roundabout which I realized in passing I'd always been semi-aware of. I reflected on how the name Henway Close was quite unsuited to the inner city location that was now closing in around me, unless it was meant as some ironic joke, and I strode into this forbidding world with my courage drawn and no flowers, my mind set on blank. I didn't think about her older brother's look of suspicious disdain from the far side of the living room, as if he were regarding an alien encroachment. I did not take notice of her mother's convenient absence or have time to take in the detail in the flat itself. Penny rushed me back outside as smartly as possible through the corridor, its walls plastered like a huge living album in family photos. I tried to concentrate on moving normally as we went down the walkway together, relieved to see that the car was still where I'd parked it, but feeling self-conscious, even this was an impossible task. I hated how it sounded as I faked assurance with the smallest of small talk, my heart all the while banging in my chest. *I should have met her in the pub,* I moaned to myself as we drove along in silence, for to call the situation awkward would not have done it justice. However, at least now I had her, and there wasn't any chance for escape. I reassured myself that the clock wouldn't actually start until we'd sat down in our places with our drinks; only then would the game really be primed to begin.

Retaking my seat at the table in the restaurant, I couldn't help but allow a little smile for myself, a little grin of congratulations on account of the fact that she hadn't bolted in my short but tactical absence. I felt eminently alive as this unreal world pricked like a drug and kept me alert, kept me on my game. She was full of light and beautiful: her blonde hair and her Irish-tanned skin; her bright blue eyes; the freckles on her cheeks and on her forehead; her soft, pink mouth, now demur and now animated; her strong white teeth and the flash of her tongue. Her head was a little higher than mine, and her long arms, which reached out to the middle of the table, tantalized with their forbidden proximity. I watched as she seemed almost wistfully to toy in silence with the cutlery: a brass knife and fork fashioned with lines to imitate bamboo shoots. An exquisite peace grew in the comfort between us until I caught her eye, and we laughed together, smiling. I continued to sneak every now and then a stare at her, as I hardly believed that this really was happening.

Perhaps the familiarity of the wonderfully exotic surroundings in my local Thai restaurant made my feeling of unreality that much greater; I had come here many times over the years. It had become a regular favourite of mine after it opened a few years earlier and I'd been back just a couple of weeks before with a broker that was visiting for work. The food was great and the staff just right, but what I particularly loved was the authentic ricketiness: the place was crafted mostly of wood where more usually you'd find metal, especially around here due to the redevelopment underway in Camden at that time. You almost felt like the place could collapse under its randomness – a railing here and an oddly hanging set of curtains there, bare timber floors throughout, and awkwardly shaped walls that provided vacant corners and alcoves to befuddle any Western sense of order. As the place grew more popular, the proprietors provided a couple of tables for additional service high up in the loft as a first attempt to cope with the overflow, but I knew from experience that woe would betide those looking for attentive service up there. With each new visit, the whole restaurant seemed to have evolved – mezzanines somehow appearing and odd steps up in the middle of a level as if to accommodate some new-sprung hillside. For such a busy venue, it was amazing how sometimes you'd be so positioned that it felt like you had the whole place all to yourself, and each time I entered it seemed that a new corner, a new alley or hitherto hidden area had been put into commission.

Here was an establishment that the usual space and motion merchants certainly had not built. That was back then, of course. Everything has a price, and nothing more so than popularity. When, a couple of years later, the space could no longer contain the custom, they commandeered the old antiques shop next door, knocking into it and redeveloping the whole building. The casually easy-going management made way for hearts and minds more suited for tourists and business, for profits and turnover, though I have to admit I'd be less sentimental if the accounts were mine to pore over – if I feasted on the takings rather than the dishes. Such is life.

Throughout the web of nooks and corridors that made up the original building, there was paraphernalia displayed which accentuated the overall theme. There were golden smiling Buddhas, images of bejewelled oriental princes, and other eye-catchers that perhaps represented eastern deities, though these brightly lit globes served only to attract my eyes and not my curiosity: my knowledge remained less well fed than my appetite, as I delighted in the surroundings without caring to research them. The restaurant had only been open for a few years, but its wooden fittings had come ready worn, red and henna-brown walls distressed by design so that from my very first visit it was like something ageless. Only in the big, open basement was there room enough for a party to gather. The layout otherwise was perfect as a date place: intimate, informal, and cosy, the welcome completed by a long bar which reached to the door on the skinny first level. From there, the happy barman served up drinks and smiles, a manner shared by all the staff, who seemed to know that they were living the life just by being there, that they were plying their trade at a place that was somehow blessed, and that they'd look back on this time as one of their finest. The customers really picked up on this mood, and though the quality and consistency of the food certainly helped, as much as anything this attitude was the clincher – this sense you had coming back each time that you were returning to a place where you were one of its own. It was this that made it a no-brainer suggestion once Penny and I had had a few drinks at the pub down the road.

Dobro Ladies

The Fusilier sits under that famously painted railway bridge which bestrides Camden High Road, its cheeky mural depicting the hanging decorators who rest with their brushes in hand and look back from their never-ending project towards the road bridge which itself spans the canal at Camden's celebrated market. I'd spent a legendary night here a few years earlier with Tim, a mate from work, the two of us keeping pace as the evening dissolved into hilarity around us, and as Penny and I stepped through the door, I felt the relief of being welcomed by the ghost of that feeling from a happy time past. After the awkwardness of the journey, it was good to have got here, finally safe on home turf. Seeking the healthy respite of separation, I went to the bar to fetch us a couple of doubles, leaving her to claim a spot at the edge of the little stage. A band in the corner were making busy with their instruments, tuning up or down or jamming or something, and the black-stained wood decor was calming and cool – so very Camden in a way that the hostile Hawley Arms just around the corner was not. We must both have felt at home here, because we never looked back. One drink turned to two and then three, and soon we were chatting in just the way that I knew that we could, laughing ironically and brooking no interruption as, complicit, we waved away the rose seller. From this very start, the match seemed a perfect one, the evening all laughter and accord, and it didn't seem to matter that we came from wildly different places. When later I suggested we get something to eat, adding as she paused that I'd better have some food and some time before getting back to driving, we left there close together for the restaurant up the road.

Coming in gladly through the door, we both shivered involuntarily as we entered the warm, our bodies trying to dispel the wintry evening which clung in our clothes about us. We were shown to an alcove with a little round table just over from the bar, but we chose to keep hold of our coats to better recover from the walk's chilly assault, and once we were seated, the change of scene brought upon us a pause that felt altogether colder. The cutting wind had somehow breached too deep, stripping from us our laughter; with a snap, we were no longer those carefree children seated side by side on the step but adults. The fragile beauty of the drooping flower in the tiny glass vase on the table between us perfectly reflected this change of mood: it seemed almost a mirage that we'd been so close. Forgetting the premise that I'd used to bring us here just minutes earlier, I ordered for us both another drink, remembering my words at the instant that I caught her seemingly reproachful eye and fearing for an awful moment that she'd call it, bring to a premature end this evening for which I harboured such high hopes. That silent moment passed, and though our chatter rekindled as soon as the waiter had retired, our lines were stilted now, polite and reserved as if the pub had never happened, and the cold still stung me and I felt too sober.

I wanted this uncommonly. It couldn't be helped, but deep down it already meant a great deal to me – all the more so for the laughter we'd shared just a little way along the road. I was no longer able just to relax and tell myself that it didn't really matter, and perhaps because of that, I could hardly settle for nerves, this unquantifiable prize remaining so close yet frighteningly stretching further and further from my reach as I sat there gaping. I needed a plan; I needed some inspiration.

"Excuse me," I said. "I'm just going to the bathroom," and saying so, I jumped up, flashing her a smile, and then strode off quickly, disappearing around the corner and beginning down the stairs. Once I knew I was safely out of sight, I paused and sucked in a couple of long, deep breaths, each one followed by a steady exhalation as I forced myself to relax. I carried on down to the bottom of the staircase, where I turned and started to marshal my thoughts, passing along the corridor side of the bamboo screen on my way to the washrooms. A table party raged in the body of the basement on the other side, and as I picked up on the voices and the overlapping laughter, I thought to myself how nice it must be – how easy to be here just for the fun in a big group of mates and not on a mission, not here to win or to lose, to succeed or to fail.

The flimsy plywood door swung open with a creak as I pushed against it, and I skipped on through just as it was shutting behind me. Entering the toilet triggered a Pavlovian response, those fluids that I'd been throwing down all evening bursting to assert their agenda and almost overtaking me with the desire to be unburdened. It was a most satisfying calling, and once relieved, with nobody else in there, I sat myself down on a closed toilet lid in one of the cubicles, freshly aware of the heavy suede jacket that hung down around me. I could already feel that the little distance I'd made for myself was starting to clarify the picture; and though I didn't exactly know what I had to do, at least I could see who I'd have to be to get where I wanted to go. It occurred to me that I might, perhaps, find something of use in one of the deep pockets, and to my delight, my right hand found the silk touch of a tight little sachet already half-empty and rolled up at one end to keep what was left of the magic secure. Carefully, I lifted it out, admiring the blessed thing like some kind of fine cigar, a throwaway stick of sugar with the taste of the finest honey. I couldn't recall leaving it there or even when I might have started on it, but none of that was of any concern: it would be perfect, neither too little nor too much, and I contemplated it silently in the palm of my hand as I weighed it against the merest wisp of a guilty sadness, all the time knowing there'd be no turning back, happily resigned and peacefully committed.

Rising from my seat, I took as if fatefully the few little steps from the cubicle to the sink. The tap was loose from the porcelain, and it wobbled slightly as I twisted it open. It shook with the force of the water and the pipe rattled against the brick wall behind, a watery habitat springing spontaneously into life. Letting it run, I watched the jet as it burst down to the sink, down to the twisting pool of its own creation, celebrated by its own fanfare. No one had entered behind me, so I smoothed out the crumpled sachet, squeezing apart the torn opening and in one movement pouring the little beads out on to my tongue. In the seconds that followed, a light, effervescent fizz delighted me by dancing in my mouth until suddenly the foam was all gummy and its vapours were banging up my nose and burning my eyes, forcing me to dive with the cup of my two hands for the fresh running water, hungrily gulping at the font that they made. Blinking through the lights and the water, I came up too sharply and, staggering back from the sink, almost tripped over myself as the blood in my veins began to bubble. One moment I was falling hopelessly, and the next I was sitting back on the seat of the toilet inside the cubicle with my hands flat on the partition walls, taking a grip as the whole place rolled this way and that. Yet even as I was becoming aware of this new paradigm, the craziest part of the ride had already begun to dissipate. With the picture now steadying, I found myself sitting there with everything about me still and in place, a huge smile lighting up my entire being as I surveyed the ebb and flow of these new settling waves inside my body growing tranquil and calm.

She caught my eye as I reached the top of the stairs. I didn't know exactly how long I'd left her there, but there she still was, and that was a positive. As I approached the table, I held her gaze with my best cocky smile, reseating myself with a conspiratorial look on my face.

"How was it without me?" I asked by way of apology. There was a momentary silence.

"At first it was OK," she said, "but as more time went by, it seemed to get better and better."

I had to laugh. "I was just checking the place out," I told her, leaning forward confidentially. "Had to make sure there was some way out of here for the both of us in case, y'know, things start getting a bit heavy. I found a window we might avail ourselves of, though it is pretty high. You'll have to boost me, but I think we might just about get away with it."

She laughed at my little foolishness, and somewhere in another part of the universe, I imagined a fault line opening – brother plates since time began breaking the vice of inertia. Sitting there with her now, it all felt right, and whenever I lifted my face, I could hardly believe it was Penny that sat there before me. I'd look away and then back again just to test it, but all fresh and lovely, it really was her; this really was happening. So many times I'd been here with friends and with colleagues, certainly with a number of girlfriends, but her being here seemed to jar with reality – jar with what before I had thought could be possible.

I remember a moment of quiet ease that fell between us as we waited for our food to arrive, sitting there trying as inconspicuously as I could to ravage her with my eyes, almost unable to convince my disbelieving self that this wasn't some dream. We must both have felt that conversation was unnecessary, and Penny took absentmindedly to looking down at the unusual cutlery on the table and toying with it, testing with her slender white fingers the points of her fork, quietly lost in a world of her own as she traced the grooves that ran along the handle of her knife. In that perfect silence, through this newly rent gap in the fabric of time and space, I became aware that fate was reaching out to me, and I knew what to do, watching as my hand slipped across the tablecloth towards hers. I laid the tips of my fingers gently on the backs of hers, and with creation standing still, I began without words to beseech her, to tell her everything that I knew and everything that I hoped for. We remained like that for the longest second, and she didn't deny me. Sensing that this impossible divide had been breached, slowly I brought my hand back and then dared to look up at her face, half smiling and beginning to blush. Seeing that colours were filling hers too, my heart skipped a beat. Though its sound from afar had yet to reach us, I knew at that moment a new world was born.

Stopping the car outside her flats, I made ready with my bravest face, the end of tonight's journey having loomed unspoken for these last few minutes as up Junction Road and around the Archway roundabout we drove, my cards all played and the lady's judgement awaiting. *Empty your mind,* I thought to myself as we rode through the gates, trying to keep a lid on the swell of emotions that could yet undo me. Amor fati *and all that,* I insisted, focusing on telling myself that whatever this had been, it had been no disaster. *Very pleasant in fact, I'm sure she'll agree?* When we stopped and she asked if I'd like to come up for a coffee, the cliché was such a welcome relief it was all I could do not to smirk. However, I did manage not to despite the cartwheels that I wanted to turn, and as we sat chatting in hushed, convivial tones in the lounge, so as not to awaken the household, I realized that it was actual coffee that she'd had in mind. Whether it was good coffee or not, I have no idea, my mind all charged now by her electric proximity and too much driven by a suffocating need to make such a judgement.

While my brain screamed for a way and, laughing and afraid, I edged closer along the sofa towards her, my conversation must have become too much absent, my motive too obvious for her to ignore.

"Look," she said abruptly with a kindly smile on her face, and I knew I was all undone. "It's been a lovely evening, and I've really enjoyed myself, but now I feel like you want ... like you're going to try to kiss me, and I don't know if I want you to do that." Gently, the knife slipped into my heart, and a moment of stillness passed between us. The night, it seemed, had come down to all or nothing, and the latter would be mine. I knew exactly what would happen if I remained in place now that the prize had been withdrawn, and I knew exactly what I'd become. Smiling a tight-lipped smile, I heaved an exhausted sigh.

"OK," I said, nodding my guilt. "I really would like to kiss you, but I get it, and I suppose if I can't, then probably I should be going." I'd said my piece, and resignedly I rose. She rose with me, and we suddenly found ourselves standing almost intimately with our faces not far from touching. My hands took themselves up to her shoulders, settling perhaps for a farewell touch on the side of her arms – but what magic was this? Without premeditation, we were spinning: I spun us around and around, and still around we went, Penny moving before me swooned and complaisant in my hands until, wobbling, we came giddily to a halt. Her eyes, which remained shut, were my invitation, and as I kissed her lips, she held my kiss, endless. The train had left the station, and we were both of us on it.

What a picture it is that I've kept in my mind: her sitting by my side on the floor with my heavy brown jacket slung across her bare shoulders, that passing lover's parting gift I'd worn until that time as my cloak of invulnerability, protection from some hurt that never arrived, never put before that moment to such a worthy use. I won't see anything as beautiful as she was that night: her long blonde hair and her soft pale skin set off by that dark suede jacket, her vulnerability both framed and protected by its contrasting heft. Another memory, a piece of sorcery I can hardly believe, was the new voice she instantly spoke with, so changed to my ear without that edge of defiance, something all of a sudden now caramel and silky, a smoothness of tone that said she was mine.

Our travels had already taken us an immeasurable distance, and long gone were we those strangers who'd sat with their coffees on that far-away sofa, placed as an exhibit just off to the side. When the time came to leave, it was a kind of creeping away that was wonderful, one without regret and full of unformed excitement. Still disbelieving, I kissed her and floated to the car, driving back to Craig's place in a dream, but as I arrived at the bottom of his road, even the car seemed to know how impossible it would be to end our journey here – the night was too full with excitement. Driving on, we passed the sleeping flats of Swiss Cottage and crossed over Adelaide Road, going on down through to Primrose Hill, where we stopped at the foot of the great mound itself. The night was cool and clear, but as I walked up to the top of the path, I could feel no cold – feeling instead how the ancient line shared my celebration, how the stars twinkling in the blackness of the sky were shining for me. As I looked all around from the top, taking in the outline of the aviary at the zoo just across the way – the Post Office Tower, that favourite landmark of mine – and then across to the monoliths of the Docklands, I felt for the first time as if this whole city were on my side. At last it was my town and at last my time.

Columbia

"You'll have to come down my way for a curry soon," says Jim as carefully he places his just-finished pint glass on to the appropriately pictured locomotive beer mat. "Sorry this one's got to be so brief. We'll do a Friday night, perhaps, get the girls together too?"

"It's perfect, really," comes my reply, "and that's a great idea. Let's sort out a date that works, and I'll look forward to it." Over the years, I've somehow garnered a reputation with my mates for being a bit of a needy one. Partly because they make me feel there's some truth to that, I always try to emphasize how laid back I actually am, how satisfied with any arrangements that we do make, especially when they actually come off. We descend the broad steps together and join the commuter hoards that mill about at the platforms below and the tourists that crowd patiently at the Harry Potter attraction, lining up for their photo at the trolley that's half set into the wall by the book shop's entrance. After a warm shaking of hands, I watch him head across to St Pancras on the other side of the road.

With no plan of a next move formed in my head, I follow in his footsteps and exit the station, breaching the cold, light evening and stopping to look around me. The station has undergone a massive redevelopment, with a huge crisscross roof which forms a dome to shield a brand-new plaza, the station forecourt with its restaurants and coffee shops and retail outlets. It extends with a lip at the mouth of the Underground's new entrance to provide cover for the new-age pariahs, a place where the lonely, disapproved smokers may tarry to draw their pleasure, saved from the elements. Looking north, I see the buildings which rise now in their steady slow motion, this brave new environment fashioned of steel and concrete before my eyes that makes everything so completely different – so far removed from what it was – that it's hard to get my bearings, and I try in vain to recall this land as I once used to know it.

Passing through here among the mammoth gas tanks and the dereliction in the mornings all those many years ago, it was drearily familiar: a mist-filled wilderness like some Shakespearean setting or a film noir landscape beset by hags. Wraiths who once had been women wandered to press their trade, appearing from the fog as if from nowhere with their shrill cry, "Looking for business, love?" It always startled me, always elicited a polite but wary refusal before soundlessly they melted back to their other world, each surreal encounter leaving in the air behind them a haunting, unholy thrill. Coming from the Tube in the lighter evenings, I'd stroll back this way to my summer garden, a patch of serenity long settled by the churchyard and so named by me because it was only during the summer months that it afforded passage home via Camley Street which ran behind it. Morning and evening, I'd celebrate the longer access that the season enabled the warden to provide by looking appreciatively about me at the trees and the flowers there as I made my way through, until winter time came round again and its permanent darkness meant a longer way home.

Back to the present, and Butterfly Walk leads north from the Underground entrance passing by the building sites which crouch hidden behind huge decorated hoardings, plastic screen borders on both sides of the stone-chip pathway that keep from view the roots of the towers that rise here. By the road that I once knew as Goodsway at the top of the path, there's a red bus stuck on permanent display like a monstrous dinosaur of transport or a prop for a film, a red metal whale left beached when the waters receded. This road, once thick with the dirt and grime that year after abandoned year had dried into its creases, is now so pristine that I struggle to believe it really is the same one. I couldn't have imagined it any more different – couldn't have guessed that this dilapidated railway land could ever be restored – but here it now stands, proud of its trees and its bright new lines, sparkling where London once chocked in its filth.

On the other side of the road, the brand-new bridge which spans the canal further disorientates me, and crossing it, I come before the relocated college, realizing it stands on the site of The Church, an infamous club where ravers once worshiped in youthful abandon, all night long. Like the central squares of old, a wide and spacious forecourt here is filled with various scattered groups of students, and a new fountain which boasts shows of both water and light stands in the centre. Over to the left, there's the newly opened restaurant for the seating of some better-heeled patrons, those who might sip their expensive drinks beneath the heaters on the metal chairs outside. Across from there, a small group of rebels are building their roll-ups on the bench with takeaway cans of beer placed in plastic bags at their feet right where the steps lead down to the towpath and, patient as ever, the canal beside it.

Taking the big block steps down to the edge of the old waterway is a journey like stepping back through the years – back to a place that's hidden from the new above, where it might be forgotten. As the street sounds fade, you will find things just as you left them, a keep and vindication here for your memories of old. The blown brick wall on the opposite bank remains draped in weeds, and its multicoloured barges still rest moored there beyond the breadth of time's regular flow. I remember making my way with my jacket slung behind on warm Friday evenings, stretching my legs as slowly I enjoyed that first lazy walk of a welcome weekend, coming round the bends to the bench where I gazed at the gliding ducks, chewing my fate on the craziest Valentine's

Day as I paused before destiny, before heading back home to the rest of my life. Looming above, the Constitution Pub still stands white and tall in the early-morning haze of my weekend with Charlie, witness to our hand-in-hand marathon on a night far from over.

A bike whizzing past reconnects me with the present, and my eyes are drawn along in its wake, watching until the whoosh that its tread makes on the stone towpath disappears around the corner. Alive again to where I am, I take a seat on the old iron bench and, after a little while, see a couple of slow-moving lovers appear from under the bridge. They move along the path towards me in their own eternity until eventually they pass me by, and I wonder at how much quieter everything seems: the noises in the air absorbed by the canal, shielded as we are by the high wall opposite that abuts the road beyond. As subtle as the soundless rippling of the water, at its own pace life goes on in this most distinctive universe in its own way.

With a gap in the traffic of wheels and lingering sweethearts, I gently draw the little steel case from the breast pocket of my denim jacket. Opening it, I look down on the stick packet inside, and for a moment, I pause, aware of a feeling almost of regret or disappointment – some kind of sentimental melancholy, maybe, but I really don't know. Perhaps it's just where I go as I savour that moment before reality changes, bemoaning to myself with rueful non-expression my habit of this sport. If that really is the case, then it's a cheap moment indeed: my mission at this point already is fixed and far beyond the point of debate. I don't think I'd want it any other way. Lifting the packet out of the case, my fingers are ahead of me and rip off the top just as my phone begins to vibrate. I'm caught momentarily trapped in a quandary with some of the tiny seeds already spilt into my hand. Cupping it all together, I twist and reach over with my other hand to pluck the phone from the pocket of my jeans, seeing on the screen as I lift it the welcome sight of Luca's face.

"Hello, mate," I say happily. "Long time! How you doin'?" After a game last week, I moaned to one of our mutual friends that he never calls me, that I don't seem to hear so much from my little brother these days. I was probably going off on one, as I'm wont to, but something about getting his call at this place now strikes me as especially poignant, here where unusually I'm steeped in the past and reminiscing on times gone by.

"It's good – all good, mate. Listen, I'm just making a few calls, letting people know that Jo's pregnant."

"What! How long?"

"Just had the three-month scan. Everything's good so, y'know, we're telling people."

I was at his wedding at the back end of last year, a really lovely affair in a little place in Hampstead. The families had flown in from their respective parts of the world, and though her lot, coming from South America, didn't have a full command of the language, their slightly baffled faces spoke most eloquently of their deeper feelings and their love for the happy couple. Matched by their counterparts and by the rest of us there present, it made for one of the nicest, most wholesome weddings I think I have ever been to. This impression, I'm sure, was largely due to the strength of those feelings that I've lodged deep inside me, to our having been so close for so long. When all's said and done, it matters not one iota that life might see us now more and more apart.

"Wow, that's fantastic. Mate, I'm so happy for you. Please give her my love. Where are you now?"

"I'm sitting outside a local restaurant. Jo's on her way, and we're just going to have a quiet dinner."

"Well, thanks so much for letting me know."

"Of course!"

"We'll have to catch up soon, mate. I'm really pleased for you. Penny will be thrilled."

"Defo. Cheers, mate. Soon."

The phone dies, and for a lingering instant, I'm stuck regarding the blank screen. Wow! How things go. First babies and then babies' babies, yet the canal stays the same, just as it was when I first discovered it and as it had been long before, current yet timeless, carrying many but unmoving itself. Turning my head, I notice that that quiet water beside me has now grown slightly dimmer as the sky above darkens.

Opening my hand, I find the beads I've been hiding already grown sticky from the heat and the moisture of my body, and pouring over the rest of the sachet, I look on as the whole coagulates into one big, gloopy mass. When I try tipping it into my mouth, it just hangs there instead, and I end up using my bottom row of teeth to lift it from my palm, battling then to send the lumpy goo down as fast as I can, already fizzling as it slips down my throat. Quickly licking what's left from my hand, I use my tongue to clean off my palate and then scrape it against the upper row of teeth, swallowing down the gummy detritus that it leaves there. In the pause that follows, I set myself against the back of the bench with my tongue continuing around my mouth for fresh saliva as I wait for the creeping hit with my mind clear and empty. Before I know it there comes a calm feeling of oneness with the universe, an understanding and an appreciation that encompasses entirety itself. This glimpse of the absolute truth is far too fragile to have any chance of holding, far too elusive to grasp and bring fully to terms, but for that flash of a perfect moment I know it's complete, the warm blood pushing out from my stomach to my limbs and then climbing my throat – that old, familiar feeling of my body sinking in beautiful relief as I wonder absently, fleetingly, with the ghost of a smile, how the cold must already have been starting to find me.

Inside the tacky infinity of my open mouth, the lolling tongue searches. I need water, but a drink's of no concern for now as the body of the canal, falling into the petrol darkness of evening, sings to distract me. The broken old towpath and the derelict bank whose smile fondly radiates from over on the other side join in this tune, and my ancient friends thus meld a harmony, lifting their song in celebration for my long-awaited return – one that's greater and more joyous for the length of my absence, for the warmth of this welcome. The block-painted graffiti that's faded on the wall above me grows starker now as I stare beyond its thick black outline to the three little stars in the heavens above, which shine brighter than ever before, delivering their cosmic message as my head sinks further against the metal at the back of the bench.

There I am, running, my stiff, mind-numbed leaps taking me up the hill from the hospital, running because I've not been here before and don't know what else to be doing, running to tell my mother-in-law of her very first grandchild, the red-faced little girl that I've left behind me down the hill in the arms of her daughter. Passing MacDonald's, I see the two of us inside passing cheerfully the time, readying ourselves as we prepare for another, a return to the hospital for arrival at last when the three of us will become four in the quiet early morning. In a matter of days, we men stand gathered around the little one as the mothers stand weeping beyond the white clinic walls, new little legs and arms attended by past generations who too were attended in times black and white. Masked and scrubbed, my proud old dad holds his new grandson's legs while, accomplice in awe, awake to the moment, I half-hold the arms as the doctor performs this made-modern blessing, the ritual no longer contentious, having been revealed a necessity for both God and man just a few hours earlier. Another baby arrives with bubbles blowing around his mouth as he lies alone, uncrying in his clear plastic shell yet nonetheless calling me, pulling me by the heart as his mother lies exhausted, the two of us shocked. Then, impossibly, that same little baby is on the stage before us, blithely at ease as he clambers the flying car in front of thousands with an angel voice booming his onomatopoeic line from the mike, "Vroom vroom, vroom vroom". Fearful, we sit rigid in the stalls, gripped by this beautiful terror.

The quiet scene of the canal and the starry sky re-forms around me as I open my eyes, the wall over on the far side much faded with the darkness that's fallen between us. I get to my feet unsteadily at first, but resolute and practised, I make my increasingly certain way back to the bottom of the steps. Finding myself there, I burst suddenly to the top and, reaching the peak, almost topple backwards towards the water beneath, my head overcome by the unexpected exertion. Catching a hold on the railings as I stop by the side of the bridge, I notice for the first time the tiny droplets that are falling, the rain that merges soundlessly with the water in the canal. I watch in wonder as I trace this mass disappearance, those blessed particles giving themselves once more to their original oneness, at last having reached their truth and shedding the illusion of individuality which our lives, spent unknowing, battle to maintain. I can almost smell how close I am to something of an answer, to some part of an understanding whereby all the world's beauty and all its seeming randomness will finally come together in a perfect, beautiful sense. Only the flimsiest of obstructions shimmers now between me and the shining light of the eternal: that last vestige of my own ignorance which will stand until evaporation, and revelation, is mine.

Turning away from the dissolving dots, I search for my bearings, staring at the college without recognition at first – it sprang up here after my time. Then I fumble with my earbuds, the tangled, obdurate mess that I've taken from my jacket and hold in my fingers. Reluctantly, almost resentfully, they yield to my fiddling with a loosening of knots, and still feeling sluggish, I find through a mind fug the initial on the left bud and twist it to my ear, following it with the other in my right. Slipping my phone back into my jean pocket with the jack pushed home, I hear Columbia's opening sequence start to play, the grinding guitar sound and drumbeat that build to a critical musical mass replete with feedback, the main line coming through anthemic as I'm drawn back over the bridge and across the road, making sure that I peer both ways into the darkness deliberately, checking for danger, my legs pulling themselves up tall and into a purposeful stride as they carry me back down Butterfly Walk.

The world's different now, all filled up with rain and dotted about with hurrying umbrella people surrounding me in their own perfect worlds as they make their way to the station. In this one, it's just me and the music which fills my mind with connections, those timeless allusions to people and places refreshed and refloated, riding with me and these soaring emotions down the new pebble path. Past the hoardings and their little square observation windows I float, reaching the Boots that seems all of glass, where I tap to pay for a plastic bottle of water, swilling it gratefully inside my mouth and around my teeth before gulping it ravenously down as I pass into the concourse. Right above me, the timetable screams in orange and Welwyn's 18.37 leaps out. It's 18.35, and before I even compute, on top of my legs I'm running through the crowds, spinning and weaving with Oasis pulsating all around me like I'm chased in a movie but one that I'm making. With the briefest of hopping pauses, I come through the barrier, my trusty oyster card lifted from its back-pocket home and gripped tight in my hand until both of my feet are on the train. I slide it back in there as I walk the two paces to the seat before me, suddenly aware as I drop down into it that I'm quite out of breath; my temples are pumping, and I feel slightly nauseous. I take big, deep gulps to catch up with myself as the song begins to tail away, its glorious work done and its legacy embossed, and just then the doors of the train start to close. As the platform through the window passes away and leaves the Butterfly behind us – this latest twenty-four-hour existence of a most modern kind which spreads further and further its wings – a new song begins to play; and my eyes start to close; and for the few seconds before I fall back again into a dream, I feel the warm touch of the rolling carriage as it slips its blanket around me.

About a Girl

Coming down from Primrose Hill in wistful contemplation as dawn broke on that first night with Penny, I felt beautifully immersed in the cool morning air, aware even then that I was stretching out the moment, indulging myself and my new state of bliss. Though feeling calm and almost immaculate as I reached the car at the bottom of the climb, I still couldn't conceive of heading back to Craig's place and was drawn inevitably instead to Shoreditch and specifically to the twenty-four-hour Beigal Bake at the top of Brick Lane – the one where they spell it correctly – that being the locale of my family's original settlement on arrival in this country and just about the only option open to me in those early hours of the new day.

Watching the steam rise above the deep-grained brisket temptingly placed on the spikes of a metal skillet right by the till, I stood in line with the other late-night Joes, eyeing the stacked-up dozens of freshly baked and boiled beigals. Steaming with bonhomie and satisfaction, my sense of sheer happiness must have been written all over my face: I couldn't help beaming at the customers who were making their way towards me – those in the snaking line who already had shuffled down the length of the shop to the kitchen at the rear. Down there, open doors revealed the bakery's busy production team, and the queue turned around and made its way back up past the row of glass cabinets filled with challahs and rye breads, a stock of made-up rolls, and those cheese cake bricks that you only find where professional eaters gather. The serving girls buzzing about in their blue hairnets on the business side of the cabinets looked like a race of their own.

"Where you coming from, then?" I asked the older guy behind me, who met my eyes. A taxi driver's identity badge hung from the ribbon around his neck, sitting on his occupational-hazard protruding stomach.

"Been up West all night, son." He smiled. "'Appen it's been a busy one, but I'm heading home now. Taking a dozen of these for the morning," he continued, pointing to the beigals behind the glass as he said so. "What about you? Any *muzel?*" I got his worldly insinuation from the little nod of his forehead, and I laughed, glad at last to have found someone with whom I could share my current delight with life, even if only cryptically.

"Yeah," I admitted with a grateful expression, "just getting some celebratory nosh so I can end this special night on another high."

"Lucky sod!" he said approvingly. Indeed.

When I awoke the following day, it was already late afternoon, and I strolled out to the high street for a lazy coffee, sitting and watching the Sunday crowd going about their business before finding a working phone box to give Penny a call. It was she who answered the phone this time, to my relief.

"Hiya," I said cautiously.

"Hi."

I hadn't thought about what I was going to say to her, but I knew that it was a call I should make and I got a welcome lift to hear that same soft tone in her voice again – such a novelty and so very changed from the way I was used to hearing her.

"It's Milo," I went on. "I just wanted to make sure you were OK, you know, after last night." I paused, but she didn't say anything so I continued. "I had a really good time, but I thought it would be better if I called you today rather than waiting to just bump into you tomorrow … as Milo from work." I couldn't help a little laugh escaping as I said it.

"That's very thoughtful of you," she replied, and she sounded genuinely appreciative, continuing with a voice that spoke straight to my heart, "but you're not just Milo from work now, are you."

"That's nice to hear," I said, beaming. "Well, I'm glad it's all cool. Maybe we'll have a drink sometime in the week?"

"Yeah, OK," she said. "That'll be nice. I'll see you tomorrow." With that, she put the phone down.

I knew that I wanted to play it cool, but in reality I was so excited at the prospect of being with her again that it just wasn't possible; and at the first opportunity when she rang me in the morning about something work related, I contrived to steer the conversation to my private agenda, convincing her to meet me that very evening at the Cafe Rouge in Hampstead so we could talk. I parked nearby and got there before her. Waiting upstairs as the clock ticked to the appointed hour and beyond, I slipped my thoughts of anxiety that she might not turn up by observing unnoticed as the local set cavorted. I was fascinated by the manners and the confident behaviour of these dark-haired Jews that made up a significant part of the area's demographic, a group that so easily I could have been part of. Seeing the way that the various characters interacted and identifying the larger-than-life roles that each one played, around which the group revolved, made me chuckle knowingly inside. All of it appeared transparent and over-the-top from where I was sitting, yet deep down I couldn't help admiring the ease with which they seemed to be able to comport themselves, the casual and unspoken certainty their manners seemed to express. Even though superficially their whole little act repelled me, perversely I knew that if I'd had the chance to be a part of this coterie – if my destiny had given me these friends and with them this behaviour – I wouldn't have denied it.

I can't adequately describe what I felt when, only about fifteen minutes late, I looked up and saw Penny arrive but when people talk about getting butterflies in their heart I know what they mean. Approaching me she noticed that I'd been waiting there without a drink and insisted on going to the bar for the first round and this left a lasting impression on me: I think I know why. While in recent times I've learnt to revel in the cheeky humour of sexism I always consider it tongue in cheek and probably find it so very funny precisely because it's exactly the opposite of what I feel. I don't doubt that plenty would damn me as complicit in an insidious, destructive poison because of this behaviour, but however I'm judged, I do truly believe in the justice of sexual equality, having done so since my impressionable eight-year-old self came under the spell of an amazing primary school teacher for whom feminism was a real cause. I've always held to the line on which she put me, even if more recently I have found myself doubting that men and women are fundamentally the same. But whether they are or not, I firmly believe that universal justice requires full gender equality. With rights come responsibilities, however, and if we want to enjoy our natural privileges, we must also be able to demonstrate that we are worthy of them. Women therefore cannot meekly accept the secondary role that men have traditionally carved out for them, certainly as far as independence is concerned, without giving away their own integrity. Mutual dependency, on the other hand, the kind that develops in the healthiest of relationships, is a very different case. Anyway, naively simplistic as ever, I took it as a bold sign that the girl would make a point of buying me a drink, and though in the scheme of things this particular example might seem a crass one, it answered for me a question that I hadn't yet thought of: a considerable haul for the price of a Budvar.

What had sprung up between us caused in me an irresistible hunger, and I think subconsciously I'd needed to see her again so soon to get a reality check to pinch myself and see if we really were as good as I thought. The next couple of hours flew by as we talked and laughed like a couple of friends who had nowhere else they wanted to be. All the other people seemed to disappear; the bar just evaporated, and all I could see was her, every pause and every smile we shared electric and exciting. As the evening moved on, I was more and more captivated; and before I knew it, closing time had drawn to a tantalizing crossroads.

"What do you think?" I asked, lingering on the long-empty glass that I still kept my hand around. "It's getting late, and both of us have work in the morning, and I know we just came out for a drink, but something in the air is saying *carpe diem* to me. I wonder if we shouldn't just go for it?"

"I don't mind," was her non-committal reply, about as committal as any phrase could be, and from that point on, the sensible route was no longer an option. Apart from anything else, I could almost sense that fate was daring me to turn down this opportunity so that I could prove what a loser I was once and for all. That wasn't going to happen.

Holding her soft hand in mine felt precious and daring as we stepped out to the pavement, the street lamps and the cars making their stately progress up the congested hill illuminating the night's rich darkness and gracing it with a frisson of delicious excitement, their bright lights a dazzling serenade as we went on our way. We found ourselves pretty soon in the reception of a hotel halfway down Haverstock

Hill, happy to accept with a carefree shrug the last room available with its single beds. Penny went up while I took a detour to the bar for a cold bottle of Moët, doling out happy smiles to the walls and the barman and anyone I saw as I waited for the silver bucket.

What memories there are of that night, and how clear they still seem – how sharp and bright they were even back then: her patterned green underwear that I took as a nod to her Celtic beginnings, the two of us on one long game as we drank and partied until three in the morning. Later, in the shower, laughing our heads off, we sprayed each other as we fought for the jet, almost pulling down the plastic curtain as our limbs kept tangling in it, drunk on the champagne of life with the floor soaking wet. The morning came just microseconds after we'd both closed our eyes, and roused disbelieving by the shocking call that we'd ordered from reception, we picked gingerly around the room for our various articles of clothing to get ourselves dressed, some bits here and others there, before driving away. Nirvana's "About a Girl" came like a love song from the car's stereo as I turned on the engine, a soundtrack that eased in effortlessly as a new era dawned as I headed for the Archway to drop her back home before going on to work.

The few weeks that followed were delicious and desperate, an unpredictable combination of joy and anxiety. There was magic in the air whenever we were together, a natural ease that made whatever we did and wherever we were exactly what the two of us wanted; yet even as this blossoming was gathering pace, we kept in our minds the crazy idea that it couldn't possibly last. Our dalliance was to be short and sweet because of where we both were in our lives, and investing our hearts seemed folly. I don't know how I stuck so long to this lazy, ill-conceived notion, but I suppose the riddle's answer lies among a web of various reasons. Partly it was a defence against falling too fast and too deep, a protection from the pain that, by this time in our lives, we'd both grown used to expecting. At the same time, creating the impression that a door was left open kept us free to enjoy these hours and hours of careless laughter without the trouble of addressing the deeper, more serious issues, giving us the idea that we could bolt if we wanted without recrimination or any regret. Without a doubt, we gave our relationship the added excitement of expiry in this spurious way, allowing us hungrily to continue our kissing and our chasing of pleasures even as we reminded each other how the clock was ticking fast, keeping set in our minds how soon we'd be over.

Life became like a dream in a whirlwind, a beautiful fantasy of magical lust. There was lust for the parties and lust for the restaurants, but most of all it was lust to be there with each other; yet still those long nights we spent tucked together in my mate's single bed always ended the same way: a declaration of our last kiss just before we closed our eyes and drifted away, sated, in each other's arms. Each night, were sure that we were finally through – that enough was enough and stopping now would mean not pushing things too far. For me, it was a perfect plan until the morning came and with it the unbearably empty prospect of losing her. Like an addict reneging on my oaths, I'd wake yearning for her lips, and then later that day, when my longing for her company had already grown too strong, I'd reach for the phone, desperately searching for the charmer inside as I dialled her number, hoping like never before that for one final time she'd answer my call.

Whatever the truth – whatever we were actually feeling – we both continued to pretend that neither of us wanted a serious partner right now, that our timing was wrong, and that finding our fun together in this moment was much better.

This is how things went on between us, date after date as weeks turned to months, keeping sacred a bizarre routine while professing our indifference and not recognizing that it was no longer what we wanted, not seeing that our hearts were changing, that we were falling in love.

Walk This World (Acoustic)

Some believe that in this world there are any number of suitable partners we could happily end up with, while others – the truest romantics, perhaps – are just as certain that we each have to find our single, predetermined one. My vote is with the former, but I also understand there is more to any match than mere personality: timing, as random a factor as it seems, is crucial. Sometimes I complain that a fourth decade was already setting its shadow upon us when first we set upon each other, that fate gave us little time as the young, carefree couple we still thought we were and a space too brief for the things that young couples do before sudden parenthood and the true step up to adult – for Penny, at least – overtook us. This is all very well, but I do need to bear in mind that as good as we were together, had we met five years or maybe even five months earlier, we wouldn't have stood a chance. Life's journey is long, and truth be told, by the time we met, I'd hardly got close to any kind of maturity. Were it not for her good sense and her patience, we'd never have found a way beyond those obstacles that later came to try us, and we would not have made the long march through to the happy family we are today.

I know why I fell in love with her, but why she fell in love with me – well, I put that down to smoke and mirrors. I kept hidden those aspects of myself that subconsciously I knew were not attractive: a natural selfishness, for instance; my family's predisposition to verbal aggression and hysteria; and of course my obsessive nature. Even back then, I was always swearing by some quirky diet – eating nothing but fruit before midday, for instance, or never mixing protein and carbohydrates – trying with tuts to impose these regimens on those around me and pouring scorn on them if they wouldn't follow. To compound the stupidity of my intolerance, I would be just as easily convinced by the next fad theory that came along, and if this meant jamming my cherished regulations into reverse, then so it had to be. Then, just as vehemently, I'd label a fool any person who stayed with the old way. Under the circumstances, I think it's a minor miracle that I managed to get her to stick around. Sometimes when she's piqued at me and wants to let off steam, I'll be reminded how some part of my character – some annoying trait or habit that was only revealed once she was safely past the point of no return – was nowhere to be found on the partner prospectus she thought she'd subscribed to.

On the other hand, her qualities that so bowled me over – her inner strength and sense of fun, her easy-going nature, her kindness, and her natural patience – are for real and remain just as they were. It isn't any wonder I had no antidote to the spell that she cast. Even though I was established in the City and doing all right, until I met Penny, my life away from the office wasn't all that it should have been. It seemed that if a problem could be made out of something, then it would be, and so where things should have been great, they were mostly only OK; where they should have been OK, they weren't even that. Due to my ignorance – my lack of understanding that happiness should be a natural state – I wasn't even aware that things were not working. I thought that was just how it was. Maybe it was me. Maybe it was due to some of the people around me. I didn't conceive that life could be lived lightly and so always managed to take the bumps horribly, never missing a pothole.

With Penny now everything was changed. It was amazing and uplifting to be with someone who laughed so much, who was so awake to all of the little treats that our life could afford us. She was such good company that her carefree nature emanated to all those around her like a sprinkling of high-grade fairy dust, and being chosen by her made me feel like a prince. Having her beside me felt like the pinnacle of my life's achievements, finally bringing home why I'd worked so hard to escape from the person I had been. The riches that journey brought me are beyond common words.

You Do Something to Me

Some weeks after that first fateful evening, we found ourselves on what I like to think of as our first weekend away, flat sitting on the early May bank holiday for a mate of mine in Neasden. I'd known Tim for almost as long as I'd been at the firm, having met him in the back office right when I joined the department, and we'd hit it off immediately. I especially clicked with his wacky sense of humour, and both of us having an ear for esoteric music, we soon stumbled upon other interests that we had in common; but the main thing that attracted me to him was his genuine friendliness, a standout quality in the dog-eat-dog world that I'd recently entered. We quickly became good friends. Our paths diverged somewhat when things at work moved on, but whenever we did get together, the reunion was always a warm one.

On the Thursday night before the holiday weekend, we chanced to meet in the changing rooms downstairs at the office. I'd just come back from playing one of the regular six-a-side games, and he was preparing for a bike ride home. After the preliminary laddish banter, he told me that he and his girlfriend were going away for the long weekend and asked what I was up to. I didn't have any firm plans and, still being itinerant, told him that I wasn't even sure where I was going to stay. On hearing this, he insisted that I make use of his flat for the duration, and after I gratefully accepted, the conversation went on. I couldn't help letting slip that Penny and I had started seeing each other. He mixed in the same work circle as she did and, knowing her quite well, was as delighted for me as I was for myself. He also seemed delighted to be made privy when I told him I was speaking out of turn because it was meant to be a secret; she did not want people at work to know about us, as we thought it was unlikely to be a long-term engagement. What I did know was that if I could trust anyone to keep something quiet, I could certainly trust him. Aside from the relief I felt just from sharing it with someone who knew her, it made me look at the thing itself afresh, and doing that felt truly wonderful.

It was no accident when I found myself speaking to Penny early the next day. Mentioning in my finest cocky attitude the conversation I'd had with Tim, I added what the plan for that night would be. Whenever I called her with a proposal, I always girt myself with this flippant persona, hiding my insecurity behind a veneer of not being bothered while silently screaming a lie. I insisted that she was extremely lucky that I'd found some amusement for her on a night that, without me, would have been crushingly mundane, but at first she wouldn't buy it. She wasn't comfortable at all about being at Tim's place or about my telling him, reminding me that we'd agreed to keep our relationship under wraps from our colleagues. As I tried to talk my way around her, I could feel the panic inside rising; the very idea of not having her with me seemed too barren to contemplate, but I was certain that Tim wouldn't betray us, and to my relief, I eventually persuaded her. I arranged to collect her from her mum's place when I'd got the keys that evening so we could drive there together.

Climbing the stairs and entering the lounge of his tidy little maisonette, which was just down the road from where my uncle and aunt lived, we found little messages and strategically placed goodies around the place – videos to watch, drinks to drink, and so on – along with instructions for the plants to be watered. It seemed that he'd gone out of his way to ensure our stay would be a happy one. We ordered an Indian takeaway with a number from one of the fliers that he'd left piled by the telephone, taking it outside to the wooden deck that was raised above the garden and filled with an array of different coloured plants in pots of

411

various sizes. We finished our dinner there as we listened to the sound of my CDs wafting through from the lounge. The world seemed totally at peace as, gazing out over the garden, we kicked back together as the sun went slowly down.

I was the first to wake on Saturday morning. Lying still beside Penny as she slept on with her back turned towards me, it slowly dawned where I was and how I'd got there. The morning light was shining into the room through the crack where the curtains joined, and I spent those next few minutes studying in silence the newly discovered galaxy of freckles that dotted the pale skin of her back. Rapt with a startling kind of excitement at the very unfamiliarity of what I beheld, I drank it all in like some newly uncovered map that would answer a universe of my questions. Before long, she began to stir, and I awakened her with a kiss. It was already quite late, and we both had things to do and places to be, so after I'd made us some breakfast and the two of us had dallied together on Tim's deck with a second cup of tea, I dropped her at the Underground.

I headed down to my parents, as we were going *en famille* to a friend's engagement party, and I remember how much I missed her that night and how I couldn't get her out of my mind. At one point in the evening, standing alongside a girl who was wearing Penny's body lotion, inadvertently I mistook the scent for the girl and almost got myself into some bother for gently laying a hand upon her. When the party was over, Dad drove us all back home, and I crashed out there. I got up in the morning and hurriedly drove across London to reach the flat by lunchtime. I don't know why I'd been in such a rush, but once inside the door, it felt like I could drop the angst that had been driving me. It was great just to chill there in peace, sitting out on the deck where the memory of my Friday night still lingered. As the afternoon wore on, I went out to get provisions and a bottle of Jack

Daniel's from the shops by the roundabout and settled down with it in front of the television to watch some of the videos that Tim had left. I might have been dozing by the time a knock at the door awoke me, and assuming the caller was a friend who didn't realize they'd gone away, I went down the narrow staircase to open the front door and inform them. It was a delightful surprise to find Penny there. She was winking at me and barely able to stand up, clearly very drunk but no less welcome for that, having come quite some way to find me, looking as she must have been to end the evening in my arms.

As we rattled around the place in the morning, she seemed slightly abashed, as if she would have liked to take back her surprise turning up, so beautifully at odds was it with the propaganda we had been feeding each other. Both the act itself and her coy repudiation of it resonated in tenderness with my own true feelings and made her all the more lovely to me. With this swell of sentiment about us, the bank holiday Monday was ours, and disguised as an everyday couple, we nipped out in the car to the big B&Q on the North Circular for a fish griddle and some fish from the supermarket, which we cooked on the terrace in the afternoon sun. It was always the loveliest feeling to be with Penny, going nowhere in tandem, nowhere better than here. Without a question passing between us, she stayed with me again that night, though when Tim and Ivy returned earlier than expected, Ivy didn't seem too impressed to catch us about to settle down into her bed. Tim smoothed things over behind closed doors, and somewhat chastened, we took ourselves and our stuff into the spare room with him surreptitiously beaming at us at every opportunity, so happy was he to be sharing our secret.

Our first real weekend away together came at the bank holiday later that month when we headed off ironically for a trip to Great Yarmouth. I'd been there on a stag weekend with some of the guys from work a few years earlier, and always remembering fondly the laughs we'd had in a sauna and Jacuzzi, I made this facility the prime requirement when choosing where to stay, managing to ignore all other criteria and booking us a room at what seemed, when we arrived, like an old folks' home. Once in our room, we made ourselves fresh from the drive with a nice soak in the bath to rinse off the cobwebs, and then, having unpacked a few items – a book, the black bottle, and a tooth brush – we headed out to see what was around. Leaving the building, our curiosity led us into some kind of television room that was right there inside the front door, a salon of decrepitude for which we were quite unprepared. Bless them, these poor elderly and the smell that marks out their turf, but we couldn't help getting out from there as quickly as possible, away and into the sunlight lest our own time of twilight come creeping too soon.

I've known others for whom my failure to ensure a better class of accommodation would have been disastrous and earned a rebuke-filled weekend with plenty of pouting, but Penny always looked to the funny side. We spent our time laughing and making jokes about the predicament, however absurd it might be, our spirits staying high even when we weren't topping them up with the hard stuff. Even the drive to get here had been a revelation, and as early as crossing over the Holloway Road I had felt quietly confused as the girl beside me made pleasant conversation and radiated content rather than the moaning and bored frustration I'd grown to expect on a journey like this. Only as we passed Lowestoft did I finally get that this wasn't a sham, and the realization was something like the sun coming out. Whatever we did, it was stitched in with happiness: the walk along the cold pebbly beach, a round of crazy golf in the wind by the old wooden pier, even the arcade hour and a tough-fought game of air hockey which I'll never admit she won before choosing fish and chips for supper when I offered her whatever she wanted.

Returning to our lodgings, we booked out the Jacuzzi for an hour, our very doing so scandalizing the aged and gently sweet receptionist, who warned us repeatedly of the cost which seemed negligible. I'd always treasured a memory from years earlier when I'd arrived rather unsure of myself one Saturday afternoon, meeting up here with a group from work who I barely knew when a guy I'd started with was getting married. On my way in, I bumped into one of the party, who told me that they were all gathered in the steam complex for the afternoon and that I should follow them there. I remember how self-conscious I felt when I did so and how happy was the transformation a couple of hours later when we all came out with some laughs and a little bit of shared history. This experience had been the inspiration for the trip with Penny, but the hour we spent floating on bubbles without and within was such a blast that it easily topped it.

After our time was up, we crept giggling wearily back to our room and created something of a vibe by putting tea lights about the place, lighting also a bigger candle from my favourite stall in Camden that I'd brought along. Polishing off a bottle of champagne, we took it in turns to reveal select little secrets, precious little pieces of our jigsaw pasts that grew more incriminating the more we drank yet nonetheless were still endearing. Each one helped us to edge a little closer together our separate presents as all the while we pretended that when all was said and done we neither of us cared. Self-delusion is a wondrous thing. The next day, with the return journey before us and wanting the weekend never to end, we went to the Sunday-afternoon showing of *Batman* at the cinema on the front, and after coming back out into the light and taking a last melancholy stroll up the pier with some more fish and chips, we set off on our way home. Coming back towards London and seeing that great orbital M25 ahead, our new city walls, I looked across at her sleeping in the seat beside me and felt proud and happy, safe and protective, worthy and yearning all at the same time.

A couple of months after the original night with Penny had started to turn my life upside down, I managed to settle on somewhere to live, a two-bedroom flat near Mornington Crescent which I'd be sharing with Luca. I invited her over on Saturday for a spot of lunch, but as I tried to fix up bits and pieces around the place to make it the way that I had imagined it, the morning ran away with me. I scaled back my grandiose lunch plans and just flew out to the local Sainsbury's for olives and pittas and dips which I laid out on a little square blanket in the tiny patch of grass I thought was a garden. Like a light summer breeze, she turned up at the flat and happily surveyed my offering, accepting the glass of wine that I poured for her and declaring it to be "all of my favourite things". Should such a simple phrase have so easily carved a valley inside me? Must I, I wonder, have come from an exceptionally hard place to have been affected so deeply by such simple ease? Those few words have stayed with me to this day, and they make me smile whenever I recall them, pretty much summing up for me exactly what she stands for. Though long years spent together have diminished their shock – have accustomed us to those things that once stood out – they've never erased my gratitude for this person who so changed my perception of what could be possible, of how life could be, of what love could mean.

Polka Dots

And so time passed. If we were short with one another and sometimes exchanged a harsh word, two sweeter ones followed it. If we were tired, then of course we could sleep, yet the game was all about burning the candle, and hand in hand, we found ourselves running just to keep up, clinging fast all the while to our mutual denial. Though oh so together, this fundamentally kept us apart, separate even though Penny was staying at mine at least three or four times a week. Everything seemed perfect, yet when I look back at how we went on, I marvel at the depths of my ignorance – how blind I was and how emotionally retarded. If gullibility is the measure of a fool, then I don't know a bigger one than I was: I had an amazing capacity to convince myself that our thing was one way when all the evidence pointed to another. Did it not occur to me that we might be looking to build a future because I couldn't imagine myself worthy of hers? Was the thought of pursuing my own dreams too terrifying to contemplate? Whatever it was that kept me so ignorant, there were moments when a beam of daylight pierced through to our idyll and it became all the sweeter for this chink of reality.

Penny was going to Ireland to tie up a few loose ends, and I kind of understood, without letting that understanding form words in my head. Flying late in the afternoon, she'd taken the whole day off, and already feeling the pain of her absence before lunchtime, I rang her at home. By the end of a short conversation, we were meeting for lunch. It was most unusual for me to stray from the office during the day, and this strange interlude found me waiting on Upper Street, looking across that wide road to the raised section of pavement on the opposite side where I knew my dad had once worked. Imagining that time with its lesser sprinkling of cars and even other times when horses held sway, I was lost to the moment and didn't see her as she stepped from the taxi which arrived right beside me. Departing, it woke me from my reverie, and there she was on the pavement in her light brown jodhpurs, her ankle boots, and a thick knit jumper, with her freshly cut hair resting on the epaulettes of a tan flying jacket. A flattish cap finished off the look, and her lightly made-up face beamed at me from beneath it. I knew where she was going and I knew why, and knowing somewhere that it meant she was moving towards me, just seeing her standing there was like a shot of adrenalin to my heart, a beautifully poignant moment. All through the lunch, I just couldn't let go of her hand. I could hardly bear to release her at all. If I'd only been able to put into words those things I was feeling!

A few days later at the flat, she lay softly sleeping on my arm. Watching her, I thought that my heart would burst. Happy to see her, I'd spent the previous evening listening contentedly to her stories: she never was short of words, and though she didn't tell me everything, it was all that I needed to know. The pocket Irish teddy bear with its big green hat she'd thought to bring back from duty free also spoke volumes, and subtly, inconspicuously, things were changing for us. The groove of drinking and abandon is a deep one, however, and we stayed true to the path. I thought I was going along with it for her, but I think we were both doing it for me; those evenings remaining a rush towards unconsciousness as we drank stronger and longer drinks. "This'd knock a horse," she would say as she tasted the next as we continued to embrace the haze and each other on those nights filled with pleasure but I guess little more. Very few at work knew yet that we were a couple, and we rarely spoke of anything beyond the coming weekend. When we did mention the future, it was only in terms that assumed we'd be strangers when we got there.

There comes a time when it's change or die, but as far as our relationship was concerned, I had no idea. Perhaps exasperated or disbelieving of my insensitivity, Penny decided she had to get on with the rest of her life and that my coming thirtieth would serve as our perfect finale, resolving to leave me once she'd seen me through it. The big day came around. Calls had gone out for a house party in our flat in Camden. Unusually, Tommy wouldn't be there; less unusually neither would Jim. Luca, of course, would be there with a few of the mates he'd invited, and I did have a couple of promises; but when the reckoning was done, Penny couldn't believe that such a big night looked likely to be so poorly attended and so likely to be flat. For my part, I was used to this and pretty much resigned to a kind of habitual humiliation, but she felt so bad for me that she swung round her plans and hit the jungle drums for her large group of friends, telling me to be sure to get plenty of alcohol. Over a jaw-dropping ninety minutes, her crowd from just up the road filled the place, and to my mind turned the evening into exactly the kind that I'd always dreamed of: the place was packed with mayhem, and those few of my mates that did come along couldn't believe what a thriving, buzzy joint they'd come to. A party at last to be proud of!

Of the memories I still have of that evening, the birthday cake features prominently, not because it was a rich chocolate beauty too good to resist but because I wasn't able to warn my invitees that it was spiked with something liberating before, too late, I realized they were helping themselves from the rack in the kitchen. That night would be my second encounter with Penny's brother, who by now seemed mildly curious rather than sullenly protective as he had when I appeared out of nowhere to collect his sister for our first date. Unsuspecting, he ate plenty of the sponge and then later became trapped in a room with the door wide open, unsuccessfully trying to effect an escape by unscrewing the window locks with the rounded tip a ballpoint pen.

By ten or eleven o'clock, there was a veritable party going on about the place with people dancing in the lounge and the corridors and even the kitchen, and excited as I was, I went at it hard and crashed out early – not for nothing am I known as a lightweight. As lasting testament, there's a picture of Penny and me unconscious together on top of the bed taken by someone who must have picked up my camera opportunistically, and if you look closely, you can see another bombed party who's lying across the bed above us like an underworld guardian. I may go down early, but at least I bounce back. I remember seeing, as I staggered dopily through the flat preparing for part two, scenes of party carnage. Bodies lay everywhere, and those less inclined to chocolate cake helped their weaker brethren in relays from the lounge to the front door and then, low-slung between their carriers like sweet, drunken chariots, to the waiting cabs, their numbers disproportionate even for a most outrageous bash.

Had things gone according to Penny's plan, she would have made herself scarce the next morning long before my family arrived, in which case a proud, dignified goodbye might have been my sad parting gift. It was lucky for me that the vodka had taken her hard and Sunday's reveille was an unwelcome one. I think maybe because of something she'd said, I had an inkling that if I got up and broke the sleepy spell, she'd quickly slip from my life. Staying still where we lay, I managed to stretch our slumber and keep her asleep, and it was only when my family arrived at midday and rapped on the front door – Mum and Dad and my sister and her husband with my niece and nephew – that we properly awoke. Roused by the sound, she blinked and looked at me enquiringly. I took the opportunity to fill her in about the birthday lunch we'd planned, asking too if she wouldn't mind coming along.

As Luca opened the front door, she gathered the enormity of what I'd dropped on her and sprang in a panic from the bed, darting with a towel pulled around her across the room to make a frantic dash for the refuge of the bathroom on the other side of the hall exactly as my parents appeared at the top end. Both parties froze where they stood, Penny and my parents finally met with surprised, awkward smiles, almost too late. After some embarrassed niceties, she disappeared to straighten herself to her own satisfaction, returning in good order as her delightful self. Good natured to the core, she agreed to come along and found herself in the midst of our family cyclone upstairs in a restaurant on Jamestown Road for chilli, burgers, and sundaes, all of my favourites things, a meeting with madness and her plans of escape foiled forever.

Another picture that comes from that midlife landmark stares down at me now from high on my wall, taken by my sister, I surmise from her absence in the frame. It shows my mum, a thin white sweatband around her forehead keeping grey hair in place, and my dad still the round-faced younger man and not yet the other I remember who grew ill and old for his final, stoic limp unto death. They look fresh from the Hampstead trek of that morning with my sister's new baby boy on Mum's lap. He's all of twenty years old now and a fortnight to the day older than his uncle and aunt's relationship. My parents at either side of the head of the table seem closest to the camera, because Luca's cut out, a mere swatch of his checked shirt allowed to carry down through the years to remind me; Dad's salt-and-pepper beard, meanwhile is carried down genetically, a gift all these years later to his doppelganger son. Next, behind the grandparents, a bubble-haired brother-in-law sits smiling with my niece on his lap, and then Penny and I resting wan at the foot of the table. Her tired visage is all patience and good manners, belying how she must have been wondering what sort of crazy gathering she'd got herself mixed up with – a first acquaintance with my secret circus and just a glass of wine for comfort. Beside her sits the birthday boy, used to the clamour and a Dos Equis before me, happily surrounded by those that I love.

When the hurricane of my family had passed, we found ourselves again alone in my bedroom sitting together on the floor, quite worn out from the emotion of the last twenty-four hours. From out of somewhere, she produced a present. I realize now that her suddenly terse mood bore a dark premonition, but weary and now newly excited, I didn't put my finger on it, feeling instead lifted with anticipation as happily I took the box from her. Opening the top, I found inside a dark metal frame, a tripod on a circular ring with a thick, blue glass bell that sat inverted upon it. Two little candles that were shaped like flat diamonds completed the set, and coming back from the bathroom with the bell filled with water, she placed the little wax boats floating gently just so.

"There you are," she said. "What do you think?"

"That's really lovely," I murmured, smiling, watching the little candle boats bobbing and rocking on the water. She set them apart on the top and pushed them both towards the middle, smiling.

"They're just like us," she said. "Don't you think?"

I smiled a tired, happy smile at her, but I was confused, not really getting what she meant. After a moment or two of thinking, I asked her.

"There," she said again, pointing as the little shapes continued to nod about on the waves, "see how they are two little ships, like us, bobbing along on the sea of life, just passing in the night."

Her delivery spoke more of what she meant than the actual words, and the doom in her meaning shivered through me like a physical blow. It was as if a hand beneath my world fell away to leave me instantly alone, helpless and adrift, and I started to cry, silently at first as my tears gathered slowly, welling in the corners of my eyes until, growing too large to hold there, they started to fall. Inconsolable sobs soon gave voice to my breaking heart. I knew that some emotional barrier had splintered inside me, but amid the pain, I felt somehow relieved, in a crazy, abandoned kind of way, to be able to feel such clarity of sadness. As I carried on crying, bent away from her with my head in my hands, she sat shocked and unmoving for a moment, watching me. Taken aback by the strength of my emotion, she soon couldn't help but put her arm around my shoulder; and as she drew towards me, I could feel the warm, entreating comfort of her kisses against my wet cheeks, grateful to be brought back into her embrace as she told me it would all be OK and her tears mingled with mine.

There was no big discussion about how we both felt, no working out of what we both wanted, and no plan set in place. Our relationship would lead us wherever it would lead us, but from that night on, we understood that we had transcended our initial, casual accident and were now on a different footing. We no longer told ourselves we were just killing time. When we awoke the next morning, we found that one of our little candle ships had sunk, and it seemed somehow symbolic: the path we'd separately been travelling was doomed, and from now on, we'd be travelling the same path together. It was easy to admit to myself how much she meant to me, but still I felt ignorant of what it would take for a properly solid, lasting relationship. I still wasn't ready to trust that we'd actually cracked it. She made me happier than I could ever remember being, and it seemed marvellous that those initial impressions of her which had seemed too good to be true were in fact no lie. Yet despite all that, I still doubted myself, still doubted that I knew what love really was. I feared deep down that it was my lack of courage and the security she brought me when I hid in her arms which made me so happy – that the man I was destined to grow into was still somewhere missing.

Wherever we were, we had gained an extension, and being more comfortable to embrace our feelings meant that we no longer needed to keep the relationship a secret. The veil was properly lifted a couple of months later. An American institution was taking over our company, and the Royal Albert Hall was booked for the grand celebration: with the building's wonderfully refined beauty and splendid history, it was a stage fit for purpose. After a painful presentation on the stage by our new joint heads – I think as painful for them to act out as it was for us to watch – we retired to celebrate the occasion in various bars around the building in our respective work groups. With all of us fragmented in our own little sections, it struck me as oddly opposed to the explicit promotion of our newly formed entity's sense of the oneness, but even so, it was never a bad thing to have a drink with the guys I worked with. The more we drank, the more convivial it became, and the more it reminded us why we should do this more often. I started off by quaffing a few champagne flutes, liking them very well, until the black-and-white waitresses who floated about the room with their silver trays began to offer only wine. I dipped then for the red ones before finally, when the servers stopped coming, moving on to the bottles of beer that were set out on trellis tables at the side of the room. What I really wanted was

Jack Daniel's or one of the cocktails which functions such as these, always billed as cocktail evenings, never feature. It occurred to me then what I really wanted, and in that same moment, a man on a mission, I set off for Penny.

Pleasantly drunk and skipping around the curving corridors, I stopped to ask anyone I thought might be able to help me if they'd seen her, delighting in the consternation this brought to some of their faces – flower that she was, they feared she might fall to this arrogant dealer. Finally entering the umpteenth bar, I found her standing with her back towards me, drinking in a group with her work friends and colleagues. The girls were already aware of our relationship, but there were some of the guys around from her floor and they definitely were not. Approaching like a determined hunter, I put my hands on her shoulders and turned her towards me, impetuously planting a big kiss on her mouth.

"Let's get out of here," I said, starting to pull her away with my hands still upon her. Surprised, she smiled and nodded, and after a couple of very brief goodbyes cut short by my impatient excitement, we fled the room, taking the stairs hand in hand. As we ran through the building, down the steps outside, and through the small crowd gathered on the forecourt, the people that saw us looked perfectly shocked that we should be together, and somehow this added to my pleasure. We jumped into a waiting cab, and I remember looking back over my shoulder, sitting on the back seat with my arm around her as our taxi pulled away, and seeing almost tangibly the frisson we'd created among the suits and the ties and the dresses that stood there looking after us.

Love Her Madly

Coincidentally or not, it was around this time that I started to cut down a bit on the drinking, taking the opportunity when I could to do more constructive things, such as toying with my guitar or writing some poetry. It was unnerving how the lines and the stanzas seemed almost to construct themselves whenever I was ready with a pen and paper, how so easily they gave form to the feelings and emotions that I'd only known in my dreams, those shadows that danced at the edge of my muddled subconscious. I found that this process of expressing them, of forging their pain into words and poems like the stripping away of stubborn old cankers, was palliative and healing.

With everything within and around now becoming more settled, it gradually occurred to me how huge were the quantities of alcohol that Penny and her friends habitually consumed. As if the scales had been removed from my eyes, I now saw her group of friends absolutely smashing it whenever the chance arose. Though she always remarked that the measures I poured were too rich – reminding me each time I gave her a drink that "it would choke a cat" – she couldn't have minded very much, because she never missed a drop. Looking backwards, I thought that my previous behaviour could have been the result of an unsettled frame of mind, so it was natural to wonder if Penny's manifestation had a similar cause. I guess with my happiness no longer hanging by such a thin thread, I had time for considerations like physical well-being, a thing that before I'd wilfully neglected.

Before that birthday watershed, our relationship had been defined by an electric uncertainty which kept our every moment together fresh and exciting, but despite the fact that things were inevitably changing, the good times still rolled on. Whether out on the town and horsing around or just chilling out in the lounge with my little brother Luca (more often than not with Penny too), the weekends and evenings had never a dull moment. Add to that a couple of games of five-a-side football a week with the boys after work and a Friday-night guitar class at the Working Men's College, and life was running with a healthy routine. Superficially, it all should have felt perfect, yet deep down inside I still had the nagging suspicion that we weren't really going anywhere. It was something I didn't quite understand, but nevertheless I knew it was holding me back. This enigmatic feeling troubled me, and I felt trapped in some kind of limbo in this chapter of my life which, however sweet, always seemed overshadowed by a sentence of death. I knew that we'd have to pass beyond this place if anything was to prosper, but for now, the way stood barred.

Perhaps on account of a newly acquired sense of purpose, I broke the habit of a lifetime and did something positive. I don't know how this good sense came to possess me or where I got the idea, but making myself an appointment to see the doctor that Wednesday afternoon was one of the smartest, most crucial things I ever did, the significance of which I can never over-estimate or give myself too much credit for. I told no one where I was going, not even Penny, leaving work early one afternoon and turning up at the surgery where years before I'd registered at the junction of York Way and Camden Road. The practice was housed in a grand old building with paint splitting away from the masonry outside in huge magnolia flakes, the waiting area large and sparse and painted in white with a high ceiling and two long sash windows facing the front out to the main road. Leafing uninterestedly through the magazines on the table, I kept wondering what on earth I was doing there, swapping occasional smiles with the receptionist as she busied herself at the desk on the other side of the room and feeling like a fraud. Ten minutes after my appointed time, she answered her intercom, and then, looking up, she smiled again.

"You may go in now," she said, so up I stood, and smiling back a little grimly as I wondered what I was going to say, I walked to the door. It cracked open as I turned the round brass handle, and pushing it wider, I stepped on inside.

I didn't know how to start, and at first I couldn't even explain what I was doing there, but I suppose doctors are used to all sorts of prevarication. He had about him an air of understanding, and prompting me, he listened carefully, getting me to open up and express myself, to talk through my feelings. I explained that I was with a girl who I knew I really cared for but that I could hear a voice inside screaming out against what I thought were my true feelings, stopping us from getting closer. I told him that I knew what the next step should be but that I felt afraid to go there and that my fear was instead pushing me to turn away, urging me to run and hide as if the prize of true love were somehow too much to bear. By the time I'd finished, I really felt that I had described the nut of my situation, and it was such an enormous relief to have got the right words out, to have heard the sentiment rather than just being uncomfortably aware of it.

Without having any killer answers, he spoke to me wisely and told me that the fact that I had come to him meant I was serious about wanting to overcome this difficulty. He then gave me a slip of paper on which he'd written the name and phone number of a counselling group that he thought might be able to assist. Infused with new hope, I shook his hand gratefully. On the other side of the door, high above the front garden on the steps that led down to the pavement and the road beyond, I felt very much lighter as I looked out upon a whole new day. Though anxious not to credit the experience too readily with having resolved my situation, I did genuinely feel less burdened, keeping the details he'd given me but knowing instinctively that I wouldn't be using them. By putting my feelings to words before him, I'd managed to untangle them, untangling also the binds around my heart. Walking the short way home that evening, I resolved to relax, to let things take their natural course, to see where they found me.

Faith is a terribly hard thing to sell – almost impossible to those who don't want it but natural and obvious for those of us who do. I guess I'd found some measure of it now, and with my fears allayed, I was happy to let myself go with the flow, to follow fate's river with the thought that I had a paddle in the water, and if I wasn't driving then at least I was steering myself as I pottered along. As it turned out, things weren't to be that simple. After a very happy Christmas, sometime in January Penny told me that she thought she might be pregnant. The blood in my body ran cold. At first, I reflexively told her that all would be fine, that she shouldn't worry, and that if she wanted to have the baby it would all work out OK. Inside, however, I grew ever more desperate. Life now seemed to be spinning dizzyingly out of my control, and the future was closing in darkness around me. All of my old anxieties intensified, and I felt choked by a sickening claustrophobia. Instead of behaving in what I knew was the right way – behaving like a real man – more and more I became the product of this panic. Though I knew that Penny felt dismayed and emotionally abandoned, it was suddenly "me" and not "us". I just couldn't bear that at this most decisive juncture of my life I should feel so helpless.

As I waited over those next few weeks to discover how my life's path would be set, as I wondered what she would decide, seeing her ultimately as mistress of the situation, I felt as if I were just blowing first this way and then that, and I longed for some respite from my ever gnawing fear. On Valentine's Day, I came home to find her already there before me, sickly and tired and wrapped up in bed. She told me wearily she'd been really unwell and had left work early. With an unmistakeable tone of resentment in her voice, she also told me that the panic was over. She was very pale, and I could see that she'd been crying. I hated it that her discomfort had resulted from what to me felt like the best news I'd ever received, but what should I do? I just couldn't share her disappointment, and though I tried to be sympathetic, I had no answer for the bitterness she now felt towards me. I knew how badly she felt I'd let her down; we both knew I had, but as much as her grief and sickness made me feel awful, I still felt like some terrible doom had been lifted. I did what I could to look after her and to try to console her, calling into work for her the next day to say she'd be off sick and trying not to feel too much the new spring in my step. But in the days and weeks that followed, there was something amiss; and in my relief, I couldn't help feeling that this whole episode was a warning: if I didn't make the important decisions, they would instead be made for me.

For a little while after that, we just limped along, still fond and close to each other but bearing the strain of our injuries. By the end of March, I'd made up my mind. But for a whisker or a kind breath of wind, I'd have been locked for life into a relationship that I wasn't sure I'd chosen. It scared me to the core to be found so ill prepared. I couldn't stand there ignoring the door which, once shut fast, was now flapping noisily open: clearly, it was my way out. Coming back from the pub one Sunday afternoon and locking ourselves away from the truth in the bedroom, I felt as close to her as I ever had, but then, as we lay cooling side by side on the futon with our skin touching and our games over, we started to talk. Our heads become clear when the other parts of our bodies grow quiet. As the conversation progressed, we both found we were tired of going the way things had been taking us, and after almost a year together, it was easy for us to agree, despite the sadness of the realization, that it was over.

Sitting at the bottom of the futon while she started to pack up some things, I regarded her quietly, watching as she readied herself for a final journey home. She looked more resigned than desperately sad, and for that moment, we both felt the same. At last, the thing was done and I was free, and a surge of relief swept over me. No longer would I be cursed by my own pathetic weakness. No longer would I be condemned in a relationship for want of the will to break myself out of it. No longer would I avoid doing the right thing for lack of the strength to identify it. I can hardly express how much this realization meant to me. I felt that I could truly believe in myself and be who I was meant to be. After a lifetime of doubts and fears of my own loathsome cowardice, I had conclusive proof that I wasn't afraid to stand on my own two feet – that I could trust in my own integrity.

Sitting there and watching her quietly pulling on her tights, I had an epiphany. Suddenly, I was clear-headed and free from doubt for what seemed the very first time in my life. With my resolution unsullied by that inveterate fear of settling for less, I knew exactly what I wanted. It was blinding and immediate and obvious: I wanted her! There was absolutely no doubt about it, and even as she continued to pack her bags, preparing to go, I was almost bursting with my new found conviction, almost grinning with happiness as I watched the girl I loved from the corner of my eye. I just had to find a way to bring this thing back around. I took the bag from her to carry it out to the car, and she followed behind me, giving Luca a quick wave as we passed the open lounge door.

"Can you do me one last favour?" she said, stopping just inside the entrance.

"Sure," I replied, "whatever you want."

"I've got a christening to go to next weekend, and I don't want to go on my own. That would just mean too many questions – getting involved in things I'd rather not get involved in. Would you mind coming with me? You won't have to stay for long."

"Sure," I said. "Of course I'll be happy to." I wanted to jump for joy at this stroke of good fortune.

Sunlight in the Rain

Opposite St Joseph's in the function room above the pub about halfway down Highgate Hill the following Sunday, I found myself gathered together with what seemed like the entirety of London's Irish community. This landmark church which, as a stranger, I'd known for more years than I'd realized revealed itself to me as an intrinsic institution to Penny and her kin, sending forth its congregation to the party on the other side of the road. Legions were there of uncles and aunts, ladies in auburn beehives and other coloured sets that came refreshed from Marybelle's, while the men, to a man, were thickset with accents that were even broader. The younger ones, who were Penny's peers and my own generation by their looks and their manners, seemed different from any group of people I'd known before. As she pointed those out to me whose names I knew from the tales she told, it was quite amazing – an encounter with fabled creatures now become flesh. It brought to life her tales of tragedy and stoicism, of fellowship and adventure such as I never could have dreamt. They all made sense now as I watched over this crowd of their subjects, this community of souls that buzzed, it seemed, with an air of comfort. They belonged together, having been to the same schools and having played in the same teams and having drunk in the same bars; they all had the same scrapes and the same history and, I imagined, the same hearts.

I stood on my own at the end of the bar while Penny was off somewhere speaking to some of her girlfriends, and I contented myself with watching the various proceedings, fascinated to see this microcosm of where she had sprung from, still shaking my head that she who'd become so familiar to me could be part of something so patently different. Though I understood that I'd been brought along only as a kind of decoy, it still felt like an honour to be at the party and to witness this happy scene as I looked out around the room, aware from time to time of faces looking back furtively at me, a stranger like a visitor at the zoo who doesn't realize that he's the attraction. A few of her friends that I'd first met at my party all those months previously came over to give unnecessary apologies for the state of their exits, and it was fun to laugh about that and more besides. A few new faces also came over to make their introductions, some of them curious and others just guarded. With the men, I mainly chatted about football, and most of them approved when I revealed my affiliation.

One of the guys who looked as distinct from the others as I did came over on his own. Swarthy and handsome, I knew him as her legendary ex-boyfriend as soon as he introduced himself. He was very polite and just as friendly as his intelligent reputation led me to expect, but I could tell that with him especially, my presence there had created a disturbance. As we chatted about not very much for a little while with the appropriate distance between us, it occurred to me that perhaps he was the reason for my being here. I didn't mind – it just felt good still to have Penny in my sight – but I knew that as things were, this could still end with her slipping away from me. I knew I had some work to do, but I felt unusually relaxed about the situation, as if destiny had coaxed fortune and they were smiling on me. Today's do was a perfect reprieve after what had happened last weekend, and though I hadn't worked out any kind of plan – though I had no roadmap for the day whereby I'd be able to get her back – now that I'd realized she was the love of my life, I just couldn't imagine any obstruction. Standing against the bar looking out happily at the crowds of strangers who were acting out together their particular rituals, I slowly sipped a Coca-Cola with my car parked outside.

As if by providence, it wasn't long before just the opportunity I required presented itself. A man called Snoopy had started playing some records, and the dancing had begun; but one of the girls on the dance floor, whom I hadn't yet met, was clearly very drunk, and her extravagant movements were causing consternation. Watching her as she flailed about, I learned that she was the godmother. Possibly overcome by the weight of responsibility that the day had heaped upon her, she took a slip after a while and fell splayed and helpless. As much for her own safety as to satisfy the bench of pioneers who were tutting their disapproval, it was decided she needed to be escorted home. Penny hadn't counted on today being a long one, and asking me if I'd mind giving them both a lift, she offered our services, the three of us then setting off with Penny beside our lolling passenger in the back, coincidentally heading for Neasden.

We drove around the streets for a while, trying to coax some positive recognition from our charge, and then, when we finally located her address, Penny tried to pull her from the car, both of us supporting her as she staggered up the drive and into the care of her father, whom we found at the front door. Saying our goodbyes, we returned to the car, and Penny thanked me, apologizing for what she called the wasted afternoon. In truth, it hadn't felt like that to me at all. Her life was so unimaginably different from mine. With her, I expected to be led from one bizarre situation to another, and I told her that, saying I had to thank her yet again for another improbable adventure, and we both fell about laughing.

As the laughter fell to silence, it was now or never. I had her to myself, and suddenly hot, nervous flames were threatening to engulf me: I couldn't wait anymore. At first, she seemed taken aback and then baffled as I struggled to convince her of what I was feeling. To her it seemed a sudden change of heart, but I explained as earnestly as I've ever explained anything that I'd come to a new me with a completely new mindset and that I'd known it even as I sat last week in my underwear on the edge of the bed where we'd just broken up. For too long a moment, I didn't know if I'd already lost her – if the turnaround was going to be too much for her to take in – and I could feel my heart getting ready to break. But maybe because I was so desperate and so desperately sincere, I finally convinced her to trust me. I remember driving back to the flat that night in a cloud of the brightest happiness and then seeing Luca's pleasant surprise and his wide-eyed smile as the two of us arrived back home together. Later that night, when we couldn't let go of each other and our mouths hung together with kisses, I remember the worlds of emotions that gushed from our eyes, those precious tears not sprung of pain that washed clean our sins as they spilled on our cheeks and ran blessed down our faces.

Three Lions on a Shirt

The christening had marked our true beginning, and we spent the months after as if in the sunshine. The doubts and fears that before had quietly haunted the air around us lifted and dispersed. A famous professor might have said we were now playing with the handbrake off, committed to each other in the way of a fully fledged couple without reservation in our minds or our hearts. It was just great. In this new spirit of comfortable maturity, we decided that as a proper grown-up partnership we could even go away together for a whole two weeks, and we duly booked ourselves an air-conditioned holiday to Turkey for early July. It was just past midnight on the Sunday morning of our departure, and I was dozing in bed with half an eye on the rapidly advancing time on my bedside clock. We had an early flight to catch from Gatwick and needed to set off for the drive across London at 5 a.m., but for some reason Penny hadn't made it home. She'd said she wouldn't be out on a long one and that I should expect to see her at ten or eleven o'clock at the latest, and I was starting to feel concern.

The day before had started like a normal Saturday. The two of us had got up in our leisurely fashion after being out for a few drinks on Friday night, and she had a couple of engagements booked for the day that she was looking forward to: one of the girls at work who, with Penny, was part of a notorious drinking gang was having a birthday bash that evening at a club just south of Oxford Street. She'd also been invited to an afternoon gathering for another birthday celebration for a colleague's one-year-old. It certainly wasn't my idea of fun to spend the afternoon at such a premature party, but I'd become newly aware that being in a relationship and seen by others as a couple meant finding yourself implicated in all manner of obligations that otherwise you would have remained blissfully unaware of. I had come to realize that my accompanying her was an ambiguous part of our new social contract. I understood that she'd like to have me along, and it was also the case that she needed a lift out to the middle of nowhere. Anyway, I was pretty happy being with Penny wherever we were. We'd set off around lunchtime.

In the event, I had absolutely no idea what I was letting myself in for: it was like visiting another planet. For one thing, it was so noisy. Some of the babies were lying quietly on mats on the floor, but others were screaming, and there was a constant conveyor belt of them being picked up and carried out and then, to my dismay, being brought back in again. Older children – babies too, I think, but bigger and able to run around and grab things – were tearing about the place and completely ignoring the futile warnings that their parents half-heartedly repeated seemingly without expectation of having any influence on their charges. Apart from being a child myself, I had no experience of being around them. I didn't relate to them – nor, it seemed, to these adults whom they had taken over. The afternoon very quickly became painful. Though I had always wanted children, I had assumed – rather hopefully, I now realise, that when my time came I'd have grown to be a different person, one that was more patient and naturally better equipped. As the person who I actually was at the time, I could conceive of no connection with these little aliens that raged all around me.

The whole environment struck me as overwhelmingly freakish. I was used to seeing these women at work without their babies. As to be expected, seeing them here in this different context was slightly strange, but what really unnerved me were the men. It almost felt like I'd wandered across to a parallel universe where the guys all had weak smiles on their faces and, never mind that it was July, all wore jumpers over their rounded bellies and softly submissive frames. Whereas the women at least seemed engaged with the other mothers as they tended to and talked about their tiny playthings – Penny herself having no problem holding and cooing over any number of them – the men just seemed apologetically to be waiting on the orders of their partners as if they'd been emasculated. I had a nagging fear it might be contagious. Trying and failing to find anyone of them with whom I could maintain an interesting conversation, I decided to focus on keeping myself moving, heading off in fifteen-minute circles as I made my way around the table nibbling from the little pots of Hula Hoops. Trying in vain to find something of interest that could alleviate my boredom, I found myself again and again inspecting the same porcelain figurines on the cabinets and scrutinizing the lavish silver picture frames with their terrible, smiling faces, all the time trying to deflect the dismal message that life clearly wanted to send me.

I had been promised that we'd only be there for a couple of hours, and the plan had been that after returning home for a bit of down time, we'd hit the West End and have a few drinks with the girls before making our excuses for a reasonably early night. By the time I'd eventually managed to extricate us from this crèche of mayhem, however, after what seemed the most excruciatingly shocking afternoon of my life, I was utterly exhausted. Dropping Penny in the West End on the way home, I took myself straight back to the flat to rest and repair ahead of the morning's drive to Gatwick. Surfacing from another chunk of fragmented sleep, the kind that is default when you've an alarm that you really don't want to miss, I turned again to check the time and realized with a feeling that unsettled me that Penny was still nowhere to be seen. She always had known how to party, and probably I shouldn't have been especially concerned; but with a flight to catch and a holiday riding on it, I couldn't help feeling vexed. It was very late, after all, and increasingly there wasn't a lot of room for error. Drifting off again, I absently hoped it would be Penny that next woke me, clumsily trying to undress after slinking in through the bedroom door.

Just a few weeks earlier, we'd had a party for her thirtieth birthday at the Irish centre where her uncle did stints behind the bar. It had been a great night with a full set of her friends and family, a group I'd started spending a little more time with, and because earlier in the day England had beaten Spain in a quarter-final of Euro 96 thanks to a disallowed Spanish goal, the spectacle capped by Stuart Pearce's penalty redemption, everywhere the mood was celebratory. Not having tickets to the game, I'd intended to watch it on the television, but with Penny's cousin going to see it at Wembley, we'd offered to help out and were minding her eight-year-old daughter. I'd seen a park just a couple of streets away from where we lived, so a while before the game was due to begin, I took the little girl over there to give Penny a bit of space. I'd got myself psyched up for it and was feeling pleased that I could help in this way, giving her a chance to get herself ready for the big night ahead. When it came to it, actually setting off in the unfamiliar role of trusted adult, I felt self-consciously as if the two of us were complicit in an outrageous ruse – as if people who saw us on the streets together would not be able to believe I'd really been left minding a child.

The little person I now found myself allied with was, to my mind, just like an adult but smaller, and not knowing any better way to communicate with a child, I thought that I should just set my mind in the present and try to see the things around me the way they would appear to her, engaging with the child on that level. It seemed to work. We ended up talking a lot, and I found that the things she said made very real sense to me. The park was warm and sunny, and being there both physically and mentally, not in the process of rushing on somewhere else for a change, meant there was so much to see and to talk about that, enjoying myself much more than I expected, I kind of got lost in this other game and the time just flew by. The match was already deep into the second half when the two of us eventually made it back to the flat.

That evening, it seemed to me that everyone who was anyone had crowded in for the St Gabriel's celebration, the contingent who'd been at the game telling their match-day tales and Penny surrounded by all of her own while I chatted contentedly, drinking plenty of booze, with anyone that would have me. There were to be many nights like this, nights when we were immersed in her big friendly group where everyone knew everyone, but I've a special memory that I keep from this particular evening: a moment when I was watching her unaware, engrossed and bubbly with her friends all around her, and she turned and, catching my eye, raised her arm above her head to send me a jigging wave as her face flashed the happiest smile just in the way that Lisa Kudrow immortalised in the opening credits of *Friends.*

The night before her party, she'd not been half so animated. I'd got us what I hoped she'd think a real treat: front-row seats for *A Midsummer Night's Dream* at the Regent's Park Open Air Theatre, but I literally had to drag her from the bar where she'd been drinking all day just to get her in the taxi. She'd been there since lunchtime, and meeting her at five o'clock for a couple after work was already pressing us for the seven o'clock show. At first she thought I was kidding when I told her about my nice surprise – that she'd have to finish her drink so we could leave – and in the state she was in, she couldn't get her head around the idea, seeming mildly disgusted at first that I would even suggest she stop drinking so early on her birthday, of all days, just to go and see a play. All the way up Farringdon road and then on past Euston, she kept going on about my having gone down in her estimations and not knowing her at all. When we did arrive and had been shown to our seats, she promptly fell asleep there, snoring loudly all the way through the first half to repay me for my obvious lack of cultural sensitivity.

The actors upon the stage were distracted by the noise she made, and from the corner of their eyes looked down on us, literally and metaphorically. All in all, it was pretty embarrassing, having to give her a little nudge from time to time when the rumbling got too much for the audience. She woke shivering at the intermission just as the night was cooling down, but I managed to purloin a blanket from the ice-cream vendor's freezer, and with that wrapped around her, she stayed wide awake from then until the end of the show. By the time it had finished, the day's warmth was well and truly a memory, and in the absence of available cabs, we almost froze there as we tried to hitch a lift from the park's cold centre. Eventually we were picked up by a gent who took pity on the pathetic pair we made, and we sat shivering together gratefully in the back of his car, thanking him all the way home as he ferried us back to our sanctuary from the cold British summer in Royal College Street.

With the tournament going on, June had always looked like it would be a busy month, and the week before her birthday I'd actually been at Wembley myself, Luca successfully having applied for a block of tickets at the beginning of the sale process. The two of us had gone up to see England play Scotland, and that's another game I'll never forget. It was the host's second match, the tournament once again having kicked off with a typically unrealistic build-up of our beloved team's expectations, which hit the bumpers somewhat on the first match day when a tough-fought draw was the result of our meeting with Sweden. I'd watched the match that day with Dad and my brother-in-law in a hotel bar while the ladies of the family were swimming and sunning themselves, Dad having taken us all away on a treat near Bournemouth. We all had neighbouring rooms, and still not having really got to know Penny by then, I remember their delightful incredulity that all they could hear from next door was her laughter; they couldn't believe anyone could be so happy and so easy-going all of the time. It made me happy and proud that they got to see her the way that I did.

Luca and I were having quite a time of it on the Wembley terrace with England leading, one-nil, thanks to a second-half goal for our super striker, Shearer, but the tide turned, and all of a sudden, everything was coming from the Tartan army. The boys standing next to me from north of the border with their chequered scarves waving were getting more and more excited about their chances, and then the referee awarded them a penalty and they became ecstatic, hugging and celebrating like they'd won the tournament, as you do. It wasn't ideal, but with Seaman in goal, I felt pretty confident.

"He saves these, you know," I said, turning to them with a smile just as the pre-kick hush fell, and sure enough, he did. But breaking our hug prematurely, Luca and I hardly had time to celebrate the keeper's excellence as we saw the bouncing ball reach Gascoigne, who then lifted it over Hendry and volleyed us two-nil up: game over. Before his back hit the hallowed turf to enact with his teammates the dentist-chair skit for which he's so famous, his very destruction represented in the midst of his triumph, the two Scots we'd watched the game with were leaving the stadium.

This stands out as a classic turnaround moment, and I was comparing it with events in my own life even as we made our way back to Kings Cross hanging from the straps on the carriage roof. How happy I was to speak of the place where life now found me! If there was just one thing that I'd done well, one time I'd been smart enough to know that it was all there – to recognize a true path I must take – it was that time a few months earlier when I had sat at the end of the bed. I am so fortunate that having what I had, I chose not to spurn it, not to run wildly away; and for that brief moment of clarity, that little hour of magic, I'll forever be grateful.

Smells Like Teen Spirit

From somewhere far beyond the limits of my sleeping mind, I could sense a growing clamour, a strange ringing that was seeping angrily through to my half-waking dream as slowly it dawned on me that the phone was ringing. More to quell the ugly banging than to answer the call, I reached for the handset, uttering a groan that was meant to be hello as I brought the receiver to the side of my head.

The clock's digital display read a stark one fifty-four, and the realization that Penny still wasn't home gave a sharp stab of panic in my stomach.

"Hello," laughed a bright voice back at me from the other end of the line, a young woman, perhaps, but not one I recognized. "Is that Mojo?"

"Eh ... Milo, yes," I replied, still none the wiser.

"We've got your girlfriend," the voice laughed again, and suddenly I was wide awake. "You need to come get her."

"What!"

"Don't worry, she's safe. I'm looking after her, but come and get her quick, yeah? She's outside the church at the bottom of Wardour Street. Do you know it?"

"I'm on my way, thanks," I said, already pulling my pants on and snatching up my socks and my jeans from beside the futon.

Still pulling on a T-shirt, I ran from the flat and jumped into the car, my mind a picture of clarity from the burst of adrenalin that it had just received – clarity that additional thought might only confuse. Knowing instinctively where to head, I locked on course, and off I sped. It didn't even occur to me to question how I could find myself in the midst of this real-life drama, a cameo that juxtaposed insanity with the calm order I yearned for like some David Lynch piece. With Penny, somehow it was par for the course.

I knew the area fairly well, but it struck me as suspiciously weird that I could picture the spot so readily with just those few words on the telephone, that straight away I'd known where to go without seeking clarification, but then as I got closer I felt some doubts creeping in. I just drove on, hoping that luck would be with me and that I'd find her, worrying that if she wasn't there then we'd miss the holiday for sure. There was no traffic to speak of, and gunning the car down Hampstead Road, I blazed through the lights and threw it round the corners, finding myself driving along Oxford Street in about five minutes and looking for a left turn. When I reached Wardour Street, there was a huge No Entry sign at the top – a cursed one-way street. All I could think of was getting to the bottom as quickly as possible, down where I was sure I'd find the church and the railings, and it just didn't occur to me to drive on and around. Right there at the roadside, I abandoned the car, jumping out and bounding down towards Shaftsbury Avenue with the crowded road full of people seemingly intent on getting in my way.

Still running and dodging, I crossed over the junction at Old Compton Street, and that's when I saw her, unmistakable, leaning with her shoulders against the railings at a cartoon-like sixty degrees. I could see she was wobbling slightly and looking about as unconscious as any person still standing possibly can. There were two policemen in front of her, one of whom was peering into the void of her face. It was such a relief to see her, but I realized I didn't know the protocol for claiming someone in this predicament.

"She's mine," I blurted out, slowing down and starting to catch my breath as I approached them, affecting as polite and apologetic a demeanour as I was able. The policemen turned their faces towards me and seemed to regard this new development with interest. "I just got a call to come and get her," I explained. "It's OK. I'll take her home. I've got her now. The car is just up the road." They looked at me, saying nothing as I put my hands under her shoulders. Recognizing me in her stupor, she smiled and started babbling about how Naomi Campbell had befriended her and set her out there. I looked to the policemen, holding her up as I waited tacitly for permission to depart, and the one nearest me smiled by way of goodbye.

"They all look like Naomi Campbell when you've had that kind of skin full," remarked the other one, and they watched after us as manfully I struggled away up the street with my giggling load.

At each turn, the short ride home was punctuated by Penny's heaving mumbles, slurred protestations that sounded something like "I'm sick" as, belted in, she lolled around the seat next to me while I concentrated on getting us home as quickly as I could. I'd fought back panic as we struggled together back up the road because, having found her, it occurred to me that I might have lost the car, just leaving it on the roadside the way I had. But it was there, and once Penny was safely inside, I could relax a little: just enough to feel a shard of anger that my plans for a nice restful evening had been brought to nought. How I wanted to sleep! As I parked the car outside the flat, there wasn't a peep from her. I hauled her up from the seat and out of the car, but she was out on her feet, so I had to carry her up the steps and into the flat and through to the bedroom, shaking my head in disbelief as I undressed her, thinking about my plans and how they'd been wrecked. It was getting on for 3 a.m., and

I could feel the clock exuding an air of sardonic contempt. And could I get to sleep? Of course not; I lay there instead thinking about how few minutes there were before I'd have to get up as Penny lay dead to the world beside me. Finally, as I continued to stare up at the ceiling, I started to relax, started to feel the relief of actually having her here at last with everything in place. I closed my eyes for an instant, and the alarm clock immediately woke me: it was time for the airport.

Luckily, our cases were already packed, and after I'd washed, I took these to the car. I'd let Penny lie for as long as I could, but when I tried to wake her, she didn't have a scooby and was still totally stocious. Feeling a little irritated, I got her dressed and back out to the car where, once in the seat, she slid easily back into a deep sleep, and off we set again, driving down through the grey early morning, down to the airport through South London's blissfully empty streets. Even with the traffic as good as it was, it felt like a long journey, but at last I got there, parking in the huge park-and-ride lot and undoing my seat belt before sitting back and breathing out a sigh. 'Almost there,' I told myself. I turned to look at Penny and gave her a little shake. Then I gave her another one. The next one I gave her was more vigorous, and she let out a long, mournful groan. Still she had no idea where she was or, I suspect, even who she was, and the fun bit was all gone now, the intoxication leaving behind it the crushing wreckage that only a long, long sleep can really allay. But there was no time to lose, so as gently as I could, determinedly I wrenched her from the car, ignoring her pathetic pleadings - 'leave me, leave me' - as she begged to be allowed to stay exactly where she was. *Is that something people do?* I was thinking to myself, *Book flights and two-week holidays and then, through the advent of an untimely hangover, miss out on it all?* I supposed there were other days and other flights, other transfers, but surely it wasn't meant to be like this.

I found out later that after I'd dropped her at the club, Penny had met up with her mates and had a couple of drinks and then a few drinks more. She had had a good night and then, seeing that it was time to leave, had come out on to the street to find her way home. Either she'd had a bit more than she realized or possibly her drink had been adulterated, but whatever the cause, the fresh air had made her head start to spin, and feeling sick just minutes after getting into a minicab, she'd asked the driver to pull over. Her memory of the time is vague, but she remembers being flung out of the cab somewhere in Soho and having her money taken, remembers being left by the roadside, where she was found and rescued by a girl who, as she peered up giddily, "might have been Naomi Campbell". I doubt that it was, but she remembers all manner of faces then that took an interest in her once inside some safe house – faces that pushed themselves into hers to offer all manner of remedies, all manner of things; and she remembers then a supreme effort to disseminate her number, giving it once, twice, and then once more, by which effort the sisters were able to call me.

After a long sleep on the plane as well as a much shorter one with her head bumping off my shoulder as the coach made its winding way along the ill-repaired mountain roads to the place we were staying, she finally came to. Then, with our fellow travellers, we sat waiting patiently in the hotel reception for the sanctuary of our room – for a wash and a bed. Her cheeks were marked by frozen rivers of last night's mascara, smudged and ghastly and all heroin chic. I'm sure I also looked shattered with my guitar slung over my back, completing our image – one that set us apart as that couple: the one that normal folk avoid and guard from the eyes of their gawping children, lest the sight should unlock in their impressionable minds a whole world full of nightmares.

So there we sat on the marble ledge together with our bags at our feet, exhausted and alone on one side of the air-conditioned lobby while the rest of our newly arrived party hung back, almost cowering, as far away from us as possible by the plants on the other side. She saw the shock of herself in the mirror when finally we'd made it to our room, and I realize looking back that this moment was her life's watershed. Initially she upbraided me for letting her look such a state, but quietly over the next few hours and days she took on board that changes were needed, and at last we'd arrived at the same place together. The path was set then for an almost alcohol-free holiday and a long-overdue reality check – the beginning of a very different phase in our lives. Life knew very well that the pair of us needed to grow up, and it was just in time too, for there was an unseen hand somewhere shifting the lever, shifting our destiny to a much higher gear.

Something in the Way She Moves

The warm days of our holiday were spent languidly under clear skies and an unfailing sun. The resort where we stayed was high up on a mountainside which overlooked the beautiful blue lagoon, and the location gave us everything we had hoped for, not least the air conditioning which, in early July, was a lifesaver. The two of us virtually collapsed down at the lagoon one afternoon from the heat's intensity, probably the hottest time I can ever recall. Up in the mountains, we swam and read and passed our time just being together, the entire fortnight as peaceful and reflective as it should have been. We didn't plan that suddenly we wouldn't be drinking, but without actually saying anything, it was understood. Though such a regime would have been a daunting prospect, we found that no longer seeking to run from our shadows, it came surprisingly easy. This alternative way of living set the scene for a two-week awakening, a time spent actually getting to know each other while growing in confidence for the life we might share.

We added some variety to our days by going on a few trips, taking a riverboat ride to see a beach where some turtles were living and then taking messy pictures at the springs on the way back when we'd covered each other in mud. On the night of my thirty-first birthday, we went to an evening of traditional dancing, and there I bumped into my old school prefect some seventeen years after last I'd seen him. He was married with a kid now and no longer the older teenager I remembered looking up to in awe, and I took this coincidence as a sign that life was tying up loose ends for me and preparing the landscape for events yet to come. When I think about how things were to move along after this, I wonder at how prophetic it was.

Whether positively or otherwise, there's always the opportunity to learn from the people around us by tapping into their knowledge and experience, and accordingly there were two couples that we spent some time with on this holiday that, for their very different illustrations, remain in my mind. After crashing out in the welcome comfort of our room on first arrival, we emerged bleary and ginger later that afternoon and gravitated to the pool, where we lay ourselves down again, by and by striking up a conversation with a man there who was quite a few years older than we were. He was joined after a while by a girl who looked a few years our junior, and with the age difference being so pronounced, we at first assumed she must be his daughter. In fact, she turned out to be a relatively new girlfriend, the two of them having decided on a last-minute whim to come away here together. Mentioning the guitar he'd seen me carrying, he told us that he was a bit of a musician, and when I let him in on the troubles I was having with my long-suffered instrument, he kindly agreed to tune it for me, offering advice about what I should do to finally get to grips with it. After spending an hour or so chatting about his musical interests, we all agreed to go out for dinner.

Arriving via the *dolmus* in the local town, he said that he wanted to go for a Chinese. I wouldn't have chosen this for our first night in Turkey, as it struck me as classic Brits abroad behaviour, but mindful that I wanted to be more of an easy-going soul than that old Milo, I shrugged off my natural objections and went along with it. There we sat at the open-air terrace behind the Chinese restaurant. Either because we were that much younger or because he was just made that way, he took charge of the conversation, and we found ourselves listening to him politely as he told us about his family, his ex-wife, and his lovely teenage daughter, and especially how happy he was that she got on so well with this new partner, who was sitting there quietly beside him. He told us about his business and his sporting achievements, and the conversation went on in this non-contentious manner until he excused himself to go to the toilet. Within seconds of his getting up from his chair – he was still so close to us that I could hardly believe he was out of earshot – his bleached concubine, who was unable to hold her tongue any longer, didn't wait to disabuse us.

"His daughter's a bitch!" she shouted, the suddenness and violence of her assertion sending upon us a wall of shock, and we could only sit there in embarrassed silence as she went on with her own version of the stories he'd recounted until he was making his way back over to the table.

I think the effect of this outburst was all the greater for me because it came so unexpectedly and so contrarily to the impression I'd formed. Here was this mature guy who nevertheless clearly kept himself in shape and who ran his own company, looking to my untrained eye with his trophy girlfriend as if he had everything sorted, yet the minute his back was turned, she was sniping at him and behaving like the daughter she looked, and a petulant one at that! As if we'd been made complicit in a betrayal, the two of us couldn't help feeling guilty when he rejoined us, and our little foursome never reclaimed its earlier innocence. I suppose he had my natural sympathy, but unfortunately, the revelation made him a somewhat pathetic character: I'd had my eyes wiped. We didn't want to do dinner with them again and so made our excuses for a few nights, and in the end, he got the message. I did see him around the pool on a few afternoons and we still chatted a bit, but it wasn't the same. She was with him less and less too, and I got the impression that they weren't having much of a holiday. I'm sure it wasn't one likely to be repeated.

This experience served as a rebuke and admonition for the simplistic way that I tended to judge the things I saw around me, but I gleaned a lot more from the other couple that we met. Roughly the same age as each other, they were quite a lot older than us, holidaying here without their grown-up children and so back to being the couple they'd originally been, many years earlier. Chatting in the breakfast room one morning, we mentioned where we worked, and she told us that she was the proprietor of a fairly well known tea room not far from our office, one that *Time Out* always recommended in glowing reports. We often found ourselves chatting with them around the pool on those sunny afternoons, enjoying the gentle breeze that blew off the hillside and skirted the gardens. I imagined they saw in the two of us a dimly lit reminder of their own story, and I think this made them feel kindly and protective towards us.

They talked about their own lives from way back when – how he'd been a swimmer who, as a young husband, used to drive off as far as his arms would carry him out into the sea before, almost at the point of exhaustion, he'd turn around and swim back in. Wistfully, he told me one afternoon how once they'd had their first child, he no longer felt at ease with such recklessness – how this new weight of responsibility had made him feel that he should desist from his perpetual man-versus-the-sea adventure. But I remember his wife then chipping in, overhearing our conversation even while she was simultaneously engaged on a different subject with Penny.

"Wasn't that the time you started getting those muscle cramps?" she asked him innocuously. It might have been a rhetorical question, eliciting a humph as his balloon deflated and yet their exchange seemed a very different example of the kind of contest that a partnership might foster, a more acceptable kind of natural banter waged between two people that care about each other and who have earned the right to a niggle.

The thing that really gave me food for thought, though, in just the same way that I'd realized all those years earlier that my parents were more than just parents, that they were people in their own right exactly like me, was the understanding that this old and worn couple had also at one time been exactly like us. Perhaps even now they were not so different. It still seemed hard to imagine that Penny and I might grow to be like these older couples around us, but it was my first glimpse of that furthest side of parenthood – the part where you can enjoy life anew once the children are older. I had never before been able to see beyond the shocking change that becoming a parent would entail. As I grasped this point, it suddenly became clear to me where the two of us were and where we were heading. For the first time since we'd got back together at that Sunday christening, I realized I had to start thinking about the future, because it wasn't far away. The way things were between us, I knew that sooner or later, planned or not, she'd likely be pregnant, and this would mean that the basis of our lives would shift irrevocably. I wasn't going to be caught out again by life's twisting and turning; I wanted to be ready for it, so now was the time to find a quiet place for myself, to search my own mind for my own conversation.

Lying there on the sun bed and looking up at the clear blue sky, listening to the sound of the waterfall as it beat down on a bed of pebbles and fed the source of the pool beside me, I posed the fateful questions. Was this it? Had I got to the place I was meant to be going? Was I going to be truly happy when Penny – inevitably, I thought – fell pregnant? Pondering quietly, I thought long and hard and tried my best to make it a real inquisition, but if I knew anything, I knew that we belonged together and that she was everything

I could dream of. Sure, I wasn't really ready and probably never would be, but with her by my side, I felt I could do it. The bottom line was that I was actually in love, and at long last, I knew it.

Don't Be Afraid of the Dark

Blink and you miss it. Lying lazy in bed one Saturday morning, tired from the week and from the night before, I was looking up at the sharp rays of sunshine that broke in through the gaps at the top of the curtains, those lengthy, shard-like patterns that stretched into our room from behind my head. I couldn't have felt any more content than I did just lying there, relaxed and quiet, not having to get up. The birds in the trees out front were twittering, making that sound which can speak to the soul but which so often goes unnoticed, filtered by the bustle of our regular consciousness. Slowly, a car made its way along the road, and its metallic thumping blocked out for a while nature's sweet song, until dipping away in the distance, it left the morning's sound palette once again clear and uncluttered for the birds to reassert themselves with their bright, chirping chorus of simplicity. Silent and still as she was beside me, I'd assumed that Penny was sleeping, so it surprised me when I turned my head to look at her and found that her eyes were already open – that she too had been looking up at the ceiling. Feeling my movement, she turned her gaze to mine.

"Allo," I said.

"Hello," she answered thoughtfully. She sounded unusually pensive, and I knew instinctively that something was wrong. Penny didn't do much silent, unless she was asleep or working on something that required concentration. I could always tell if she'd woken up, because invariably she would be talking to me. I hadn't realized how true it was until this very moment, but it was a fact, and it was unnerving to think that she'd been lying there awake but saying nothing.

"What's up?" I asked.

She started talking to me about the previous evening. I knew she had gone after work to a benefit, a fundraiser for the son of one of the long-timers in her department, who suffered from a wasting disease. The boy worked in our post room, but as his condition had deteriorated, it had become increasing difficult for him to carry on normally; it was terribly sad. She hadn't been going out nearly as much lately and had arranged to go with the girls who were her erstwhile drinking buddies, planning on a big one, but she told me that when, in her normal way, she had started on the vodkas, for some reason she just couldn't get them down. Ever resourceful, she had switched to wine, but still she had found that she just couldn't get a taste for it. While it made her perplexed, the girls had taken it as a lack of will and had been short with her, so she'd left there early and headed for home. I'd turned up at the benefit later, and it had struck me as very odd that I hadn't found her still there. Her mates had told me that she'd left to go home, but they hadn't been in a condition to elaborate, and anyway, when I had got back to the new flat we were renting, I had found her fast asleep.

"I think I'm pregnant," she now quietly announced in the flattest tone, looking back up at the ceiling and not at me. For a few moments, she remained in that position, and then without further ado she rose from the bed and left the room on her way to the toilet.

Our holiday was history. Almost three months had elapsed since we'd returned from Turkey, but we had been away just a few weeks earlier – a weekend trip to Berlin which I'd arranged in secret partly to make up for the fact that I'd been studying for a regulatory exam and she'd been effectively banished from the lounge for the duration. I had stealthily packed her a bag with some clothes and cosmetics, but I'd forgotten about her pills, and becoming aware of my mistake as I was chasing her around the bed on our arrival at the hotel, in half-jest she warned me, but to both of us it really had seemed like a joke. I thought it must be virtually impossible that she'd get pregnant just for missing a couple of her little pills, so I carried on chasing her. Between the two of us, we had dared life to do its worst.

That night, after an exhaustive and exhausting walking tour around the city led by a stick-thin English expatriate who had the small group of slightly overweight American tourists crying in their sneakers, we'd taken a dip in the hotel pool. That had been the final straw, because afterwards we both felt so knackered that we decided to get food sent up and spend the night in even though we were flying home the next afternoon. We were back now to drinking moderate amounts of alcohol. Even if it wasn't a patch on what we used to put away, Penny could still hold her own, but when we cracked open the duty-free bottle of champagne that we'd bought at the airport, she didn't even manage to finish her glass. Having to finish off the whole bottle, I'd ended up pretty drunk, but I wasn't complaining. Before we left the city the next day, I remember Penny stumbling as we were walking down some steps to the river, and she tore her tights on a stone. Without any reason for thinking so, I remember that her losing her balance struck us somehow as odd at the time.

So there I lay, unmoving on my back just as I had been when Penny left the room, thinking to myself what a surreal morning this was turning out to be. After a little time, she re-entered with a white predictor stick held in her fingers, a look on her face of silent concern.

"We have to wait for a few minutes," she said as she got back into the bed beside me, and I don't think another word passed between us as she took occasional glances at the tiny indicator window and gave it the odd shake. I just continued to lie there looking up at the ceiling, waiting out the silence without any feeling of panic and wondering whether I really was as calm as I seemed to be.

"It's positive," she said finally before turning to me and looking anxious.

"It's good," I said, nodding.

"Is it? Are you sure?"

"Yup. I've thought about this, and I knew it would happen. Great! We'll have a baby. Give us a cuddle." So saying, I wrapped my arms around her naked body.

She tells me that she spent almost the entire nine months waiting for me to awake from my trance, to repudiate at last my calm acceptance and make for the hills, but that never happened. Her fears were unfounded.

Dragonfly Summer

This is the trip – the best part - I really like, because aside from those startling bursts of excitement and my sense of fulfilling a duty just by being here and performing this habit that serves as a link in the long chain of tradition, what I really crave in attendance is that slow, sweet pleasure of watching victory unfurl: a match incomplete yet all but won playing out before me. What could be more relaxing or more totally satisfying than a ball in the back of the net? It's like money in the bank, and the confidence it affords – the sense of sunny superiority that it gives us – displaces effortlessly the tense anxieties that might otherwise be rippling through our terraces, the wolf that stalks when times are tough. To a man, we stand happily buoyant, watching over this longed-for finale, enjoying at the same time the flat resignation of the fans huddled in the opposite corner. We are secure enough as impending conquerors to give them the nod that might be their due, the polite round of applause for our plucky losers as they attempt to lift a last cheery tune, changed in our minds for accepting their fate from bitter foe to a body deserving of a measure of our commiseration and possibly respect.

My memories here form a landscape pocked by such magical moments, such spires and farms as when Denis, breaking his duck, puffed out his gaunt, maestro cheeks as he took to the air with relief right before us or when, with finest aplomb, he lifted the ball over the two-tone defence for Freddie's timed burst, poking it home to breach staunch resilience. Turning to my left, I still see Henry with his back to the goal, flicking the ball up for a shot on the turn as it flies right over the crossbar, over that is until the very last moment, when unbelievably it dips down into the net – a rippling instant, that slightest of pauses before ecstasy reigns. This one today is another game that means so much, another match that tested our nerves, but they're all forgotten now, for the season is won and our glory is wrought. It's a fairy tale for the scrapbooks, crowned by Adams striding regally through a flat back four, their arms up against him unheeded. His chest meets the rising ball and places it, obedient, on the prize grass before him, and then he lashes a screamer past the keeper stuck still. In the few disbelieving paces that follow, our captain comes to rest with a smile on his face and looks all around him, raising his arms in limp satisfaction as the terrace disciples unleash all their joy.

What a privilege it is to be here today, to witness in the flesh this rarest of spectacles which the majority of supporters can only ever dream of. I was watching the game on television the last time we won the league. It was May eighty-nine, and I was sitting at home in the lounge with my dad. No one gave us a chance that night, and sure enough, in those agonizing final moments, our chances were ticking away. A great opportunity had just gone begging, and it looked like our last – but wait, Thomas was bursting through on Grobellar's goal, and we held our breath as the ball found the net and we were two-nil up at fortress Anfield: the margin to win. The pitch was a carnival of joy-filled cartwheels when, in speechless incredulity, I turned to my dad. He was still there sitting but high off his chair, arms raised and clenched fists almost touching the ceiling. At that very moment, my mum stepped in, carrying a tray and a look of surprise. I carry still that picture of the two of them frozen in time.

The players give their customary show of appreciation with a lap of the ground as they pass between them the coveted trophy. Each of them glows as they take turns holding it aloft as if it were the hero. This clapping and picture taking seems perfection itself as I take in the air – huge, gulping drags of this glorious satisfaction, this rarest of days that was so long in coming. The fans begin to make their way, and with handshakes and mutual congratulations, the afternoon attendance slowly dwindles, the rows by degrees emptying to reveal the white letters on the seats opposite as the crowd becomes sparse. Enjoying the warmth of the Highbury sun, the remnants of the fire that has blazed here this afternoon, the two of us kick back in our seats as we continue to savour the moment until I feel it's time for me to speak.

"Well?" I say at last, breaking a silence that felt almost holy. "Are we going to get a move on?" Though we'll be back in our colours for the FA Cup final the following weekend, we've arranged to meet some of the others for an end-of-season bash at the pub by the railway land, and I fancy a drink. Tommy turns to me with a look of supreme happiness on his face.

"You go on ahead, bruv" he says. "I'm older than you; I reckon I'm right where I need to be just now. Might never see the like of this again, so I'd better take in as much of it as I can." For a few seconds, he continues to look into my face, and then a slow, wry smile appears. "Anyway, I think you know where you're going" he adds. "You'll not be getting quite so lost without me now."

With a tired, happy smile – one full of long-spent emotion – I assent. "Right you are then," I say, getting myself up and making my way past him to climb the empty staircase. "I'll see you up there."

Trying to pass through the opened exit gates, the going is unusually slow. Because I thought that everyone ahead of me was long gone, I'm surprised to find this obstruction of people still there milling. Looking out between the heads, I can see that a crowd has reformed on the other side of the doors, a group of supporters who are looking back up at the stadium windows, waving and shouting. When eventually I manage to burrow to the point where I too can turn around, I see the attraction: a shirtless Ian Wright, almost hanging from the changing room windows, is waving the trophy above our heads with a big, toothy smile that says it all, milking the moment for himself and for the players and for all of us fans; and together, just as we belong, we celebrate in the shadow of the old listed building. For as long as this special moment lasts, we are all of us transfixed – a little squeezed, perhaps, but nothing out of the ordinary and far too captivated to have any concerns as we all think with one mind, beat with one heart, happy to be held by the gentle embrace of the crowd's easy pressure.

Some of the other lads above us take their turn, but eventually we see them drawn back inside, and the offending window is pulled closed by what looks like a commissionaire, if the singularly long shadow behind the frosting is anything to go by. The spontaneous show is over, but it's still hard to leave, still nigh on impossible to lower our sights from those opaque windows while the shadows of our heroes shimmer there on the other side, though our necks now ache and our faces feel distended by our ecstatic smiles. I loiter for a while, breathing this finest ninety-eight vintage until eventually I'm almost alone and have shared the final looks of happy disbelief with those few of us remaining.

Reluctant to draw myself away, I dawdle along in a bath of late-day sunshine, thinking about all that has passed as I slowly proceed to where my crowd is gathering. There's hardly anyone about now on the pavements or in Blackstock Road's shops; even the post-match traffic jam has dispersed, the street long cleared of cars as the area slides lazily into its summer mode of relaxation, a three-month holiday of careless midweek calm. Reaching the crossing at the top where the one-way system comes in from Finsbury Park, I feel a gentle vibration against my thigh and instantly experience a spark of excited curiosity, the delight of being wanted. Lifting the phone from my pocket, I see Luca's smiling face upon the screen.

"Congratulations, mate. I saw it – incredible. You guys really deserve it." He speaks earnestly with that definitive twang in his voice. What a lovely call this is!

"Thank you. Yeah, I'm just floating. Thought we'd get there, but now we have, I can't quite take it all in."

"What you up to?" he asks, and I tell him I'm on my way to the post-match party. He tells me to have a couple for him. "Anyway, just wanted to call, say congrats," he finishes.

"Cheers, mate. I'll see you soon," and the line goes dead.

Just Now

Outside the pub's doorway, I stop for a moment, hearing out of nowhere the birdsong and noticing the detail of the stained-glass windows which decorate the sides of the building with their storied depictions: giants and dragons, ogres, a maiden with a pointy hat. The beautiful collage of primary colours is no less delightful for being obvious, and it obscures the melange I will find inside. There was a time when I could hardly have set foot over the threshold of the Head and Heart and certainly wouldn't have done so alone. Back then, this kind of place was so foreign to me that I wouldn't have known how to breathe its air or to answer the gush of self-doubt and questions that such an environment inevitably would have thrown up. The path of my youth travelled a parallel track which didn't account for this particular education – the education of the crowd. The fact that I can stand here now is a testament to the lessons a different type of life has taught me, the protocols I've more lately achieved. Once inside the pub, I'll make certain to coarsen my accent just a little, to be a bit brash, fashioning myself to an easier humour so I can be better company. The patrons inside will not smell the fear off this new, improved Milo, who knows the binding power of a drink and how being like others does much to assure. It may be a gift to know one's weaknesses, to be able to pick over them and find out what they can tell us about ourselves, but it's a more precious one not to have to dwell with them, to be able to shake them from one's thoughts in order to join the common flow, allowing it to guide us to that place we're all so desperate to find.

My hand grasps one of the big brass handles. It's cold in my grip, and as I lean back my weight a little, a gap cracks open. As I pull the heavy doors further, the picture inside widens, and I see across to the far side of the salon, where some acquaintances I recognize are lined along the bar with their drinks in their hands. They've all got their faces on, various groups of friends who have long known one other – who grew up as kids in the same place in the same way. They'll bear me around them in the bar with easy smiles and words bought cheap for the occasion, even if it's a different story outside in their lives. It helps that I understand better now why I'll never be one of them and know too how differently we are all made – how surprisingly at odds they are even with each other. With that insight, I am far more able to accept the truth without feeling I'm to blame.

As I step inside, the whole salon's before me. In the corner to the right of the long bar stand others enjoying themselves, delirious in their clusters as they should be on a night like this. There's no sign of Banksy – he may have come and gone already – but Wolfie, Raj, and the brothers are still very much up and running, laughing and smiling. Polo's there too, obviously in the middle of one of his tales, because his hands are flying and his audience is wrapped around him entranced. Without any indication that I've caught his eye, he suddenly stops and turns his head theatrically to give me one of his loaded glances. I give him back a nod, and he turns to his captives and resumes the narrative. Near the entrance to the private bar on the other side of the room, I see PJ standing with the other guys who originally formed our block when first we took up position down by the Clock End. He's even got his little brother with him tonight; he's not been around for ages, and he's not so little now. It takes me back just to see him.

From my position just inside the door, I stand and watch them all for a while. There's certainly a kind of comfort in having arrived at this place, a feeling of security and of being wanted that comes from having people I know around me. I know that I could go over to one or the other for a cursory welcome and at least hover there on the edge with a drink and a smile, taking a little part in their fun; and yet for the moment I hesitate, nagged by a sense that somehow tonight it wouldn't be quite the thing. Instead, I decide to maintain the little bit of separation I have, to allow myself for a few more seconds or minutes, maybe, the pleasure of nurturing alone this night's special feeling. I always feel a strange power in standing on my own. I relish the brazenness of this social nudity, which in its way reassures me and empowers me, the needing no one but myself which means I can be in the moment with my own thoughts, not having to play another or make the air uncomfortable for failing to do so – a thing which would inevitably find me wanting away as soon as I got in. Despite my solitary conviction, however, as I observe those around me, I still sense the shadow of jealously as it flits across my consciousness. Wearing my burden, I can't help but envy what always appears to be the ease of those others, their simple comfort which looks to work so smoothly with the people around them and even with the way they live with themselves.

I sometimes forget that looks can be deceptive and that all of us must translate what we perceive through our own prejudices. For some, the inner self is the ultimate stranger, a precious treasure which, for many reasons, they'll never know. Truth, therefore, is difficult to gauge, but the one thing I'm quite certain of is that most of these people are fundamentally different from me. For them, there is no dogged commitment to pick at self-doubt, to embrace rather than to avoid their troubles, and to seek a perverse refuge in a confounded life. The luckiest are blessed with an easy nature, an inner peace that's at rest – perhaps their journey's gone further and deeper than mine. Others are fortunate to enjoy the kind of peace that only lack of intellect can provide. For better or for worse, neither one of these is for me. Then, as if on cue, I become aware that I've switched inside again, overcome without realizing it by the feeling that groans in my heart – that hollow, yearning moan which sucks my thoughts to the vacuum within.

The doors open sharply behind me, and startled, I jump around, finding myself suddenly face to face again – or at least face to chest – with Tommy.

"What are you doing just standing there?" he laughs. "Haven't you even got yourself a drink yet, you dingbat?"

"I just got here," I lie. "What took you so long, anyway?"

"I've got something for you. Penny asked me to give it you when we got to the pub." So saying, he produces a manila envelope which he puts in my hands. Holding it, I stand there confused, not knowing what to do next. "Open it then," he says. I slide the card from its sheath and, opening the cover, reveal a colour photo inside.

"What's this?" I say, seeing my little girl's bonny face made round by her big baby cheeks. Grimly she stares out from between the FA Cup and the Premiership trophy, sitting with them on a trellis table as she holds the red-and-white sash in the little fist of her left hand.

"Wow, that's amazing! How did she get this?"

"She had to queue up for hours, but she knew you'd like it. Must really love you, eh? You've got a good one there." The two of us stand lost in the picture and the thought that's gone into it.

"Right, give it here," he says after a moment, taking the picture and the envelope and putting them carefully away. "I'll keep this safe. You follow me." So saying, he strides off towards the private bar, and following behind him, PJ and I exchange glances as I pass through the door.

"I'll see you in there later," he says, and the thought makes me smile.

The atmosphere is different in this smaller salon. It's more of a dining area and is much less dominated by the bar – only a small part of the long main one rolls in by the doorway, just poking through so that drinks can be served. In their respective corners, the close-knit groups sit around each separate table. The Finsbury lads are variously sitting and standing as they hold their drinks or have them placed before them on the polished table surface, engaging all together in shared conversation.

"You hom!" exclaims the Big Man as he sees me enter, never missing a trick and ever ready with a heartfelt welcome.

"You wish," I jeer back at him, a knee-jerk reply as I mosey on over.

"Where's your drink?" says Pele almost suspiciously, simultaneously offering me whatever I'm having, but declining gratefully, I tell him that Tommy is getting me one. By the manner of his acceptance, it's clear that his offer's sincere, as is everything about him. There's no confusion with these guys, friends that they are. The warmth that we share is a blessing to us all.

At the tables lined up on the far side of the room sits Gloria like a caricature of me but with much longer hair; and there too are her kids; and my mum with my uncle and aunt; and my dad's cousin, who's flanked by his grown-up boys, all of them tucking into a meal. On the table before them among the plates of rice and the bowls of half-eaten curry, the metal jugs of water and the little plastic tumblers, a couple of framed photographs stand out. The first one I recognize as the picture we reproduced to decorate Dad's seventieth birthday cake on that hot, happy day of celebration and thanksgiving when family and friends all came together dressed up and sweated. It was a picture of him taken on holiday in Spain in a cool corner of the Cat Bar, which was halfway down the stairs to the cove we called Bubi's beach. The panama hat on his head shields him from the Mediterranean sun, and a multicoloured tablecloth contrasts with the plain blue half-sleeve which covers his portly stomach: a picture of health. I don't think I've seen the other photo before, a black-and-white one which stands before Wayne and his boys of a beautiful woman with skin like porcelain, hair curled perfectly like a picture of Hollywood, and a long and flowing dress. It's in the same style as pictures I've seen of my nana when she was a young woman, so I assume that this one is of my great-aunt, her sister, brought to dinner tonight by her son.

Here is one family or at least a selection of it, with multiple dynamics playing out among its protagonists. Gloria's at the loud end, trash talking with her daughter in the bombastic way that we share. She nods in disbelief as she listens, impatient to talk, the certainty of her convictions fuelling anger that she's sure is righteous.

"He wouldn't have stood for this if he were alive today," she asserts, taking up the photo of our dad and holding it close while shaking her head. Putting the picture back down, she helps herself to a little more chicken and takes a sip from her glass. My niece, who sits beside her, listens and learns, and my mum listens too, keeping her counsel on the words she's already heard too many times before. She flashes me a smile as she sees me, and we both understand. My mother-in-law sits there quietly beside my uncle and aunt, who nod, trying to be supportive and encouraging even while finding that a little awareness and balance is wanting, having a while since untangled the peculiar conundrum of things on our side. That their own doted-upon child and grandchildren now are so far away makes our sometimes-unhappy turn all the more ironic. Further afield, and not unhappy to be thereby removed, Wayne and his boys observe calmly from their end, the occasional invective that carries across passing somehow beneath them. Like all lovers of harmony, theirs is an appreciation that being here brings true happiness with an understanding borrowed from those that are gone and those that are yet to come.

Tommy appears beside me with a steaming bowl carefully cupped in his hands, and as I watch, he lifts it to obscure his face as he drinks it in deep. His fill taken, he lowers it again from his lips and smacks his chops, smiling as he lets out a contented sigh.

"You'll need both hands for this, bruv." He winks, passing it towards me, and as I look down over the bowl between us, the misty vapour warms my face.

"And what mysterious brew is this?" I ask, furrowing my eyebrows, but he's as inscrutable and as assured as ever.

"You do trust me, don't you?" he laughs, so I take the bowl from him. What else can I do? I take a small sip. Actually, the liquid is not too warm, and the initial, strangely bitter taste seems to turn somehow sweet as it passes from the mouth.

"Hmmm. Strange, but very nice," I tell him.

"Get on with it," he commands. "Fill your boots."

So, looking down into the bowl again, I shrug and lift it back to my lips. Pouring it into my open mouth, I gulp it down until the bowl is empty. A warm sensation pervades my whole body, and I give him my best thank-you smile. As he takes the bowl from me, his smile mirrors my own.

Another table is added, more chairs and more places for uncles and aunts and cousins with their husbands and wives, and there's more drink than food down at this new end: pints of porter and bottles of vodka. The noise of the party grows louder, almost covering the voice of my sister in the hubbub. Mainly it's the female voices that stand out, perhaps because they are the shriller, but overall the sound is strange to me – a chatter that's lighter and seems to carry less concern, less contention than I'm used to. Now there are even more chairs and tables, and they continue to fill with family from far-away places and far-away times. Friends now are here, taking up their special places for a bewildering mix that seems to stretch on forever in a blur of care and noise. Tommy puts his hand on my shoulder, and I jump.

"I've something to show you," he says. "You better follow me. Are you ready?" and without waiting for an answer, he disappears from the room under the flap at the bar, leaping multiple steps up the stairs beyond without a backward look. As he's disappearing, I notice that others have arrived: Jim has made it, and Luca's here too, mingling with the Finsbury boys and recounting already shared times on the pitch. I see Chloe along with Billy, who looks surprisingly well: a heart-warming sight. Casting a quick smile at them by way of an apology and a promise to return, I nip under the bar and hurry along in Tommy's footsteps.

Lament 1, "Bird's Lament"

Scampering to the top of the carpeted staircase, I chased him along the seemingly endless corridor as if he were an overgrown hare, just about keeping him in my sight but able to make up no ground. We were flying past door after wooden door, and I could see that each bore a shiny brass plate with letters engraved, but though my curiosity was roused, there didn't seem to be time to stop and read them. Eventually, I saw Tommy slip in through the very furthest door at the end of the corridor. Entering just moments behind him, inexplicably, he was gone. There didn't appear to be any other exit from the small and fairly sparse room: just a built-in wardrobe and what looked like a dressing table and a large brass bedstead in the centre. Dumbfounded, as I took in the little space, I noticed the reedy strains playing in the air above me, the deep rasp of an oboe, which seemed to allude with mysterious resignation to something I felt was incredibly familiar yet just beyond my grasp. As I continued to listen, a slightly higher counterpart joined in, and lighter notes of the brightest hopefulness further overlaid these siblings, like the beams of the sun breaking through a cloud or the chirps of a brave little bird on an uncertain morning, proud and satisfied and prepared to let go. It was then that I saw him – the figure of an elderly man I hadn't hitherto noticed lying asleep beneath the duvet with only his head showing where it rested on the pillow by the ornamental bars. Intrigued, careful not to disturb him, I paced around to the far side where he lay with his eyes closed and his breathing easy, and looking down, I beheld the face of my father, quietly sleeping. It struck me that I hadn't seen him for the longest time, and somewhere in the distance, I felt the great joy that it was to find him here. I placed my hand gently on the duvet where I could see his chest rising and falling, and he opened his eyes, smiling at me.

"My lovely boy," he uttered in a mixture of pride and happiness, and for a moment, our souls spoke as we gazed at each other.

"Are you having a nice rest?" I asked him, hearing my voice almost overcome by a helpless simplicity. His answer came in his smile and the blink of his eyes. He exhaled as he closed them again, and I watched as he drifted back to sleep. At that moment, it crossed my mind that these were as fine a set of last words as I could ever have hoped for – words that forevermore I would save in my heart.

Looking away, I saw a door that I hadn't registered earlier opposite to the one where I'd entered the room. Lifting the metal latch, I pushed the door open and was immediately aware of carnival music playing outside – banging steel drums and blowing horns along with the shrill sound of whistles that seemed to interrupt rudely and then disappear. I stepped out over the threshold and took the three wooden steps down to the gravel yard below. With my eyes not yet accustomed to the night, I peered out over the vast emptiness, trying in vain to locate where the music was coming from. Taking slow steps into the darkness before me, I began to distinguish what looked like a stage that had been set up just beyond a small bonfire, where I was now able to distinguish figures dancing and gyrating, throwing themselves around to the rhythm of the music in some kind of hedonistic celebration. The sky above was cloudless, and the silent heavens were alight with the twinkling of a thousand stars. As I continued to search the area ahead of me, I noticed a small group of people slowly approaching the stage from the right-hand side. A tall figure emerged from among them and, moving as if weighed by a heavy load, took the few steps on to the rostrum alone. Up there before me, she was revealed as an elegant and smartly dressed woman heading towards a microphone which stood on a stand in the middle of the stage. The music began to subside, and the crowd fell silent. She seemed to hold herself naturally tall, and though her face was partially covered by a veil, her expression was nonetheless clearly visible; it spoke of a controlled dignity, resolute and sad. She bore in her hand a little book, and having seen it correctly opened, she looked up and turned to address the people that gathered expectant before her.

"Thank you all so very much for coming here today to celebrate the memory of my son, my poor, poor Billy," she began firmly before faltering for just a moment, quickly regaining her composure and then carrying on. "I would like to read to you a passage from this book," she said, indicating the copy of *The Prophet* that she held amid cheers of support that went up from the people around me and from those closer to the stage.

"Your children are not your own," I heard her say, and as she continued the piece in a calm, clear voice, I began to notice that some of the strange faces around me were shooting me looks. I could hear them whispering among themselves, and I had the uncomfortable feeling that it was me they were talking about.

Looked around the yard quickly, to my relief I caught sight of Tommy standing over at the edge by a wide exit with a road just beyond it. Looking back at me, he beckoned me over.

"What's all this about?" I asked as soon as I came within earshot. "What's happening?"

He looked at me, surprised. "Don't you know what's happening?" he said, his voice disbelieving.

"What? Has someone died?"

"Billy died. You were there, remember?"

"That was a dream, wasn't it?" I asked, confused, as he stood there looking at me with a half-sad, half-serious look on his face.

"It's all a dream, brother, but it doesn't make it any less real. The two of you were way out there, and you just got lucky – caught that wave back at the very last moment while he was carried away. His body came out a couple of days later round the coast somewhere."

I stood there dumb as the music started up again, and regarding the shock on my face, he too stood silent.

"I'm sorry, Milo," he said eventually. "I thought you understood – thought you knew what day this was."

A shiver ran through my body. It felt strange being here with all these people I didn't recognize, people who were dancing and celebrating Billy's passing. It wasn't like any kind of funeral I could relate to or imagine, and it seemed so wrong now that I should have been one of the last people he shared breath with, singing our songs on the sands like the end of the world wasn't waiting in the water. Suddenly, I needed to get some distance from all of this noise, and I really needed some cooler air.

"I do remember," I told him. "Of course I do. How could I forget? I just didn't think that it really could happen; I thought death was for older people. Every year when this day comes around, I give guilty thanks that it was him and not me, think how strange it is that things could have turned out so differently as I pay tribute to his memory with a moment – with a private little nod. It's so easy to get carried away, especially when there's a few of you, and it's so hard to get back in – impossible, maybe, once the tide has really turned, once you've let yourself go and you're out there far from the shore. I suppose we've all got it in us to self-destruct, but we can hardly say that we didn't know the risks. Choosing to ignore them is the sin – thinking that things are so bad that anything else would be better. Maybe it's the not thinking that gets us in the end. I don't know, but my head hurts. Give me a minute. I just want to get away from all of this noise."

"You OK, brother? I wish I could have been there for you. I wasn't around much then, was I?"

"It's my bad, mate," I said sadly. "I know I messed up, but I'll be fine in a minute. I'll see you back here soon." So saying, I took a few steps outside the brick compound and then continued along the sandy road, listening to the sound of the sea as it lapped along the shore. The infinity of palm trees I went by leaned out over the water, better to admire the reflection of the moon.

After a little walking, I came upon a car. It was parked on the beach under the night shadow of one of the overhanging trees, and as I approached, I could see by the glow of the moon that it was a light blue convertible with its roof down, empty but for an elderly man in the passenger's seat wearing a baseball cap with its peak facing backwards. He sat bolt upright and was stock still. The noises from the lot behind me had now grown distant, and the slightly wet crunch of my boots on the sand seemed so loud that I expected him to turn with each fresh step I took, yet he remained unmoving and seemed not to register my presence. I drew level and, for the last time, beheld my father's profile. As I stood there, I could see he was completely detached and separate, far removed from any worldly communication. As he stared off somewhere beyond the horizon, I could tell by his gaze that he was no longer a part of this time and place, following his soul to the ends of eternity.

Thirteen Days

Walking back up those three wooden steps, I felt so weary I could barely lift my legs. Tommy was nowhere to be seen and must already have gone back inside: I just wanted to get there myself, return to all the others who, I hoped, would still be enjoying themselves in the bar. As I entered and closed the wooden door behind me, I turned and saw a now-empty bed, the sight amplifying a vacuum inside me and making me feel dizzy and sick. Exhausted and washed out by the emotional overload, I stood there, unable to forge my way on to the doorway. Sitting down, with what felt like the last drop of my energy, I wrestled the boots from my feet and swung myself around to lie down on the duvet. I listened to my breathing as gradually it slowed to nothingness. Feeling myself sink deep into the bed, I allowed my eyes gently to close.

A muffled noise from the corridor awoke me when what felt like mere seconds had passed, a noise that seemed to come from just beyond the door. It grew more distinct as I listened, and I began to think that I could discern a female voice calling my name. Entranced, I continued just to lie there listening as the call became clearer and clearer, hearing it for the moment without reacting until, able to delay no more, I twisted my legs over on to the floor and stood up, looking urgently for my boots. They didn't seem to be where I'd left them, but it couldn't be helped; I couldn't delay for another second. Dashing around the bed to the door in my socks, I snatched for the handle and pulled the door open as quickly as I could.

Where the corridor had been was now a narrow paving-stone pathway. The white slabs bisected a front garden, and standing in the doorway of the house at the end was a woman who looked to be about my age. A small grey boulder with a white number four painted on it sat on the step by her feet. The woman smiled as she saw me, and she held out her hand, softly repeating my name. Racking my brain, I was sure that I knew her voice from somewhere; I searched her face and my mind desperately as I walked down towards her. As I reached the doorway, I took her hand, and suddenly stepping down to the path, her face moved towards mine and we kissed – a long, slow kiss that closed my eyes. I knew the smell of her perfume and the warmth of her cheeks. When our lips finally broke from each other's, I took half a step back and, feeling light-headed, refocused on her face as she waited there flushed and smiling at me. My eyes fell upon the little red mark on her left cheek, and at last, I recognized a look deep in her eyes.

"Rachael?" I almost gasped.

"I didn't want you to forget me," she smiled. "I made sure that you wouldn't, didn't I?"

"But –" I started, and she put her finger to my lips to silence me.

"Shush," she said, "it's not for words. This is just how it is. Don't you ever forget me," and putting a playful kiss on the end of my nose, she stepped back up and into the house. "Goodbye," she said as she gave me one final smile, and closing the door, she was gone. I stood there for a long time hoping that it might open once again, but it did not, and as I wiped away the tears that brimmed and turned to go, the salt stung my eyes.

I did wonder if I'd somehow come the wrong way as I stepped back into the bedroom, but that just wasn't possible. The bed was no longer there, however, people instead sitting on the newly revealed carpet where previously it had held sway. Groups were spread about the floor smoking and talking intensely to each other, and the gentle sound of "Thirteen Days" was drifting in the air among the spiral smells of incense. As I looked to see if I could relocate my boots, without introduction, a hand was thrust into my face, and it startled me. I looked around to see someone I didn't recognize bidding me to take a lit cigarette, and doing so reflexively, I found myself sitting down cross-legged in the centre of the carpet. I took a long, deep drag, noticing a beautiful couple opposite who were casually posing. He was dressed in skinny blue jeans and a plain black T-shirt, its little sleeves slightly furled. A pair of sunglasses was clipped to the neck of the T-shirt by one of its arms. His light brown quiff was mussed just so, and his reddish lips were set almost to a pout. Beside him, just barely touching as she sat facing away at a ninety-degree angle, was Maddie, her dark, wavy hair; thick, dark eyebrows; and black, flowing dress all set off by her pale skin. Her lips wore a deep red lipstick, and her countenance, although dumb, seemed overflowing with fun and energy.

Despite myself, I was really excited to see her, and taking another puff of the cigarette, I waited for her to recognize me and to register her own surprise. Though her face wore a smile as she sat looking right at me, projecting what wonderful joy was within, she continued just beaming and saying nothing.

"Hello," I tried at last, yet still there came no glimmer of recognition, and wondering if something else in the room might give me a clue as to what the hell was going on, I looked around and caught sight of myself in the dress mirror by the door. What a truly pathetic vision it was: I looked like a subject trying to pay court to an oblivious queen! Feeling myself suddenly overcome by anger and self-loathing, I crushed the cigarette into a beaker that sat on the floor beside me and, shooting a final sneer that was aimed at the both of us, rose quickly to my feet, heading off through the door without so much as a backward glance.

It was a relief to be back in the corridor that I recognized as the way I'd arrived – also to be away from that room which had been so vexing of late. I started to make my way towards the doors I'd passed earlier, beyond which I knew was my way back into the pub; but coming to the first one, I saw the name Tracy engraved in capital letters on the brass plate, and I stopped to take note. Just like all the other doors I'd run past with their brass plates and their rounded brass handles, I noticed now how the wood was stained with a pinkish hue. My curiosity impelled me to try the handle, but it was locked and wouldn't budge at all, which only served to make me more curious. I gave it a really good shake just in case that might do the trick, but it was to no avail, so I found myself moving on down the corridor to try the next one. Once again, the brass plate bore upon it a single word; once again, that word was the name of a girl, this time Claire, and once again, the door was locked and couldn't be opened. Once again, I moved down to the next. Again and again, I tried successive doors and was frustrated. The silence that seemed to me to lurk with baited breath behind them was pregnant with significance, and I wondered what secrets were on that mean other side. On the sixth or seventh attempt, now more in hope than in expectation, I tried the handle of a door which had the name Charlotte engraved on its plate, and it turned in my hand. My heart gave a skip as I opened the door and pushed on inside.

The room was a picture of devastation, and the stench was abysmal. Furniture drawers lay tossed upturned on the carpet which was ripped and in some places completely worn away, while others still hung from their wooden chest carcasses with rifled contents spewing out over the floor. Jars and bottles of creams and lotions lay strewn uncapped on their sides amid the chaos of a unit which might once have served as a dressing table. The glass of its vanity mirror was smashed up and jagged, reflecting multiple views of the wardrobe on the other side of the room with its doors left yawning wide, one barely hanging on by the thread of a single twisted hinge. At the base inside, beneath where a hanging rail seemed once to have been, the wardrobe floor was piled with dirt-smeared garments and oddments of clothing. What looked like a white sweater dress lay balled and abandoned at the top of the pile, a rag covered in grime. Broken pieces of black plastic hangers lay about the place like so many shiny twigs, and the sash windows on the far wall were old and crumbled and flaking, their bare wood decaying and eaten away. Rife too were the cobwebs that entangled the filthy net curtains, yellowing and torn.

Like the macabre scene of some ghastly crime, this awful vision stung me, shocking me with dread and with a sudden, sinking guilt. I knew instinctively, without understanding how, that this room fitted much too neatly a place in my heart. Automatically, I moved to right the dressing chair which lay facing towards the dilapidated wardrobe on its side, but even as I was doing so, the futility of the act occurred to me, and checking myself, I let it slip back down to the floor: a tiny, irrelevant detail where such devastation had been unleashed. Standing upright and in a quandary, I looked disbelieving at the room around me. A piece of paper on the desk caught my eye. Edging closer to it, my sense of revulsion momentarily overcome by my curiosity, I saw the writing in her unmistakable hand. It was then that the sickening realization hit me that the pink, tear-pocked paper was that last letter Charlie had sent. The air was suddenly charged with the icy bitterness of accusation, and recoiling involuntarily, I almost fell over the chair, hopping back from it to find my balance and landing with a dull crunch on glass that lay concealed on the floor beneath another tangled mess of detritus. Everything here was broken, everything rotten and poisonous, but what did it all mean? I couldn't take it in, but my head was exploding and the air was growing darker and more malevolent by the moment, the walls closing in around me. Backing out from the room as quickly as I could, repeating, "I'm sorry, I'm sorry," I bumped into Chloe, who was standing guard in the doorway.

I spun around startled with my heart in my mouth, but recognizing her there was a huge relief and the perfect antidote, as if prescribed, to the pain and confusion I was feeling. Looking at me, however, she wasn't smiling.

"Horrible," was all that I could utter as I stood there shaking my head, beseeching her comfort.

"What did you think?" she snarled at me. "You're not an idiot. You can't run around like you are one and expect that everyone will somehow end up fine anyway!" The violence of her anger surprised me, but she was all I had and I felt much too unsettled to allow her to stay angry. I needed her and so threw my arms around her neck and hung there entreating her, despite her resolve, until eventually I felt her arms close around me and the sigh of her stiff anger subsiding. For a moment, I allowed myself to bask in the penetrating relief of her embrace, and then, pulling away, I stood back and looked at her. I still didn't know what to say.

"Look," she said at last as she leant beyond me and pulled closed the door, "what's done is done. Forget it. Everyone's coming from a different place anyway: it's where we're all going that serves as the reckoning. The remorse you're feeling is positive, because it speaks of how you're not that person anymore. Just accept what you've done, and with that, allow yourself to let go – to move on. We both know you'd do things differently if they came around again." I knew she was right, but even as I stood nodding and showing her that I felt it too, I couldn't help staring towards the doors arrayed beyond her, the brass plates with their names that went on back down the corridor. She seemed to read my mind.

"It's enough now, Milo," she said firmly, taking me by the hand and leading me back to the room at the top where the bed and my boots were waiting. Without speaking a word, I let her undress me and then climbed back into the bed, watching through a haze of weariness as she neatly folded my clothes: my jeans, my T-shirt, my shorts. Tucking the duvet under my chin, she left me with a kiss on my forehead and was gone.

A gentle music drifting about the room awakened me. It was something classical, something melodious and soothing, and coming to, I felt calm and relaxed from the rest I'd had. My neatly folded clothes were pressing down on the duvet by my feet at the end of the bed, and sitting up, I reached for them and started to dress. Pulling on my socks, I noticed that, unusually, my back was a little stiff. As hard as I tried to rack my brains, I had no concept at all of what time it was or what day or how long I'd been here, and just as it occurred to me that exploring a little might provide some answers, I noticed that the door in the corner was slightly ajar. Slipping off the bed and moving round towards it, I passed the dressing table and couldn't help but take my habitual peek in the mirror there: what I saw arrested me, and I sat back on the bedcover confused. I continued to stare transfixed at the glass, where an old man with long grey hair and a deeply lined face stared right back at me. His lips seemed formed with a faint smile, and there was a light shining in his bright blue eyes, a light that spoke of knowledge and perfection. As my head tumbled with thoughts in confusion, we both sat staring at each other. I pinched myself: no, I wasn't dreaming, and yet this surely wasn't quite real. The face in the mirror had to be mine, but it couldn't be.

"Who ... who are you?" I asked. As much as I'm convinced I'm speaking to myself, another part of me is equally sure I'm not.

"This is you, Milo. You know this is you."

"Then who am I?"

"You know who you are. You are precisely he who is asking the questions. And of course you are me, a fragment of the eternal, here and now a guardian for what has gone before and what is yet to come."

"Where are we?" I ask, perplexed. Some of the events since I followed Tommy up here are coming back to my mind, and many things are occurring to me that can hardly make sense – even this room itself which I'm starting to understand has been so fluid and insubstantial. The face in the mirror smiles and gives a nod of acknowledgement as if reading my thoughts.

"You are here. You are always here, everywhere, and nowhere, the place where the life you've lived and the friends you've had have brought you. You find your own friends every day, and you must find your own answers too, once you've found the right questions."

Everything I heard seemed to carry the perfect ring of truth, and yet I didn't understand any of it enough even to begin to sense the sniff of a meaningful answer. I knew no more than I had before the conversation began.

"Look, let me explain to you what I can. You know enough now to stop asking some of the more basic questions, and these are the most important. You know what you are here for – that life is about finding happiness in equilibrium by living honestly and being happy with what you have. You understand too how little you actually need – your health and a few good friends – and that that's where you'll find peace of mind."

The words sounded simultaneously profound and obvious, but I could feel the clouds breaking in my head. It was as if there were a light, warm and nourishing, at last shining through.

"Soon enough you'll see it all, Milo. Just know that one way or the other, the river always finds its way to the sea. It really isn't something that you have to worry about."

"But wait. What ... what really ... what am I here for? What can I do?"

"Be loved, and give back to the world with the love that's your own. You care, Milo. That's all you ever need, so don't block it out. You give with your cares: to the world, to your friends, to your children."

"I don't have any children," I protested.

With a broadening smile, he replied, "But you do – of course you do."

The door to my left creaked open, and a head swung around it. It was Penny, and her smile lit the room. She wore a chain of flowers on the crown of her head, daisies fashioned of silver.

"I didn't want to wake you," she said, shooting me a look. "You needed a rest. Have you quite finished talking to yourself now, you eejit?" She laughed, and I looked back at the mirror. The face that I saw looking back was my face, young and old together in one.

"Come on – it's time," she said, and as the door opened further, I saw that she wore a long white dress made of shiny material which fit tightly around her waist and her hips and ran straight down her legs to the floor. There was a wide opening at the top which showed off her neck and the ridge of her shoulders. From behind her dress, three little hands stretched into the room – three little children with excited smiles on their faces. There was a girl in a flouncy white smock and flowers around her hair just like her mother's. The two little boys wore suits and shirts with grown-up ties that were far too big for them.

"Come along, Daddy," they said as one. "It's time."

Taking a last look in the mirror, I saw that a tear was making its way down my cheek, and it made me smile, glad to find an old friend at such a happy time. For a few seconds, I held the searching gaze of my reflection, and we dived deep into my eyes. Neither of us appeared to have any definitive answer. Nothing I could feed my brain would have been as profound as the words I'd just heard, as eternal as the peace I'd felt then in my heart, but the road ahead was obvious, and it filled me with joy at last to be upon it. Slipping from the chair, I knelt to embrace the three little children, the bubbling mass of life that would soon be my education and make everything clearer. Then, rising, I took Penny's hand, and we led each other to the little white hall. Slowly past our families and friends we made our way towards the table at the top where, looking back beside Tommy, I stood smiling and humble, watching my bride make her graceful approach. My heart and my eyes were full again, and as the harpist began her nimble-fingered melody, both overran with a freshly flowing joy.

Fate of a Fool

After that soporific train journey, the walking and the fresh air nurse me gradually back towards my proper senses, the night wearing off as I come over the crest of the hill that sits above our station. I love the bend and the gentle undulation; I love the houses; but most of all, the trees make each part of this way so special: old and established, each an individual, reaching out to the heavens as variously they shade and shelter, decorating this final leg of my evening's journey home. Their leaves are something else, as diffuse and startling as a language I don't yet speak but, hearing it everywhere, somehow understand. It's a world I know almost nothing of, an ecosystem hidden before my eyes that I too rarely notice, yet infinity is on show here in the ever-changing shades of green. As I grow, the palette grows subtler too. It's when the sun shines that really I like this part of the journey best – when I smell summer's fragrance as I amble along with the rays on my skin. It darts away behind the leaves and the branches I pass under, and there's nothing in the world sweeter than when it returns.

I love walking along this road. I think of my father, because he never saw us living here, and I know how much he would have loved it. When it crosses my mind, I think how proud he would have been, and I grimace slightly as I hope it is so. I remember what he always said when I described some great achievement that I insisted he'd have been proud to witness – usually an especially ripping goal that I'd scored on that very evening, catching up with him with a call as I made my way home. He always replied with a smile in his voice that he was proud of me already, and we both felt happy: satisfaction indeed! Though he is gone now and I grow older, I still like to try to make him proud of me. I look up to the stars in the sky, and I wonder – to the planes that cross the heavens carrying innumerable people to innumerable destinations – knowing that all of us might be somehow connected and that something somewhere can make it all come together to a perfectly formed sense. I know that it yet lies beyond me.

Still a little lifted, I feel as if I'm being carried to the end of my journey in the restful pit of a sigh: lifetimes can pass by looking in vain for such a state. As I top the final brow, our twin baton lights come reassuringly into view, the markers of our entrance that guide me in and tell me that I'm all but at home. As I step on to the drive, there amid the silver birch and the horse chestnut, I find Penny overloaded with some more bags of rubbish for the morning collection. It's a timely reunion, and she smiles as she sees me. We'll go inside together now and kick back, perhaps, in front of whatever we're currently engrossed in, see our little satellites buzzing around in their own close orbit, and I can ride the fading tail of today's comet peaceably until my bed. Thanking me as I lift from her a bag, as if continuing with a conversation that I should already be appraised of she carries on chatting, and listening to her happily I nod, already at home, and I smile.

Lightning Source UK Ltd.
Milton Keynes UK
UKOW04f2325040316

269654UK00001B/1/P